SCANDAL TAKES
A HOLIDAY

SCANDAL TAKES
A HOLIDAY

LINDSEY DAVIS

Warner Books Edition
Copyright © 2004 by Lindsey Davis
All rights reserved.

This Warner Books edition is published simultaneously by arrangement with Century, The Random House Group Limited, 20 Vauxhall Road, London SWV 2SA.

Mysterious Press
Warner Books

Time Warner Book Group
1271 Avenue of the Americas, New York, NY 10020
Visit our Web site at www.twbookmark.com

The Mysterious Press name and logo are registered trademarks of Warner Books.

Printed in the United States of America

First Warner Books Printing: September 2004

10 9 8 7 6 5 4 3 2 1

Library of Congress Cataloging-in-Publication Data
Davis, Lindsey.
    Scandal takes a holiday / Lindsey Davis.
      p. cm.
    ISBN 0-89296-812-5
    1. Falco, Marcus Didius (Fictitious character)—Fiction. 2. Gossip columnists—Crimes against—Fiction. 3. Rome—History—Vespasian, 69–79—Fiction. 4. Private investigators—Rome—Fiction. 5. Scribes—Crimes against—Fiction. 6. Political corruption—Fiction. 7. Ostia (Italy)—Fiction. 8. Kidnapping—Fiction. 9. Pirates—Fiction. I. Title.
    PR6054.A8925S28 2004
    823'.914—dc22

2004008551

In Memory of Sara Ann Freed

Who are you, sirs? From what port have you sailed over the highways of the sea? Is yours a trading venture, or are you cruising the main on chance, like roving pirates, who risk their lives to ruin other people?

—Homer, *The Odyssey*, tenth century B.C.

Piracy, like crime on terra firma, has its great syndicates and its petty criminals. On the high seas, neither is an easy catch . . . No one, apart from ship owners, their crews and insurers, appears to notice that pirates are assaulting ships at a rate unprecedented since the glorious days when pirates were "privateers" protected by their national governments . . . Piracy is a historical problem . . . It is rooted in these societies . . . Despite all the information now available on piratical attacks, there are hardly any cases where these attackers are arrested and brought to trial. Piracy is a high-profit, low-risk activity.

—Charles Glass, *The New Piracy*, A.D. 2003

The Roman Mediterranean

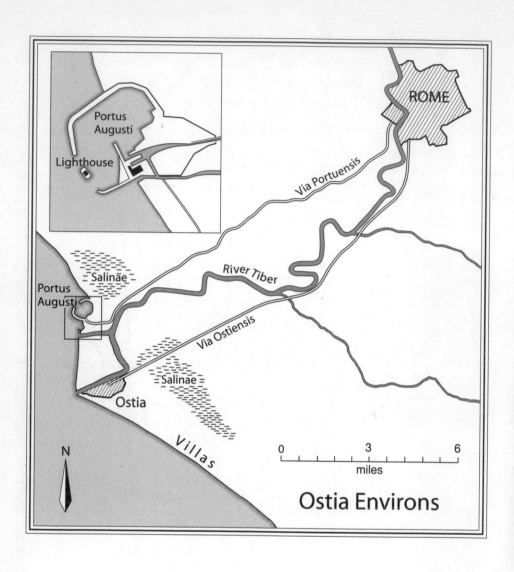

Ostia Environs

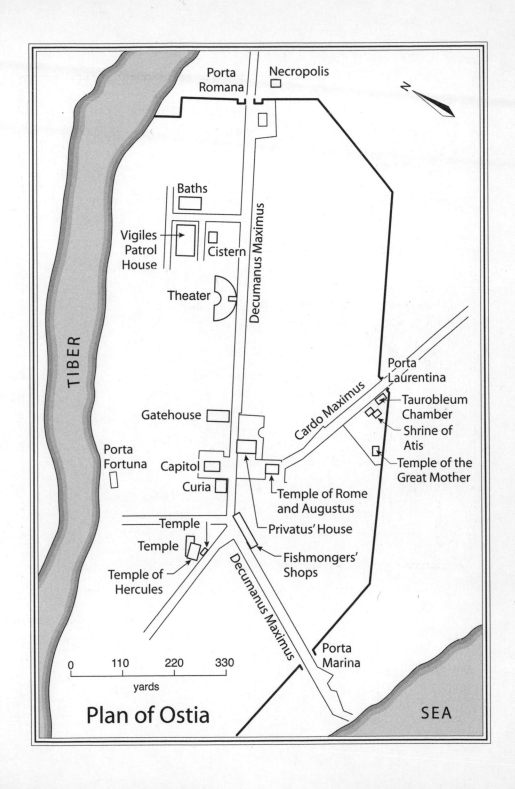

Plan of Ostia

EXTRACT FROM THE FAMILY

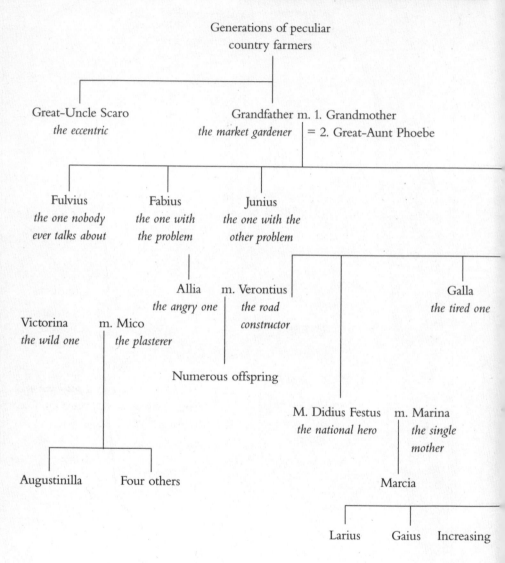

Generations of peculiar
country farmers

Great-Uncle Scaro
the eccentric

Grandfather m. 1. Grandmother
the market gardener = 2. Great-Aunt Phoebe

Fulvius
*the one nobody
ever talks about*

Fabius
*the one with
the problem*

Junius
*the one with the
other problem*

Allia   m. Verontius
the angry one   *the road
constructor*

Galla
the tired one

Victorina   m. Mico
the wild one   *the plasterer*

Numerous offspring

M. Didius Festus   m. Marina
the national hero   *the single
mother*

Augustinilla   Four others

Marcia

Larius   Gaius   Increasing

TREE OF MARCUS DIDIUS FALCO

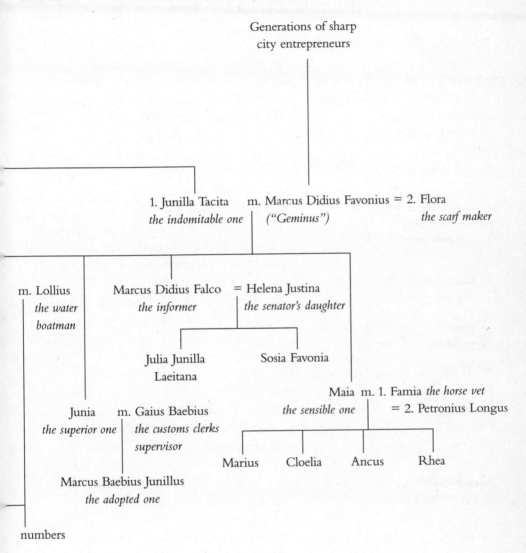

Generations of sharp
city entrepreneurs

1. Junilla Tacita   m. Marcus Didius Favonius = 2. Flora
the indomitable one   *("Geminus")*   *the scarf maker*

m. Lollius   Marcus Didius Falco = Helena Justina
the water   *the informer*   *the senator's daughter*
boatman

Julia Junilla   Sosia Favonia
Laeitana

Maia m. 1. Famia *the horse vet*
the sensible one   = 2. Petronius Longus

Junia   m. Gaius Baebius
the superior one   *the customs clerks*
supervisor

Marius   Cloelia   Ancus   Rhea

Marcus Baebius Junillus
the adopted one

numbers

PRINCIPAL CHARACTERS

Relations (see also Family Tree)

M. Didius Falco	an informer on summer vacation
Helena Justina	catching up on her holiday reading
Julia Junilla and Sosia Favonia	their children, struggling for attention
Albia	their British foster child, a treasure
Nux, Ajax, Argos	furry friends in need of training
Ma	rising to difficult situations
Pa (M. Didius Geminus)	sinking to new depths
Junia	Falco's sister: the irritating one
Gaius Baebius	her well-matched husband
Maia	another sister: the coping, caring one
Fulvius	an enigma whom nobody talks about
Cassius	a mystery nobody knows about
D. Camillus Verus	Helena's father, an off-duty senator
Julia Justa	her mother, always on the alert over:
A. Camillus Aelianus	her sons: who certainly need
and Q. Camillus Justinus	watching

Staff of the *Daily Gazette*, Rome

Holconius	the political reporter
Mutatus	the sports commentator
Diocles	fun correspondent; a family man
Vestina	his only family

The Vigiles

L. Petronius Longus	on independent secondment (a maverick?)
Brunnus	leader of the VI Cohort's Ostia detachment; a rival
Marcus Rubella	tribune of the IV Cohort, a thinking man
Fusculus, Passus	members of the IV, regular good lads
Virtus	a public slave, the vigiles' Ostia clerk
Rusticus	the vigiles recruiting officer

Persons about town in Ostia

Landlady	double booking
Titus	her slave, a liability
Caninus	a naval attaché; a drinking man
Privatus	president of the builders' guild; fraternizing with Petro

Staff of the Damson Flower Hotel, the Venus, the Clam, the Dolphin, the Aquarius, and other establishments
A fishmonger and his mother

Chaeron	a funeral flautist, who will tackle anything

Colorful overseas businesspeople

Damagoras	an old Cilician, not necessarily a pirate
L★BO	his topiarist, slightly overpruned
Cratidas	a violent Cilician, but innocent, honest
Lygon	another Cilician, but honest, really
Pullia	a mother (from Cilicia) with a bad habit
Zeno	a neglected boy (from Cilicia)
Cotys	an Illyrian, too scrupulous to be a pirate, he says
Theopompus	another Illyrian, in love—no, genuinely
The Illyrian	an intermediary
Antemon	a sea captain who has never met a pirate
Banno, Aline	ship's owners, too scared to admit that piracy happens
Posidonius	an importer, not so scared—but now regretting it
Rhodope	his daughter, who thinks one Illyrian is wonderful
Lemnus from Paphos	just a concrete mixer

Ostia, Italy:
August, A.D. 76

I

If he chucks a stone, he's done for," muttered Petronius. "I'll have the little tyke . . ."

It was a hot day along the waterfront at the mouth of the Tiber in Ostia. Petro and I had badly needed a drink. It was so hot we only made it to just outside the vigiles patrol house and into the first bar. This was a sad backtrack. Our principle had always been, "Never go into the first bar you see because it is bound to be rubbish." For the past fifteen years or so, since we met in the queue to enlist for the legions, whenever we sought refreshment we had always strolled a good distance away from home and work, in case we were followed and found. Actually we had sat in numerous bars that were rubbish—but not many that were full of associates we wanted to avoid and very few that our women knew about.

Don't get me wrong. We two were pious Romans with traditional values. Of course we admired our colleagues and adored our womenfolk. Just like old Brutus, any orator could say of us that Marcus Didius Falco and Lucius Petronius Longus were honorable men. And yes; the orator would make that claim with an irony even the most stupid mob would understand . . .

As you can see, in the heat I had drunk up too quickly. I was already rambling. Petronius, the experienced inquiry chief of the Fourth Cohort of Vigiles in Rome, was a measured man. He had his large hand clamped around his wine-shop beaker but his heavy right arm was currently at rest on the warm boards of our sidewalk table while he enjoyed a long, slow descent into tipsiness.

He was here after putting his name down for detached duty. It was a pleasant life—especially since the villain he was waiting for never turned up. I was here to look for someone else—though I had not told Petro.

Ostia, the port for Rome, was vibrant but its vigiles patrol house was falling apart and the bar outside was terrible. The place was little more than a shack leaning against the patrol-house wall. After a fire, the vigiles rankers would block the side street as they crowded around with mugs of liquor, desperate to soothe their raw throats and usually just as desperate to complain about their officers. At present the street was almost empty, so we could squat on two low stools at a tiny table with our legs stuck out across the sidewalk. There were no other customers. The day shift were having a lie-down in the squad house, hoping that nobody set fire to an oily pan in a crowded apartment, or if they did that nobody sounded the alarm.

Petro and I were discussing our work and our women. Being still capable of two things at once, Petronius Longus was also watching the boy. The little lad was too intent; he looked like trouble. A giggling group would be annoying enough. But if this loner did hurl a rock through the doorway of the patrol house, then shout abuse and run away, he would run straight into my old friend.

Mind you, he was only about seven. Petronius would probably not break his arms or legs.

After Petronius had narrowed his eyes and watched for a while, he carried on talking. "So how's your billet, Falco?"

He was teasing and I scoffed, "I can see why you don't want to stay in it!"

Petro had been assigned a room inside the Ostia patrol house. He refused to occupy it, but had loaned the grim cell to me this week. We two had had our fill of barracks life when we were in the Second Augusta, our legion in Britain. Even marching camps in that remote province had been better organized than this dump. Ostia was mainly a four-month assignment, on rotation among the seven Rome cohorts; the provision was constantly under review, and it showed.

Off the Decumanus Maximus a short way inside the Rome Gate, the buildings had been thrown up in a hurry three decades ago when Claudius built his new harbor. He first brought some of the rough-and-ready urban cohorts to guard the spanking new warehouses. Fires in the granaries subsequently caused a rethink; they had upped the provision and replaced the urbans, who were general troops, with the more professional vigiles, who were specialist firefighters. Rome's vital corn supply ought to be safe with them, the people would be fed, the city would be free from riots, and everyone would love the Emperor, who had arranged it all.

The same happened here as in Rome: while on fire watch, especially at night, the vigiles found themselves apprehending not just arsonists but every kind of criminal. Now they policed the port and kept an eye on the town. The Ostians were still trying to get used to it.

Petronius, who knew how to run rings around his superiors, only got involved in day-to-day issues when it suited him. His special operation had no time limit, so he had brought his family with him. Nowadays Petro cohabited with my sister Maia, who had four children, and in Ostia he had a young daughter of his own with whom he wanted contact. To house them all he had managed to fiddle the loan of a mansion, borrowed from a very wealthy local contact of the vigiles. I had not yet worked out the angle there. But as a result, his unwanted room in the patrol house was mine. Lucky me.

"This squadron coop has well outlived its usefulness," I grumbled. "It's too small, it's dark, it's cramped, plus it's full of bad memories of villains who have been dragged in through the gate and never seen again. The latrine stinks. There is no cookhouse. Equipment is left all over the exercise yard because every detachment thinks if they are only here for four months they can leave it rotting there for the next group to tidy up."

"Yes, and there's mold in a big cistern underground," Petronius agreed cheekily.

"Oh, thanks. Don't tell my mother you have stuck me above some stagnant sink."

"I won't tell your mother," he promised, "if you promise not to tell your wife." He was frightened of Helena Justina. Quite rightly. My high-rank sweetheart had much stricter morals than most senators' daughters and she knew how to express her views. Petronius faked a contrite look. "Well, the room is rough and I'm sorry, Marcus. But you're not staying long, are you?"

"Of course not, Lucius, old pal."

I was lying. Lucius Petronius had welcomed me as if I had just come on a visit to see how he was. I was withholding news of my own commission in Ostia. Last year, when the Emperor sent me to Britain on some murky Palace errands, Petro had followed me out there. Only by chance did I learn that he was the lead player in a serious hunt for a major gangster. It still rankled that he had kept quiet. Now I was paying him back.

He drank his wine. Then he winced. I nodded. It was a filthy vintage.

Without a word, Petronius stood up. I stayed put. He walked slowly over to the little lad, who was still motionless outside the gate. They were about five strides from me.

"Hello, there." Petro sounded friendly enough. "What are you up to?"

The small boy had a thin body under a worn tunic. It was fairly clean, a muddy shade, a size too big for him, with one sleeve of a white under-tunic showing. He did not look like a native of Ostia. It was impossible to tell his nationality, but the layers of clothes suggested Mediterranean; only crazies from the north strip off in the heat. He wore no belt, though he had beaten-up brown sandals with their straps curled by age. His hair was too long and there were dark circles under his eyes. But he had been fed. He was fit. His was the normal look of a lad from the artisan classes, maybe required to work hard at the family trade and then allowed to stay up far too late on long summer nights.

He stared up at Petronius Longus. What the boy saw was a big man waiting silently with a friendly expression, someone who might throw a beanbag about in an alley with the local children. The boy seemed streetwise yet clearly unaware that this was an officer whose slam-bang interrogation methods were a legend. All vigiles are hard, but Petronius could persuade incorrigible criminals to bleat out damning evidence against their favorite brothers. He could make them do it even if the brothers were innocent, although mostly he did prefer confessions of real guilt.

"What's your name?" I heard him ask.

"Zeno." The worst Zeno would suspect was an approach from a pervert. He looked the kind who knew to yell loudly and run.

"I am Petronius. So what's up, Zeno?"

Zeno said something, very quietly. Then Petro offered his hand and the boy took it. They walked over to me. I was already dropping coins on the table to pay for our wine. I had heard the boy's answer, and I knew what my friend would do.

"Falco, Zeno says that his mummy won't wake up." Petronius hid his foreboding. "Shall we go and see what has happened to her?"

From long experience, he and I reckoned that we knew.

II

The boy led us, with Petronius still gripping his grubby little hand. We walked along the Decumanus Maximus. Ostia was a long habitation, so it had a long and very hot main street. As a major route for trade commodities, it was already packed with an endless line of carts jostling their way out of town, in order to arrive in Rome at sunset as the daily ban on wheeled vehicles ended. We were walking against the traffic. They were heading toward Victory Square and the Rome Gate. In our direction, far ahead and way beyond the Forum, lay the Marine Gate and the open sea. Roads to our left passed through mixed habitation toward the Laurentine Gate, the exit into the lovely countryside on which our forefather Aeneas set his sights. Short roads to the right led to the Tiber. It would be chock-full of boats and ferries, bound for the markets and the great Emporium. Beyond the Tiber lay another road to Rome, which would also be jammed with laden transports, those too all trundling toward the Golden City on the Transtiberina side.

"You're not from hereabouts," Petronius probed. "So where is home, Zeno?" Zeno had been trained to look dumb or daft. "Far away?" This time the child let himself nod. "Did you come on a ship?" Too specific: Zeno relapsed into vagueness.

Petro glanced at me over Zeno's head, then stopped asking. Questions would be better when we had seen whether the unresponsive mother had been battered by her husband or lover or whether (less likely) she had just faded away in her sleep from some natural illness.

We passed the Theater. Opposite that tight-arsed Augustan edifice were various old monuments and guild assembly rooms. Then came a podium holding a neat row of four little temples, all elderly in style, just before the approach road to the massive granary built by Claudius. We stayed on the Decumanus to the end of that block. Then the boy turned right, facing the river. He stopped in front of what had once been a fortified gatehouse, when Ostia was much smaller and much, much older. This would have been the boundary wall of the original settlement. It probably dated back to the supposed founding of the port by Ancus Martius, one of the traditional Kings of Rome. They built to last in those ancient times, using massive square blocks. The stolid gate, made redundant when the town expanded, had now been redeveloped into shops. Above them were a couple of rooms rented to visiting foreigners.

Petronius left Zeno with me; he made a brief inquiry at one of the shops, then went up alone by an outside stair. I sat on the curb alongside the child, who meekly squatted by me.

"Who told you to come to the vigiles for help, Zeno?" I asked nonchalantly, as we pulled in our feet in front of a heavy cart full of marble blocks.

"Lygon told me, *If anyone ever doesn't wake up, the vigiles will want to know.*"

Lygon instantly became a key suspect. "Is he one of the family?"

"My uncle." The child looked embarrassed. There are uncles and uncles. Some uncles are no relation, as children understand.

"Where is he at the moment?"

"Gone away on business."

"When do you think he will come back?"

Zeno shrugged. No surprises there.

Petronius stuck his head out of a window on the top story.

"Come up here, Falco." He sounded annoyed, not like a man who had just found a domestic tragedy. "You can bring the boy."

"Sounds as if your mother is all right, Zeno." We went up.

The gatehouse contained a warren of small rooms, all kept cool by its massive construction. Zeno lived in a cheap let, a single airless room with no amenities. The mother was unconscious on what passed for a bed. It was the only one; Zeno must either sleep with her or on the floor.

She was from the scrag end of womanhood; we had suspected that. She was dressed, in several layers—a traveler who wore all her wardrobe, as a deterrent to theft. The folds of cloth were richer than I expected, though when sleeping it off she wore them in bedraggled swathes. Sprawled face-up on the mattress, she looked sour and middle-aged, but I guessed she was much younger and had fallen pregnant with Zeno in her teens. That was the type of ménage it was. "Uncle" Lygon would be her latest lover; we could guess what he was like: some scrounging swine who was now playing the big fellow in a wine shop by the port. Presumably they both liked a tipple. Zeno's mother had imbibed so much she had passed out cold. I guessed that was yesterday.

"Drunk as a dog." Petronius (a cat man) closed her drooling mouth with his thumb. This was a gesture to spare her young son. He wiped his thumb on his tunic at thigh level, with an expression of weary distaste. Much of his working life had been spent among this sad level of society, and he despaired of it.

Had the child been any older, that would have ended our interest. Instead, since my sister was only around the corner in the loaned house, Petro made me stay at the gatehouse while he fetched Maia to sit with the mother until she came around. We would look after Zeno.

Maia was furious to be given this task—but she had children herself. We took Zeno to play with her brood; Petro and I claimed that both of us would need to supervise them. Cursing, Maia stayed behind. Two hours later the woman revived. Maia came home with a ripe black eye, cuffed Zeno around the ears, told him to go and keep his mama out of trouble, then made us feel guilty all that evening.

"Your lush is called Pullia. The family come from Soli, wherever that is. There's a man no one ever sees much. Pullia is dumped on her own while he goes out and has his fun; she's bored, but she never leaves the apartment. The child roams the streets. A neighbor in the cushion shop told me."

"That's more than I found out," Petro soothed her admiringly. "I didn't even notice that it was a cushion shop!"

"Eyesight qualifications don't apply to the vigiles? Drop the flattery." Maia and Petro were in love. Happiness had failed to soften the cut and thrust of their repartee. Maia distrusted men who tried to ingratiate themselves and Petro was finding out fast just what he had fallen for.

They were made for each other—though that did not mean this relationship would last. Petronius had always sought out fair-haired women previously—apart from his ex-wife. Arria Silvia looked a little like Maia, who was dark and smart, with a fiery temper and a brisk manner even when nothing had offended her. My Helena reckoned Petro had married Silvia because Maia was married herself at the time and refused to look at him. I knew Petro, and I could not believe it, but I saw the similarity.

"Do the tipsy family pay their rent?" he asked Maia, pretending he was only making conversation.

"Find out for yourself," snarled Maia, as she prodded her battered cheekbone.

She was my favorite sister. I made sure Petronius applied soothing liniment to her eye as soon as Maia calmed down enough for him to get near her. I wouldn't risk it myself.

The feckless folk from Soli were a typical splash of color in the hectic marine society of Ostia. The place was awash with temporary visitors from all ends of the Empire. Attached in some way to nautical trade, they stayed weeks or months, awaiting a cargo, awaiting a payment, awaiting a friend, awaiting a passage. Some found work, though mostly the locals had the jobs and clung on to them. Now that Pullia had had a meeting with officialdom, her little group would probably be up and off.

I was off myself, back to the patrol house. I could have stayed to dinner. The moneybags who had lent Petro the house had left his slaves behind, in accordance with the hospitality rules of the rich. They served up regular meals of excellent quality, for which Petronius was not billed. "The food is here—eat, don't let it go to waste!" the steward urged. No one needed to be told twice.

It was not for me, however. I was hoping that Helena would arrive that evening. The patrol house was somewhere no well-brought-up young lady would want to find herself alone.

III

A donkey cart was standing outside the gate: Helena had already arrived.

She was just inside the entrance, keeping her cloak tightly around her. In late July it was far too hot for cloaks, but a respectable woman's duty is to be uncomfortable in public. The Sixth Cohort duty boys would not have interfered with her, but nobody made her welcome either. The vigiles rankers are ex-slaves, doing a horrid job as the quick route to citizenship; their officers are citizens, normally ex-legionaries, but few and far between.

Helena glanced around the quadrangle, with its many shadowed doorways; they led to equipment stores, the bare cells where the men slept, and the offices where they skillfully brought pressure to bear on witnesses. Even the entrance to the shrine at the far end looked forbidding. As harsh voices sounded loudly from indoors, she flinched. Helena Justina was a tall, spirited girl, who could always fend off trouble by citing her position as a senator's daughter—but she preferred to avoid the trouble in the first place. I had taught her some tactics. She disguised her nervousness, though she was glad to see me.

"Luckily no suspects are screaming in agony just at this moment," I teased, acknowledging the atmosphere that hung over the yard, especially at dusk. We went to the room I had been using. The false excuse was to fetch my belongings; the true one was to greet my lady privately. I had not seen her for a week. Since everyone I knew swore that she was bound to leave me one day, I had to reinforce my feelings. Besides, I liked getting excited when Helena showed her affection for me.

Even we felt too uneasy there to dally. I promised greater relaxation at an apartment I had found for us.

"Aren't we staying with Lucius and Maia?" Helena was fond of them both.

"Not likely. Petro has been loaned a flash mansion by a damned construction magnate."

"What's wrong with that?" Helena was smiling. She knew me.

"I hate handouts." She nodded; I knew she too preferred our family to live quietly, with no obligations to patrons. Most of Rome operates on favors; we two had always made our own way. "But we can go and have a free dinner!" There were limits to my high-mindedness.

Back at the town house, Petro and Maia were already eating in one of their host's frescoed dining rooms. He had several. This was made airy by folding doors, currently flung open onto a small garden, where a tiled turquoise niche housed a sea god statue. A child's hat was hanging on his conch shell. Small sandals, clay animals, and a homemade chariot littered the garden area.

Space was quickly made for us on the large, cushion-strewn couches. Maia gave us a calculating look, as she rearranged the children: Marius, Cloelia, Ancus, and little Rhea, who were aged between twelve and six, all four of them bright as new carpentry nails, together with Petro's quiet daughter Petronilla, who must be about ten.

"Are you staying or what?" demanded my sister. She and I came from a large, loud, quarrelsome family whose members spent much effort avoiding one another.

"No, we've taken a holiday apartment, just the other side of the Decumanus," I reassured her.

Maia did not want us cluttering up her already busy household, but she went into a huff. "Suit yourselves!"

Petronius came back from stabling Helena's luggage cart. "It looks as if you've come for the rest of the season by the amount you have brought!" he said.

"Oh, it's holiday reading." Helena smiled calmly. "I was rather behind with the *Daily Gazette*, so my father has lent me his old copies."

"Three sacks of scrolls?" Petro asked her, in disbelief. Clearly he had poked through Helena's luggage without shame.

Everyone knew that the strange girl I had chosen would rather have her nose in literature than tend to her two little daughters or walk to the corner market for a mullet and some gossip like a normal Aventine wife. Helena Justina was more likely to neglect me because she was deep in a new Greek play than because she was having a fling with another man. She did tend our daughters in her own fashion; Julia, at three, was already being taught her alphabet. Fortunately I liked eccentric women and was not afraid of forward children. Or so I thought so far.

Helena fixed her gaze on me. "The news all looks rather dull at the moment. The imperial family are at their country estates for the summer—and even Infamia has taken a holiday."

Infamia was the pseudonym of whoever compiled the salacious scandal about senators' wives having affairs with jockeys. I happened to know that Infamia was shifty and unreliable—and if he really had taken a holiday, he had forgotten to clear the dates with his employers.

"If there's no scandal," Maia announced crisply, "then there's absolutely no point in reading the *Gazette*."

Helena smiled. She hated me being devious and was trying to force me to say what I knew. "Infamia must have a hotspot villa somewhere. Think of all his payoffs from people who don't want their secrets told. What do you think, Marcus?"

"Are we missing something?" Maia hated to be left out. She sounded tetchy. Nothing new in that.

"Falco, you rat. Are you down here on one of your crackpot investigations?" demanded Petronius, also catching on.

"Lucius, my dearest and oldest friend, when I am commissioned for work, crazy or sane, I shall report it to you immediately—"

"You *are* on a job!"

"I just denied it, Petro."

Petro turned to Maia. "Your tight-lipped bastard brother is hiding a commission in his hairy armpit." He scowled at me, then gave his attention to capturing a tureen of gingered shellfish the children had been scooping up like ravenous gulls. He had to deal with the squeals as they watched him emptying all the good bits into his own food bowl.

"What job?" Maia quizzed me rudely.

"Secret. Clause in my contract says, 'Don't tell your nosy sister or that interfering boyfriend of hers.'" I relieved Petro of his trophy and served Helena and myself the last prawns.

Maia snatched one from my bowl. "Grow up, Marcus!"

Ah, family life. I wondered if the man I had come to look for had any close relations. When you are looking for motives, never neglect the simple one.

IV

Helena and I had one evening to ourselves. We made the most of it. Tomorrow we would be joined by Albia, a young girl from Britain who took care of our children while we tried to take care of her. Albia had had a poor start in life; running around after Julia and Favonia took her mind off it—in theory. She had experience of family travel from when we brought her to Italy from Londinium, but controlling a toddler and a growing infant on a two-hour jaunt in a cart would be a challenge.

"Are we sure Albia can find her way here all on her own?" I sounded wary, but not too critical.

"Settle down, Falco. My brother is bringing her."

"Quintus?"

"No, Aulus. Quintus stays with Claudia and the baby." Gaius Camillus Rufius Constantinus, our new nephew aged two months, was making his presence felt. The world and all the planets revolved around this baby. It could be why Helena's other brother was very keen to leave the family home. "Aulus is coming on his way to university. He expressed an interest in law; Papa seized the moment and Aulus is being packed off to Athens."

"Greece! And studying? We are talking about Aelianus?" Aulus Camillus Aelianus was the unmarried son of a senator, with money in his pocket and a carefree outlook; I could not see him gravely attending jurisprudence lectures under a fig tree at an antique university. His Greek was awful, for one thing. "Can't he be a lawyer in Rome?" That would be more useful to me. Expert knowledge for which I did not have to pay was always welcome.

"Athens is the best place." Well, it was traditionally the place to send awkward Romans who did not quite fit in.

I chuckled. "Are we certain he is going? Do you and I have to check that he goes on the boat?" At a little short of thirty, the favorite pursuits of the noble Aulus Camillus Aelianus were hunting, drinking, and gymnastics—all done to excess. There must be other, equally vigorous and disreputable habits, which I tried not to discover. That way, I could assure his parents I knew of no nasty secrets.

"This is a serious shock for my parents," Helena rebuked me. "One of their children can at last be mentioned at respectable dinner parties."

I held back the jokes. Their daughter had left home to live with a lowlife—me. Now that Helena and I had daughters of our own I understood just what that meant.

As parents we had better things to do than talk about Aulus. Freed for once from the threat of little visitors in the bedroom, we tested out our apartment with passion. I had hired one of the identical room-sets in a small block set around a courtyard with a well. There were balconies on the street side, for show; tenants could not access them. All around us were other visiting families; we could hear their voices and the knocking of furniture, but since we did not know them we did not have to care if they were listening in.

We managed not to break the bed. I hate being at a disadvantage when the landlord comes to check the fixtures and fittings schedule before he lets you leave.

After a short deep sleep, I awoke abruptly. Helena was facedown and dreaming beside me, pressed closely to my side. I lay with my right arm along her long bare back, my fingers lightly splayed. If there had been a pillow, it had gone missing. My head was back, my chin up. As always at the very start of a mission, my brain was full of busy thoughts.

I had been hired to find the absent *Daily Gazette* scribe. It was a mission I was foolish to take on, like most jobs I do. The only advantage to this one was that there were no dead bodies—or so I reassured myself.

As I lay quiet, I thought back to how it had started. Back in Rome, the request first came obliquely via the imperial secretariats. There was a top man there called Claudius Laeta, who sometimes gave me business; the business always turned sour, so I was glad that Laeta's name was not attached to this. Well, not obviously. You could never be sure, with that smooth swine.

At home two weeks ago, someone on the Palatine had recommended my investigative skills to the scribblers at the *Gazette*. A scared little public slave was sent to sound me out; he wasn't telling me much, because he knew nothing. I was intrigued. If this problem had any significance, then as Chief of Correspondence, Claudius Laeta should have been made aware of it: the *Daily Gazette* was the official mouthpiece of the government. In fact, when the slave appeared in my office being secretive, one attraction was the delicious idea that scribes at the *Gazette* might be trying to work a flanker on Laeta.

There was something that would make me even happier than going behind Laeta's back: putting one over on Anacrites, the Chief Spy. That glorious hope seemed a possibility. If there was a hitch at the *Daily Gazette,* then, like Laeta, Anacrites ought to have been told about it. His role was protecting the Emperor, and the *Gazette* existed nowadays to burnish the Emperor's name.

Anacrites was away at his villa on the Bay of Neapolis. He had told my mother, whose lodger he had been briefly, and she had passed it on to me so I would be jealous of his prosperity. Stuff his prosperity. Anacrites upset me just by talking to Ma, and he knew it. What he did *not* know, apparently, was that the scribes who produced the *Gazette* were asking for expert assistance. He was away, so they had come to me. I liked that.

Initially I was only told by the messenger that there was a problem with an employee. Even so, curiosity grabbed me; I told the little slave I would be happy to help, and would call at the *Gazette* offices that same afternoon.

★   ★   ★

In Rome I worked from an office at my own house on the Embankment, just under the cliff side of the Aventine Hill. At this period of my informing career, I had two younger assistants nominally, Helena's brothers, Aulus and Quintus. Both had their own preoccupations, so I was on my own with the *Gazette* inquiry. I felt relaxed; it had all the signs of a nice little escapade that I could handle blindfolded.

That fine day two weeks ago, therefore, after my usual lunch with Helena, I had taken a pleasant walk to the Forum. There I did some preliminary homework. Most jobs came to me without warning; this time, it was good not to have to make the usual snap decision about accepting the work.

At the column where the news is hung up daily, a handful of idlers were telling one another utter nonsense about chariot-racing. These time-wasters could not decide which way four horses were facing, let alone work out the odds on the Blues making a comeback with that snotty driver they unwisely bought and their new quartet of knock-kneed grays. In front of the column, a solitary slave stood copying headings, using big letters for his extracts so it would fill his tablet and look good. His master was most likely an overfed slug in a palanquin who never read the stuff anyway. When I say "read," I mean "had it read to him."

It was late in the day for perusing the column. People who needed to keep up to date would have acquired the news hours ago. Fashionable politicos would want to start outmaneuvering their rivals before the rivals were up and networking. Adulterers would have to invent a good alibi before their spouses were awake. Even innocent householders liked to be abreast of the edicts: Helena Justina's father always sent along his secretary in time for him to bury himself in his copy over breakfast. That, I was sure, had nothing to do with Decimus Camillus wanting to avoid conversation with his noble wife as he blearily ate his nice white morning rolls.

I checked today's familiar list. Most just made me yawn. Who cares about the number of births and deaths recorded in the city yesterday, or money paid into the Treasury and statistics relating to the corn supply? The election lists stink. Occasionally I found an intriguing nugget among

the magistrates' edicts, wills of famous people, and reports of trials—
though not often. The *Acta Diurna* was instituted to list the doings of the
Senate—tedious decrees and toadying acclamations; automatically I
skipped that. I sometimes consulted the court circular, if I needed to see
the Emperor and did not want to waste time hanging around on the
Palatine only to learn he had gone to his granny's villa for a festival.

Now I skipped to the end, the most popular section. Here would be:
prodigies and marvels (the usual lightning strikes and calves born with
three heads); notice of the erection of new public buildings (hmm); con-
flagrations (everyone loves a good blaze in a temple); funerals (for the old
women); sacrifices (ditto); the program of any public games (for everyone; the most consulted section); and privately submitted advertisements
from snobs who wanted the whole world to know they had a daughter
newly engaged to a tribune (boring! well, boring unless you had once
flirted with the daughter) (or with the tribune). At last I reached the best
bit: what the scribes discreetly call "amatory adventures." Scandal—with
the names of the parties robustly revealed, because we are an open city.
Deceived husbands need to be told what is going on, lest they be charged
with condoning it, which is statutory pimping. And the rest of us like a
bit of fun.

I was disappointed. Where the gossip should be was just a note that
Infamia, the columnist, was on holiday. He often was "on holiday."
Everyone always joked about it. Let's be blunt: it was thought that senators' wives whose affairs he discovered sometimes gave him a free ride to
shut him up, but the senators who knew about it then hired thugs to
track down Infamia—and the thugs sometimes caught him. "On holiday" meant our scandalmonger was laid up with wounds again.

With no juicy stories to delay me further, soon I was being interviewed by the rather dour scribes who run the news service. Or so they
thought. I had more experience. In reality, I was interviewing them.

There were two: Holconius and Mutatus. They looked about fifty,
worn-out by years of deploring modern life. Holconius, the elder and
presumably senior, was a seamy, thin-featured stylus-pusher who last
smiled when the story came in about the Empress Messalina plying her
trade in a brothel. Mutatus was still more po-faced. I bet he never even

chuckled when the Divine Claudius pronounced his edict that farting was legal at dinner parties.

"Let's go through your problem," I probed, fetching out a note-tablet. It made them nervous so I held the waxed pages upon my knee, with the stylus at rest. They told me they had "lost contact" with one of their number whose name, they said, was Diocles. I nodded, trying to give the impression I had heard, and of course solved, such mysteries before. "How long has he been missing?"

"He is not exactly *missing*," Holconius demurred. I could have scoffed, *Well why call me in then?* But those who work for the Emperor, putting an imperial gloss on events—skewing everything to look good—have a special way with words. Holconius had to send everything he wrote for Palatine approval, even if it was a simple list of market days. He then had every pearly phrase redrafted by some idiot until its impact was killed. So I let him be pedantic—this time. "We do know where he went," he murmured.

"And that was?"

"To stay with a relative in Ostia. An aunt, he said."

"That's what he told you?" I assumed "aunt" was the new term for fancy woman, but I thought no worse than that. "And he never came back?" So the fancy woman was tasty. "Is this unusual?"

"He is a little unreliable."

Since no details were supplied, I embroidered it myself: "He is lazy, drunk, feckless, he forgets to be where he should be, and he's always letting people down—"

"Why—do you know him?" interrupted Mutatus, sounding surprised.

"No." I knew plenty like him. Especially scribes. "So the job for me is: go to Ostia, find the bonny Diocles, sober him up if he'll let me, then bring him back?" Both of the scribes nodded. They seemed relieved. I had been gazing at my note-tablet; now I looked up. "Is he in trouble?"

"No." Holconius still hardly raised a sweat.

"*Any* trouble," I repeated quietly. "At work, involving work, trouble with women, trouble with money, health worries?"

"None that we know of."

I considered possibilities. "Was he working on a particular story?"

"No, Falco." I reckoned Holconius was telling me the big fibs. Well, he was the political hack; Holconius, I knew, took the shorthand notes in the Senate, so untruths were his stock-in-trade. Mutatus just listed this month's program for the games. He could do stupid inaccuracy with effortless grace, but he was weaker on pure lies.

"And what section of the *Gazette* would Diocles normally produce?"

"Does it matter?" asked Mutatus quickly.

I deduced it was relevant, but I said sweetly, "Probably not."

"We do want to be helpful." Reluctance filled his tone.

"I would like to be fully informed." Innocent charm filled mine.

"Diocles writes the lighthearted items," stated Holconius. He looked even more somber than before. As the edict reporter, he disapproved of anything light.

I could tell that before I arrived today Holconius and Mutatus had held detailed conversations about how much to confide in me. I worked out what that meant. "So your absentee writes the shock-and-horror society news?"

The two scribes looked resigned. " 'Infamia' is the pseudonym of Diocles," Holconius confirmed.

Even before they admitted it, I wanted the job.

V

In my first week of inquiries in Ostia, I made a slow start. I reported my lack of progress to Helena, the morning after she arrived.

"If Diocles' landlady is his real aunt, I'm the back legs of a Syrian camel."

Helena and I were eating fresh bread and figs, sitting on a bale near a ferry that took workers to and fro between the main town and the new port. We had risen fairly early. We were entertained by a stream of loaders, negotiators, customs men, and sneak thieves going to the port for their morning's work. Eventually a host of newly landed merchants were ferried in, along with other foreigners in multicolored hues, looking bemused. The merchants, fired with know-how, raced straight for the hired mules. Once they realized all the transport had been taken, the general travelers milled around aimlessly; some asked us the way to Rome, which we pretended we had never heard of. If they were persistent we pointed out the road to take, and assured them they could easily walk it.

"You are being childish, Marcus."

"I've been sent on fifteen-mile hikes by horrible locals in foreign parts." I had been deliberately misdirected by roadsweepers in Rome too. "You thought of it first."

"Let's hope we never see them again."

"Don't fret. I'll explain you are a senator's daughter, brought up in ignorance and luxury, and have no idea of distance, direction, or time."

"And I'll say you're a swine!"

"Oink."

Our room nearby came with neither a breakfast menu nor a slave to serve it up. The accommodation had a bucket for the well and a couple of empty lamps, but not so much as a food bowl. One reason we were out and about was to buy basics for picnics before Albia and the children arrived. My little daughters might be fobbed off with "Let's all go hungry for fun on this holiday!" but Albia was a ravenous teenage girl; she turned nasty unless fed every three hours.

At least we were in the commercial hub of the Empire. That helped with the shopping. Imported goods were piled in mounds everywhere and helpful negotiators were only too happy to drag items from the bales and sell them cheaply. Some actually had a connection with that cargo; one or two might even pass the price to the owner. I had already bought some winecups an hour ago, and thus considered my part done. There was no need to order up amphorae; provision had been put in hand by me. Helena pointed out that after a mere week on my own I had reverted to the classic informer. I now reckoned a room was fully furnished if it contained a bed and a drink, with a woman as an optional extra. Food was something to snatch at a street caupona while on watch.

So far I had nobody to watch. My case was going nowhere.

"You found out where Diocles was living, though?" Helena asked, after finishing a mouthful of fresh bread.

I picked olives from a cone of old scroll papyrus. "A hired room near the Marine Gate."

"So staying 'with his aunt' was a fiction. He is *not* with his family?"

"No. Commercial landlady of the forbidding kind."

"And how did you discover her?"

"The scribes knew the street name. Then I knocked on doors. The landlady soon popped out of her hidey-hole, because Diocles had left owing rent and she wanted it. Her story matches what the scribes already told me—Diocles arrived here about two months ago, seemed set to stay for the summer season, but vanished without warning after about four weeks, abandoning all his stuff. It came to light because the *Gazette* had an arrangement to send a runner once a week to pick up copy. The runner couldn't find Diocles."

Helena gurgled happily. "A weekly runner? So is there plenty of scandal at Ostia?"

"I'd say Diocles just sits at the seaside and giggles as he makes it up. Half the people he libels are away themselves and never hear about it, luckily for him."

Helena licked her fingers. "You paid the rent he owed and obtained his baggage?"

"No chance! I'm not paying some truant's rent, especially for a room he hasn't occupied."

"The woman has not relet the room?"

"Oh, she relet all right. I refused to pay, and I've sent to the *Gazette*."

"For the money? She shouldn't be paid twice." I explained to Helena that port landladies traditionally double-charge, under an edict that dates back to when Aeneas first landed and was put up at a ludicrous rate in a fisherman's spare room. Helena still looked disapproving, but now she disapproved of me. "Be sensible. I am trying to take an interest in your work, Marcus."

I gazed at her. I loved her very much. I pulled her closer, paused, carefully wiped olive oil from my lips, then kissed her tenderly. "I have sent for a very stern docket which will say I am to be allowed to take away Diocles' property as it belongs to the state."

"The landlady will already have searched it; she knows it is dirty undertunics," Helena demurred. She was still clasped to my chest. Passing stevedores whistled.

"Then she will be impressed that the state is so interested in this man's underwear."

"You think there may be something more useful in his luggage?"

"I was brought up rough," I said, "and I confess to some fetishes, but so far I have not sunk so low that I go sniffing at people's old tunic stains."

"You want note-tablets." Helena Justina snuggled against my shoulder and was silent for a while, watching the ferry. "Pages of helpfully scribbled clues."

Eventually, because she knew I was waiting for it, she murmured with polite curiosity, "My darling—what fetishes?"

VI

The arrival of our children occupied the rest of the morning. Aulus and I had a jocular chat about his planned trip to Athens while Helena and Albia talked gravely about why the dog seemed off-color. The girls toddled and crawled around on their own, looking for things to destroy in their new home. The dog, Nux, raced with them for a while then tired of the frenzy and hid under a bed.

There was a lot to unpack. Everyone tried to avoid being the fool who ended up doing it. The person who sorts out the luggage on arrival always gets blamed for everything other people have left behind.

Yes, of course it is unfair. *Life* is unfair. After ten years as an informer, that was the one philosophical certainty I still held.

For Aulus, two hours in a hot cart with a cantankerous mule, supervising my retinue, had used up all his reserves. A fit and thickset young fellow who should have had endless energy, he soon put his feet up on a window ledge and fell asleep. Before he dropped off, he handed me the docket from the scribes, which gave me authority to obtain Diocles' possessions. Aulus declined to take an interest in reclaiming the loot.

I would have thought he was staying behind because he had taken a fancy to Albia, but she was far too young for him, and had a past too full of uncertainties for a conservative like Aulus. She came from Britain; she had been found in a gutter as a baby, during the Rebellion. She might be graced with Roman parentage—but equally might not. No one would ever know, so in society she was damned. As for Aulus, he had lost an heiress when his onetime fiancée, Claudia Rufina, married his brother instead; he was now determined only to cast his big brown eyes on a gilt-edged virgin with a line of pickled ancestors and moneybags to match.

Albia might have had a crush on him, had she not suffered serious abuse before we rescued her. She avoided men now. Well, that was what I told myself, though, for all we knew when we took her in, her past might have made her promiscuous. Helena had faith in the girl. That was good enough for me.

Domestic anxieties would once not have troubled me. Once, I had no ties. My only worries were how to pay the rent and whether my mother had spotted my new girlfriend. Becoming a husband and father had doomed me to respectability. Single informers are proud to have a racy reputation, but I was so domestic now that I could not leave two un-married persons alone without soul-searching.

Helena had no qualms. "If they were going to sleep together, they would have managed it on the way here."

"What a shocking thought." I hid a grin.

"Marcus, you are just startled that I still remember what you and I would have done."

I reminisced nostalgically. Then I consoled myself, "Well, Albia hates men."

"Albia *thinks* she hates men."

I could foresee trouble in that.

"He is too fat," commented Albia herself, coming in unexpectedly. How long had she been listening? She was a slender teenager with dark hair that could be Mediterranean and blue eyes that could be Celtic. Her Latin needed polish but Helena had that in hand. Soon Albia would pass for a freedwoman and the questions would stop. With any luck we could find her a husband with a good trade and she might even end up happy. Well, the husband might be happy. Albia had lost her childhood to iso-lation and neglect; that would always show.

"Who is?" asked Helena disingenuously.

"Your brother!" quipped Albia.

"My brother just has a heavy frame."

"No." Albia had reverted to her normal wounded seriousness. "And he is not serious about his life. He will come to a bad end."

"Who will?" asked Aulus, appearing in the same doorway in turn.

"You will!" we all chorused.

Aulus showed his teeth. He drank too much red wine and he tried to eliminate the stains by scraping his fangs with emery powder. The teeth would fall out, but he no doubt believed they would look very pretty in the dentist's discard dish. He had all the normal vanity of a lad-about-town—and enough cash to be a fool every time he went into an apothecary's shop. At the moment he reeked of cassia. "A bad end? I hope so"—he leered salaciously—"with any luck in Greece!".

When he bothered to smile, Aulus Camillus acquired sudden good looks. It could have worried me, in relation to Albia. But we left them together anyway. For Helena and me, having someone to look after the children while we went out in tandem was too good a chance to miss.

It was a hot day and the walk to the Marine Gate took us plenty of time. We stayed in the shade, dodging off the Decumanus and down shady side streets wherever possible. For a pre-republican town, Ostia possessed a good grid system and we found our way through its quiet alleys easily. It was afternoon, siesta time. A few lunchtime bars were still serving extended snacks to regulars, with furtive sparrows pecking at leftovers from previous clients. Thin dogs slept against doorsteps and tethered mules stood with their heads down at water troughs, tails flicking listlessly as they pretended their owners had left them abandoned. The owners, like most people, were indoors. They were enjoying normal lunchtime life: a quick bread and sausage snack, or a fast hump with their best friend's wife; aimless conversation with a pal; a game of draughts; asking for more credit from a loan shark; or a daily visit to an elderly father.

Helena and I walked around the back of the Forum and its associated public buildings; we passed fullers and temples, markets and inns, as we headed for the cooler breezes and the sound of gulls. I allowed Helena a rapid glance at the ocean vista, then dragged her to see the landlady. We knew that the woman would be sleeping and bad-tempered if we disturbed her, but at least at this time of day no whey-faced slave would inform us that the mistress was off out shopping or being beautified, or that she had gone somewhere miles away to pick a fight with her mother-in-law. A sleepy seaside afternoon, when the noon sun has baked the morning's fish scales to papery transparency on the harbor wall and the cormorants are sunbathing, is the time to find people.

I watched Helena sum up the woman, who was broad-shouldered and florid and wore a plum-colored gown that was a little too long around the sandals, and a not-quite-matching stole. Her heavy gold earrings were in a hooped style and she had a snake bracelet with sinister glass eyes. Rouged cheeks and tinctured eyelids, with the color settled crudely in the creases, were clearly routine ornament (for her, not the bracelet snake). She was either a widow or it suited her to appear so. She was certainly not the helpless kind of widow. I would have accepted her as a client—though the prospect would not have excited me.

I knew from my previous visit that her manner was one of pleasant efficiency but she was out to make money. Play her right—and pay her far too much—and she would be all sweetness. She wanted no trouble, so on production of my docket she scowled heavily but did lead us to Diocles' belongings. She was keeping them out in an old chicken shed. There were predictable results.

"I can see you are looking after everything." No chickens now scratched around the tiny kitchen garden, but they had left mementos of the usual kind. There are worse things than feathers and chicken shit, but it seemed a crude repository.

"I am not a luggage dump."

"No, of course not," Helena assured her, soothingly. The woman had noted Helena's clean vowels and consonants. Accustomed to sizing up would-be tenants, she was puzzled. I was an informer; my girlfriend should be a pert piece with a loud voice and a pushed-up bust. After six years together, Helena and I no longer explained. "Diocles had mentioned that he was coming to see relatives," Helena murmured. "Do you know if he had any visitors, or contacted anyone in particular?"

"His room was in my building next door." The landlady was proud that she owned a couple of houses, one where she lived herself and one variously let out to seasonal visitors. "He was free to come and go."

"So you saw no one with him?"

"Not often. The slave from Rome, who alerted me that the man was missing, seemed the only one." That was the slave who came to pick up *Gazette* copy. "So long as there is no trouble, I don't pry."

"Ah, you're as helpful as a goat with three livers to a novice augury-taker," I commented.

Helena caught the woman's eye. "It has endless possibilities—but no obvious story to tell," Helena explained, then both women sneered at my joke.

I busied myself with the baggage. There were unwashed tunics, as Helena had prophesied. I have smelled worse; public scribes who work in government offices do know how to use the baths. Diocles' laundry had been sitting around for a month, then placed in a poultry hut. There was never a chance of sweet scents of balsam.

"Did you believe Diocles was in Ostia to work?" Helena had a quiet persistence, which people never felt able to challenge. The landlady hated answering so many questions, yet she was drawn in.

"He said so."

"Did he tell you his occupation?"

"Some sort of record-keeping, I think."

"Seems right." I confirmed the half-lie, having dug out a bundle of note-tablets. They looked almost empty. Just my luck. Diocles was a scribe who kept everything in his head. Witnesses can be so selfish.

I did find one name. "There is someone down here called 'Damagoras.' Looks like an appointment . . . Do you know this Damagoras?"

"Never heard of him," said the landlady. At least she was consistent.

VII

Helena and I walked slowly back. This time we went straight up the Decumanus. I was carrying the scribe's laundry and other possessions, collected together in his cloak. Apart from the whiff, which was a strange mixture of male sweat and old mortar, being in possession of what was clearly a clothes bundle made us a muggers' target. Dresswear is the most popular item for thieves. Half the vigiles' casework comprises reports of filched tunics from changing rooms at the baths. I bet you didn't know that.

Wrong! I bet you have been a victim at least once.

There is no such thing as a bathhouse with good security. Look no farther than the owners. Most proprietors are taking your ticket money with one hand while they feel the nap on your garments with the other, prior to a transfer of ownership. Many have a cousin who is a fuller. Your prized tawny tunic will be redyed bull's blood red, making it impossible to identify, while you are still strigilling off your chosen body oil and moaning that the water isn't hot enough. I take the dog to guard my togs. Since Nux guards clothes by lying on them, the disadvantage is that I get clean only to end up smelling like my dog. Nux is *never* clean. However, unlike one unfortunate man we passed in Ostia, I have never had to scuttle home naked, covering my assets with a borrowed hot-room water scoop.

The Decumanus was the short route back, but it was full of other people. The nervous nude had his own problems dodging jibes and guffaws. We were little better off. All the porters with handcarts had bagged the shady pavement, the roadway was crammed with wagons, and the hot side of the street was baked. Diocles' property was not heavy, but it included a little folding stool, washing gear, a half-empty wine flagon, and a stylus box; the knotted cloak was an awkward shape to maneuver in the confined spaces of a main road with its afternoon traffic jam. Helena was no help. She was carrying the tablets, and as an insatiable reader that meant she was already searching through them as she walked.

"His doodles are useless. He must just scribble a memory aid like 'Tomorrow,' without saying what for . . . This Damagoras you found is the only name—"

There were about five bound sets, each with four or six double-sided wooden tablets, so keeping her grip on all these writing-boards, while struggling to open them one at a time, kept Helena busy. She dropped a couple once, but that was because a water-carrier barged her. Helena stooped to retrieve the fallen tablets, thwarting any "helpful" passersby who might have pretended to help pick them up for her while palming the odd one. As she bent down, a lecherous snackbar waiter clearly planned on goosing her, but Diocles' bundle made a good guard, under cover of which I kicked the waiter. He reeled back with his empty drinks tray. Oblivious, Helena carried on reading. "Juno, this man was a bore . . . here he's added up a bar bill. In the last set he sketched what looks like a grid for solo draughts."

The bar bill came to so little it could only have been cold stew and a beaker for one. The scandal scribe dined out alone. At least that saved us feeling frustrated about untraceable meetings with anonymous contacts. The apparent board game could have been a map for a rendezvous, but if so, Diocles had missed out all the street names. That was no help.

"Maybe he was the kind of sad bastard who spent his leisure time drawing imaginary cities," I speculated gloomily. Nothing I knew about him suggested he was King of Atlantis in his spare time, however.

"Marcus, from what I've been reading so far in the *Daily Gazette,* he had enough fun applying his creativity to '*Flavia Conspicua seems to have grown bored with marriage very soon. Hardly has she been snatched from her mother's arms by the eligible Gaius Mundanus, than rumour has it Flavia (heiress to the Splendidus estates and an experienced amateur flute-player) is already seeing her old love Gaudius again . . .'* I invented that," Helena assured me.

"Sounds good. Your Flavia is hot stuff?"

"Always popular on the bachelor circuit."

"Blonde?"

"Auburn, I should say. No figure, but a lovely nature; she'll do anything for anyone."

"You can take that several ways . . ."

"Oh quite!"

"Tell me, is 'flute-playing' some ripe shorthand in scandal column terms?" I queried.

"Very much so," said Helena, with the gravity I loved so well. "You would think all Rome would sound like a wind instrument orchestra, given the prevailing loose morals. Flavia's fingering is legendary, her breath control is lovely, and it's thought she even sometimes has a go at the double-ended tibia."

To avoid encouraging my loved one's filthy mind, I concentrated on squeezing the bundle of clothes between a temple portico and a mason's cart that had been left parked rather tight against the streetside building line.

Hot and weary, we stopped by at the house where Petronius and Maia were living, where we allowed Maia to fan us and furbish us with mint tea.

We were forced to be introduced to the owner, who was visiting to oversee the installation of a fountain. It was a statue of a naked Young Dionysius; in the throes of his early wine-drinking lessons, the handsome god (who I thought looked rather like me when young) made the waterspout by peeing. Since the house-owner was a building contractor, I assume this tasteful artwork had been pinched from some unfortunate client. Perhaps it had been chipped slightly on the bunch of grapes as it was delivered, and became a "return," with no visible refund on the final account.

Petro's benefactor was called Privatus and had a shiny bald head, over which he had drawn long strands of thin graying hair. They crossed on top, creating a loose darn of fake locks that would blow apart in the slightest gust of wind. Not tall, the builder was bony and knock-kneed. I had met men who were more flash, but he reeked of social ambition and consciousness of his own success. You guessed: I did not take to him.

Petronius was out. In an uppity mood, Maia took great delight in explaining to Privatus that I was an informer, in Ostia to find a missing scribe. I prefer to keep quiet about a mission, until I have the measure of a new acquaintance. Maia knew that.

"So, what would you say are your chances of finding this Diocles?" asked Privatus. It was a fair question. I tried not to bridle.

"At the moment it looks unlikely I can go much further." I sounded more pleasant than I felt.

"Marcus Didius is being modest," Helena declared loyally. "He has a long history of solving difficult cases."

Privatus looked nervous. It takes people that way. "So what do you reckon happened, Falco?"

"At this juncture, it's impossible to say."

"How does an informer—excuse me asking so much, by the way— how do you go about finding a lost person, Falco?"

People are always curious about my work. I sighed, then went through the rigmarole: "Before I left Rome, I checked at the Temple of Aesculapius in case he had been hospitalized—or dumped there for burial. Here, I asked Petronius Longus to see if my man has been arrested by the vigiles for some reason—negative—and now the patrols are looking out for him. They should spot him if he's wandering in a daze. If he just changed lodgings because he couldn't stand his landlady, my task will be much harder."

"Sounds like hard work!" exclaimed the builder, clearly unconvinced.

I smiled bravely. "Have you ever heard of anyone in Ostia called Damagoras?"

Privatus posed, pretending to think. "Afraid not, Falco."

I should have asked Privatus about *his* work. Still, he had probably heard that informers are famous for their bad manners. His life presumably was one long happy round of rebuilding the docks when holes he left the last time started letting in water.

Helena and I quickly drank up our mint tea, then I took her home. She remembered the note-tablets. With skill, I managed to leave behind Diocles' dirty laundry, which I had left standing on the well-swept marble floor, in the atrium of Privatus' tasteful home.

VIII

Next day I went back to the scribe's lodging—this time in the morning. With luck, the landlady would be out then, and I could ask her new tenant to show me the scribe's room.

I left Helena continuing her task of reading old copies of the *Gazette*. She was doing this in the presence of our daughters. Julia Junilla, aged three last month, could start a riot that required quelling by the urban cohorts when she felt obstinate; at the moment she was playing cute. She did it with style and my heart melted. Sosia Favonia, a somber thug of only fourteen months, was standing up naked in her crib, having learned how she could pull herself upright even as it rocked. Next trick: falling out and cutting her head open. Still, Albia had laid a rag rug beside the crib to limit the damage. In order to read, Helena resorted to the old wheeze; she produced a new toy (all the doll, ball, hoop, whistle, and wooden animal makers in Rome knew and adored us), then she moved away quietly as the children grew absorbed. She was safe with her scrolls until the next screaming quarrel started.

I kissed the girls. They ignored me; they were used to me leaving home. Sometimes they seemed to think I was just the greengrocer's delivery boy. No; he would have been more exciting.

★　　★　　★

With Nux darting through my ankles in an attempt to trip me up, I returned to the Marine Gate. It was a long way to walk, only to find the new tenant was out. Depressed, I went to knock on the landlady's door, and at this point the Fates took pity. She was out too, so I finally met her all-duties slave, Titus. A snub-nosed, scar-faced rascal in a loose-fit one-shouldered tunic, this Titus had been kept away from me on previous calls. He was sharp as a nail; like all his tribe he knew exactly his value to a man in need. The pittance the *Gazette* scribes were paying me would not go far around many like Titus, but according to him he was unique. So that was all right.

It was Titus who had actually cleared the room after Diocles went missing.

"Excellent news. Now earn those tinkling coppers you just squeezed out of me, Titus. I know what Diocles is supposed to have left behind—a few used tunics and some empty note-tablets. Now you tell me what else was there, and don't hold back."

"Are you saying I nicked something?" Titus demanded indignantly. Always eager to join in a rumpus, Nux walked over and sniffed him. The slave eyed her uneasily.

"You are entitled to perks, young fellow."

"Well, that's how I see it." He settled down. Nux lost interest. "He had a couple of other tunics—clean ones. As he wasn't coming back, I had them off him."

"Sold in the secondhand market?"

"Too right."

"Diocles came to Ostia for the summer," I mused. "He wouldn't have walked in with just one knapsack and a packet of squid dumplings, but even if he did—"

"What you saying, Falco?"

"Where did his knapsack walk off to?"

"He had two. I got a good price for them."

"Were they empty?"

"Oh yes." It sounded true. I looked at him steadily. "I shook them out, Falco."

"Where did his cash go, then?"

Titus shrugged. "No idea, honest." There was no point pressing it. I noticed the slave had not asked me, *What cash?*

"How much luggage did he have when he first arrived? Would you say Diocles could have moved gear to some other lodging?"

"What he brought with him was left when he bunked off. A stool, and stuff—"

"Forget the stool!" I had retrieved it. The folding stool was wobbly and I had pinched my finger when trying it out. "Was there a weapon?" I growled.

"No, sir!"

Now, that was wrong. In Rome it is illegal to go armed (not that that stops people) but when traveling we all tool up. I knew from Holconius and Mutatus that Diocles always carried a dagger, and sometimes he took a sword too. The other scribes had told me these were standard precautions, in case he ran into an offended husband or a furious wife's huge whip-wielding driver. "I don't want them back, and I won't report you, Titus. I just need to know."

"There was none."

"Right."

"You don't believe me!"

"I believe you."

I believed no slave would ever confess to stealing anything with which he could arm himself, even if he had sold on the weapon. Slaves and swords don't mix.

"So is that it?" asked Titus, looking hopeful.

"Almost. But since the new tenant has gone out, I'll have you show me the room, please."

Knowing he was on shaky ground over the stolen goods, Titus agreed to this. But we found that while I had been talking to Titus, the tenant had returned. He was a run-down furtive corn factor, now sitting on his narrow bed eating a cold pie. Nux ran in as if she owned the place and he jumped up looking guilty; maybe the landlady forbade food indoors. While he recovered—being mainly ashamed that he had gravy all down him—I showed I was tough. I searched the room, without bothering to

ask permission. The corn factor must have known that the previous tenant had vanished; patiently he let me do what I wanted.

He and Titus watched, as I went into all the special places where travelers hide things in hired rooms, from obviously, under the mattress, to
more subtly, on the top of the window frame. The floorboards were all
well nailed down. The wall cupboard was empty apart from dirt and a
dead wasp. I found nothing. I ordered Nux to search, which as usual she
declined to do, preferring to sit staring at the factor's pastry. I thanked him
for making his facilities available. He offered me a bite of pie, but my
mother brought me up to decline food from strangers.

I dragged Nux and Titus outside, put the dog on a string to stop her
going back inside to beg for food, then grilled the slave further. I wanted
to know Diocles' habits. "Did he sit in his room waiting for an earth-
quake to happen, like that quiet soul you're renting to now?"

"No, Diocles nipped in and out all the time."

"Sociable?"

"He was looking for work, he said, Falco. He kept going off and trying places. Never had no luck, though."

As a slave, who would make a copper on the side whenever possible,
Titus did not think this odd when Diocles was already employed.
"Where did he apply?"

"All sorts, I think. He went to the docks, of course. Everyone does. All
the jobs there are well sewn up. Once or twice he hired a mule and trotted off to the countryside; he must have fancied lettuce-picking. He
wanted to be a hod-carrier one week, but he was no good at it and they
kicked him out. Vulcan's breath, I reckon he even tried joining up for the
vigiles!"

That was a facer. "Surely not?"

"No, you're right, Falco; he must have been ragging me. No one is that
daft."

"Anything else?"

"Not that I can think of."

"Well, thanks, Titus. You've given me a picture of his movements."

It was a faint picture, and one in which Diocles had either gone nuts
and was trying to run off to another life or had laid a false trail to hide

whatever sensational story he was looking into as Infamia. Several false trails, by the sound of it.

I was not quite discounting the first possibility. The man had disappeared. Whatever the other scribes thought about Diocles being irresponsible and whatever I suspected about his work having gone wrong, he could still have deliberately chosen to vanish. People do run off without warning. For no obvious reason, some decide to start afresh and it is often in a new role that would amaze their friends. I had an uncle who bunked off like that—my mother's eldest brother. He had been even more odd than her other two weird brothers, Fabius and Junius. Now he was the one nobody talked about anymore.

IX

There was a large, mad-eyed, paw-scrabbling, tooth-baring black-and-white dog tied up on the landing when I went home for lunch. Hades: it was Ajax. I knew what that meant. Nux growled at him with long-term animosity. I patted and shushed Ajax, who was desperate but harmless. On hearing my name called, I dutifully slunk indoors.

Lunch was on the table; Julia was hiding under it. Favonia was trying really hard to clamber out of the crib. Helena looked frosty.

Julia was hiding because we had been visited by her cousin, Marcus Baebius Junillus, an infant who was deaf, rather excitable, and given to sudden shrill exclamations. Favonia was frantic to play with him; she loved anyone eccentric. Helena was frosty because little Marcus (and also the slavering dog Ajax) had been brought to see us by my sister Junia: famous for her unlovely temperament, for her ludicrous husband, Gaius Baebius the customs clerk, and for ruining Flora's, the one-time hotspot caupona that she had inherited—which was how Junia saw it—when my father's mistress died.

"Hello, brother."

"Hail, sister. You're looking a picture."

Junia squinted at me, rightly suspecting I meant a picture I would not find a nail for. She dressed formally—every pleat in place—and primped her hair into regular fat rolls. A self-righteous snob, she had always imagined her stiff mode of attire made her look like the matrons of the imperial family—the old-fashioned, severe ones that never slept with their brothers or the Chief of Police, the ones nobody cares about. No amount of forcing would groom Junia's spoiled little son to be an emperor, however. That was why Helena always made me be polite; lacking children, Junia and Gaius had willingly adopted Marcus when he was abandoned as a baby. They had known he was deaf. They tackled it stalwartly.

Junia milked this act of charity every time we met. I had never liked her, and my patience was close to evaporating. That was even before she said shamelessly, "We heard you were on holiday in Ostia and all the family are planning to come and stay with you. I rushed down to get in first."

Gaius Baebius worked here at the port. He had done so for years and anyone else would have acquired an apartment by now; instead, meanness made him sleep on a pallet at the customhouse when he stayed overnight. For him, the lack of an apartment must have the extra benefit of preventing Junia visiting.

"I'm not on holiday," I said curtly.

Helena made haste to add, "Sadly, I have had to say we don't have space for you, Junia. Albia and Julia are in our second room, the baby has to sleep with us, and poor Aulus is having to stretch out on the floor in here—"

Straightening her numerous strands of necklace, Junia brushed Helena aside. "Oh, don't fret. Now that I've seen Maia's living arrangements in that lovely house, we shall all stop with them."

I said Maia would be thrilled. Junia glared at me.

"If you're not having a break here, Marcus, I suppose you are on one of your daft exploits. What is it this time?"

"Missing person."

"Oh, you should ask Gaius to help. He knows absolutely everyone in Ostia—" Who thought that one up? My brother-in-law was completely unsociable; people fled his company. He was a ponderous, pontificating, boring, boasting drone. He knew how to wind me up too. He always insisted on joining me if he caught me in a wine shop, then he always let me pay the bill. "Have you any leads?" Junia preened herself for know-ing the right jargon.

"Ask Gaius if he's ever heard of someone called Damagoras," Helena told her, rather more crisply than usual.

"He's bound to know. Your case is solved already."

If there was one person who was unlikely to provide me with infor-mation it was Gaius Baebius.

Her son was fractious so we managed to get rid of my sister. That was just as well, because Petronius arrived soon afterward, urgently needing to rage about Junia booking herself in with him and Maia.

"Privatus can't be expected to put up all your bloody family, Falco! I can't stand that woman—" When he calmed down, I asked him to check if there was a Damagoras on any vigiles list. "We don't keep lists!" he in-sisted.

"Don't be unreasonable, Petro. You have lists of prostitutes, actors, mathematicians, religious maniacs, astrologers—*and informers!*" We all chorused the last one, an old joke. Not so funny if you thought your name was in the files. As mine was, undoubtedly.

"So, Falco, are you looking for an evangelical astrologer who hires out his body and appears in tragedies?"

"I don't know what I'm looking for, and that's the shitty truth."

"Should be easy to spot."

"Never mind," Helena soothed us gently, as she placed lunch bowls before us. "Junia is planning to ask super Gaius Baebius to help you, so everything will be all right." For an instant Petronius stared at her, almost taken in.

"Donkey's arse! I can't wait to get rid of them." Petronius might be liv-ing and sleeping with my youngest sister, but he thought the same about the rest as I did.

Mind you, I always thought something funny had happened between him and Victorina. But when she was alive, you could say that about Victorina and pretty well anybody masculine in Rome. Had she been a person of note, my rowdy eldest sister could have kept Infamia in dirty stories for months at a time.

So had some siren lured the scribe to a seashore love nest and kept him trapped in sexual bondage? That should be fun to investigate.

Later, Helena told me that from her research so far into the *Gazette,* several females of quite illustrious lineage were current favorites for mention.

"Empty-headed socialites seem to enjoy the attention. Silly girls made pregnant by outrageous boyfriends almost court discovery."

"What's new, sweetheart? But these lasses are in Rome, not Ostia."

"The big story ought to be how Titus Caesar is living openly at the Palace with Queen Berenice. That will never be mentioned."

"For one thing, they are in love," I said. Helena laughed at my romantic streak. "Well, Berenice is so gorgeous he can hardly hide her. Every male at the Circus Maximus thinks that Titus is a lucky dog—and Titus has no objection to them knowing all about his luck."

"The Emperor disapproves," replied Helena with some sadness. "Vespasian is bound to persuade Titus to end it one day. That won't be mentioned either, except as a note under diplomatic events, when the poor woman is sent home. 'The Queen of Judaea has concluded her state visit and returned to the East.' How much genuine heartache will that leave unsaid? 'The Queen of Judaea is far too exotic to be received in stuffy patrician homes. Her oriental origins make her unacceptable as a consort to the heir to the Principate. The mean-spirited snobs with "traditional" values have won; lovely Berenice is to be torn from her lover's arms and dumped.'"

"Meanwhile," I agreed, "there will be awful legates' awful daughters holding orgies with the charioteers at the Consualia Games, and senators-elect going up the skirts of the priestesses at the Temple of Virgin Diana like geckos under rocks."

"While for light relief Infamia will say that the rumor is false that pirates are operating again off the Tyrrhenian coast."

I laughed.

"No, that was real," Helena said. Then she laughed too. The one thing every Roman schoolchild knows is that the seas were all cleared of pirates a hundred years ago by Pompey the Great.

My old teacher, Apollonius, used to add thoughtfully that fewer people remember how Pompey's own son, Sextus Pompeius, a contender for the highest seat of power, then lured some of the same pirates from peaceful retirement and joined with them to cause upheaval, during his quarrels with Augustus. One place the noble Sextus and his colorful cronies had then raided was Ostia. Their stay on land, with its merciless rape and thoroughly well-organized pillage, remained a horrific folk memory.

"Don't let's get too excited, love. Not if Infamia says the pirate rumor is false."

"True." Helena dug me in the ribs teasingly. "But there are all kinds of shorthand ways to make insinuations in the scandal reports."

Now we were back to flute-playing. And it was giving me ideas.

X

Beset by family, I needed escape. We informers are tough men. Our work is grim. When not treading a solitary path, we like to be surrounded by other grim, tough men who feel that life is filthy, but that they have mastered it. I sought fellow professionals: I went to visit the vigiles.

A weary group was hauling back a siphon engine after a fire last night. Begrimed and still coughing from the smoke, they trundled in listlessly through the tall gate of the squadron house. A couple dragged charred esparto mats. These seem crude, but used in quantity they can suffocate a small blaze, long before water can be fetched. One squat soul with meeting eyebrows, who must have been on punishment duty, was laden with everyone's axes and crowbars, and had all their ropes slung around him in diagonal coils; the others were joshing him as he dropped his load just inside the entrance and collapsed. They clanged down their empty fire buckets, and straggled off to wash. Ex-slaves to a man, they were used to exhaustion, dirt, and danger. Each knew that if he survived for six years, he would receive a diploma of citizenship. Quite a few did not survive. Of those who did, some madmen would even choose to stay on afterward. Self-preservation took second place to the free meals and camaraderie. And maybe they liked roughing up the populace while on the crime roster.

I followed them inside. Nobody challenged me. Somewhere there should be an officer of the day, like Petro an ex-legionary who wanted a secure job with a few thrills and plenty to moan about. He was invisible. I could hear the troopers exchanging insults as they cleaned up indoors, but the parade ground was deserted. It added to the impression that detached duty out at Ostia was the free-and-easy option.

I walked around the porticoes in the heavy shade cast by the barrack-like buildings. In one of the rooms a handful of prisoners, burglars captured during the night watch, were being processed by a wizened clerk. He kept them subdued by his competent personality. When I coughed, he looked up from his charge sheet; he knew me, and when I inquired about applicants, he suggested I might find Rusticus three rooms down.

"Who's he?"

"Recruiting officer. Your lucky day. He comes once in two weeks, Falco." I had not reminded the clerk of my name. "Rusticus will find time for you. He's never busy."

Rusticus had taken over a cold office, outside which he had hung a slate with a picture of a stick man and an arrow to say: Enter here. Fresh from Rome, he kept up appearances. He was awake. There was no visible evidence of him eating his lunch or playing board games. He had unpacked a scroll for oaths of allegiance even though he had no one queuing. He would need an officer to witness any enlistment; I guessed he had one on call.

Whimsically, he pretended to think I was an applicant. He gave me the open-faced grin of welcome, though I noticed he did not bother to pick up his stylus.

He knew perfectly well I had some other errand. At thirty-six, I was too old, for one thing. I had a well-exercised body that had seen too much action for me to volunteer for more. My laundered oatmeal tunic with bilberry braid was a custom fit, my dark curls had been tamed by a half-decent barber, and I had treated myself to a professional bathhouse manicure. Even if he failed to notice my firm gaze and tricky attitude, once I stuck my thumbs in my belt he should have seen that it was a damn good belt. Visible on my left hand was a gold equestrian ring. I was a free citizen, and I had been promoted by the Emperor to the middle rank.

"The name's Falco. Friend of Petronius Longus."

Petro was in the Fourth Cohort. Rusticus must be from another, though not necessarily the Sixth, who were currently on duty here. He conceded, "Yes, Petronius Longus has supervised enrollments with me."

"A good lad."

"Seems it. What are you after, Falco?"

I sat down on a spare stool. It was lower than his, so nervous recruits would feel vulnerable as they pleaded to join. This basic ploy failed to worry me. "I am making official inquiries about a man who has gone missing from a Palace secretariat." Although "official" was pushing it, the *Daily Gazette* was a Palace mouthpiece and the scribes would pay me from public funds.

"I'm surprised they noticed!" Rusticus and I were not friends yet. I thought we would never be. But he took an interest.

"Quite. Rusticus, this may be a false lead, but someone has told me my fellow recently tried to join the vigiles. His name is Diocles. If he gave a falsie, of course, I am stuck."

Rusticus shrugged, then he leaned back on his stool, arms folded. He made no move toward the scroll in which newly enlisted recruits were formally recorded; he did not even look at it. "Diocles? I turned him down."

Obviously nobody much was rushing to join up in Ostia. I kept that to myself. "Can you recall the circumstances?"

He pursed his lips. He could not resist playing with an informer. "I do remember, because unless he only has one leg—no, we took a Moesian amputee once, and he hopped around brilliantly—until he fell through a floor—turning one down is a rarity."

"Something not right about him?"

Rusticus took his time again. "Diocles. Thin fellow. Unobtrusive sort of maggot. He trotted in, and he had all the patter. Had been a slave but was manumitted. Had forgotten to bring his certificate, but would be able to produce it. Wanted a new life, with a chance of citizenship and the corn dole. Even said he wanted to serve the Empire. Some of them regard being a patriot as a recommendation, though personally I find it more natural if they are trying to get free dinner and fun with flames."

A cynic. I grinned my appreciation. Maybe he warmed up slightly. Or not. I decided he was just an unpleasant bastard.

"Was he too old?"

"I think he said thirty-eight. Not too far gone if they are tough."

"So why did you reject him?"

"No idea." Rusticus thought about it, as if amazed at himself. "Palace secretariat, you say? Fits. His Latin was a touch too nice. But it was instinct on my part. Always trust instinct, Falco."

I said nothing. Instinct can be a fickle friend. That significant "feeling" often only means your last night's dinner has played up, or you're getting a cold sore.

The recruitment officer leaned forward suddenly. "So what is the bastard? Special bloody audit?"

I laughed. He thought Diocles was investigating the vigiles, some corruption inquiry. "You're not far out. He's Infamia." Wasted. The vigiles never keep up with the news. "He writes the scandal section of the *Daily Gazette.*" I was taking a chance; Rusticus might now close ranks and clam up. But as a recruiter, I reasoned that he was a half-day visitor, not bonded with the Sixth. "So," I said, lowering my voice, "do we conclude that someone in the current detachment is thought to need scrutiny—in the public interest?"

There could be a number of reasons. Swiping funds. Having perverts for playmates. Blatant inefficiency . . .

Wrong: inefficiency does not make exciting news.

"A skirt?" asked Rusticus, looking keen as he thought up his own ideas. "No, sleeping around is allowed! The *wrong* skirt."

"Possible," I agreed. "I stayed here briefly. Things seem positively prudish. I've seen hardly any late-night visitations from women with togas." On a female, the toga is the badge of a prostitute.

"No; it would have to be big," said Rusticus. "An officer in bed with a town councillor's wife?"

"Or sending very large presents to a superior officer's mistress?"

"Or cozying up to a crook's floozy—even then, only if the crook was under special investigation."

"For at least import tax evasion—"

"With backhanders—"

"Above-average ones!"

We both subsided, at the limit of not-very-shocking offenses to name. "I can't see it, Falco," sighed Rusticus. "Wouldn't raise a flicker in Rome."

I was ready to leave. "You're right. It's tame. I don't know why he came here, but I don't believe Diocles was looking into the vigiles themselves." He had gone after other jobs, for one thing. "So; is there anything else you can tell me about my missing man?"

"He was fine when he left here. I said we had no vacancies but I'd keep his name listed. He took it quietly enough."

I had reached the door before an impulse made me turn back. "Did he give you a contact address? A room by the Marine Gate?"

Rusticus looked surprised. "He said he'd come in that day from out of town; I had the impression he stayed somewhere on the coast. Afraid I didn't bother to take down the details. I wasn't interested in him, after all."

I did find the officer of the day. As I left, he was entering through the main gate, in company and laughing with Privatus, that builder with the stranded hair who was giving Petro houseroom. Maybe he was seeking a contract to rebuild the squadron house. The builder acknowledged me pleasantly, looking vague about where we had met. He seemed at home here. It was too much to hope that it was because he was regularly arrested.

I managed a private interview with the officer and asked whether any "Damagoras" featured in their special lists. He said the lists were confidential. He refused to look them up.

Sick of unhelpful blockheads, I went home for lunch. There, my very intelligent and normally helpful girlfriend was awaiting my return. But even Helena Justina looked as if she might turn nasty.

XI

Albia was playing with the children, head down, not meeting anybody's eye. For once, the two little girls were keeping very quiet. My brother-in-law Aulus was acting unconcerned, as if whatever had happened was none of his fault; he greeted me with a silent grimace, then stuck his head in a note-tablet. I could not even see Nux. They all seemed grateful that I had come home, to fend off the ballistics and rescue them.

Helena Justina continued for a moment to slice leeks on an unpleasant wooden board we had inherited with the apartment. Leeks are an Ostia speciality. I had been promised my favorite recipe. It looked as if grit would be left in among the fronds. On purpose.

"Helena, dear heart! Shall I go out and come in again, more contrite?"

"Are you suggesting there is something wrong, Falco?"

"Of course not, fruit. I would just like to make it plain I never touched that barmaid, whatever the girl may be saying, and if somebody has left a dead rat in the gutter overflow, it wasn't me; that is absolutely *not* my idea of something funny."

Helena took a long, deep breath, and looked up from her knifework with a stare that said she was considering the barmaid suggestion very, very thoroughly. Maybe that joke had been too big a risk.

She was still holding the knife. I really could not think of any reason to feel guilty, so I stayed quiet and looked meek. Not too meek. Helena was easily irritated.

She was still holding her breath too; now she let it all out, extremely slowly. "Nobody should be blamed for their family," she announced.

"Ah!" It was one of my relatives. No surprise. I could have run through the possibilities mentally, but there were far too many.

"Your sister came," said Helena, as if it had nothing to do with the atmosphere.

"Maia?" I did not even bother to mention Allia or Galla. They were useless lumps who tried to borrow things, but they were safe in Rome.

"Junia."

Right. Junia came back. How typical. "Whatever she did or said, I apologize for her, dearest."

"It wasn't what *she* did," snarled Helena, my mild, tolerant, diplomatic partner. "It never is what Junia *does*. It's what she damn well *is*. It's how she sits there in her neat outfit, with her careful jewels, and her struggling son in his very clean tunic, and her slobbering dog, who gets himself everywhere, and I can't actually say what leads it to happen, but maybe her trite conversation and self-satisfied behavior just—make—me—want to scream!"

Now she felt better.

I sat down, nodding sympathetically. Helena went back to chopping. For a girl who had been brought up to consider kitchens as places into which she was only expected to wander to give orders about recipes for patrician banquets, she could now wield sharp knives adeptly. I identified a handy cloth that would stanch blood, then I watched with caution. I had taught her to try and avoid chopping off her fingers, but it seemed best not to distract her until she finished. Helena had long, beautiful hands.

After a time she threw the leeks in a bowl of water, rattled them about to clean them, wiped the knife, banged down a pan on the cooking bench I had improvised, looked for the olive oil distractedly, and allowed me to find it for her. I took hold of the pan handle. She snatched it away from me. I stood aside politely. She elbowed me back into position and allowed me to take over cooking. Aulus, with unheard-of domestic sense, unwound himself and poured a beaker of red wine, which he placed formally in his sister's hand.

Helena leaned against the table, sipping. Her frown relaxed. Soon she told me glumly that Petronius had called that morning; he had looked up the lists of undesirables kept by the vigiles and found no mention of any Damagoras. Then we got to the nub: Helena added that the reason Junia had called was to gloat that Gaius Baebius did have some information on the name. Being Junia, she would not tell Helena what. Well, that was why Helena was annoyed.

I would have to see Gaius Baebius. Now I was annoyed too.

Still, the leeks were good. I crumbled in some goat's cheese and de-stoned black olives, frisked it all around with a little salty fish-pickle, served it into bowls, and topped off with a dribble of extra oil. We ate this with yesterday's bread. Helena had been too angry to go out to the baker for fresh.

XII

I took the ferry to Portus, where Gaius Baebius worked in his capacity as a customs clerk—or, as he would pedantically add, a supervisor. The vital labor of harassing importers for their tax took place at the main harbor, the big new one planned out by the Emperor Claudius and finished by Nero. Meant to replace the clogged facilities at Ostia, Portus had been inadequate for the task since the day it was inaugurated. I knew Gaius would explain that to me all over again, whether or not it affected my inquiry and despite me reminding him that he had moaned on about it before.

I had promised Helena I would use the ferry trip to calm down. Instead, as I sat in the boat being rowed slowly over, stress gripped me.

Portus Augusti had been constructed about two miles to the north of Ostia itself. I tried to concentrate on geography.

Ostia was the only real harbor on Italy's western coast for many miles in both directions, or nobody would ever have made land here. You probably had to go up as far as Cosa to find a decent berth to the north, while to the south, grain ships that came from Africa and Sicily still often unloaded at Puteoli on the Bay of Neapolis, after which the corn was transported overland to avoid the difficulties here. Nero had even wanted to build a canal all the way from Puteoli, as a "simpler" solution than trying to improve the Ostia maritime gateway.

Rome had been founded upstream on high ground at the earliest bridgeable point on the Tiber—but that presupposed ours was a useful river. Romulus was a shepherd. How would he know? Compared with the grandiose waterways in most major provincial capitals, old Father Tiber was a widdle of rat's piss. Even at Ostia, the muddy river mouth was not much more than a hundred strides across; Helena and I had been given much amusement the other morning, watching large ships trying to maneuver past one another amid shouts of alarm and clashing oars. And the river was unfriendly. Swimmers were regularly plucked out of their depth and swirled to their death by drowning. Children did not paddle on the Tiber's brim.

The small, meandering Tiber was too full of silt, its current was unpredictable, and it wound all over the countryside. That said, although it flooded often and suffered droughts, it was rarely impassable. Vessels could make their way inland to moor right up alongside the Emporium in Rome, and some still did. However, rowing upstream meant the fast flow was against them. Sailing was ruled out because of the bends; square-rigged ships lost the wind at every turn. So they were towed. Some were hauled by draft animals, but most were dragged up or down the twenty-mile distance by teams of despondent slaves.

That imposed a weight limit. And it was why Ostia, together now with Portus, was so important. Many ships had to moor and unload when they arrived at the coast; then they had to lay up, while they awaited their outgoing loads and passengers. So Ostia had always served as a docking anteroom to Rome. Unhappily, it had been chosen and founded by saltpan workers, not sailors. The Tiber mouth was perfect for an industry that required shallows, but there had never been deep moorings. Worse, it was an unsafe landing point. The largest trade vessels—including the huge imperial corn transporters—had to disembark at least part of their cargoes into tenders out in the open sea. That was dangerous, and only feasible in summer. Two currents met, where the river dashed out into the oncoming tide. There were treacherous west winds to contend with. Add in the coastal shoals and the sandbar at the mouth of the river, and merchantmen arriving from foreign lands had a good chance of foundering.

Meanwhile, for more manageable shipping that ventured straight to land there were still problems. As it finally reached the coast, the Tiber divided into two channels, both nowadays too choked with silt for ships of any size. Portus had been designed to relieve the problem, and to some extent it did. Many trading vessels now docked in the Portus basin. The muddy Tiber channels were still busy with traffic, especially the four different ferry services, all run by dour, toothless men whose families predated Romulus, who charged separate fares for locals and for visitors, and who could diddle your change in all known foreign currencies.

I braved the ferry, then hitched a lift in a vegetable cart across the Island, a flat area of market gardens with rich soil through which a busy road now ran. I had been here several times over the years, usually making Portus my starting point for overseas missions. Each time I had found more and more building work, as the warehouses expanded and people chose to build new homes out here where they worked.

The new harbor was heavy-duty imperial magnificence. Encircling walls surrounded the great basin, forming two moles that thrust out to sea. On their far ends stood temples and statues, and between them lay a man-made island. This was famously formed by the sunken ship that had once brought from Egypt that enormous obelisk that now graced the central divide of Nero's Circus in Rome. The delivery ship had been scuppered in deep water, while laden with ballast, and onto this base was planted a four-story lighthouse, topped by a colossal statue of a monumental nude; to me it looked like an emperor, only lightly draped for modesty. Below him, shipping sailed in through the north passage and out through the south, with sailors and passengers staring up at the imperial never-you-minds and thinking ooh, what a dramatic sight.

The giant Julio-Claudian goolies were even more dramatic when underlit by the pharos at night.

The harbor itself was crammed with every kind of vessel, right down to summer visitors from the Misenum Fleet. On a famous occasion, the flagship had called in, the gaudy hexeris called the *Ops*. Today I saw a line of three deserted triremes, which were clearly military, in among the oceangoing traders. Tugs, each with sets of chubby oars and a sturdy towing mast, slowly shunted around large vessels as moorings needed to be rearranged. Bumboats skidded over the water like fleas, amid shouts of abuse or greeting. Skiffs pottered aimlessly in the hands of those inevitable old harbor bores who hang about wearing seafaring caps and trying to cadge drinks off people like me. From time to time large vessels silently entered or left the harbor beneath the shadow of the lighthouse, then there would be flurries of interest among the cranes and offices on the moles. I could not count the forest of masts and towering beaked prows, but there must be sixty or seventy sizable ships tied up inside the harbor, plus a few strays anchored offshore and various vessels plying up and down at sea.

I had traveled the world, but seen nowhere like this. Ostia was the hub of the widest trade market ever known. The Republic had been an era of modest prosperity that ended in civil war and hardship; the emperors, who were backed by legendary financiers and flush with spoils, soon taught us sumptuous spending. Rome now gorged itself on produce. Marbles and fine timbers were bought in endless quantities from every corner of the Empire. Artwork and glassware, ivory, minerals, jewels, and oriental pearls poured into our city. Fabulous spices, roots, and balsams were brought in by the shipload. Brave men imported oysters from the northern waters, carried alive in barrels of murky salt water. Amphorae laden with salt fish, pickles, and olives jostled for notice among thousands upon thousands of other amphorae brimming with olive oil. Dusky traders coaxed elephants down gangplanks, among cages of furious lions and panthers. Whole libraries of scrolls were delivered for great men who were too busy to read them, along with refined librarians and papyrus menders. Cloths and exorbitant dyes arrived. Slave dealers brought their human traffic.

Some of these commodities were reexported to enlighten distant provinces. Goods created in Rome were sent abroad by smart entrepreneurs. Italian wines and sauces were dispatched to the army, to overseas administrators, to provincials in need of educating in what Romans valued. Tools, household goods, turnips, meats, potted plants, cats, and rabbits went out in mixed cargoes of lawyers and legionaries to places that had once lacked all of them, places that would one day be exporting their local versions back to us.

When they did, a treat awaited. Gaius Baebius would be here. They would find him lying in wait on the quay at Portus, seated behind his customs table with his soft smile and his maddening attitude, ready to give them their first long, slow, unbearable experience of a Roman clerk.

Only if they were very, very lucky would I turn up to drag him away.

"Come and have a drink, Gaius."

"Steady on, Marcus; I have to be at my post—"

"You're the supervisor. Give your staff an opportunity to make mistakes. How can you put them right otherwise? This is for their own good—" The underlings gazed at me with mixed feelings. A small queue of traders let out an ironic cheer.

Oh Hades. Junia had made Gaius have Ajax for the afternoon. When I pulled him from his seat behind the tablets and money caskets, the dreadful dog came too. An uncontrollable tail knocked over two inkwells, as Gaius lifted off his wide-beamed backside and stood up reluctantly from his stool. That enormous wet tongue caught the back of my knees as the loopy creature bumbled after us. Every time we passed a porter with a handcart, Ajax had to bark.

"Leaving the desk is bad practice, Marcus—"

"Have a breather. Enjoy bumming off for once, like everyone else."

"Ajax! Drop it! Good boy . . ."

Portus was Elysium for an excitable dog. The harbor walkways were stuffed with bollards to pee against, sacks to jump on, amphorae to lick, cranes to wind a leash around. Short men who looked suspicious lurked everywhere, begging to be harassed with growls and bared teeth. There were wild smells, sudden loud noises, and unseen vermin scuttling in dark corners. Eventually the dog found a bit of ragged rope to carry, then he calmed down.

"He needs discipline, Gaius. My Nux would be walking sedately at my side now."

Gaius Baebius was annoying, but not daft. "If that's true, you must have gotten a new dog since I saw you last, Falco."

He sidetracked himself, wondering when our last meeting had been: Saturnalia, apparently. Julia had broken one of her deaf cousin's toys, and Favonia gave the dear little boy a nasty cold. Well, that was children, I said callously, dragging the brother-in-law to the counter of a streetside foodshop. I ordered. I didn't bother upsetting myself by waiting for Gaius Baebius to play the host; we would have ended up being asked to leave the counter to make way for paying customers.

I asked for a small dish of nuts and a spiced wine.

Gaius Baebius held a lengthy debate about whether he wanted the lentil mash or something they called the pulse of the day, which looked like pork chunks to me. Gaius, unconvinced, expressed his uncertainty at great length, failing to interest anybody else in his dilemma. I had tried solving problems for him in the past. I had no wish to end up dribbling with delirium again, so I just ate my nuts. Meat stews were banned in fast-food outlets, in case enjoying a decent meal incited people to relax their guard and express disapproval of the government. No food-seller was going to admit to Gaius Baebius that he was flouting the edict; every word Gaius uttered gave the impression of an inspector sent by some unpleasant aedile to check on infringements of the Emperor's hotpot regulations.

Eventually he decided on a bowl of nuts too. The proprietor gave us both a filthy glare and banged it down, only half full, at which Gaius caviled stubbornly for a while. Dark plans for murdering him seeped into my brain.

One customer edged away from us, declined a refill, and fled. The other walked aside in a huff, and lapped up his potage while leaning on a bollard and shouting insults at seagulls. Ajax joined in, barking so loudly that heads popped out of the nearby grain and spice negotiators' offices, while the bouncer at the Damson Flower Boarding-House (which looked like a brothel) came outside to glare. Ajax had been imbued with my sister's stiff morals. He hated the brothel bouncer; hurling into attack mode, he dragged at his leash until it pulled so tight he was frothing and half choked.

Oblivious, Gaius Baebius fixed me, wagging his finger. "Now come on, Marcus, stop holding up the issue. You want to ask me about that fellow called Damagoras. So why can't you get on with it?"

*   *   *

It took me some time to stop choking on my wine, then a few more moments of reflection on why it would be unwise to throttle Gaius Baebius. (Junia would turn me in.) Then I solemnly asked the crucial question, so Gaius Baebius gravely told me what he knew.

I thought he told me everything. Later, I knew better.

My brother-in-law mentioned a large maritime villa somewhere out of town. Holiday homes owned by wealthy grandees and the imperial family had long occupied the stretch of coast near Ostia. There was an attractive mix of forests full of huntable game and an ocean panorama; holidays could provide exercise and relaxation—and when they palled, Rome was only a few hours distant. That property-lover, Augustus, had owned a spread that passed to Claudius, who kept elephants in the grounds. A nosy tourist, Gaius Baebius had once taken a trip to gape at these places, which were mainly deserted nowadays; a local had pointed out one great house that was actually occupied, where a man called Damagoras lived. "I remember this, Marcus, because of the rather unusual name; it seemed to have a foreign ring—"

"So give me directions to the incomer's villa, Gaius."

"You'll never find it. I'll have to take you there."

"I wouldn't hear of it."

"Oh, it's no trouble," declared Gaius (implying it was enormous trouble, so that I would feel guilty). "As you said so wisely, Marcus, my work can wait. They very much rely on me, but I should take time off occasionally."

I was stuck. My dead-weight relation was now looking forward to a leisurely seaside day out. There was no alternative. I had no other clues to the whereabouts of Diocles. The mysterious Damagoras was my sole lead.

XIII

Once I prized him from his desk, Gaius decided to make the most of it. He suggested we take picnics, sunhats, and our families. I said that would look unprofessional. Respecting the work concept, he agreed even though he had always thought my sphere of activity had all the glamour of the mighty mound of horse manure outside the Circus Maximus. I managed to persuade him we still had enough daylight to hire donkeys, visit the villa, and be back before dinner. We could make up a bathing party some other day . . .

Time was with us when we started. We left through the Laurentine Gate, riding fast through the enormous necropolis that lay outside town. Farms and orchards covered the plain, then when we hit the Via Severina, the main road to Laurentum, there were fancy villas every half a mile. After Gaius had lost himself down several wrong turnings, we were pushing it for time. Off-duty fishermen had stared at us in a tiny seashore village when he took us off the main road. Returning to it, we had ridden through miles of light woodland.

Gaius rejected numerous villas built for people with too little leisure time and far too much money. The Laurentine coastline south of Ostia is a continuous ribbon of guarded homes set in elegant playgrounds, and we had ridden past many of them. The sun had mellowed and shadows were long when we took one final lumpy track off the high road, headed gloomily toward the sea, and turned up at the place we wanted: a large fenced property that by chance had no one at the gate.

The gate was closed. We tethered our donkeys out of sight and climbed it. I wanted to go exploring by myself, but nobody went on a solo foray when they were out with Gaius Baebius. He had no idea of diplomacy, and no intention of covering the rear.

We walked up the entrance drive, keeping our ears peeled. If the owner of this place was the usual rich enthusiast with a menagerie that roamed loose, we were sitting targets. Our boots sank into warm sandy soil on a soft track, where the coastal air was richly scented with pine needles. Cicadas whirred in the great trees all around us. Otherwise there was silence, except for the distant whisper of the waves, breaking in long low combers on the so-far hidden shore.

The villa we reached was built so close to the sea that it must often be uncomfortable to unfold the panoramic doors on its various dining rooms, lest the sea view came in a little too close and spray reached the serving tables, tainting the rich contents of the silver dishes and tarnishing their heavy decoration. Sea breezes would waken sleepers in the lavish guest bedrooms. The salty air was already drying my skin. It must cause horticultural problems in the kitchen gardens beside the bathhouse, the trellised arbors covered with tough vines and ornamentals, and the wide, formally planted parterre where we ended up. There the paths had been graveled, but sand constantly blew over them, and some of the box edgings had suffered from too harsh a climate. Nonetheless, a dogged gardener had produced a green area where he let his imagination run riot on topiary. The estate did boast wild beasts—a half-size elephant raising his trunk (which had to be on wires) and a matched pair of lions, all clipped out of bushes. So proud was the topiarist of his careful handiwork that he had signed his name in box trees.

He was called Labo. Or Libo. Or Lubo.

L BO

stood neatly at the end of the garden. But the topiarist was unlucky. The villa's owner had wanted to see his own name in box trees. The missing vowel had just been beaten down to a stump by a furious man who now seized the topiarist by his hair. As Gaius and I arrived, he was about to cut off the screaming L bo's head with his clipping shears.

XIV

Nobody had seen us. We could still scram out of the way.

"Excuse me!" Gaius shot forward, a righteous clerk at full pelt with his chin up stubbornly. He was interfering dangerously and I should have abandoned him.

The shears may never have been sharp enough to decapitate the gardener, but they had drawn blood. The furious man was gripping the blades together one-handed, digging them into the neck of the topiarist as if he was tackling a stout branch. He was strong and handy.

Pompous and plump, Gaius Baebius shook his finger like a feeble schoolteacher. "Now I suggest that you stop right there." Judging by the furious man's expression, we were next for having our fronds lopped. Gaius carried on calmly, "I'm all for chastising errant slaves, but there are limits—"

The man with the shears hurled the gardener to the ground, where he lay gurgling as he clutched his throat. Killing your slave is legal—though unless you catch him screwing your wife, it is generally frowned on.

The attacker stamped on the topiarist and marched toward us. He was not Roman. His clothing was rich and colorful, beneath a patina of careless grime; lank hair tumbled down to his shoulders; gold glinted at his throat. Most knuckles on the hand that gripped the long-bladed shears were armored with gemstone rings. He had dark skin, weathered in some open-air occupation; from his manners, he had reached the top of his career by trampling on subordinates and bludgeoning rivals. Whatever that career entailed, I did not think he earned his living by delicate silk-thread embroidery.

I tried to defuse the tension: "Your fellow looks in need of help," I called, still at a distance and keen to stay there. "He may never clip a spiral again—pity. His work is a fine standard . . ."

It was debatable whether this man could understand Latin, but he clearly disagreed. I expected trouble—though not what happened. He threw the shears straight at me.

The tool came flying at neck height. If he had targeted Gaius, Gaius would be dead. As I swerved aside, my brother-in-law shrieked. "Hey, this is Didius Falco! You don't want to mess with him!"

That was a challenge—one I myself would not have issued. I feared that our attacker had very sharp knives tucked into every fold of his richly layered tunics and cummerbunds, but that he could kill an enemy with his bare hands anyway. Now he was going to kill me.

Experienced in conflict, I made a quick decision: "Gaius—*run like mad!*"

We both took off. The furious man roared. He pounded after us. So did the gardener, now staggering to his feet to join in. As we reached the end of a hedge, several other men appeared.

We ran past a detached sun lounge and guest suite. We reached the limits of the grounds. We hit the beach. The sand was dry powder, hopeless for running. Gaius Baebius carried too much weight so he was floundering; I grabbed his arm to haul him along faster, and as I glimpsed his flushed face I saw that this was the most exciting thing to have happened to my staid brother-in-law since Junia broke her toe on an empty amphora. To me, it felt like disaster. We were unarmed, way out in the country where they make their own rules about strangers, a long way from our donkeys, and heading in the wrong direction. Our pursuers caught up with us five yards across the beach.

Some slaves overpowered us first. I ordered Gaius not to fight. Quickly

I owned up to trespassing at the villa, and appealed to good sense. I had just had time to introduce myself when the furious man strolled up, glaring. On his side the courtesies were basic. I was thumped. Gaius Baebius suffered the fate of the foolish: he was thumped, knocked to the ground, and given a kicking. Then he made the mistake of scolding the topiarist for ingratitude—and got kicked some more. By the topiarist, this time.

We were dragged back to the main villa and pushed somewhere, headlong. When our eyes grew accustomed to the dim light filtering through an air vent above the doorway, we knew we were locked up in a small empty storeroom.

For a while I did not want to talk. Gaius Baebius shrank into himself; temporarily, he too stayed silent. I knew he would be feeling sore, hungry, and terrified. I was in for a lot of complaints, none of which would help.

I did think that if they intended to kill us, they would have done so. But there were plenty of other horrible things that could yet happen.

Although Helena Justina knew vaguely where we were going, it would be some time before she realized we must be in trouble. Then we would have to wait for her to alert Petronius Longus, and for him to find us. It would soon be too dark for him to search. Given our captor's brutality, an overnight stay as his prisoner did not appeal.

I wondered if this was what had happened to Diocles. If so, he might still be here. But somehow, I felt it more likely the scribe was long gone.

"Marcus—"

"Get some rest, Gaius."

"But won't we try to escape?"

"No." I had scanned around for possibilities. I could see none.

"All right. So we'll jump them the next time anyone comes in?"

I was thinking of that, but would not forewarn Gaius in case he messed it up. "There's nothing we can do; try to save your energy."

We lay in the gathering darkness, trying to work out from a vague, unsettling smell what had been kept in this store before us. Gaius Baebius groaned as our hopeless position finally struck him. Then conscience made my sister's ridiculous husband confess something. He had kept to himself one very important fact about this villa and the man who owned it.

"I was told something curious about Damagoras . . . Is now the time to mention it?"

"Gaius, the time for information was way back. Before we climbed over his gate, I'd say. What do you know about this man?"

"I was told he is a retired pirate," said Gaius Baebius. He had the sense to make it a simple statement, then not to goad me anymore.

XV

Torches announced a new arrival. This was no swine of a pirate in theatrical robes, baring his teeth wildly in the flickering light. Instead, the door swung open to reveal a tall, big-bellied, elderly man, wearing a clean white Roman-style tunic, and accompanied by two neat house-slaves. I would have thought him a retired banker. There was an air of money about him, and I don't just mean that he lived in a minor palace with bayside views. He was sure of himself—and very sure that he despised us.

We were lying on the ground, Gaius lolling against me for comfort. Unable to shift him in time to jump the new people, I stayed put. Extremely depressed and subdued by this stage, Gaius followed my lead.

"What are you?" asked the big man bluntly as he stared down at us. He had a thick accent that I could not place, but spoke Latin as if he was used to it. He could be a trader—a successful one.

"My name is Didius Falco. I am a private informer." There was no point hiding why we were here: "I am looking for someone."

I noticed that Gaius did not try to mention his own occupation. As customs officers go, he was good at his job and even bright. Piracy and collecting tax don't mix. Well, not unless you think the Treasury is a bunch of pirates.

"And your colleague?" The man with the debatable pedigree missed nothing.

"He is called Gaius Baebius." Gaius had gone rigid. "My brother-in-law." That was accepted, but I felt Gaius stay tense.

We waited for reverse introductions, but none came. The man jerked his head for us to get up and follow him. I ignored it. He turned back and said rudely, "Stay there and rot, if you prefer."

I stood up, wincing at my aches. "Whom are we addressing?"

"Damagoras."

So who was the short-tempered maniac who captured us? Not Damagoras. Then he was gone. The slaves with the torches followed him, so I pulled Gaius to his feet and we set off stiffly after them.

Damagoras had returned to a sun lounge, recently occupied. I could not tell if he had been here previously on his own, though I doubted it. There was no sign now of the furious sidekick; I assumed the two of them had discussed their strategy for dealing with us. Damagoras seemed quite casual. That could be a ploy.

The villa was stuffed with high-quality furniture and fancy objects. My father, an auctioneer and fine art dealer, would have grown ecstatic at this chaotic jumble of marble seats, silver lamps, and gilded statuettes. The stuff was sourced in many countries, all from the upper end of the cost spectrum. Pa would have loved raising a sale for it.

There were slaves everywhere too; they went about their business, looking efficient, while their master stumped by them without acknowledging their existence. He had brought us to a room that was heated by braziers against the night chill, even though the folded doors were still half open, admitting the smell and murmur of the sea. Frugality had no place here. Light blazed from many lamps, some the inevitable pornographic phalluses, others tall and tasteful candelabra, plus some everyday oil lamps that were shaped like boots or double shells. Cushions with rich coverings and fringes padded out the sofas almost to excess. Rugs runkled untidily on the geometric marble floor. Expensive things were crammed everywhere, but not displayed to cause envy as in so many wealthy households; like my own father's, these objects were part of the life their owner had always lived. They gave him security. They were a hedge against needing loans from financial sharks. Property as collateral, instead of land; portable; fashionable; fast profits when required.

There was no thematic unity in the collection. This room contained both Egyptian stools painted in jeweled colors and a carved ivory box from much farther east. Baltic amber was housed in a display cupboard. One very large Greek bronze water container sat in a corner.

Maybe Damagoras collected people too. A woman who was clearly not one of his slaves came in. Younger than him, she was wearing a dark crimson, long-sleeved tunic over which were many gold necklaces and rows of bangles. She topped up a cup he had been drinking from and kicked a footstool nearer to his slippered feet; she glanced at Gaius and me, making no comment, then left the room. A relative, maybe. Maybe the man who had nearly killed the gardener was a relative as well. All of them were similar national types.

Members of the household must have had their evening meal. Gaius was growing fidgety. He had a fixed routine. He would be panicky about staying out all night without prior warning to Junia, and he needed regular nourishment. I preferred to ignore my hunger and anxiety until I had the measure of the game.

Damagoras looked over eighty. To survive so long he must have led a life of luxury. Numerous brown age spots mottled his rather loose skin, but he remained handsome and fit in appearance, with large bones. He was less tanned than the other man. What hair he had left, probably white, had been cut very short. He leaned back, surveying us. "You have invaded my house," he said.

"I apologize for that," I replied.

Now the householder was all smiles. "Forgotten!" he assured me. I liked him less now that he was friendly. He sounded like my father, who was as devious as they come. "I am an old man, no time for grudges. I'm a happy soul, generous, easy to get along with. Now, what's that look for?"

I had let my skepticism show. "Men who profess easygoing ways, Damagoras, tend to be narrow-minded despots. However, I can see you are a wonderful character, all warmth . . ." I too could fake the charm. "Who was your friend who apprehended us?" I asked him lightly.

"Oh, just Cratidas."

"Is he always annoyed?"

"He gets a bit hot."

"Relation?"

"He happened to be here." Damagoras evaded the question. "I don't go out these days. People drop in to see if I am still living."

"How nice. They bring you the news and a punnet of pomegranates—then half kill your slaves, demolish your garden, and batter any visitors?"

Damagoras shook his head at me. "Now then!"

"If Cratidas is a mere acquaintance, you are very tolerant."

"Cratidas is a fellow countryman."

I sensed a tight-knit community clustering together in this remote villa. Few strangers settle on the Ostian shore. I felt uneasy about where they had come from—and why. "So he lives here with you?"

"No, no. He has his own concerns. I am an old man, completely retired from the world. So what do you want, Falco?"

I gave up waiting for an invitation to sit, and made my way to the nearest couch. Gaius, like a tame lamb, tailed me and perched on the other end. He looked lumpish, unhappy, and out of his element. All his pedantry had been crushed by the beating.

I kept it neutral. "I am looking for a man who has gone missing. I found your name in a note-tablet he left. He's called Diocles."

Did Damagoras modify his attitude? Probably not. He looked unperturbed. He stretched one arm and thumped it down along the back of the couch he was sitting on. He supped wine, slurping audibly. Then he crashed down the beaker on a three-legged bronze side table. Both the arm position and the crash seemed normal behavior. Not significant. Even at eighty he was a big, relaxed man whose gestures were large too.

"What's he done, this Diocles?" His curiosity was straight nosiness, as far as I could tell.

"People who know him are concerned. He vanished and left all his stuff in a lodging house. Maybe he fell ill or had an accident."

"And for that, an informer gets paid?" Damagoras scoffed. Clearly he held the widespread view that informers are money-grubbing leeches.

"That's rich, from a man who is said to be a pirate!"

Damagoras took it well. In fact he laughed his head off. "Who told you that rubbish?"

I smiled back at him. "Can't be true, can it? Everyone knows that Pompey the Great swept the seas clean of pirates." When Damagoras made no reply, I added, "So did he?"

"Of course."

"Good old Pompey. How did you acquire your exciting reputation then?"

"I come from Cilicia. Every one of us is believed to be a pirate by you Romans." True. Cilicia had always been the pirates' most notorious base.

"Oh, I hate easy generalizations. I had dealings with a Cilician recently. He was just an apothecary . . . So what part of Cilicia are you from, Damagoras?"

"Pompeiopolis." Damagoras made the declaration with mock pride. Anywhere with such an overblown title had to be a dump.

I chuckled. "I can guess who your hometown is named after!"

Damagoras shared the joke. "Yes, it is one of the settlements where reformed pirates all took to farming for a living."

"So now you come from farming stock?" I grinned. "Of course it's past history, but wasn't it all rather neat: Pompey sails out with his grand mission to remove the scourge. At his fearsome approach the whole pirate fleet says they are terribly sorry for being a nuisance to shipping, and will be good boys now?"

"I believe," said Damagoras, "Pompey explained very carefully where they had been going wrong."

"You mean, he bribed them? In order that he, with his inflated ambitions, could look good back at home?"

"Does it matter how or why? It was a long time ago."

"I really do come from farming stock," I said. On my mother's side it was true. "Well, my grandfather had a market garden, which two of my uncles still try their best to ruin . . . We're country shrewd. I take the cynical view, I'm afraid. I cannot believe a whole nation suddenly gave up a lucrative trade, one they had been plying for as long as human memory, and all sat down to herd bloody goats. For one thing—take my word, Damagoras—goats don't bring in much."

"Ah, you upset me, Falco!"

"With my attitude to husbandry—or my view of human nature? Come on, you must agree. Laden cargoes are still sailing past Cilicia— more than ever, in fact. I never heard that Pompey burned the pirate fleet—that in itself is curious and it smacks of complicity. So popping out from inlets and snatching the loot must be second nature. Once a thief, always a thief."

Damagoras still demurred. "Don't call it theft, Falco. Anyone who engaged in the old occupation would have seen it as business. Acquiring goods and selling on."

"Past tense?" I challenged.

"Oh, very much so." As if to disturb my line of questioning, Damagoras abruptly turned to Gaius. "You are quiet! Are you an informer too?"

"No, I work with accounts. Just dull work, adding up figures all day . . ." Aha—the upright Gaius Baebius! I would enjoy teasing him later about his reassuring half-lies. "How did Diocles happen to know you?"

I sat up, startled, as Gaius turned the conversation back to my quest. "Yes, tell us, Damagoras. What is your connection with my missing person?"

The big man shifted and lowered his arm from the seat back, but he still looked relaxed. "He came out here a couple of times. We were discussing a project, working together on it."

"What project? A man of your years ought to be spending his days asleep under a blanket in his orchard. What *do* you do, Damagoras?"

"I was a ship's captain. Obviously I gave up years ago. Haven't been to sea for decades."

"Why was Diocles interested?"

"Maybe he wasn't. I assume he lost interest but didn't want to offend me by saying so. Just when I thought we were off to a good start, he stopped coming here. That would be . . ." Damagoras paused, thinking. "I'm losing track of the date these days. I imagine it was about a month ago." It was now just over a month since Diocles had disappeared from his lodgings at Ostia.

"How did you meet him?"

"Someone must have told him I was looking for assistance. He approached me."

"So what was the project?" Gaius asked, with his usual dogged persistence.

Damagoras smiled and looked down at his hands in his lap, almost coyly. "Oh . . . it's no secret really. I'm eighty-six, Falco. Would you believe that?"

"You're a credit to whatever you drink," I hinted, gravel-voiced from sand in the air and tiredness. Still no offer of refreshment was forthcoming. So much for the hospitality of seafaring men.

Damagoras was a talker who ignored interruptions. "Anyone who says I was a pirate can expect a call from a libel lawyer. I've lived long enough in Italy to know how things are done! I told you, the old trade is dead nowadays. Absolutely. But I had a long life at sea. Plenty of adventures. Met some odd characters. I have opinions on all sorts of things. I had success—that's a story that's always worth telling. I have a large family; I would like to leave something of my knowledge to future generations."

"So why Diocles?" I had a queasy feeling.

"He is a clerk of some sort, isn't he? Well, he told me he wanted work. He was going to help me write my memoirs."

I pointed out that, from what I knew of commercial publishing, the memoirs of a sailor who had *not* been a pirate might fail to attract a readership.

"That is exactly what Diocles said," replied Damagoras, sadly.

XVI

M aking yet another claim that he was an old man, Damagoras retired
to rest. I imagined him having more drink, freshly warmed for him with
fine spices, and snacks on a galley tray. It would not surprise me if his
bed was warmed by a couple of lithe young women, scented with high-
quality Persian oils and skilled in the performance arts.

Very basic pleasures awaited us. We were allowed to stay the night in
a guestroom. It had two narrow beds, with a plain coverlet on each, and
no exciting comforters. A dusty jug of water, which could have been
there since last market day, was the only refreshment.

We were no longer prisoners, but they stopped us wandering. We were
led to our quarters by slaves; more slaves were hanging about in the corridor every time we tried putting our heads out. There was no chance to
explore the villa.

In the morning, a minimal breakfast was delivered by a silent wench.
We had barely time to wash the crusts down with more brackish water,
then we were led outside to find our donkeys waiting. An escort to the
gate ensured that we left the property. We did not see Damagoras again.

"We could sneak back later," claimed Gaius, emboldened by a night's
sleep.

"You'll go on your own, then."

"Oh, right," he capitulated wistfully. "Best to be sensible."

"Junia will wonder where you are, Gaius."

"No, Marcus," my brother-in-law disagreed. "Junia will be expecting trouble. She knows I am with you."

It was still early when we entered Ostia by the Laurentine Gate. Late-night revelers would only just have fallen asleep down in the dingy bars by the Marine Gate; holiday visitors must still be lying in. Traders and regular inhabitants were going about their business. The baths would not open until noon, but thin columns of smoke marked laundries and fullers as their furnaces were brought back to life, while the scent of fresh loaves and rolls wafted delectably from the bakeries. Mullet and sardines were being laid out in rows by fishmongers beneath heavy swordfish, hung head down from metal hooks; baskets of fruit and vegetables were arranged in neat patterns; commodity shops had their big front doors pulled half open while owners sluiced the outside pavement clean. As we rode through the narrow side streets, above our heads busy housewives already had their bedding hung over windowsills to air.

I imagined how in the building contractor's house, Junia would be up and bossing the slaves about as she fretted over the missing Gaius Baebius. Hiding in bed, Maia would bury her head against Petro's back, pretending to ignore the bustle. At my apartment, Helena would be lying fully awake, trying not to worry about where I was.

Anxious about our reception, both Gaius and I wanted to hurry, but we were delayed by a blocked street. There had been a fire. Early morning was so often the time for gawpers to view the remains of a blaze, a frequent result of lamp-oil accidents. A small crowd had gathered by a burnt-out house from which cindered furniture was still being dragged. The owner slumped on the remains of a ruined chest, with his head in his hands; his wife, deep in shock, simply stared at the blackened frontage of their home.

"Looks like they have lost everything!" Gaius Baebius greeted other people's tragedy with relish.

We were in a residential district not far from the Forum. It lay some way from the vigiles station house, so maybe there had been no time to summon them when the flames were spotted. Instead of the proper fire brigade, some local men were overseeing the action. They seemed pretty well organized. As we arrived we saw them removing equipment amid the acrid smell of smoke and clouds of filthy dust. We could hear loud crashes of walls and stairs being dismantled with grapplers; presumably they thought the interior had become unstable. They gave the impression that this situation, with civilians in charge, was normal in Ostia. Worn-out now, they had become bad-tempered. A group strode into the street and started to move back the crowd; people scattered fast, as if they were expecting rough treatment. Gaius and I were slower to respond.

"Shift yourselves, idiots!" The burly brute gave us no chance for backchat. A colleague angrily slapped the donkey Gaius rode; it was a vicious blow, so the donkey reared, tottering almost upright on its back legs. We had our work cut out controlling the beast, while Gaius clung on; then mine played up. It was easiest to carry on down the street, calming our animals as we went.

Next we had to mount the pavement and squeeze against house walls as we ran into a short convoy of builders' carts, rattling toward us. They were empty apart from workmen, who were no doubt going to effect demolition. This was all extremely efficient. I could not say why I experienced unease.

We returned our donkeys to the hiring stable and I managed to shed Gaius at Maia's house without being lured inside. The last thing I could face was an altercation with Junia.

Helena was in fact waiting when I entered our apartment. She was sitting at a table opposite the door, leaning her chin on her hands. She was dressed, in a short-sleeved light blue dress, but with her fine hair loose and minus jewelry. Her great brown eyes met mine, asking if I was safe. I smiled wearily, acquiescing. When I went across to her, I just managed to put down the new bread I had bought, before her arms went tightly around me. I could feel her heart pounding as she absorbed my presence and settled down.

"It's all right, fruit. Something delayed us last night."

"Oh, I knew Gaius Baebius would look after you!"

Helena Justina leaned back to inspect the bruises from the hammering I had received from Cratidas. I was home now and as an informer's girl-friend Helena had seen far worse damage. She was almost calm. Only the fierce compression of her lips spoke of hidden emotions.

"So he *is* a pirate," she commented, fingering my sore cheek. While I was away, she must have persuaded Junia to confess what Gaius Baebius knew about Damagoras.

"He says he is not."

Helena Justina surveyed me with her intelligent dark eyes. Rueful thoughts were working in that clever brain. "I think he is a pirate who tells lies."

"That will be part of his calling. But he claims he is merely an honest, longtime-retired sea captain—who wanted Diocles to help write his life history."

Helena took me in her arms again. Against my neck she murmured, so the words tickled me alluringly, "A pirate who lies about his past . . . so did he want the missing ghostwriter to *fake* his memoirs?"

We agreed that it seemed ludicrous.

But as Helena and I talked it through, we wondered if Diocles had started the project innocently to make extra cash while on holiday—only to discover an unexpected story. Had Damagoras stupidly hired the wrong person? Did the scribe learn something that aroused his investigative instincts, and had he been about to expose a scandal in the *Daily Gazette*? That could have gotten him into serious trouble. Would Damagoras then have harmed the scribe? He certainly had cronies—Cratidas, for one—who could be vicious.

I went back a stage. Might Diocles all along have suspected there was a story here? Did he come to Ostia deliberately, intending to expose Damagoras? I had allowed the scribe's two colleagues to fob me off regarding his motives—or their colleague might have kept them in the dark on purpose.

Either way, I would have to find out for myself whatever the scribe had learned at the villa. I needed more information on Damagoras' background—and I needed it fast.

XVII

I met Petronius at the vigiles station house shortly afterward. We had made no specific arrangements. With Junia and Gaius causing a bad atmosphere at his lodgings, I knew he would have rushed to work. I walked around to the station house, and found Petro sharing a room with the officer in charge. Petro feigned surprise at seeing me, but he was being daft.

The officer heading up the Sixth's Ostia detachment was a short ex-army heavy with a beard—the same caricature of leadership whom I met yesterday. The unhelpful one. I had asked his background so I knew he had been a legionary centurion and was intent on higher things. According to him he was taking the vigiles route to a post with the Praetorian Guard. No doubt it would happen. He looked like a clunk to me. He would fit in nicely.

With this delight, whose name was Brunnus, Petro acted as an intermediary. I explained my interests with regard to piracy. Brunnus blustered. "Well, if this villa-owner is eighty, and supposed to be retired, no wonder I couldn't find him in our lists of deviants."

I refrained from reminding Brunnus that he had refused to consult the lists at all. Petronius had done it for me privately so there was no need to cause friction. I could save crushing Brunnus for later; good things are best allowed to take their time.

"What's the official stance on pirates nowadays?" I followed Petro's lead in handling the man civilly, even though I wanted to poke his vine-stick somewhere dark and personal.

"No pirates exist," stated Brunnus. "Officially."

Petronius rephrased the question, with a peaceable smile: "What's the *un*official position?"

"Pirates never went away. Pirates are a filthy rash that will always reappear. But they operate out of Sicily, Sardinia, Cilicia. The vigiles are a land force, so, thank the gods, we don't have the bastards in our remit."

"I can see that a retired old pirate who never leaves his seaside home would be of little interest," I suggested, "but doesn't your undesirables list for Ostia include current leaders, should they come ashore?"

"We have enough to do," grumbled Brunnus, "guarding the corn supply and catching dockside pilferers."

"No watching brief?"

"The navy cover it." He was terse; I detected jealousy. Inevitably for someone so intensely ambitious, who was not an idiot, Brunnus knew more than he had said: "I can suggest a naval contact with expertise," he offered. "He happens to be at Portus with some of the Misenum Fleet." I remembered the three triremes I had seen there.

Petronius, with his free access to chamberlains, chefs, and huge dining couches, volunteered to ask the naval contact to dinner. Since Brunnus was our go-between, we ended up inviting Brunnus too. At least we were confident he would not steal the household linen; Brunnus was so keen to advance himself, he was bound to own his own dinner napkin, ready for when he was allowed to attend fancy banquets with the elite. He was not sufficiently aware to know that the real elite give you one to take away.

I bet Brunnus already had a Praetorian uniform, and tried it on in secret every night.

When dinnertime came, both Brunnus and the contact were late. Maybe they had wives somewhere, but away from home base they behaved like single men. I reckoned they had gone for a drink on the way here. Possibly they would go for more than one. Petro and I were soon in trouble over their casual behavior. We were a large family party that included infants, children, and other young people, all clamoring to be fed at the right time—not to mention women who grew frosty when we messed up their domestic plans.

Luckily the building contractor's house had several dining rooms. While we hung about waiting for our visitors, Petronius arranged with a steward to feed the family group at once. We would have a small men-only dinner served up separately. Getting restless in our party clothes, Petro and I morosely had a drink ourselves.

Brunnus arrived, solo. The naval attaché must have gone for a drink on his own. The two men were less pally than we had supposed.

We gave Brunnus some wine. As we picked at nuts, to make conversation I mentioned the fire that Gaius and I had passed that morning. The brusque behavior of the men who were clearing up still bothered me.

"Sounds about right!" Brunnus nodded sagely.

"I was surprised the firefighting was not being done by the vigiles," I hinted, with one eye on Petro. I wondered if the Sixth's detachment were slackers.

"If only! What you saw is standard practice in Ostia, Falco. Goes back to before the vigiles came here. Prior to us, the builders' guild always put out fires; they had the right equipment, see. They have retained the role."

When I raised my eyebrows, Petronius explained further. "Only for fires in domestic property."

"I don't get it," I said.

"There was local resentment about the Rome vigiles being stationed here. Some prefect decided we would respect sensitivities, so we let the builders' guild carry on as before, in residential areas."

"I gather your landlord, Privatus, is top of the guild? Is that why he is so willing to be hospitable?" I tried to sound nonjudgmental, though it seemed an awkward situation.

Brunnus poured himself another silver winecup of Privatus' elegant table liquor. "We don't necessarily want to cuddle up."

"Problems?" I asked.

"The guild can be a bit pushy," Brunnus admitted.

From what I had seen of their street behavior, that was an understatement. "How powerful is this guild?"

"Too powerful!" growled Petronius.

"Look, Ostia is packed with craft guilds and associations," Brunnus told me. "They do no harm; we tolerate them. You know how it works—the leading lights in a trade meet for dinner parties; they club together for burial funds; they raise civic statues. The wine merchants have their own forum; when I want to spend a happy afternoon, I descend to check their licenses. The shipwrights are traditionally the biggest mob—but the builders are coming up fast due to all the public works contracts in and around the harbor."

I could see that. Our absent host Privatus was rolling in money. This dining room opened onto a small interior garden, which was frescoed in ocean scenes. At the far end stood a grotto made from intricately patterned seashells. Floating lamps drifted among water lilies on a long pool between the couches. I had a horrible feeling our dinner would come served on pure gold model ships.

"I can see Privatus is raking it in."

"Privatus hasn't even started," moaned Petronius. "He wants to redevelop the whole bloody town. So tell us, Falco, was there any unacceptable pushing and shoving at this fire you witnessed?" I guessed he and Brunnus would like to collect evidence of bad behavior to pressure the vigiles management into ditching the builders as firefighters.

"Now Lucius, old pal, if you're so keen to jump *out* of bed with Privatus, why did you ever agree to be put up here in his house?"

"Rubella." Rubella was the tribune of the Fourth Cohort, Petro's chief. Rubella knew that Petronius Longus was a damn good officer, but suspected him of subtle insubordination. Rubella would not usually provide letters of introduction.

"Rubella's a joke to you!"

Petronius pretended to have a nervous tic, brought on by stress due to mention of his senior officer. But then he said, "Have to admit, he fixed me up very nicely."

"What's he up to?"

"Official initiative to improve relations with the builders. Rubella asked me to fraternize."

"So where have *you* been fixed up to socialize?" I asked, turning to Brunnus.

"We're not that fraternal. I have to rough it at the station house." There was a pause, during which we all fraternized mentally with the wealthy Privatus by swigging more of his fine wine. "Go on, Falco—what upset you about the bastards on fire duty?"

"Well, be fair; they were rough lads and it was an emergency situation."

"Being rough was justified?"

"All they really did was jostle the donkey Gaius was riding."

Petro and Brunnus looked at each other and laughed. Jointly they decided that this was acceptable: to find Gaius Baebius in your way counted as provocation. "The vigiles would probably have shoved his donkey backwards all the way to the Marine Gate," scoffed Petro.

"With Gaius Baebius tied upside down under it," elaborated Brunnus.

Petronius had gone quiet, watching me. "You think we need to watch those builders, Falco?"

"I do." We let the subject drop.

XVIII

The naval man was older than I expected, a white-haired, fussily dressed type, with a meticulous way of speaking. He looked like a freedman who had previously worked as the Emperor's wardrobe master: when the Emperor was not the old soldier Vespasian, but one of the dissipated young divinities—Nero or Caligula—who liked incest and murder. The marine came laden with hostess gifts to beg forgiveness for his late arrival; he carried in a whole armful of garlands for our womenfolk, who were unimpressed.

"Charming," I murmured to Petro, who grumbled back under his breath.

Caninus was the sea biscuit's name. We were not surprised that a contact recommended by Brunnus turned out to be a liability. Caninus obviously arrived hours late everywhere he went and believed a few blossoms would absolve him. Maia was barely polite as she passed the floral gifts straight to a slave; Junia sneezed loudly; Helena had a defiant glint. Only the children fell screaming with excitement on the long streamers of roses, which would be torn apart in moments.

At last we could eat.

"I hope the cook can find you something that's still warm," Maia called after us sarcastically.

"Your sister's a dour piece!" observed Caninus, too loudly.

"Bit of a drink habit," Petronius lied, in a more cautious undertone. "Try bringing her a half-amphora of Falernian next time . . ."

Unfortunately for him, Maia had not disappeared yet, but was leaning on a faux marble column with a purse-lipped intensity that reminded me of our mother as she overheard the libel.

It was a good dinner. I let Petro enjoy his food without telling him what trouble from my sister lay ahead.

When the slaves removed the serving tables after three elegant courses, we signaled that we would pour our own wine now; they left us plenty, being well trained from times when the builders' guild settled down for a long night discussing measured rates for waterproof concrete and how to fix the voting for the next guild elections.

"We hear you're a pirate specialist." Petro was hoping to pick Caninus' brains, then shed him. No such luck; he liked to talk too much.

"Oh, I'm your man!" Caninus intoned, flinging his right arm madly toward the ornate figured plasterwork of the ceiling and its coving above, like some slurred orator in the afternoon court session. He was left-handed. I noticed that. He kept his left hand clamped firmly around his goblet, so the brimming wine barely rippled, despite the frenetic posing. My physical trainer, Glaucus, was a devotee of keeping your main body still while exercising legs and arms until your eyes watered; he would have loved Caninus.

"Naturally, it depends how you look at it," Caninus raved. "Let us land and beat up the locals: you are a pirate; I am a heroic warrior with expansionist pretensions on behalf of my city-state . . . Goes back at least to Athens—"

"The Greeks. Great seafarers," Petro agreed. From him this was no compliment.

Caninus seemed not to notice. "Piracy was the fast alternative to diplomacy. Same with the damned islands. Rhodes, Crete, Delos—Delos in particular—nothing more than enormous free markets where plunderers could sell off their booty, no questions asked. Think of the Delos bloody slave market—ten thousand souls shifted daily, in peacetime or war. They say prisoners are sold as soon as a captain unloads them, and nobody asks were these once free men and women, who never ought to be in chains."

"Still?" I managed to get in.

"Still? What do you mean still, Falco? Has some joker told you the slave trade ever stopped?"

"No, Rome's enormous appetite for slaves has kept the Delos market going—"

"With donkey bells on!"

"Tingaling! I meant, are *pirates* still the slave merchants who supply the bodies?"

"Who else?" Caninus slammed down his cup. He could do this in safety because it was now empty. Brunnus, who had introduced him to us, was starting to look nervous at the man's capacity. At least seeing Brunnus sweat made the evening worthwhile. "We have the Pax Romana, Falco. No war, no prisoners of war."

To save his host's wine cellar Petronius tried ignoring the empty goblet—so Caninus poured his own. In fairness, he was not selfish; he poured for all the rest of us too. "Drink up, young man," the nautical lush chivvied Petro, as if to a novice. Fortunately my old drinking partner could pretend to be tolerant.

"Tell us more," I croaked, although I was now so drunk I had lost interest in research.

Caninus obliged happily, like some awful philosopher groaning into the next part of a three-hour lecture. "Let us have some definitions: piracy, characteristics of—"

"We can send out for a slate if you need to do diagrams." Brunnus stopped taking this seriously.

Caninus ignored him. "Risk; violence; plunder; death. The four pillars of organized sea theft. Death is the best one, for your average sea thief. Raids on land, setting on merchant ships, they all involve robbery with violence and part of the thrill is—" He stopped himself, puzzled that he could have overlooked a vital element. "Thrill . . . Risk, thrill, violence, plunder, death—the five pillars."

Brunnus had a lamp table beside him, on which he carefully arranged three apples, a fig, and a half-eaten hard-boiled egg to represent the crucial quincunx. Quincunx was his word, and I was frankly surprised that he knew it, or was capable of summoning it from his bleared brain.

"Especially death," intoned Petronius. He was lying on his back on the dining couch he shared with me, inspecting the ceiling. Petro's dough-colored tunic with the rope patterned braid, his favorite off-duty wear, had crumpled around the armpits. He had a glazed expression that I had not seen since our last night in Britain, the night we left the army. A story in itself.

I felt sick. I told myself it would pass.

"Killing," Caninus informed us, "is your pirate's favorite party game."

"Rape?" suggested Petro.

"Rape is good, but killing is best."

"In perspective," Petronius applauded. "Thanks."

"To these people"—Caninus could burble for hours without thinking about it—"their way of life is just business. Piracy equals trade. Ships equal investment. Plunder equals profits. That's profits from legitimate activities, to your pirate."

"Do you"—Brunnus woke up suddenly—"do you do this talk for recruits?"

" 'Knowing the enemy,' " confirmed Caninus, tapping his nose. "My grand speciality. Every time we get a new bloody admiral who has only been a shore woozle until his best friend the Emperor gives him a fleet to play with—on such an ill-starred occasion, I have to do this talk for the woozle. I wear my best whites then. Sometimes I even stay sober while woozle-waffling. In between, I do it once a year for the trierarchs at their Saturnalia bash. Extremely drunk, all parties; with gestures."

"At Misenum?" queried Brunnus for some reason.

"No, I'm at Ravenna—" Brunnus, who had previously told us Caninus was from the fleet at Misenum, looked annoyed.

"Tell me," I begged. "Before I pass out beneath this tasteful lamp holder—" A hairy bronze satyr with a large willy. Privatus, who owned it, had pitiful taste. "Tell me about Cilicia."

Caninus gave me a deep, suspicious stare. Once again he possessed an empty goblet yet this time he refrained from filling it. Petronius supplied wine for him. I waved Petro to stop, but he refilled my cup too. I noticed that he left his own empty.

"What's your interest in Cilicia, Falco?"

I forced a smile. "If I knew, I would not be asking for clues."

"Ever been there?" Caninus demanded.

"No."

"Unusual for Falco," Petronius inserted loyally. "This is a much-traveled man. Didius Falco is a name that makes barmaids blush in wineries as far apart as Londinium and Palmyra. Say this man's name in burning Leptis Magna and, I have heard, twenty landlords will rush forward, expecting a very large tip for hay and oats."

"I think you've confused me with my brother, Petro."

"Sounds like I'd like to meet your brother," said Caninus. Thank the gods he could not have an introduction; my brother, who loved deadbeats, was long dead.

"I never tip for oats." I cut across the nonsense: "Cilicia," I reminded Caninus.

"Cilicia," he replied. Then there was a long silence, in which he did not even drink.

"Cilicia, Pamphylia, Lycia. The three mobsters of the eastern seas." Caninus let an awestruck note feed into his voice. "Rock-bottom countries. They are neighbors; they give shelter to each other. You will find harbors in Pamphylia which have been set up specifically for Cilician pirates' use as selling posts, and whole Lycian villages which are occupied by Cilician sailors. Cilicia itself has been for a long time the most notorious of all these hideouts. Between the mountains and the sea. The people up in the mountains claim to be entirely agricultural. Maybe they are. But there are endless small harbors on a rocky coast, ideal bases and markets—the two things pirates need."

"And in these rocky docks," I suggested, "live people whose ships Pompey the Great did not burn—for some reason. People who say they have turned to farming and who claim they keep ships for occasional fishing and a little light yachting in summer?"

"Ships which just happen to be very fast, very light, often undecked vessels with a lot of zip," Caninus agreed drily. "Every single one with a big beaked ramming prow."

"Just something to hold on to as they lean out with shrimp nets!"

"You're a character, Falco."

"What's the word on Pompey then?" I pressed him.

Caninus helped himself to one of the apples Brunnus had placed on his side table. I could not remember if it represented "thrills" or "death." "Pompey," he mused, chewing. We immediately knew his take on the Great One. "Ambition with flippers."

"I like the new definition," I murmured.

"Pretty!" smirked Petronius. He shared my views on famous men.

"Want my opinion of the Forty-Nine Days?"

"Better define that first." I had no idea what the Forty-Nine Days were, though I was beginning to think we would be trapped here that long.

Caninus sighed. "Let's go back, then. It's the dying days of the old Republic and Rome is beleaguered. Pirates are skidding about all over Mare Nostrum. Our sea is their sea. Pirates are ravaging the coasts of Italy—attacking our cities, coming right into Ostia. Anywhere low-lying and prosperous was an attraction—" He had suddenly changed tense, but this was not the moment for editing. "The corn supply was seriously threatened. With the Rome mob raging because they were hungry, the coasts were bloody dangerous. Enough rape and death to fill a novel—and what was worse (this was their big mistake, in fact), whenever the pirates captured a notable man, they subjected him to insults."

"Ouch!" cried Petronius, laughing.

"So after enough highborn victims have suffered humiliation, Pompey goes out to rid the seas of the pirates," I said. "And it takes him forty-nine days?"

"I'll come to that." Caninus refused to be rushed. I was right about the forty-nine damned days, though. "First Pompey secures the corn supply—he garrisons legates in Sardinia, Sicily, and North Africa. Funnily enough . . ." Our mentor ran off at a tangent. "Young Sextus Pompeius, when he later fell out with the triumvirate, used exactly the same tactics as his great papa, but in reverse. He joined up with some pirates, then put a stop to trade from the east, the west, the south. How did he do it? He settled himself in—"

"Sardinia, Sicily, and North Africa!" Petro and I chorused, still trying to hurry him. "But how did Pompey senior manage his spectacular coup?" I insisted.

"It *was* spectacular." Caninus sounded serious. "From what I know, he had not more than a hundred ships. To police the whole Mediterranean it was pissing in the wind. Only half the contingent would have been decent. Some were bound to be barnacled hulks dragged out of retirement. It was a rush job. A classic. But somehow Pompey drove the flotilla of pirates all the way to Cilicia. There was a bit of a battle, though nothing for the annals. Then he dealt with them by that special Roman miracle. Clemency!"

"You are joking?" Even Brunnus woke up.

"I am not joking. He could have—you may say he should have—crucified them all. They knew what was due, and yet he put no one to death if they surrendered. They fled home, scared of his reputation. Then, as you said earlier, Falco, Pompey did not burn their ships. He let it be known that he saw many had been driven to evil by poverty, and he offered the best deal to those who turned themselves in."

"Penitent pirates flocked to submit?"

"Pirates are sentimental bastards. Pirates will slice your bowels out—but they all love their mothers. Pompey set them up with little farms. All within sight of a river or the coast—that must have been in case the pirates felt homesick for salt water. Adanos, Mallos, Epiphania. A large contingent at Dyme in Achaea. Then of course there was Pompeiopolis—just in case anyone ever forgot who deserved all the credit."

"New town?"

"No time to build new. Just an old one renamed, Falco."

"I've been talking to a man from Pompeiopolis," I told him. "A curiosity called Damagoras."

"Never heard of him. He's a pirate?"

"Oh no, he claims he never has been."

"He's lying!" Caninus scoffed.

"Seems likely. He has a huge house, stuffed with rich loot from all over the Mare Nostrum, and no visible explanation for his acquisitions . . . So despite the little farms, they still plunder the seas?"

"Rome needs her slaves, Falco."

"You mean, we want pirates to operate?"

Caninus feigned shock. "I didn't say that. It is treason to suggest Pompey failed. He solved the problem. It's a Roman triumph. The seas are clear of pirates. That is official."

"It's official bollocks, then."

"Ah well, Falco, now you're being political!"

We all laughed. Mind you, since some of us were strangers to one another we did it cautiously.

XIX

Nnone of this was helping me find Diocles.

My restlessness communicated itself to Petro. He rolled suddenly, and stared at Caninus. "Brunnus said you were a pirate specialist. If they don't exist officially, how come?"

"That's the navy," said the sea biscuit, looking coy.

"What are you doing here in Ostia?" I made the query as light as possible. He was a long way from Cilicia, if Cilicia was the pirates' heartland.

"Goodwill mission."

"With three triremes?"

Caninus looked surprised. I let him wonder how I knew. It was hardly a secret. Anyone who wandered around Portus could have seen them and counted them. "Never a warship when you want one, then a whole bunch turn up." He grinned.

"For a shore exercise?" Petronius, a typical vigiles man, wanted to know what was being arranged by other units in the patch he currently occupied.

"We just flit about from port to port and shout the Emperor's name. When the high-ups decide we deserve shore leave, they let us come here and join the squash docking at Portus. We're showing the standard to foreign traders—"

"You haven't chased some pirate ship ashore?" Petro demanded.

"Jupiter, no. We don't want ugly scenes on the Emperor's doorstep."
Until the conversation became political, Caninus had spoken with heat
and passion. Now he was blustering in clichés. I did not believe the
change was caused by drink; he had shown himself impervious to wine.
He was hiding something.

"I'll be straight," I said. I was too tipsy for anything complicated. "I
was hoping you could explain why a scribe who writes notorious sections
of the *Daily Gazette* would have contacted a man who is reckoned to
have been a pirate."

"Why don't you ask him?"

"Sorry; I thought I had explained that. The scribe has disappeared."

Perhaps a change darkened Caninus' face. "You think he's been captured? Well, you know how they used to work it in the old days: if pirates had taken a prisoner who was worth something, a note would be
brought to people who knew him, by an intermediary, naming a very
large ransom."

"You think that's possible?" It had never occurred to me that Diocles
might have been taken by pirates. In fact, I disbelieved it.

"Of course not," said Caninus drily. "Ransoming captives is history.
We have the Pax Romana now. Lawlessness only exists outside the
boundaries of the Empire. Anyway," he added, almost sneering, "a scribe
would not be worth much, would he?"

It was what he knew that might have been important, though I did
not trust Caninus enough to say it. "So someone must have bopped my
scribe on the head and buried him under a floor after a tavern brawl."

"All you have to do is find out where he used to drink," Caninus
agreed, as if to an amateur. "Then bring a chisel to lift the floorboards.
He won't have been writing about pirates," Caninus assured me; he
sounded far too bland. "Your scribe can contact as many Cilicians as he
likes, but now they are loyal Roman citizens. The scribe is bound to say
that. The *Daily Gazette* is a government mouthpiece. He is supposed to
enhance the glint of the Pax Romana."

True. Infamia *would* be allowed to publish, however, if he was reporting that the glorious Pax Romana had come under threat.

Had it? Did that explain Caninus? Was that why this expert, working in what he implied was a defunct area, had berthed at Portus with his three triremes?

There was no point in me asking. Caninus would waffle all night about what had happened a hundred years ago. He had no intention of telling us what was happening this week.

I glanced at Petronius. We had our own situation to contend with. If we descended any further into tonight's debauchery, Petro and I would both be under threat—from Maia and Helena. Somehow we had to encourage our tedious guests to go home. Tomorrow would be soon enough to think up excuses for Privatus about the depletion in his wine supplies, which was far more than the laws of hospitality would support. Tonight we had to get rid of the men who drank it.

Believe me, the rest of the party was laborious.

In the end the sea biscuit left first. He departed with a fairly full amphora of Rhodian red on his shoulder. The steward, good fellow, had ensured that as the joy continued, the quality and cost of the drink diminished, to limit the damage. His last choice was appropriate. Rhodes had been one of the historic venues for the piracy Pompey stamped out. Rhodian red is a passable table wine that travels; that's because this tangy island vintage is traditionally cut with seawater.

Brunnus was harder to shift than Caninus. When his contact left, he slithered from his couch to the marble floor; Petro and I were beyond lifting him. Slaves appeared, however, which made me think they were used to clearing up after lengthy dinners. I also guessed they had been eavesdropping.

"Caninus—" slurred Brunnus, desperate to communicate. "My contact—"

"Yes, he's excellent," I assured him. I was sitting on the edge of my dining couch, unwilling to exert myself lest the results were volcanic.

"Man of few words . . ." Petronius was still capable of wit.

"Lot of misleading ones," Brunnus spluttered, as a couple of large slaves gathered him together and made ready to remove him. "I don't trust him, I've decided. Solo artist. Absolutely not sharing. Absolutely not liaising. Absolutely— "

Brunnus fell silent at that point, absolutely drunk.

I stayed with Petronius. We slept there in the dining room, unable to move.

XX

I shall omit what was said in my household next morning.

XXI

Let us pass swiftly to luncheon (which I did not eat), then on into the turgid afternoon. I spent some of it lying down with my eyes closed, on the floor, out of sight behind a baggage chest.

I struggled upright when Aulus returned from a trip to Portus with information that he had found a ship to take him to Athens—and other news. As a member of Falco and Associates he was trained to keep his eyes and ears peeled. I had taught him to stay alert in commercial quarters, in case he was beaten up or robbed. I did not want his mother, a forceful woman, to blame me if anything ever happened while he was working for me.

"There was something going on, Falco." Aulus could spot interesting situations; in his snooty way, he was a nosy swine. "My ship's captain was having a real upset—"

One of my daughters pushed by him, so she could stare at her unusually withdrawn papa. "Don't bother him," Helena admonished coolly (aiming the barb at me). "He is poorly today. Your father has been ridiculous."

"Ridiculous!" Julia Junilla lisped her first multisyllable ecstatically. She was three, and all woman.

"Ridiculous," repeated Aulus, with awe. "A hot night, Falco?"

"Even you would have thought so."

"Oh I wouldn't have dared join in. In case you wondered." He grinned. "I fetched Helena home."

"Thanks," I croaked.

"Junia offered to accompany me," Helena remarked coolly. "Ajax would have protected us. But Gaius Baebius needed her. Junia is nursing him full-time. He has been badly laid up since your jaunt to the seaside."

"He's feigning."

"No, Gaius has had to take sick leave. He wants you to look out for the man who attacked him, so he can claim compensation for his injuries."

"He won't get it. The thug was brutish, but if it goes to court I'll have to say that Gaius Baebius asked for everything he got."

"Unfair, Marcus. You just hate him because he's a public servant."

I hated him because he was an idiot. "His stupidity at the villa was dangerously real, my love. You're talking as if Gaius will never work again. Has the customs service lost its star?"

"If Gaius has been really hurt, this is not funny."

"I am not laughing."

Whatever I thought of my sister Junia, no Roman woman wants a husband who can no longer work. If Gaius was ever laid off from tax collecting, the family would have only their savings—and they had always been spenders—plus a token income from the unpleasant snackshop on the Aventine that Junia ran as a hobby. Only part of the profits ever reached her. Apollonius, her put-upon general waiter, fiddled the figures; in better times he had been a geometry teacher and he could easily persuade my sister that an obtuse angle was acute. He had been *my* teacher, so I would never snitch on him.

I forced my bleary brain back to the original subject. "So what's this ship, Aulus?"

"Well, come and have a look, Falco. I want you to ask the captain about what was going on when I took him my payment."

"You paid your fare before going aboard?" The lad knew nothing. Even I had failed to teach him common sense. Aulus Camillus Aelianus, son of Decimus, heir to a life of luxury, had been an army tribune somewhere or other and worked on the staff of the provincial governor in Baetica. Who knows how he managed to reach those overseas postings? When I took him to Britain, he had me to make all the arrangements.

"I am a senator's son," he retorted. "The master won't cheat me—not if he wants to return to this port. He makes a fortune from passengers; he has to keep his good name."

"It's your money!" It was his father's money. Still, Aulus was probably right about the captain. "So what's the story?"

"Are you up to taking the ferry?"

"Only to pursue a really good story."

"The best!" he assured me. I was too hungover to quibble. He clinched it, however: "That blusterer Caninus who got you sozzled had his nose right in it. It sounded to me as if there had been a run-in with some pirates."

I agreed to go to Portus.

The vessel selected by our traveler to carry him in search of his legal education was a large transporter in which he had been promised speed, stability, the next best thing to a cabin, and food prepared by the captain's own cook. If the weather blew up rough, there would be no food and little shelter, but Aelianus was his usual overconfident self. Well, he was going to Greece for education. Let him learn, I thought.

I had assured Helena I would check over this transport and ensure that her brother would be as safe as it was ever possible to be, riding the route to Greece amid the summer storms that thunder out of nowhere in the Tyrrhenian and the Aegean. The ship, called the *Spes,* was indeed solid. These days Rome was using the biggest traders ever known. This one had just brought a cargo of fish, olives, and luxury goods from Antiochus via the Peloponnese, and was apparently awaiting wine and pottery to take out again.

The captain, Antemon, was a calm Syrian with big feet. He had three warts on his left cheek and a birthmark on the right. While he found time to see us, Aulus briefed me on what he saw that morning, so I went straight into the attack. "Antemon, my name's Falco. I hear one of your passengers has had a wife go missing. Has she run away with your first officer, or is she getting her leaks plugged by the ship's carpenter?"

"Nothing to do with you," the captain told me, looking grim.

"It is now. Please be honest. While Camillus Aelianus was waiting to book his passage, he heard your blow-up with a distressed passenger. When Aelianus came back to pay you his money"—it would do no harm to establish that Aulus had a witness—"a naval attaché was asking you more questions."

"He was making a huge fuss," Aulus backed me up. "And you hated it, Antemon."

"The navy nark is called Caninus," I said. "We know which rockpool he swims in. He told me himself, only yesterday. So, captain, were you troubled by pirates on your voyage to Rome?"

"No!" Of course Antemon was anxious to avoid deterring passengers. "I have never been bothered by a pirate ship in all my career. I told Caninus that—before I told him which gangplank to jump off."

"Caninus endorses the myth that before Pompey lost his head in Alexandria, he turned all the Cilician pirates into farmers," I said. "Caninus says ex-pirates are lovely men who now feed goats and adore their mothers. But if so, why was Caninus on board your ship? And why were you so keen to give him the fast fly-swat?"

"I was only looking after my passenger."

"With whom you had been arguing?"

"No, I was trying to calm him down so he was fit to deal with the situation."

"Your passenger is in trouble?" The captain looked stubborn, so I added lightly, "Of course he is. We know the man has lost his wife. Well, he may be new to Ostia and careless in giving her directions to their shore lodgings . . . Or what happened, Antemon? I'm still supposing the woman had a dirty fling."

"Mind your language. He is my owner!" growled Antemon.

"This is his ship, you mean?"

"He's a highly respectable charterer. His wife, poor woman, is chaste, dutiful, and probably scared witless. He'll get her back. He needs to be left alone with it. He doesn't want a crowd of uninvited advisers—"

"Advisers on what?" demanded Aelianus.

Last night's conversation helped me work it out: "You're talking kidnap!" The captain was silent. I pressed him again angrily. "Your owner's wife was taken from your ship on the voyage—"

That finally riled Antemon. "No, she was not! No one boarded my ship. No one interfered with my passengers," he protested hotly. "I brought them here perfectly safely. They left the ship. The only reason Banno came back here to consult me was that he reckoned they were set up when we first landed and he wanted to know if any of the crew saw anything. He and his wife only went ashore yesterday. He reckoned someone watched the ship on arrival, sized them up and decided they were wealthy, then followed them and snatched her."

"He thought you were in on it!" Aulus rashly accused him.

"No, no. Settle down, Aulus." I trusted the captain. He was annoyed at his own bad position in this—not least because he could lose his job if the vessel's owner blamed him. If he really had been passing information about his passengers to kidnappers on shore, he would have had a rebuttal ready and a more brazen manner. But it would be madness to finger the ship's owner. "Antemon, I take it you have sold your cargo and your owner has the money?"

He nodded. "Banno will be able to satisfy the people who have his wife."

"And they know it!"

"Of course they do. Keep out of it. Don't mess things up for him."

"Answer this, then. Ever come across an old Cilician called Damagoras?" No. "A younger one called Cratidas?" No. "Has Banno any names for whoever took his wife?" No again. That was to be expected. Kidnappers use anonymity to build fear. "And when Caninus poked his nose in, how come he knew something had happened?"

Antemon was terse. "This is a port."

"You mean everyone in Portus knows that Banno's wife has been grabbed for ransom?"

"Only navy spies, with narks sitting in the taverns, men who have been hanging around on the docks for months, waiting for a whisper that it has happened again."

I picked up on "again." "So it has happened before." I remembered how Diocles had inserted that taster in the *Daily Gazette*: "Rumors of piracy reviving are said to be false." Not false enough for Banno.

"I am a private informer," I told the captain. "I can be discreet. My trade relies on it."

Antemon still hesitated. "You can trust Falco," said Aulus quietly. A senator's son has influence, and Antemon may have weakened.

I twisted the awl. "Look, I was already working on a case which may connect with this. Let me know where I can find Banno. This is for his own sake and the wife's safety. Somebody does need to help this couple," I said. "If you don't want to cooperate with Caninus and the navy, maybe I can do something for Banno unofficially."

The captain was still unhappy, but muttered to us where Aulus and I could find his ship's owner ashore.

XXII

Banno was a pale, tense man, at a guess at least half Egyptian, a negotiator for the salt fish industry. He worked fast: he had already paid up and retrieved his wife.

He made out to us that nothing had happened, but he was not prepared to discuss the matter. We glimpsed the wife, Aline, sitting in a basket chair at their lodgings, deep in shock. Our raised voices in the doorway made her cover her head with her mantle. Aulus and I were kept out of their apartment by Banno, who blocked the doorway. He was certainly jumpy, as if he had had a close brush with fear.

Banno and Aline were leaving for Rome within the hour, and if they came back to Ostia when leaving Italy, they would pass straight through and board their ship. They might very well prefer now to pick up the *Spes* at Puteoli, or even take the long overland route to the deep south and rendezvous at Brundisium.

I said quietly, "The only way these criminals will be stopped is if you tell us what you know."

Banno replied, even more quietly, trying not to let his wife overhear: "They will know if I talk to you. We don't want to be killed."

I offered to arrange protection. He shut the door in my face.

★   ★   ★

We returned to the ship. This time the captain had taken defensive measures: a sailor maintained he had gone ashore, nobody knew where. We were sure Antemon was skulking belowdecks, but it was impossible to look. An extremely large deckhand, coiling a rope in a way that showed off his biceps, made us aware that sneaking around on the *Spes* without permission would be inadvisable.

Not wanting to end up crammed head down in a row of tightly packed amphorae with another heavy row on top of us, we turned around for home.

It was departure time for everyone who worked daily at Portus. Appalled by the queue for a ride back across the Island, I led Aelianus to the bar where Gaius Baebius and I had chatted two days ago. A carved sign, tail up, indicated its name was the Dolphin. A welcome sight to travelers, it had a large stock of wines and a decent array of food pots. I guessed it served plenty of breakfasts when the early morning workers arrived, and it certainly had a sidewalk full of punters in this evening rush hour.

With nothing to lose, I asked the proprietor what he had heard about kidnappings. He claimed ignorance, but loudly asked his regulars. These barnacles all instinctively feigned puzzlement; to them we were slick town boys. When I said a wealthy woman, newly landed, had been captured and ransomed only that day, they shook their heads and declared it was terrible. But gradually one or two admitted that they had heard of such things happening. After Aulus bought drinks all around (he borrowed the money from me, on the excuse that this was a business expense), they lost some of their scruples and we became as friendly as I ever wanted to be with short sweaty men who manhandled fish-sauce containers all day.

Between them, they were able to recall at least three stories of abductions. Since the victims wanted secrecy, there could have been plenty more. Details were skimpy: women were taken, their male relations pressured. A common thread was that afterward the ransomed women were traumatized. The tendency was to leave Ostia fast.

"You don't know who does it?"

"Must be foreigners." Anyone who came from outside Ostia was a foreigner to this lot. They meant that the kidnaps did not form part of the age-old pilfering, skiving, cadging, diddling, dawdling, and mislaying that were regarded as normal trade practice by the long generations of intermarried families who worked in the ports.

One gnarled stevedore with a lopsided shoulder did suggest that someone had reported the problem to the vigiles. "Give those Rome boys something else to think about!" He grinned gummily. These men who worked on the docks and in the warehouses preferred not to be policed.

"Have you seen anyone hanging about around here?" I asked. "Other than us two, of course?"

There was muttering and a little laughter. Somebody mentioned Caninus. Someone else turned his back on the conversation, disgusted. They loathed the navy even more than the vigiles, it seemed.

"I know about Caninus. I was thinking of a clerkish sort, a scribe looking for something exciting to write about. His name is Diocles. Ever seen him?"

Apparently not.

Aulus and I finally hitched a lift back to the ferry on a slow cart, but all across what they called the Island the traffic jam was terrible. Like many others, we soon jumped off and walked. At the ferry dock we herded with the crowds, with people's toolkits jammed in our backs and elbows in our sides. On the boat, we were hanging off the gunnels, clinging to any handhold, and bruised every time the oars made a stroke. The oarsmen had their work cut out. Accustomed to this frenzy, they just stopped rowing when they were impeded too much. That added to the torture, as we drifted downstream and had to be brought back. The haze of garlic, wine, and perspiration from work tunics formed a breath-stopping miasma above the low-slung boat as it crept across to Ostia. Charon's filthy punt must be more pleasant. At least there you know you are heading to interminable rest in the Elysian Fields.

Another thing: Charon makes every dead soul pay. Aulus and I were the only men from Rome in this ferry, and we seemed to be the only two who had been asked to cough up fares.

At last we landed, and walked straight back home. It was too late to achieve anything more. I wanted to think first, because I had not come to Ostia to investigate kidnaps; no one would thank me—or pay me. I had to keep sight of my target. My brief was to find the scribe Diocles. So far, I had linked him to a possible retired pirate, but the Damagoras connection led nowhere definite. I had no cause to think Diocles had known about the kidnaps we had just uncovered. He would have *liked* to know, yes. Kidnap for ransom was an old pirate tradition, but I couldn't prove Diocles had realized it was going on here.

For all I knew still, he might really have come to Ostia to see his auntie as he told the other scribes. Once here he may have considered moonlighting on the Damagoras memoirs while he was invisible to his Rome superiors. Perhaps he dropped that idea when he realized he would earn better pocket money on a building site. In the end I might find him alive and well, mixing mortar for a construction team and unaware of the fuss he had caused.

Mind you, he would find construction hard labor; he was no stripling. I possessed some personal details. The vigiles recruiting officer had said Diocles was thirty-eight—a few years past retirement for an imperial freedman. Palace slaves were normally manumitted and pensioned off with a bag of gold when they were thirty. Holconius and Mutatus had told me the only reason Diocles was still working at the *Daily Gazette* instead of marrying and setting up a scrollshop behind the Forum was that the Emperor wanted reliable old hands buffing up the imperial name.

Why did Vespasian care about the Infamia column? According to Holconius, the court circular would constantly display good news affecting members of the ruling Flavian dynasty—impressive deeds in the fields of culture, adorning the city, and bashing barbarians. But Vespasian, famous for his old-fashioned ethics, also wanted tales of immorality toned down in the *Gazette* so that he—as the Father of his Country—would appear to have cleaned up society. The old spoilsport needed to feel the scandal column was no longer so titillating as it had been in Nero's day.

I could not see—or could not see yet—how piracy came into that.

True, if there really were pirates still roaming the seas, Vespasian would clear them out again. But would he want to be "the new Pompey"? Pompey was an unlucky politician, murdered in Egypt for the delight of his rival, Caesar. In the end the great Pompey was a loser. Vespasian was too canny for that. Wrong message from the signal post. And wrong messages were not Vespasian's style.

XXIII

First thing next morning I was off to the vigiles station house.

Petronius was not there. In fact, no one much was around. I addressed myself first to the clerk. He told me Brunnus was out somewhere. At the time I took that for a good omen. Ignoring cries of protest from the arsonists and thieves who would have to wait longer to be freed on bail, I extracted Virtus (the clerk's name, I discovered) and drew him to the open courtyard where nobody would overhear.

"You'll know this," I complimented him. "You're the only one here I can rely on to be up to date with casework—"

"Stop buffing the bronze, Falco. What's the score?"

"Kidnap."

Virtus shook his head. He turned to go back to his duties. I grabbed his arm. I told him there had been several victims, and I thought some at least had made vigiles reports.

Virtus assumed the vague expression clerks do so well. "Maybe the snatches occurred months ago when the last cohort were here."

"Which preceded the Sixth?"

"I forget. The Fourth? No, the Fourth are due to replace us next week. They are Petronius' unit—"

"I'm well aware of that," I said. "But it's an ongoing crime—and you're a permanent clerk. Don't mess me about. Now, the kidnappers apply frighteners, but people do get angry when their shock dies down. Victims have been here—and somebody has interviewed them."

Virtus wavered. "There's only one place these records may be, Falco."

I produced a sweetener. Sometimes clerks tell me secrets because they like my approach; sometimes they hate their bosses and are glad to cause trouble. For Virtus, his job would be endangered if he talked (he protested), therefore a bribe was essential.

I paid him. I liked him, and I reckoned it would be worthwhile.

He was still nervous.

We walked to the end of the exercise yard, and right into the shrine. It honored the Imperial Cult. Indoors, we were shadowed by busts of the current Emperor, flanked by his sons, Titus and Domitian Caesar, along with older heads of Claudius—who first brought the vigiles to Ostia—and even the disgraced Nero. That was quite enough witnesses. I made sure no one else was lurking.

Now I was nervous too. The way Virtus and I had entered must look suspicious. Anyone who had seen the two of us skulk up the portico and nip in here would imagine we were planning indecent acts. Sodomy was not my sin, and the Fourth Cohort would have known that, but to the Sixth I was an unknown quantity. I had just handed over money to a public slave, then led him to a murky place. Such an act might ruin my reputation—and since this was a shrine, there could be a blasphemy charge.

"Get on with it, Virtus."

Anxious to flee, Virtus muttered, "It may be in the Illyrian file."

I groaned. Just when I had done enough research to master a Cilician angle, here came another provincial bundle of trouble. Illyria, in Dalmatia, is much closer to Italy but yet another rocky coast, also full of inlets and islands, also harboring a nest of pirates in every cove where fishing fails to bring in enough money.

"What's with Illyrians, Virtus?"

"We keep a set of notebooks that gets passed to each new officer at cohort handovers. Don't ask what's in it."

"You don't know?"

"It's top-secret, Falco." Not the straight answer to my question. This vigiles clerk was falling back on tricks of bureaucracy: "I always thought it was a dead subject. Just because it comes with a high security category, doesn't mean the case is live—" He was waffling.

"Case, or cases?"

"Can't say. There is another set of notes just like it, on Florius—" Florius was the gangster Petronius was pursuing as his special subject.

"Florius is irrelevant. You're telling me another secret bunch of notes relates to someone with an Illyrian background. Is there a special navy contact on this issue? I had the impression Caninus only covers Cilicia."

"No, it's the same. Caninus."

"You sure about that, Virtus?"

"Every time a new detachment arrives, Caninus makes contact with their officer. Brunnus, for instance, had to be told to give Caninus special respect."

"Who told Brunnus?"

"I did. It's my job to brief the officers on sensitive issues."

"So who told you Caninus was sensitive?"

"He did."

"Caninus instructs you, 'Tell any new officer: I'm an important secret contact'? But you don't know what secret issues you are briefing them about?"

Virtus laughed. "So what? I'm a clerk. I do that all the time."

I failed to find it funny. "How can I get to see the Illyrian notes?"

"Not possible, Falco."

"More cash help you?"

"Still not possible," said Virtus—with regret. "Brunnus slept with the Illyrian notes under his pillow last night. Don't ask me why he suddenly took an interest." I guessed our party with Caninus had aroused his curiosity. "Today he's gone off with the tablet in his satchel. I suppose he is chasing up the old cases . . . Problem, Falco?" asked Virtus, innocently.

"It's a little inconvenient."

"If you don't want Brunnus to know that you have an interest . . ."

"Yes?"

"Don't you want to know what I can offer?"

"If you swindle me, you'll regret it. But I've reached my limit, cash-wise. So just tell me."

Virtus demurred. I got tough. He submitted.

No officer wrote out his own case-notes, however confidential. If a clerk was preparing a top-secret report which would have a long forward timeline—that is, notes that would eventually be handed on to other co-horts—the officer would want them to look good. So the clerk would draft out a rough version, then rewrite it neatly.

Unless the officer was extremely efficient and demanded to see the rough copy being destroyed, then naturally if the case was exciting the clerk preserved his rough copy.

"If I liked you enough," said Virtus, "I could show you my drafts."

What a bastard. He had known all along that he could give me what I wanted.

An hour later I was happy, as I clutched my own note-tablet. I had cribbed several names of complainants, some with addresses in Ostia at the time, though they had probably moved on by now. I had dates of ab-ductions. A couple had happened in the Sixth's term of duty, but there were others before.

It looked as if only one captive was ever held at any time. That might be to lessen the risk, or there might only be one safe house available. All the reported abductions were of women. On return to their husbands they never knew where they had been held, and they seemed very con-fused. In most cases the husbands paid up at once; they were all carry-ing large amounts of cash for business purposes. Sometimes the wife had been snatched immediately after the husband had arranged the sale of a large cargo, at the very moment when he was flush.

Each time the clerk's notes said that now the distressed family were either leaving Ostia for Rome, or leaving the country. If Brunnus had gone out today to double-check their Ostian lodgings, he would have little luck; judging by the couple I talked to, Banno and Aline, nobody stuck around. Perhaps the kidnappers actually ordered the victims to leave.

Those who complained to the vigiles had been brave. They were try-ing to protect others from sharing their anguish.

Helpfully, Brunnus had had his thoughts summarized. He calculated that there were several people involved in the abductions and holding the prisoners. All were shadowy so far. Brunnus suggested the victims might be drugged to ensure they would not recognize anyone.

One of the captors could write. Husbands were always contacted by letter.

One significant lead came out of these notes: there was a go-between. All the husbands had dealt with a mediator, a man they found very sin-ister. He asked them to meet him at a bar, different each time; there was no regular venue. He would be a stranger to the barkeeper—or so all the barkeepers claimed afterward. He was very persuasive. He convinced the husbands he only wanted to help, and at the time they somehow believed he was just a generous third party. The contact letters (which he always took back from them) would tell the husbands to ask the barman for "the Illyrian."

The Illyrian stuck to his line that he had been brought in to act as an intermediary. He implied he was a neutral, respectable businessman doing victims a good turn. He warned that the actual kidnappers were dangerous, and that the husbands must avoid upsetting them, lest the missing women were harmed. His advice was: pay up, do it quickly, and don't cause trouble. Once this was agreed, he took delivery of the ran-som. He dispatched his runner, a young boy, to tell the kidnappers he had the cash, kept the husband talking for a while, then suddenly sent him back to his lodgings, where as promised he would find his wife. No hus-band ever stopped to watch where the Illyrian vanished to.

"He's a member of the gang, whatever he claims . . . Well, thank you, Virtus," I said. "Tell me, is Brunnus dealing with this personally?"

"He is. It doesn't tax him, Falco. There are no leads. By the time some brave husband comes to report a new abduction, it's all over. They always beg Brunnus not to have men visibly investigating. Brunnus agrees to that, because he thinks that if any victims are attacked for reporting the crime, *he* will cop the blame. He knows in his water he'll blunder. You have to admire it," said Virtus. "Whoever planned this out is very clever."

"And Brunnus is playing along with them."

"Tell me something I don't know!" said his clerk. "But be fair, Falco. Brunnus listens when anyone brings information direct to us—but official policy is that he should leave it all to Caninus."

"So—do we trust the navy to handle this?"

The clerk raised his eyebrows expressively. "What—a bunch of sailors?"

Armed with this new information, I went back to my apartment. It had taken me the first part of the morning to extract the kidnap notes from Virtus—long enough for some new family arrivals to reach Ostia from Rome. I saw a cart, sensibly parked under a fig tree's shade in the courtyard. Then I found my nephew Gaius, sitting on the steps, looking as if he had earache. Always keen to try new fads, he was poking at his bare chest, on which were infected needle marks from a recent foray into woad tattoos; one thing the poets don't tell you when they extol the blue Britons is that woad stinks. I looked sick; Gaius grinned ruefully. We did not speak. Upstairs I could hear my elder daughter squealing, and from past experience I guessed she was having her hair combed and pulled into tight fancy plaits—an older generation's fad. Nux was whining in sympathy.

Indoors, a large mullet was sitting on a dish I knew from home, with its tail lolling up against a well-trussed bag of leeks. Only one person I knew bought fish in Rome even though they were coming to the seaside. Only one person had access to a market garden which produced better leeks than those at Ostia.

"Marcus!" cried Helena, smiling brightly. "Here's a big surprise for you."

As surprises go, this was eerily familiar. I shoved my note-tablet casually under a fruit bowl and braced myself. "Hello, Mother."

"You look as if you have been up to no good," replied Ma.

"I'm working." Somehow it sounded as attractive as if I had said I was in quarantine with plague. Helena would have told Mother the details. Small, shrewd, suspicious, and convinced the world was full of cheats, my dear mother would not be impressed.

My sisters and I had spent thirty years trying to fool Ma, and only managed to annoy her. It was my late brother, her favorite, who had consistently managed to deceive her; even now, Ma never acknowledged what a lying cad Festus had been. "I'm so sorry to say this, Mother, when you've only just arrived, but I must flee back to Rome to follow up a lead, and I need Helena to come with me—"

"Lucky I came then!" my mother retorted. "Somebody has to look after your poor children."

I winked at Albia. Albia had met Ma before; she managed to ignore the insult to her babysitting.

"So what is behind your visit?" I ventured.

"You keep your nose out of other people's business, young man!" commanded Ma.

XXIV

My mother was up to something, but Helena and I did not bother to investigate. We knew the answer might have worried us.

We were able to travel that same afternoon. Having escaped Ma, the first person we found on returning to our house in Rome was my father. You never lose your parents. Pa was in our dining room, munching a takeaway stuffed half-loaf, which had leaked purple sauce onto the couch cushions.

"Who let you in?"

My progenitor grinned. He had let himself in. According to Helena, my father's grin is a twin to mine, but I find it deeply irritating. I already knew that whenever we were away, my father treated our house as if it still belonged to him. We had done a house swap a couple of years before; give Pa another decade and he might actually honor it.

"Marcus, tell Maia Favonia to leave that big daft friend of yours and come home to look after her poor old father's business," he wheedled.

"I'll tell her you said so. Maia will do what she wants, Pa."

"I don't know where she gets her attitude."

"I can't think either! So now you're here, when are you leaving?"

"Don't be so unfriendly, lad. I heard you were in Ostia. Did your mother turn up?" My parents had not spoken to each other for nearly thirty years, since Pa ran away with a redhead. Nonetheless, each always knew what the other was up to.

"Arrived yesterday. Galla's Gaius brought her; he's a right little barbarian. I wasn't with Ma long enough to work out what diddles she's planning."

Pa, who was a wide-bodied, gray-haired old trickster full of deviousness himself, looked pleased. "Oh, I know. She heard her brother has slunk ashore at Portus."

"Who—Fabius or Junius?" My two uncles from the family farm took it in turns to abscond in a huff, often over woman troubles, always due to some huge slight involving the other brother. They each liked to hone grand, embarrassing schemes for a new life, mad ideas like becoming a gladiator or running a cuttlefish firm. (That was Fabius—ignoring the fact that shellfish brought him out in a rash.)

"Neither of them." Pa dropped this news, and waited for my amazement. I gasped. "Not . . . *the one no one ever talks about?*"

Helena came in behind me. "Hello, Geminus; this is a surprise." She was excellent with irony. "Who do you not talk about, Marcus?"

"Much too long a story!" Pa and I replied, with rare unanimity.

Helena Justina smiled and let our enigma pass her by, knowing she could pull the answer from me like a splinter in the finger later.

She coiled herself gracefully on the couch beside my father and helped herself to his oozing snack. It smelled delicately of saffron; he could afford luxuries. Strands of green vegetation dangled from the piece of bread she pulled off. Helena managed these with elegant long fingers, while Pa just sucked his up like an enthusiastic blackbird gulping bits of live worm.

"Geminus, now that we have you here . . ." Helena managed to make this sound inoffensive, yet Pa looked at her sharply. "Do you know a man called Damagoras?"

Pa was the one person I would not have asked. Still, Helena saw him as a man with useful contacts. He answered at once, "Big old brigand? I have bought things off him."

"What things?" I barked.

"Rather good things, normally." "Rather" meant exceedingly good. And "normally" meant always.

"Is he an importer?"

My father laughed coarsely.

"You mean he peddles stolen goods?"

"Oh, I imagine so." My father was an auctioneer and art dealer; the size of his profits signaled to me that he accepted goods for sale with little regard for provenance. Rome had a flourishing repro market, and Pa was adept at pretending he really believed a bare-faced copy was original Greek marble. In reality he had a good eye, and plenty of genuine statues that had evaded their real owners must have gone under his hammer too.

I explained that Damagoras had told me he was too elderly to venture from his villa. My father spelled out for me, as if to a priest's little altar boy, that wicked people sometimes lie. He saw Damagoras as pretty active still.

"Active in what, Papa?"

"Oh—whatever he does."

Helena toyed with an olive bowl. Annoyed, I recognized the olives. It looked as if Pa had opened up the Colymbadian giant queens that I was saving for special occasions. My shameless father would now take big scoops of the luscious green gems back to his own house. I would be lucky to find a lick of marinade at the bottom of an empty amphora.

"Geminus, we think Damagoras is a pirate." Helena gazed sternly at my father. For her, he always pretended to be a reformed character. He was right; people lie. "If pirates still exist, that is."

"He's a bloody Cilician," retorted my father. "What more do you need to know?"

"You regard all Cilicians as pirates?"

"It's the only life Cilicians know."

And why should they abandon it, so long as crooked auctioneers in Rome would fence their plunder? I resented all my father stood for, but if he had information, I wanted it. "I regret to say I need your help, Pa. Might Damagoras or his close associates be connected to a kidnapping racket that seems to be centered on Portus?"

"Oh, that!" exclaimed Pa.

★   ★   ★

He might be bluffing, but my father always had an ear to the ground. He now said he had heard of people being held to ransom, though he was unable to link these kidnaps to Damagoras. He swore he knew the old villa-owner only as the seller of a particularly fine "Aphrodite Surprised," a couple of years back. "Beautifully modeled drapery!"

"Wearing a wet chiton, you mean?"

"Not wearing much of it!" Pa smacked his lips.

When I produced my list of the kidnap victims, the first result was depressing: Pa knew for sure that one man called Isidorus, an olive oil merchant, had left Rome about a month ago. The other names were strangers to him, apart from a certain Posidonius, whom Pa said he could probably find for me. He already knew Posidonius had been a victim; the man had been moaning all around the Emporium about having to ransom his daughter—and my father added the detail that Posidonius believed one of her captors had interfered with the girl. Forewarned about this, Helena Justina came with me next day, after Pa did provide contact details and I went to interview the victims.

Posidonius was a timber merchant who specialized in exotic woods from the eastern end of the Mediterranean. He shipped in the baulks for manufacture in Rome, where they were used to make enormous tables for millionaire show-offs with palatial homes. There was a high returns rate, owing to the fact that eager purchasers forgot that the heavyweight tables had to be delivered and installed. Fine art mosaic floors had crumbled under the massive display pieces, and slaves in two different households had suffered heart attacks while trying to lift tabletops through doorways. One had died. Posidonius was now trapped in Rome, awaiting the outcome of a compensation claim against him. But it had done him good. The publicity had brought in new business.

His daughter, called Rhodope, was about seventeen. She traveled around with her father, who was a widower. He had brought up Rhodope single-handed since her birth. He seemed intelligent and cosmopolitan, much annoyed with himself for being caught out by an old routine. She looked quiet; not that that meant much.

Helena took the girl aside while I discussed the abduction with her father. Pa had described him talking freely to Emporium colleagues, but with us he clammed up. Perhaps he had now realized the risks. He would only confirm to me that what had happened fitted the case-notes Brunnus had drawn up. Mention of the Illyrian, the sinister go-between, made Posidonius shudder. He was reluctant to discuss his fears for Rhodope, perhaps because if she had been seduced it might affect her marriageability. Besides, he complained that she refused to talk to him.

Helena had more luck. She told me afterward that in her view, the girl had definitely lost her heart and all that traditionally goes with it. Helena had found her extremely naïve. My glimpse of Rhodope had been of a wide-eyed teenager with that guileless look that usually means a young girl is hiding dangerous secrets from her worried parents. I should know; I had been the secret sometimes, in my younger days. While Rhodope pretended to be preoccupied with eye paint, she was probably hoarding her dress allowance for a flight from home. Helena had discovered that the girl, completely infatuated, believed that the captor who had paid her attention was coming back to find her, so they could elope.

"His name is Theopompus. Apparently he is virile, dashing, and *very* exciting to know."

I said, "I bet his breath stinks and he already has three wives."

"If you point that out," replied Helena sadly, "Rhodope won't hear you."

"So how did you persuade the loopy lummock to talk?"

"Oh . . ." An uncharacteristic vagueness afflicted my beloved. "She's sweet, and perhaps rather lonely." It could have been Helena herself when I met her—though in her case I would add: furious with men, ferocious with me, and extremely bright. Among the girls I knew at the time, she shone. If I had had any wives, I would have socked them all with divorce notes. "That was what made her vulnerable, I suppose, Marcus. She may have opened up to me because I confessed I had once fallen in love with a handsome brigand myself."

I gazed at her benignly. "Helena Justina, what brigand would that be?"

Helena smiled.

Retailers of fashionable household goods are not my favorite citizens, but as a father of girls, a deep chasm of sympathy for Posidonius opened in my heart. I left him a note of how he could contact Camillus Justinus in Rome if he needed professional help; I did not say, if Rhodope ran away. With luck she would just mope, and by the time she realized Theopompus was never coming, some other appalling fellow might be hanging around to take her mind off it.

Rhodope had been ransomed some weeks before, during the period when Diocles was still staying at his lodgings in Ostia. I checked and no approach for information had been made by the scribe to this family, either at the time or since.

Diocles could have been in Ostia for some completely different purpose, or else he knew about the kidnaps but had been prevented from following up the story. The way the mysterious "Illyrian" always stressed that the kidnappers were violent worried me. If Diocles had dabbled in this, I started to feel anxious about the missing scribe's fate.

XXV

All the other names on my list were dud throws of the dice. Pa introduced me to people who knew some of them, but the men I needed to talk to, the husbands who had paid up ransom money, had all left town. Most originated overseas, and had gone back there. Perhaps now they would never return.

To the kidnappers these victims were just faces in the throng, but if traders were rich enough to fleece, they had had something to offer Rome. The city was losing valuable commerce. I was more angry about the human cost, though. People at the Emporium all spoke of pleasant, knowledgeable commodity traders, good family men, which was why they traveled with their wives. When Helena and I chased up addresses, we felt the victims had left a strong aura of distress and fear behind them.

After some thought and discussion with Helena, I walked over the Aventine to the Twelfth District to the vigiles headquarters of the Fourth Cohort. I went alone. Petronius Longus would not thank me: I was going to see Marcus Rubella. Rubella was the cohort tribune, Petro's loathed superior. I generally found him not so bad, if you could ignore a few flaws: he was an ill-qualified, overfastidious, self-serving rule-stickler who tidied his desk and ate raisins all day. Rubella was a fellow

Petro and I never wanted to go for a drink with—which was just as well, because he never asked us.

I was better-known among the rankers from the other half of the cohort, those who patrolled the Thirteenth, my home district, but even in the Twelfth my face was familiar. Barracking met me; I returned the banter, then I was allowed in to see the tribune at once. Rubella never had much going on in his office and he knew I only went to see him if there was some big event I could not handle by myself. He was aware that if Petro had been here in Rome I would have consulted him instead.

"Marcus Rubella, I have been working in Ostia. I believe the Fourth is off there soon."

"On the Ides. So what can't wait, Falco?"

"I've stumbled on a scam. It must have been going on for some time; the other cohorts have failed to get a grip—" Rubella bared his teeth, shark-like, as if he saw through my flattery. He enjoyed thinking his lads had an opening to show up their rivals.

I outlined the kidnappings, never suggesting they went back in time too far. Pardon me for sounding like a schoolboy's arithmetic problem, but if seven cohorts are working four-month shifts in rotation, then they must each return to the outstation every two years and four months. I happened to know that Rubella had joined the Fourth, as a new appointment by Vespasian, three or four years ago, so I had to create a pretty panorama where all members of the glorious Fourth had kept their ugly noses blown the last time they served at Ostia and no hint of these kidnaps could have reached their tribune then. The whole point of me being here in Rubella's office was to stir him to action now.

It worked. After I described the situation, Rubella decided to implement the officers' answer to everything: a special exercise. In order to lend it gravitas and impetus (and in order to escape the burning heat of Rome in August) Rubella would head up this exercise himself.

Hades. Rubella was coming to Ostia. Now Lucius Petronius would really hate me.

I carried out one last task during my flying visit to the city. I was supposed to meet Helena at our house, but after I left Rubella, I took a long detour and made my way down to the Forum. I checked the *Daily Gazette* column; of course it told me Infamia was still on holiday. Then I went to see Holconius and Mutatus in the *Gazette* office.

Neither was there of course. Most of the *Gazette*'s readers are away in July and August. Nothing of note happens. Everyone is at the coast. Everyone with any money goes into the hills for cooler air, or south to the sea.

"You could create a special edition called the *Neapolis Exciter*," I fantasized to the slave who was slowly plying a damp sponge around the otherwise deserted rooms. "Seaside gossip. Sandy Surrentum secrets. Baiae bathing-pool outrages. Hints that there may soon be a shortage of scallop omelets, unless senators on holiday curb their maritime villa banquets."

"Market day in Pompeii is Saturn day," replied the slave glumly. It sounded as if a *Campanian Companion* had already been considered—and rejected as too boring. "In Nuceria it's Sun day, in Atella it's Moon day—"

I told him I took the point. As I was leaving he revived suddenly. "Falco, how is Diocles? Is he still at his auntie's?"

I paused. This was unexpected. The gentle Fates had handed me a bonus. "Holconius and Mutatus gave me the impression that was just a ruse. I thought Diocles didn't really have an auntie."

The slave looked scornful. "Of course he does. He goes to see her every year."

"How come you know?"

The slave looked swanky. "People talk to me." He probably wanted to be an investigator when he was freed. If I failed to find Diocles, there might be a job going.

"So—Auntie what?"

"Auntie Vestina."

"Know where she lives?"

"Near a temple."

"Portus or Ostia itself?"

"Ostia."

"Ostia is a very religious town, my friend; any clue to which temple?"

All the slave could come up with was that water had something to do with it. Well, that should be easy in a town on a river mouth, down at the coast.

I gave him a half-denarius. He didn't know he could have just put an end to my nice little summer commission. Infamia was no longer missing; he was swanning on a sunbed while a loving relative plied him with cool drinks and homemade olive pâté. All I had to do now was locate the right temple, collect Diocles from his Auntie Vestina, and bring him home again.

Ah, if only it had been that easy.

XXVI

I had told the slave the truth: Ostia had always been very religious. There were temples absolutely everywhere, some spanking new, some that harked back to when the town was just a cluster of salt workers' huts in a marsh. If the Ostians had space for any sort of dedicated enclosure, they whipped a wall around three sides and put up a podium in a pillared shrine. Their motto was: why build one when there is room for four? A cluster of altars was better than a solo. When they ran out of gods, they threw honors at allegorical concepts; near our apartment stood a row of four little temples, dedicated to Venus and Ceres, plus Hope and Fortune too. I for my part had no time for love, and with two very young children under my feet in a small apartment I was dead set against any further fertility. As I failed to track down Diocles, I was soon cursing my bad fortune and running out of hope.

On my return, the quest for the scribe's aunt took me all over town. I reckoned I could omit the giant temples to Jupiter and to Rome and Augustus which dominated the Forum; anyone who lived there would describe their house as near the Forum. Pompous types might call it the Capitolium. Vague ones would say they lived in the middle of town.

Otherwise, I had to visit the lot. I became adept at scenting out smoke from sacrificial offerings. I also became a real nymphaeum bore. The Ostians liked gracing wayside walls with water-troughs, and though some were plain drinking points for beasts of burden, many were set up as decorative shrines to water gods. Helena had to listen to me counting up each day's haul as temples became my obsessive collecting fad, worse than the time I tried to explore all the Seven Hills of Rome when I was only eight years old and not supposed to leave the Aventine by myself. Now I would be death at a party: I kept note-tablets jotted with details of temples I had spotted, like some ghastly tourist's diary. At the slightest encouragement I showed people my sketch map with shrines marked in red.

My mother, who was staying with Maia, became very excited when she thought Helena had begun sacrifices to the Good Goddess. (I was absolved from taking part; men are too Bad.) Bona Dea was for a while our favored divinity in the conundrum, as her neat sea-view temple lay outside the Marine Gate. We did wonder if Diocles had chosen lodgings in an area he knew—though if his auntie was in that vicinity we could not explain *why* he went into lodgings . . . We failed to track down Vestina near the Bona Dea, so my search moved back to the center of town.

Top deity here was Vulcan. A straightforward anvil god with a fetching limp. Helena and I spent a pleasant day at his ancient complex; we took Albia and the children, making it an excuse for a picnic, which was just as well because as a work exercise our trip was pointless. We could only associate Vulcan with water via a long-winded link involving the vigiles dousing fires. Tenuous. For reasons nobody knew anymore, the fire god's high priest was the most important man in Ostia, lording it over the cult's own praetors and aediles; it was a lifetime appointment of ancient derivation which carried, as far as I could see, no advantage nowadays except being groveled to by sycophantic town councillors, all hoping that the current pontifex of Vulcan would quickly drop dead so they could jostle for his post.

That night Helena Justina sat up suddenly in bed with a shriek of "Cybele!" This did not enthrall me. Eastern gods are generally deplorable and I really wince at the Great Mother with her self-castrating sidekick, Attis. No man with a love life can think calmly of a consort who cut off his genitalia. Anyway, I had done the Eastern cults already. I had examined houses all around the Temple of Isis. Seemed a good bet: Isis equals

Nile god equals very important water if you live in Egypt. Isis is also a sea goddess, and protects sea voyagers. Her temple was in the west end of town, on the riverbank. To match the slave's description, this was about as likely as anywhere could be, so I scoured the neighborhood thoroughly. Always uncomfortable with the sistrum-shaking priests, the dubious priestesses in their topless, see-through pleated linen, and the unnerving portraits of dog-headed fellows with their arms folded, I was glad to escape.

I had had no luck searching around the Isis enclosure for waterfront houses where a scribe's aunt might live. To cheer myself up, I bought a good hanging lamp in the form of a ship, and only noticed when I got it home that it had three little shrines of Isis, Anubis, and Serapis. Ours was not a household that liked statuettes of gods. We did not even own our own Lares. (Thinking of that, I went back out and checked around the Forum shrine of the town Lares.)

"No, it's Cybele we want," Helena insisted that night. "The cult statue was brought from the East to Rome by sea when Claudius decided to legitimize worship. There's that story of the young woman with the soiled reputation—"

I perked up. "Oh, my kind of girl!"

"Think again, Falco. The ship got stuck in the estuary. Whatever-her-name-was went and claimed that if her chastity remained intact she would touch the ship with her girdle—"

"She did the girdle trick: the ship moved off up the Tiber. Now can I go to sleep again?"

"You can go to the Temple of Cybele tomorrow, Marcus."

I did; I found nothing. Cybele had a huge enclosure by the Laurentine Gate where she was attended by various associate gods in their own little shrines but, as far as I could discover, no aunts. Helena allowed me to resume my dogged search elsewhere. I investigated temples of Castor and Pollux, Mars, Diana, Neptune, Liber Pater, round and rectangular temples of divinities whose names were not even obvious, Pater Tiberina, and the Genius of the Colony. The craft guilds had their own temples, prominently the Temple of the Ship Builders and a temple in the Forum of the Wine Growers (I enjoyed that morning).

I was running out of podiums.

At this point, my dedicated religious trek must have caught the eye of some softhearted Olympus deity. I had been poking around backstreets on the west side of the Forum, where somebody had suggested there might be a shrine with ships on it. I never found them. Despondent, I headed back to a road that would take me to the Decumanus. It had a couple of small temples which I had already dismissed. Squashed in on the same site was one major temple: to Hercules Invictus. Empathizing with any other hero afflicted with hard labors, I paid it more attention than previously and walked right up the steps. There were nine. On a hot day it was a steep climb, which was why I had omitted this last time. I entered the sanctum. There I had my breakthrough.

In the interior, a set of friezes depicted how the cult statue had been discovered years before: Hercules had been dredged up from the sea by some fishermen. Probably some ship carrying works of art had foundered in the shoals off Ostia, taking the statue down, club, bearskin, beard and all. I tipped my forelock to the hero's smooth, handsome torso.

"Thank you, delectable demigod. And by the way—nice arse!"

I began a fast search of the neighboring area. Parts appeared to be in the process of redevelopment; there were cleared spaces and a couple of elderly atrium houses standing empty. In a side street, I finally found the place where Diocles used to stay. I learned that his Auntie Vestina, a freedwoman of the imperial house, had lived for many years right beside the Temple of Hercules Invictus. The aunt's house had burned down about this time last year. The first woman I spoke to had not seen the aunt since.

That would have been bad enough, but if Vestina had escaped and re-located I might have tracked her down eventually. Sadly, I found another neighbor who knew the whole story. The fire had started at night. Help took a long time coming. Vestina had been crippled with arthritis and she was asthmatic. She could not struggle out of her burning house quickly enough, and was killed by the smoke before she could be rescued.

XXVII

Feeling melancholy, I cut back toward the Forum and started walking home. I hit the Decumanus Maximus at a crossroads, where it took a slight bend as it turned from its original axis toward the Marine Gate. This was a major junction with a shrine and market stalls, old established fishmongers and butchers. Ahead were public buildings, first the Basilica and then the Forum itself. Those bore the marble stamp of Augustus, telling locals and new arrivals how exceedingly rich the spoils of Egypt had made him, and how determined he was to be seen as ruler of the world. The area where the streets met was full of life. It made a sad contrast to the dead spaces behind me—though when the empty lots were redeveloped, that part of town would be a fine place to live: central and probably select. Some builder was due to make a killing if he could get his hands on the land, and it did look as if a steady acquisition program was in progress.

Around one corner from the Decumanus, in a scaffolded block that seemed to be already earmarked for redevelopment, I found a small group of vigiles. It was unexpected; Petro had never mentioned an outstationed unit, though we were a long way from the creaky patrol house, so it did seem a good idea. It was miles to run to the main patrol house to report a bathhouse on fire or to ask for reinforcements when someone had left his wife sitting on a captured burglar.

They had a deserted shop set up as an office. The frontage of what must once have been an artisan's workshop was now a gaping hole, minus its pull-across doors. There were four men on duty, not the liveliest bunch I had ever met. At a beaten-up table they lolled around while awaiting citizens with complaints. I could see bits of chewed old loaves on the floor, which was rubble. There was a smell of wine, though none in evidence. I made a mental note to warn Petronius this bivouac needed sharpening up.

"Name's Falco."

"What's your problem?" I had not expected to be offered chamomile tea and an almond fancy. Even so, the approach seemed belligerent.

"Can you supply some information?"

"We are not encyclopedia salesmen." The pallid oaf who was addressing me showed too much of his surly slave origins.

"Whatever happened to shmoozing the public? I pay my taxes, you washed-out bucket of whey!" Well, I was supposed to pay, and in a previous job for the Emperor I had made many wealthy tax evaders say they were sorry and cough up. That was much more useful to the state than if I had paid my own.

A new face homed in. "Now then, sir!" This one must have attended a neighborhood-relationships lecture. "What were you wanting?"

"Apart from a bit of courtesy? I'd like to know about a fire in the next street where a woman died last year."

"We can give you courtesy, high-class saluting, and a very hard kick up the arse," said the second man—the charming, witty one—while his idiot cronies ogled. "We don't know anything about that fire. Details of past incidents are not made available to the public."

"Not unless you pay the record-search fee," inserted a third specimen. I saw his partner thump him, telling him to shut up.

"Search fees?" I folded my arms and looked thoughtful. "Whose bright idea was that one? I know Vespasian needs to raise money for his civic building program, but this is new. Is it special to the Sixth? Does it only apply when you cheerful lot are on duty, or is the procedure cohort-wide? Is this Ostia only? Or Rome-led?"

Mistake, Falco. The mood grew sinister. Two vigiles who had so far only chewed apples now closed in on me. The loon who had asked for fees squared up. The main spokesman was already only a foot from me. None of them were tall. All were sturdy and wide. By definition they came from rough backgrounds and were employed for hard labor, fearless of danger. They were ill-shaved, dirty-tunicked heavy-duty boys, who reeked of smoke and building dust—and none were frightened of me. They were off their home patch, twenty miles from Rome, and confident that their actions here were unlikely to be criticized. I could see why the people of Ostia must have ambivalent feelings about them.

The spokesman placed a muscle-bound arm in front of two others. "Now then, lads. This seems to be the sort of grand fellow who will tell us he is best friends with the Urban Prefect." He made it plain that did not worry him.

I kept cool and looked him straight in the eye. Prefects are too remote to count, even if I knew any. I could have mentioned Brunnus—but most likely they hated him; citing their officer could be a very bad idea. I wondered what their names were, but thought better of asking.

"We don't know anything at all about any fires last year," the spokesman repeated, inches from my face. His filthy finger prodded my chest. "So, Falco—" He repeated the poke, much harder. "We would like you to remove yourself!"

The others all took a step toward me. Behind me, my exit was clear so I took it. I heard them laughing.

I continued home, feeling soiled and disconcerted. On the first stretch of the Decumanus I kept looking over my shoulder, and I made sure I mingled quickly with the crowds once I reached the Forum. The moron who talked of search fees had plainly asked me for a bribe. The general threat of violence was real. I wondered whether this showed the reaction local people had met when they called for help, the night Diocles' aunt found her house on fire.

Then I wondered whether Diocles had been staying with her, last year when the blaze happened.

*　　*　　*

When I returned to our apartment I was gloomy and introspective. Any joy at finally locating the scribe's aunt had vanished when I learned of her death. My confrontation with the vigiles added to my foul mood. I told Helena about the episode, playing it down.

We discussed the aunt's tragedy. "I can see," I said, "that if Diocles had always stayed with her in summer, he may have come back automatically this year. Once he got here, he could have booked into lodgings and then started brooding about what happened to his aunt. If he's sensitive, this could be why he has gone off somewhere."

"You think he can't stand being here again, so he's taken himself to have a holiday at Lake Nemi instead?" After Helena asked, "You don't think Diocles was applying to join the vigiles so he could expose some inefficiency that caused his aunt's death?"

I pulled a face. "I know what Petro would suspect if Diocles has a fascination with fires: he'll think Diocles is an arsonist."

"No!"

"Arsonists don't just start fires, you know. Some like to hide in a portico and watch what happens, but some want to show themselves as heroes who can save people and put fires out. Types like that regularly apply to join the vigiles. Smart recruiting officers have a nose for it and reject them."

"You met a recruiting officer. You thought Rusticus was smart, didn't you, Marcus?"

I pondered that. "Yes, I did. But thinking back to what he said, he was uneasy—Rusticus was fazed himself and didn't know why he had said no to the scribe. Diocles was a puzzle, not a phenomenon he recognized."

"Doesn't sound as though Rusticus suspected he was an arsonist. You still think Diocles was up to something?"

"Yes, love. But it may have been nothing to do with his aunt."

Helena was silent for a moment. Then she said, "His aunt was on his mind, Marcus. When Diocles told Holconius and Mutatus he was coming to Ostia, he said he would be staying with her."

"True. Maybe subconsciously he forgot her death. Maybe his mind played a trick on him."

Now Helena and I were both worried that Diocles might have come here and had a breakdown.

"Talking of breakdowns," Helena said, smiling and changing the subject as she tried to cheer me up a little. "I had a surprise today—I met your uncle!" I raised an eyebrow, sensing what would come next: "That's right, Marcus. The one nobody ever talks about."

XXVIII

It was a quarter of a century since I had seen Uncle Fulvius. He did have a name; it was just damned to the memory. Had Ma's family been able to commission statues, his would have been broken up and reused by Fabius and Junius to build a pigsty.

I was curious to know how he had weathered.

"We hardly exchanged more than a few words," said Helena. "He wanted your mother; I told him Junilla Tacita was staying with Maia now, as they have more room than us, and I gave him directions." In the act of repinning an enameled shoulder brooch, she paused for a moment. "Mind you, I did gain the impression he was slightly odd."

"In what way?" I asked, grinning.

Helena merely shrugged, unsure. "I just felt happier when he left."

Albia looked up from the floor, where she was playing with the children. "What has your uncle done, Marcus Didius?"

I suspected I had been too young to be told the full story. I supplied the safe part: "He ran away to Pessinus, but he got on the wrong boat."

"And now he has come back? That took him over twenty years?" exclaimed Helena, amazed. "Surely when his brothers are restless, they just disappear for a couple of seasons and then come sidling home?"

"Fabius and Junius are normal, compared to him. My uncles quarrel with each other," I explained to Albia. "Fabius thinks Junius cheated him over his share of the farm when my grandfather died; Junius is certain that Fabius will ruin everything through his unwise friendship with a neighbor's wife; Junius got depressed when the walnut harvest failed and he hates his brother's plans for intensive chicken-rearing—he is a filthy-tempered rat's tail anyway. Fabius knows he could be something big in the world if he could just find the right medium for his so-far-undetermined talents. Junius is looking for love, specifically; he thought he had found it but he had to go to market with the eggs because it was his turn that week—there are a lot of eggs because Fabius really has cracked it with his chickens in baskets—and the girl left town." I ran out of breath.

"Auntie Phoebe told me the girl Junius wants is engaged to a sewer contractor anyway," Helena put in.

"Great-Auntie Phoebe, my grandfather's freedwoman, keeps the farm together while the brothers are messing about. She stanches the blood when they attempt suicide. She keeps them apart with a pitchfork when they try to kill each other."

"I see!" Raising her finely feathered eyebrows, Albia went back to playing with my daughters. I took Helena to Maia's house, hoping Uncle Fulvius might still be there.

Since he was the elusive one, Fulvius had been and gone.

Instead, I ran into Gaius Baebius. Junia was trying to persuade Ma to take the invalid back to Rome in her cart. Ma very crisply disabused Junia. She seemed low in spirits; whatever she wanted from Fulvius, he must have been difficult about it.

Now that she had talked to her brother, Ma was returning home to the Aventine, but there was no chance she would share the journey with my sister and her whining husband. Ma thought one benefit of being elderly was that she no longer had to be polite about Gaius Baebius. This presupposed she had ever been polite in the first place.

"Ah, Marcus!" Rebuffed by Ma, Gaius latched on to me. "I am thinking I shall go out to the Damagoras villa and place a formal complaint about the way we were treated. I shall never be the same man again—" An amateurish cough confirmed it.

Junia rounded on me too. "You will have to go with him! I cannot put myself in danger among a group of violent pirates, and Gaius is no longer fit to drive."

I saw my mother pin her skeptical gaze on Gaius. Wickedly, I heard myself promising to go to remonstrate. I had a fair idea what Damagoras and Cratidas would say if asked for money. I had no intention of antagonizing them, but thought I might have another look at the Cilicians for my own purposes.

"You ought to have a strong word with Uncle Fulvius too," Junia instructed me. "You are the head of the family." Since my grandfather died, that ought to be Fulvius himself, but he declined the duties. From what I knew, he would sell off the busts of our ancestors (had we owned any). "Here's poor Mother trying to mediate and bring him back into the family, but he just refused to have anything to do with us. He upset Mother very badly."

"I am not upset," lied Ma. She liked to choose for herself when to play helpless.

"Do Fabius and Junius really want him back?" I queried.

"Fulvius is the clever one," Ma retorted as if the farm needed someone with intelligence. It was true, but I saw that as the very reason why his brothers might be happier if Fulvius stayed in exile.

"So what is he doing, Ma, and why has he come to Ostia?"

"He never said."

"What—and you failed to screw it out of him?"

My mother must be holding back. Obviously Uncle Fulvius had found yet another wild career that would cause us huge embarrassment. Ma read my mind. So she quickly muttered, "He told me he had taken up shark-fishing." She had a way of making a declaration so you were never intended to believe it to be true.

I was none too sure how old my mother was, but Uncle Fulvius was known to be ten years her senior—a bit geriatric to wrestle with deep-sea man-eaters. It was typical of my family. Their craziness rarely led to real harm, but they never knew what was appropriate. I could have sat back and seen them only as good entertainment—but nowadays members of the family were always pressuring me to reform other relatives, under that deathly edict, "You are the head of the family."

Informers who play up their feckless side avoid this. I looked back to my irresponsible days with sudden fondness.

Once again next day I hired a donkey and rode out along the coast. The gate to the so-called pirate's villa had a guard this time, but he let me in without trouble. As I rode down the sandy path, I passed a man leaving. He was going at a crazy pace, feet-out on a small mule like desert tribesmen in Syria, who liked to race off from oases in this madcap way. Because of the dustcloud, the rider had a long scarf wrapped around his face, but as I coughed in his wake I glimpsed a coat-shaped robe of Parthian cut, a balding dome, and eyes that looked sideways at me curiously.

Damagoras received me. Perhaps his claim was true that he never left home, so he welcomed visitors. Little bronze cups on a matching tray were being removed by a woman in beaded slippers after his previous caller. No replenishments appeared for me.

As I expected, Damagoras crushed any suggestion that my brother-in-law deserved help with his medical bills and recompense for his time off work. We quickly abandoned that conversation.

I pressed him again on the subject of Diocles, but that too hit a dead end.

Then I mentioned the kidnaps. The old rogue became a little more attentive, but I could see he reckoned I had very few leads. "So what makes you link this to the Cilician community, Falco?"

He was right: none of the victims had mentioned any provincial nationality, apart from "the Illyrian." I left Illyria out of it. When there is a viable bunch of suspects, why complicate matters? "I am making a direct connection between Diocles' interest in the kidnaps and his visits to you."

Damagoras gave me his honest-fellow laugh. "We never talked about kidnaps. What interest in kidnaps was Diocles supposed to have had?" I noticed the past tense. Perhaps Damagoras knew what had happened to the missing man.

"The longer he is missing, the more closely all his interests will come under scrutiny," I warned.

"This is bad, Falco! Trying to frighten an old man who has done nothing wrong."

"You don't scare that easily. But don't let's quarrel about it—or not yet! Now I'd like you to give me a contact address, please, for your pugilistic crony Cratidas." Damagoras went vague on me. "Better to let me discuss what that angry swine did to my brother-in-law, Damagoras, than for Cratidas to find his name is on a surveillance-of-aliens list, being monitored by the vigiles."

I was a Roman, so Damagoras took the threat as real. Coming to the notice of officials is the last thing a provincial in temporary residence ever wants. Any seafarer has quite enough to do, dodging import taxes and protection rackets, and haggling with the negotiators who try to dun him out of all his profits in an unfriendly market. To be marked for constant investigation and harassment is deadly. Unable to risk it, the old man reluctantly told me a bar where Cratidas could be found in Ostia. I noted the name.

"And would you happen to know an adventurer called Theopompus?"

Nothing changed in Damagoras' expression. "A common name among sailors," he said. "What has this Theopompus done? Is he one of your kidnappers?"

I felt I had made a mistake. At least I had not mentioned the girl, Rhodope. There was no particular menace in the so-called pirate's tone, but if he knew anything about the ransom racket, I had just fingered a gang member who must have broken the anonymity code. Word of this stupidity by Theopompus would get back. Mind you, if the young girl's seducer was thrashed as a result, I had no qualms.

"I suppose one of the female victims says she slept with him?" Damagoras read my thoughts as cunningly as my mother. "Falco, I'll tell you—the woman will be lying. It was always a rule with the old pirates never to touch their guests." Calling them "guests" was a glossy euphemism. And of course he was still pretending piracy had died out. "The whole point was to convince friends and relatives to pay up, knowing that they could be sure the . . ."

"Victim," I supplied, as he paused.

Damagoras smiled, but still left the word unsaid. "Would be returned to them, alive and unharmed."

"Women," I commented. "Always tricky commodities."

"They lie," he said, again baldly. "They want to believe they have had a romantic love affair. It was well-known, Falco. Women were trouble. The experts at ransoming never took women, if men were available. That way, they avoided untidy consequences."

"All the victims here have been women. It is a very particular scam."

"Craziness," said Damagoras.

"Maybe it will end like the most famous kidnap of all."

"Who's that?" demanded Damagoras. He squinted at me keenly, just like a man who thought I had insulted his trade.

"Julius Caesar. He promised his captors that as soon as he was ransomed he would come back and crucify them all. He was true to his word."

"A noble guest," observed Damagoras. "A hard man, very tricky to do business with!"

I had distracted him from the Rhodope angle. There seemed nothing to gain from him, so I left.

XXIX

Cratidas drank at a tavern called the Aquarius. I had a feeling he probably lived there. It was by the Gate of Fortune, which was close to the bank of the Tiber and fairly near to my apartment, so after I rode back, I diverted and found it. I was expecting a verminous hovel where day would be as black as night, and night unspeakable. However, the house with the name of the zodiac water-carrier was a large establishment with a pleasant exterior and several shady interior courtyards. It lacked a river view, but being set back from the bustle of the waterfront made it seem more gracious.

Casual trade used the snackbar, standing up at streetside counters on two sides of a corner. The servery there was larger than most, well equipped with shelves of flagons and bowls. The odors from the sunken pots of food inset in the marble counters were less repellent than the low fast feeders in Rome; the bar-girl was neat and clean, and she said I was welcome to pass down a short corridor to the ground-floor courtyard area. Here, tourists sat about on benches under pergolas, congratulating themselves on finding such a good hotel, right near the Portus ferries. A businessman who clearly knew the place of old passed through on his way to a room upstairs, led by a burly slave carrying luggage. He was something big in corn; we were in an area of grain measurers and associated government officers.

In this slightly unlikely setting, I found Cratidas. He was talking to another man, probably subordinate to him in the Cilician hierarchy. They
had seats at a table under a fig tree, where they had established themselves
in a way that suggested this courtyard was their private office so the
tourists had all better use the other spaces. The tourists had taken the
point. Maybe they thought Cratidas owned the Aquarius. In fact, for all
I knew, he did.

Maybe, though, people avoided him because there was just something
about Cratidas that told them he was dangerous. I had met worse bullies,
certainly more obvious ones, but he carried himself with an air. He was
coiled for action. Clearly, he was just looking for an excuse to take offense, and he expected to win his fights. That would probably be because
he fought dirty—but complaining about his methods would not be
much help after he had sliced off your hand or blinded you. He had scars,
including a long knife wound, which had healed years ago in a silvered
crease, running from his eyebrow to his jaw. The end of one finger was
missing.

His companion looked fairly presentable until he laughed; then I saw
he had very few teeth. Cratidas was still wearing the long crimson robe
he had flaunted when he attacked Gaius and me at the villa; this one was
in a dull greenish ensemble. It looked filthy, but the braid on the neck
and the edges of the long sleeves included genuine gold thread. I recognized his balding crown and the long multicolored scarves flung around
his thick hairy neck.

Nobody would mistake this pair for philosophy teachers. They were
rough. Very rough. As I approached, I had heard harsh voices and abrupt,
coarse laughter. That was before they noticed me. After that, their hostil-
ity hung between us as tangibly as woodsmoke.

"Nice base you have here! Remember me? I'm Falco." Cratidas turned
to his companion and said something in a foreign language. Evidently he
did remember, and the recollection caused them both to grin nastily.
"Sorry to interrupt," I said. "Is this a Greek symposium?"

"Oh yes, we were discussing literature!" Cratidas replied. The pair
laughed at some huge private joke. I raised an eyebrow coolly.

The other man stood up. He was Eastern-looking, and when he

swayed past me, looking sideways with a sneer, I definitely recognized him. I had last seen him riding away from the Damagoras villa at a cracking pace. Now he left us too, once more grinning at Cratidas as he went.

I had been standing with my thumbs in my belt, but I now joined Cratidas. Spreading myself, as I took a bench opposite him at the table, I moved one end of it away from the table to make myself more room. I began discussing the disability he had inflicted on Gaius Baebius. I knew it would be a waste of time. Cratidas spat fiercely at the fig tree. After that, he slammed a dagger into the table. The point just missed my hand. I kept my hand motionless, not even flinching at the noise. He could decide for himself whether this was because I was stupid, or so stunned I couldn't move.

"That's an old trick." I made it dry and languorous. "Did you mean to miss, or are you just incompetent?"

Then, under the table, I jerked up one thigh to trap his knees against the boards so he had no leverage; I used my other foot to kick away the bench he was sitting on. He crashed down to the floor; it must have jarred his back. Of course he was up again instantly. I threw myself right over the table and grabbed him by his long hair. (Never have hair long enough to be grabbed by an assailant, as my trainer says.) When Cratidas lunged at me, I went with the motion, but swung him around and got him facedown on the table with an arm up his back. I was pinning his head down with my body weight. His nose was so bent he must be finding it difficult to breathe.

"Now listen!" He seemed helpless, but I was not intending to stay that close in case he wrenched free and took off some part of me. "I think that you and your sidekick in the dirty Parthian dressing gown are part of a racket to kidnap merchants' wives. Probably Damagoras runs the racket. Other people are looking into it, so you can take your chance with them. I want to know, and I want to know now, Cratidas, what happened to the scribe, Diocles?"

"I don't know!"

"Oh, I bet you do! Was he investigating your ransom scam?" He made another negative gurgle. I lifted him up partially and banged his face against the table. As a favor to Gaius Baebius, I bashed him down really hard. If Cratidas was impressed that I could match him in brutality, he didn't show it. "Where is he, Cratidas? What have you done with him?"

I felt him tense for action. I was vulnerable, lying half on top of him, so I flew off him as he burst free. He spun around, teeth bared. We had fallen apart a couple of yards distant. He saw I had snatched his knife from the table. He was one blade down (though I reckoned he had others), and he had yet to discover what weaponry I carried.

He hauled up the bench he had previously fallen off. People were taking notice of us now, though. Cratidas probably wanted to continue his stay here so he needed to calm the situation, or the nice people who were sitting under the pergolas would huffily ask the affable tavern landlord to evict him. He swung the bench around, about the height of my head, but then placed it back down. The fight was apparently over—not that I trusted him.

"I don't know," he said, in that coarse voice with the rasping tone, "what went on with the scribe. Damagoras toyed with him, but even he lost interest. You can find out where the man went or what he wanted for yourself, Falco!"

"I will," I said. "And then I'll be back, Cratidas."

We omitted good-byes.

As I left the Aquarius I gave the bar-girl a sample of imperial coinage and my best smile. She knew I had not ordered any food or drink. So she accepted the money and returned the smile delightfully—then when I asked if she knew the name of the visitor in the dirty green robe who had come to see Cratidas, she told me.

He was called Lygon. I had heard that name before. When I hit the street outside he was long gone, but that did not bother me. There was no need for me to tail him home. I already knew where Lygon lived— or at least, where he had lived until recently.

XXX

When I consulted Petronius, I thought he looked shifty. I had left a message at the station house; he called in at our apartment late that afternoon. I told him how I had identified Lygon—the same Lygon, I was sure, who had been named to us as the boyfriend of Pullia, young Zeno's mother. I had decided the Cilicians had placed her in the gatehouse room where we found her unconscious so that when they took a victim, Pullia could be their jailer until a ransom was paid.

"Apparently the women seem confused after their ordeal. Brunnus thinks that while they are being held, they are drugged—remember how the boy said to us, 'Uncle' Lygon had once told him that if anyone didn't wake up, the vigiles would want to know?"

"How do you know what Brunnus thinks?" Petronius demanded.

I feigned deafness. "Zeno must have misunderstood what Lygon meant. Lygon was talking about the risk of being hunted down for murder, if any victims were accidentally given an overdose. In fact, Pullia may have overdosed herself instead. That time the boy took us to see his mother, she wasn't drunk, as we thought. I bet she got bored and sampled the drugs herself."

"So by chance, we stumbled on the racket, way back!" Petronius sucked his teeth in annoyance.

"Missing it doesn't matter. Now we can break the ring."

"I'd like to hold back on that, Marcus. We need to gather evidence—"

"When did evidence feature in a vigiles arrest?" I scoffed.

"Don't be like that! We need to be certain—" Prevarication had never been Petro's style. I guessed his motive, however.

"We are waiting until the Fourth Cohort arrives in Ostia?"

"End of the week," Petronius said briskly, unaware that Rubella had already told me.

I mentioned that Rubella might accompany the detachment. I had to explain why. Petronius Longus told me what he thought of me. His dissertation was not pretty.

Eager for action now, we reached an accommodation. "I'll get you for this, Falco!"

"Fine. In the meantime, old pal, what's our plan?"

"We can take turns to watch the old gatehouse. We'll establish whether Lygon and the woman are still living there."

"It's just around the corner from where I saw Lygon with Cratidas."

"Yes, the gatehouse is ideally positioned." Petro had quickly thought it out. "It's near the river, when they snatch victims from Portus. It's also centrally located if they take them in Ostia, and good for returning the women after ransom."

"I thought our involvement that time would put them off the place."

"Pullia may never have owned up to the others about what happened. Even if she did, once the gang saw we were not suspicious of her, why sacrifice a good location? So we can observe the place until the next time they bring a victim back there. Then it's arrest time."

As always when I had made a neat connection, I found myself wanting to test it: "Pullia and the boy come from somewhere called Soli. Remember, Maia found that out. Do we know if this Soli is in Cilicia?"

Helena Justina was reading, so quietly we had forgotten she was there. Now she looked up from the scroll. "Yes," she said, as if she were already part of our conversation. "Soli used to be on the Cilician coast."

"Used to be?" I was skeptical. "What happened? Did the town sprout wings and fly off into the puffy clouds? Sounds like an abstruse metaphor, in an Athenian satire."

Petronius was grinning—too much, I thought. I was better acquainted with Helena's research skills. I gave her a look. Her dark eyes betrayed a modest triumph. Roman matrons do not gloat. Particularly over their spouses, of course. "I brought a map of the Empire with me, Marcus."

"Of course you did," I answered. "We want to be equipped, if one of our very advanced children starts asking cute questions about remote provinces."

"I expect," Petronius mocked us gravely, "Julia Junilla Laeitana can already recite all the rivers in Germania."

"Germania Ulterior *and* Inferior," I assured him. "Rhenus and all its tributaries, in order, north to south."

"Should be south to north, Falco. Go with the flow, man."

"I know, but I was holding the map upside down when I taught her. We are working on Germania Libera, but the little sweetheart is frightened by the thought of untamed barbarians." Julia was three; she still had problems reciting all her own names. I had been rather carried away when naming my firstborn.

Helena waited quietly for Petro and me to stop fooling.

"I think you will like this; it fits your theories. Soli was officially renamed a hundred years ago." She lifted her right hand, a characteristic gesture, freeing up the group of bracelets she wore on her forearm. They tinkled against one another as she twisted her wrist, unconscious of the movement. "Soli, you crazy pair of jesters, is now called Pompeiopolis. Now, Marcus, isn't that where your old pirate comes from too?"

We took it in, then both graciously applauded her. Helena had just provided our first link between the kidnappers and Damagoras.

Inspired, Petronius and I took turns at watching the gatehouse.

"You'll have to be careful," I warned him. "What if the Soli group have already noticed you? You only live about two doors down. You've been sauntering right past their place almost every day."

"I'll take the night watch then," he volunteered. As a father of small children, that suited me. I could be telling bedtime stories, while Petro endured the drunks and caterwauling whores.

★   ★   ★

We started straightaway, and observed the place for the rest of the week.

Lygon, a relaxed lover with a callous attitude, hardly ever bothered to visit his drab ladyfriend, though I spotted him once and Petro reported another sighting two nights later. Pullia was always there. My worst problem was avoiding her boy, the seven-year-old Zeno. He played in the street, looking bored. He had no toys, but threw stones, stared at passersby, and kicked his sandals on the curbstones. Pullia rarely went out, but sometimes she sent him on errands; at mealtimes she would call him indoors, shouting his name abrasively. He was no worse treated than some of my elder sisters' children, but his way of life meant there was a strong chance he would notice one of us while we were lurking across the street on observation. He seemed an intelligent child, who would probably remember us.

Someone did eventually spot me—though the way it happened was unexpected. It was my watch. Helena, with Favonia in her arms, was just bringing me a lunch basket. I had stationed myself almost opposite the old gatehouse. There was an empty block, perhaps earmarked to be an overflow forum. Sometimes a mad old woman brought crumbs to feed the birds, but they were a standoffish flock and she shuffled around keeping well away from me. There were two houses on the other side of the street where the occupants kept looking out as if they thought I was a prospective burglar. At least when they saw Helena with me, they could comfort themselves that I must just be dawdling in the hope of an adulterous liaison. It was a good excuse for us to cuddle in public—always a cheap thrill. Meanwhile Sosia Favonia practiced toddling.

The Ostians were not great humorists and disapproved of us canoodling. Fortunately our curly-haired child looked so sweet in her clean white tunic and tiny bead necklace, our behavior was soon overlooked. We stopped being lewd and passed ourselves off as proud parents parading their infant.

I did not believe in using my children as props in a disguise. My mother would have been furious. *Helena's* mother would have seized Favonia and sought sanctuary in the nearest temple.

In my days as a lone informer, I had had other methods. Here, I would have sat against a pillar, huddled in dirty rags—except that Petronius had bagged this role of down-and-out for his observations at night. I had tried pretending to be an artist, but when I sat on a stool drawing town-scapes in my note-tablet, the inevitable group of gawpers assembled behind me. They made it clear my sketching was awful. Several advised me to give up and get a proper job. It was not a situation where I could answer that I already had one, and ask if they knew Diocles.

In the end, I assembled ropes and poles, with a bucket and some sponges, set up a barrier against the exterior of Privatus' house (which lay on one side of the open area), donned a one-armed unbelted tunic, and pretended to clean the stonework. That would be accepted by everyone as an endless job, and one where I, as the useless workman, was bound to be a slacker. I was safe then so long as Privatus himself never came around, demanding to know who gave me instructions to ruin the patina of his building.

I was still lazing there in my role as a renovator when Helena brought the lunch basket. To observe the gatehouse opposite, I had had to plant myself right on the street line. Down the Decumanus Maximus came all the day's busy traffic. Plenty of carts and donkeys were entering the town, while the usual slow buildup accumulated in the other direction, all heading out to the city with their goods that evening. Then driving against them, rattling in from Rome and causing a fine drama, came a driver with no sense of social timing. Cursing him, the working teams who were trying to go the other way all slowed up and banged against one another.

He was flash trash. In a bright crimson outfit, thirties, louche-looking, proud of his luxuriant hair, and wearing pounds of gold, he cut an expensive dash. He had a girl with him. Of course her admiring presence made him whip up his horses—there were two, clearly excellent and well matched in color (inevitably glossy black). In case anyone failed to notice them coming, they had bells on their harnesses. They were pulling the latest model in chariots for show-offs. A garish Medusa covered the front, with pseudo-Greek hoplites all around the sides, whose oversized helmets and long phallic spears were apparently laid on in real gold leaf. The equipage must have been a special order, and its salesman was probably sunning himself in Neapolis on his commission.

The girlie was screaming with glee. When she saw us, she could not help waving wildly, even though she had to cling on tight as her lover swerved from side to side, causing as much havoc as he could. She wanted us to know how proud she was to be tearing along through Ostia with this wondrous man. Her hero loved her. He had come to fetch her. She was absolutely radiant at being with him.

He must be Theopompus. The passenger he was so busy impressing was Posidonius' daughter, Rhodope.

XXXI

They did not stop. That was just as well. Rhodope might be ecstatic, but Helena and I saw it differently.

"Oh, Juno! She looks in her element. Marcus, her poor father!"

"I should have warned him to keep a guard on her."

"If she was determined to run off, she would have escaped somehow."

"You're the expert on young girls with dreams." I had always had the impression that Helena Justina, a shy and reserved young woman, had nonetheless led a wild imaginative life before I met her.

She never confirmed it. "Oh, *I* was scrupulously sensible—until I met that informer in Britain. The dark, dangerous one with that look in his eyes and the way with words . . . You have gone quiet, darling."

She always understood me. I was smitten with fear about this adventure.

Among the more mature female prisoners who were usually taken, Rhodope must have been a one-off. When he bedded her, however, Theopompus could never have been serious. Afterward, we had been sure that only heartache awaited the besotted creature. Rhodope was not bad-looking—but not good-looking either. From what we had seen, she was a pale little character, completely inexperienced. She lacked the fire to ensnare a man of action, and yet she had too many romantic expectations to be suitable for the hard life led ashore by the worn-out women-folk of pirates. The fact that Theopompus had gone back for the girl seemed out of character.

"She offers easy pickings, though."

"Yes. She was young, an easy lay who would not argue—making it awkward for her father to pursue a seducer afterwards."

"I meant, she is the only child of a rich and loving widower," Helena remarked astutely. "Theopompus can bleed Posidonius dry. The father knows it; I saw the dread in his expression when we talked to him. It is not just that his daughter has lost her virginity and is unlikely to agree to a good marriage while she's pining."

"No, you are right. Posidonius has paid heavily to get her back once—and even if Theopompus returns her to him this time, it is bound to involve cost."

"The father is helpless, Marcus; he knows the girl is making a horrible mistake. If Theopompus is a real villain, he will string Rhodope along, maybe even marry her, then expect her papa to pay out a permanent retainer to save her being hurt."

"Or worse."

"Or worse," agreed Helena, shuddering.

After a moment I confessed my real anxiety. "I just hope Theopompus has not picked her up because Damagoras told him to."

"You think that would be your fault." Helena loved me, but was an unsparing critic.

"Admitted. I am scared that Damagoras was annoyed when he found out—from me—that Rhodope had named Theopompus. The old villain may want her put out of the way."

"Want her *killed,* you mean?"

"Let's hope not. Theopompus may just have been told to bring her into the clan where they can keep her quiet."

Helena bent to Favonia, who was dragging at her skirts. Holding our daughter on her hip, she gave me a long look. "Can't we believe the warmhearted Damagoras has allowed a new tryst because he likes to see love triumph over adversity?"

"What adversity?" I scoffed.

"All right. A silly wretch has thrown herself at a lout who wastes cash on garish transport—"

"Helena, she is rich and ridiculous, but she's up against worse than she knows. And I don't just mean she's in danger of crying her eyes out when her cupid dumps her."

Helena sighed. "You must find her, Marcus. Go and see Petronius. At least tell her father where she is."

That was my intention. I wanted to hear whether Posidonius already knew the whereabouts of the eloping couple. If he had been informed of their plans by Theopompus, then I could relax. That meant Theopompus was holding the girl now in order to rake off more of her father's fortune. The father had his troubles and for him they might be long-term ones, but at least the girl would stay alive.

Since the contractor's house stood right alongside where I had been on watch, I abandoned my position, and rushed to see if Petronius was at home.

"Oh, look; now we have the whole set of dice!" Maia greeted me. I took it for affection. She let me kiss her cheek.

"Who's here?"

"Roll yourself into the second courtyard and you'll see."

Petronius was talking to Marcus Rubella. They looked at ease, reaching up for grapes from a pergola and speaking in quiet voices. The tribune must be so intrigued by what I had told him of events at Ostia, he had come a day in advance of the rest of his detachment. As men talking together professionally about their unit, he and Petro both looked annoyed at seeing me.

"Sorry to interrupt."

They had the seats. Petro was in a woven chair that Maia normally used; her wool basket sat on the ground at his feet. Rubella had sprawled on a marble bench, with one leg along the full length of the seat. He did not move up. I stood. I was too impatient to wrangle about his manners, and merely told my tale.

"I already knew the girl, Rhodope, was missing." Rubella stayed calm.

"The father came bellyaching at the patrol house. Relax, Falco. We are onto it."

"Well I've told you she is in Ostia. No need to thank me," I sneered. He did not blink.

"That's a bummer." Petronius was more forthcoming. He even pulled out a cushion from behind him and tossed it to me so I could sit on a low wall. "She's put the whole operation at risk." So it was an "operation" now, was it? Rubella in charge, and even Petronius Longus following his chief's orders. I knew where that placed me. "The charioteer didn't stop at the gatehouse, Falco?"

"Theopompus never looked at the place. That may have been to conceal the hideout—or he may just have been enjoying himself too much with his crazy driving."

"And you believe this girl is at risk?" Rubella's tone was ponderous; he reminded me of Gaius Baebius. When I spelled out my fears that Damagoras would eliminate Rhodope, the tribune's interest was cursory. "There has been no direct threat to her?"

"No, there has been no threat. But what villain issues a statement of intent when he is about to snuff out a witness?"

I knew what Rubella would say. Even Petronius would support him. "We can keep a watching brief on the girl. But we can't go in and fetch her. There is too much at stake," warned Rubella bluntly. "Until we identify the others and position ourselves for a swoop, Rhodope cannot be my priority."

Petronius Longus then gave me the fixed stare treatment. "I know what you're thinking, Falco. Don't do it!"

Rubella also jumped on me: "Falco, I don't want you carrying out an independent mission. Leave the girl and her boyfriend strictly alone from now on, do you hear?"

"We'll do the drama." Petro reinforced his words.

"So what about the watch on the gatehouse?" I demanded.

"Leave that to us," said Rubella.

I stood up. "Well thanks, both of you. I would like to say that if the girl dies, her blood is on your hands. Unfortunately, I can't let myself off so lightly. If she dies it will be my fault—my fault for having foolishly trusted the vigiles to defend law and order."

"We are accountable to the whole community." Rubella's tone was so bland I could have pushed his teeth down his throat. "I don't want to see the girl harmed—I don't want to explain that to her father."

"You know the score, Marcus," Petronius said. "She must take her chance." It was tough. That's the vigiles for you.

Rubella was making statements: "I want to round up the entire gang and put a stop to this kidnapping, once and for all."

"Once and for all" is political jargon—which makes it absolutely meaningless.

As I took myself off from the contractor's house, who should I meet coming in but Brunnus, the Sixth's detachment leader.

"What are you doing here, Brunnus?"

"Marcus Rubella has arrived in Ostia. We have a meeting arranged, Falco. Handover and joint strategy discussion."

Joint balls-up, more likely. After Rubella and Petronius had both expressed a wish to show up their colleagues in the Sixth, I could hardly believe this. "Inter-cohort liaison? Whatever happened to rivalry?"

Brunnus grinned happily. "What rivalry, Falco?" He was an innocent. Rubella was probably picking his brains, prior to shafting him and his cohort. "We have to interleave our efforts on some critical initiatives—"

"The kidnaps," I stated.

As far as he knew, I was chasing pirates over Diocles but had never heard of the kidnap racket. Fired up, Brunnus failed to notice. "Be wonderful," he gloated, "if the vigiles can get ahead of Caninus and the navy!"

No doubt Caninus had some other navy unit *he* was hoping to outwit. The Ravenna and Misenum Fleets were bound to be rivals. So it would go on: each branch of the services locked into doing down the next. Never mind Posidonius losing his daughter. The important thing was to establish cohort supremacy. All any of them wanted was an honorable mention from the Emperor.

Brunnus headed in to see the others, but I caught his arm. "Word of advice," I said, feeling tetchy and wanting to land someone in muleshit. "You need to jolly up that dozy group of bullies you keep farmed out in the west sector."

"We don't have any farmed-out men, Falco. I don't believe in it. Leads to lack of discipline."

"I saw them myself. Four great laggards. Streetside, sleeping on the job in an abandoned lot, chucking their weight about, just beyond the main Forum."

"Not ours," Brunnus assured me.

"Then get there and arrest them. You've got impostors, using a fake guardpost to defraud the public of bribes. Isn't impersonating the vigiles a crime?" Taking a bribe was a crime too, though that was theoretical. The gang I met would never have succeeded in their ploy, had the real vigiles been lily white. They were behaving as the public expected.

Brunnus could not be bothered. "Frankly, we have more exciting things on. You must have been dreaming, Falco."

I pulled up and smacked myself around the ear. "You're right. I must have seen some ghost troopers left behind decades ago by the Divine Emperor Claudius . . . Forget I mentioned it."

Now Brunnus looked worried. But it would not affect him long. Brunnus had a thrilling afternoon ahead, plotting joint exercises with Marcus Rubella and Petronius Longus of the Fourth Cohort.

Relegated to the role of an outsider, I found myself something else to do. If the men who had threatened me the other day were nothing to do with the vigiles, I was free to challenge them. The vigiles were accountable to the community; as a private informer, I was accountable to no one—but I had a social conscience. I could back it up with intellect, cunning, and if needs be fisticuffs. I marched off to confront the bastards, all set to wreak havoc.

No use.

I walked along the Decumanus to where I had seen the fake patrol house. At the same time, I kept one eye out for the crass chariot Theopompus drove; it made me feel better to be looking for him, and Marcus Rubella could not stop me using my eyes.

The empty shop near the Temple of Hercules was now completely abandoned. The impostors were no longer to be seen. They had packed up and vanished. I was relieved Brunnus had not sent an inquiry team, or I would have looked stupid.

But the old crusts still lay on the rubble-strewn floor; liquor fumes still hung in the air. So did the rank smell of deceit. The fraudsters had been here. Now they were hunkered down somewhere else, preying on new people in a new locality. I would find them eventually. And next time, I would put them out of business.

XXXII

Back at the Decumanus I crossed the junction to a run-down row of fishmongers'. There was no chance of me and mine eating with Maia and Petronius this evening. Taking Rubella's part against me was utterly hypocritical. The vigiles may look down on private informers—but when it suited, we were good enough to help them out with their clear-up figures. Petronius Longus damn well knew that.

Stuff him. I would take home something to cook up myself for a supper with my own brood. It was a few days since we had enjoyed my mother's mullet. I decided I was ready for pan-fried sardines. They were a favorite of mine, and easy to prepare even in an apartment with limited facilities. Back in the old days at my dilapidated Fountain Court rental, I ate sardines all the time.

The stall I chose had been here for a century. Surely soon some emperor who wanted to look good would provide new premises with smarter fish tanks and big marble slabs. In the meantime, they gutted fish on a wooden table which they scrubbed each night. The produce was fresh and the stallholder friendly. I asked if he had known the scribe's aunt.

"Oh, Vestina was a regular until she got too creaky. Then she used to send her maid—unless she had her visitor. He would help her along here herself."

"Her nephew? Diocles?"

A woman appeared from the cramped living quarters in the rear. Elderly and nosy, she was introduced to me as the stallholder's mother. It was no surprise. They shared similar squashed noses. "That was a terrible night," she said, clearly referring to the fire.

"Can you tell me about it? I heard there were problems getting help."

"Of course there were. We all hate fires."

"Vigiles too far away to fetch?"

"Oh, much too far. People around here would never go to them," said the son, betraying the Ostians' suspicion of the men from Rome.

"Who do you call on? The builders' guild?"

He shook his head. "Not unless we're desperate."

As I raised my eyebrows in query, the mother rushed to moan about the guild. "Nasty lot. Looking after themselves, you know."

"How's that?"

The son gave the mother a warning look and she subsided. I stuck it out, now looking into the crayfish bucket as if I was considering a starter course tonight.

"I wouldn't want to say anything bad," murmured the mother, helping me to flip good specimens into a piece of sacking. Then she went ahead: "The firemen go into people's houses and come out with their knapsacks filled."

"They help themselves to valuables?"

"Famous for it," said the son, now willing to blacken them. "And worse."

"Worse?"

"Well, nothing can be proved, but some say when the builders' guild are putting a fire out, they don't try very hard." I pretended to look blank, so he explained: "If the property is completely destroyed, there will be a nice profit, putting up a new building. They would rather obtain a contract than save a house or business."

"I noticed a lot of empty plots over the other side of the junction. Is that builders on a redevelopment plan?"

"Could be. No sign of much happening. I reckon it will be years before they start."

"Any hint of foul play in all this? Do the builders ever deliberately help fires to start?" Both mother and son swore they had never heard it suggested. They had a less cynical attitude than me. "So the night Vestina died, who did turn up to fight the flames?"

"Locals," said the fishmonger. "We had to get water from the baths, and they were closed so that took time."

"Wasn't there a vigiles guardhouse hereabouts?"

"Oh, them!"

"Would they not turn out?"

"No, Diocles asked them."

The son had been terse; the mother elaborated: "They just laughed at him. He begged in vain."

"First most of us knew, he was running about from place to place screaming for help—"

"Well, you know why he was so upset," said his mother. I turned to her and she said flatly, "It was all his fault. He was always feckless; some men are, you know. He caused the fire."

"Accident?" I asked her, still thinking that Petronius Longus would wonder if the scribe was an arsonist.

"Oh yes. He let a lamp fall off a shelf, he admitted it. The poor man was hysterical about that. His aunt had been such a nice woman—quite cultured, you know; she had worked for an empress when she was a young girl. I think Vestina and Diocles were the only family each other had—freed slaves but perfectly respectable, with royal connections. He was left all alone when he lost her. And such a terrible way for her to go . . ."

"Have you ever seen him back again? Has he been this year at all?"

"Oh no. I don't expect he'll ever come here again," said the fishmonger's mother. "He wouldn't want to remember what happened, would he?"

I sorted out more crayfish thoughtfully. Some were just large prawns but they would still be tasty. Now I had the full picture, my anxieties about Diocles were leaping up again. Whatever work motives had brought him here, he was asking for mental anguish. Or were his motives personal?

"I'm worried about him," I told them. "He stayed in lodgings by the Marine Gate this summer. Then he disappeared suddenly."

"He'll be dead in a ditch," said the fishmonger's mother. "He couldn't take the nightmare any longer, if you ask me. He'll have done for himself. I can see him now, his torment was shocking. Tears streaming down his face, all blackened from the fire where he had tried to get back in the house. People had to drag him away. There was nothing he could do, the heat had gotten too intense. So he sat in the street then, whimpering to himself, over and over, 'the bastards, the bastards!'—He meant the men who laughed at him, those ones in that guardhouse. He meant, they could have come to help when he begged them, but they just let Vestina die."

XXXIII

Subdued, I bought my fish, then walked slowly home.

The crowds jostling in the main street seemed garish and crass. All looked vibrant and thriving in this multicultured port, but corruption ate at the heart of the local fabric, stinking like rotting seaweed. Many towns have a stench in the back alleys. Here it was subtle, but universal. The bullies from the builders' guild preyed on their own people; the vigiles left them to their own devices. Interlopers from barren provinces homed in as parasites on other foreigners. A young girl had had her life ruined. She failed to see her loss, or how it would ruin her father. An elderly cripple had died because no one would help her. A scribe had vanished. All these busy people in the streets pushed and shoved, all these heavily laden vehicles rattled and bumped, along the sunny streets in the name of commerce, heedless of the polluting tide that sucked to and fro in the darkness under the warm wharves of Ostia and Portus.

I walked half the length of the Decumanus Maximus, one silent man amid the bustle. I was thinking about someone else who had passed along this street in solitude. I wondered if bereavement was the only force working on Diocles' emotions, or if he too had burned with anger over this town. If he knew of the stench, I wondered what he did about it. I could not tell if I was any closer to finding him, but as I thought of

Diocles that evening I knew that what had once seemed an easy, light-hearted task for me had assumed a blacker character.

I hoped he was here. I hoped he was nearby. I wanted to find him, merely maudlin and drowning his sorrows at one of his solitary suppers in a bar. But increasingly I feared for him.

It was just as well I had lashed out on the extra seafood. We had a house-ful of visitors. Having shed my mother, we had suddenly acquired Helena's mama—not to mention her father and her younger brother. They had all come to see off Aelianus, whose ship would leave for Greece the next day. Fortunately, I was not expected to cram in extra people. Senatorial families always stay in some noble friend's villa when they travel around; they have the knack of finding one where the friend is not in residence to bother them. Unlike my own family, today's relatives were going on to a nearby estate for the traditional patrician customs: criticiz-ing their friend's bedlinen and his favorite slaves, before leaving a very short thank-you note and mounds of unwashed foodbowls. Slaves had gone ahead to ensure there were beds ready and hot water in the bath-house. Tonight, the travelers were staying to supper with us. Decimus Camillus and Julia Justa wanted to see their granddaughters.

Cooking arrangements in the apartment were not up to this, so we built an open fire down in the courtyard, over which I cooked the fish in relays: they were succulent and scented with herbs. Man's work; I had to fight for my position against the senator and his sons. They had no idea how to keep a wood fire going, and I was skeptical of their skewering techniques. Never mind where our firewood came from—though I did hear the local baker had problems getting his oven fired up next day.

We took over the whole ground-floor outdoor area; other tenants of the apartment block could only gape jealously and mutter about us blocking access to the well. Helena and her mother went out for more provisions; there was a little market just inside the Gate of Fortune. Senators' wives never normally shop in person, but Julia Justa had a pretty good eye for a bunch of dill. They were extremely cheerful when they came back laden; it was probably the first time for years they had been on an expedition together.

In fact there was so much giggling, I wondered whether the two of them had stepped into the Aquarius for a little spiced wine toddy. Far be it from me to sniff my mother-in-law's breath for cinnamon, or anything stronger. It is probably treason for an equestrian to suggest that a senator's wife has been drinking in a public place. I could certainly have got myself smacked—and I knew that women who have had a tipple lose all sense of how hard they are hitting. I remembered when Maia, as a young girl, used to come home hysterical from a screaming night of fun at the loom-workers funeral club.

When I told this to Helena and Julia Justa, it caused so much merriment, I was quite sure about the hot toddy.

It was a very warm evening. Back in Rome, the Camilli might seem diffident, in comparison to their stately colleagues, but once they were let out of their town house on a spree, they knew how to throw themselves into a country feast. We could have been at an olive harvest. We were loud, we ate heartily, we laughed and talked until it grew so dark we had to light oil lamps and start batting at insects. The children scampered about. Nux sniffed and snuffled around people's legs. Nervous at first, but then happier than I had seen her, Albia allocated bowls and spoons. Aulus hauled water from the well; Quintus opened up the amphora that had somehow found itself strapped in the luggage box of the senator's carriage without Julia Justa knowing why there seemed so little room for her possessions.

The senator sat in the middle of everything, looking as if he wished he could retire to a vineyard in the sun.

"Classic," I said, handing him a dish of prawns to pick apart for Julia and Favonia. He was a devoted grandfather. Like many, he probably had more enjoyment from the younger generation than he had allowed himself with his own children. "You are a traditional Roman, devoting yourself to city politics as a duty, while yearning for the simple life when our ancestors were robust farmers."

"And if they had stayed farmers, Marcus, we would all be tenants under the thumb of some Sabine elite!"

"Working all hours to pay the rent to our heartless masters."

"I thought you were a republican, lad."

I wondered who had told him that. "It's easy to be a republican when you live in a thriving empire," I admitted. "I'm not sure that I really fancy the hard old days of plowing and porridge."

Decimus posted a peeled prawn into little Favonia's mouth, while she sat on the stone bench beside him, looking up patiently for the next morsel. "Gone soft!" he said, grinning. "When I first knew you, you were as cynical as Diogenes, a moody loner with a black soul."

"Now I'm staid? Your daughter's mellowing influence." On the other side of the courtyard, Helena and her noble matron mother, who were unpacking vegetables, appeared to be tossing radishes at each other, in fits of laughter. The senator and I thought best to ignore it. Men dislike too much uncharacteristic behavior. Women should stick to the rules we have learned.

"Now you are rather sensible," said Decimus. "You still do good in the community—but you don't resent yourself for it. On a night like this, Marcus Didius, I think you manage to be happy with life."

"True. As I said, thanks to Helena." I always gave him credit for the way he had brought her up. He was a fair man, but secretly Helena was his favorite. He liked her willingness to rebel; he may have felt proud of it. "I wouldn't give Favonia any more shellfish, not until we've got some plain bread into her—"

Favonia saw the game was up. Without a backward glance of thanks to her grandpapa, she wriggled off the bench. She toddled straight over to Aulus, steadying herself against his knee with sticky fingers; she had spotted that he was peeling the really big crayfish. Favonia only liked the best. Aulus, always a standoffish uncle in his own mind, would be entirely at the mercy of those big pleading eyes. Nux saw the scrounging in progress, and squirmed in alongside Favonia, adding her own silent pressure.

The senator gave another prawn to Julia, who snuggled up to him, pretending to be much better behaved than her little sister. "I know you don't want to talk about work tonight, but make sure you speak to Quintus at some point. A man came to see him. Quintus will tell you."

It could wait. It would have to. There was a sudden flare-up of the bonfire. I had a crisis with my fish.

★ ★ ★

Later, when stars were lighting our good-byes, I did snatch a moment with Justinus. The senator was supervising packing up with his carriage driver. Helena was soothing a sleepy, whining child. Aulus had to calm his mother, who had definitely supped too much of the red wine, so she had become weepy about losing him tomorrow.

"Quintus! I hear you have things to tell me."

Camillus Justinus was leaner and cleaner-cut than his elder brother, a quiet and thoroughly stable young man on the surface, though I knew he had another side to him. He lived at home with his parents, his serious wife, and his new son—but he had adventures abroad behind him. Too many, in my opinion.

He leaned on my shoulder; to save carrying empties, he had helped ensure the amphora was empty. "A good night! A wonderful send-off for Aulus. Oof!" He puffed out his cheeks, sobering up quickly. "I should have brought Claudia."

"You never bring Claudia. You're very unfair to her."

"Ah well . . . Of course she could have come. She chose to stay with the little chap." I knew why that was. It had nothing to do with feeding the baby or keeping his routine. Claudia had once been betrothed to Aulus. He had learned not to be rude about being dumped, but she found the situation awkward. It was possible she now thought that when she married Quintus, she had chosen the wrong brother. Sad to say, in her lowest moments, that pleasant, grave young woman probably thought she should not have married either of them.

"How are things, Quintus?" I asked carefully.

"Things are fine, Marcus."

"I'm glad to hear it."

"Things are just fine." People never mean that.

Quintus rallied from a brief fit of melancholia and told me his news: he had been visited by Posidonius. (I had myself told Posidonius he could contact us.) After he reported to the vigiles that Rhodope had eloped with her lover, he had felt dissatisfied and decided to seek further help from us.

"The situation is depressing," said my young partner, now in efficient professional mode. "He knows there is little he can do. Theopompus has already demanded cash for a wedding, plus more money for the couple to set up house together."

"So the pressure is on—'Surely you don't want your little girl to be unhappy, Posidonius?' Appeals to his love, backed by unspoken threats. Theopompus claims to adore her—while making sure the father knows he *could* make her really miserable."

"Exactly, Marcus. Poor bastard. Posidonius is being begged for a trousseau and dinner service already, and knows future bills will mount. The vigiles had sparse consolation to offer him—"

"Are we surprised?" I asked bitterly.

"Anyway, the girl thinks her dreams have all come true but the father knows better. He won't simply take it, though. He intends coming to Ostia to search for Rhodope; he is bringing people he knows in Rome. A group at the Emporium are getting together . . ." Quintus paused, unsure how I would take this. "I think your father may join in."

"Heaven help us!"

"Anyway, I told Posidonius where to find you." Now Pa would know too. "I can stay if you want, Marcus, but I would rather go back and head up the Rome office." He had a fancy way of putting it. Our Rome office was just my house, with whoever knocked on the door bringing their troubles. "Claudia would be happier," Quintus confessed.

I said, whatever made Claudia happy would make me happy. With one associate bunking off to Greece, I had to keep the other sweet. Otherwise I would go back to pounding the pavement night and day as a lone investigator.

The senator had been right: I liked to enjoy life nowadays.

As Aulus helped their mother into the carriage, which she achieved with less agility than normal, I muttered to Quintus, "When your mother comes to Portus tomorrow, warn her to leave her jewels behind."

Julia Justa was always smart in a restrained way. She chose her tunics to tone or contrast aesthetically with her overmantles; today she was in two shades of violet. Even for a journey and an informal alfresco fish supper, she wore a necklace formed from two rows of suspended gold spindles, large earrings with big central pearls and pearl drops, bracelets on both arms, and various finger rings. If she used the public baths, her embroidered girdle would be a magnet for pilferers; likewise her beaded shoes.

"You don't think my mother will fall prey to kidnap!" Quintus guffawed. "They'll get more than they bargain for. They would end up paying *us* the ransom, pleading for us to take Mama back!"

"The point is," I suggested, "she looks wealthy—and since your father eagerly throws off his purple-edged toga when he leaves Rome, nobody will know she is the wife of a senator. Don't scare her, but make her be sensible."

Decimus himself had now clambered into the vehicle after his lady, and was waving cheerfully through the small curtained window. Originally, theirs must have been a marriage of convenience. I knew Julia Justa had brought in money—though less money than the impoverished Camilli really needed. Nonetheless, they had made it a marriage of affection and stability.

"She's safe if they do know her rank?" Quintus was moving to join them.

"This gang is clever. They don't invite trouble. They choose merchants from overseas, to limit the support their victims can call on here in Italy. Then they scare them so badly they just want to flee back home. It works. Picking on outsiders, they have—up until now—avoided an outcry."

"Was Diocles going public on them?"

"Maybe he just inadvertently gave that impression."

Quintus waited while Helena leaned into the carriage to kiss her parents. "So what's happened to Diocles, Marcus?"

"Maybe some frank Cilician seafarer has explained that he would like Diocles to keep quiet."

"And carried him off?"

Maybe—but I still had the feeling that Diocles had not gone far from Ostia.

After we waved off our visitors and peace descended on the street, the others went on up. I stood alone for a few moments breathing in the night air. Helena and Albia would be indoors, washing the children and putting them to bed. I would be needed soon for my tucking-in duties.

I stood in the darkness and felt aching sympathy for Posidonius, who had lost his only daughter to an adventurer.

XXXIV

Next morning we all trooped out to Portus with Aelianus and saw him board the *Spes*. The last time the Camillus brothers went abroad, they had come with us on a trip to Britain. Helena and I, always keen to travel, felt a shared pang now as we braced up to seeing one of her brothers venturing abroad without us.

"Try and find a mystery for Marcus!" Helena quipped. Her mother shook her head, but her father sighed as if he would quite like to come too. Quintus looked on with special yearning, as he thought of his sibling loose among the wine, women, and cultural riches of Greece. At least, I knew the first two were on his mind.

If there is one certainty when you have been given a sailing time, it's that the boat will never go when you expect. If it is not sailing out of the harbor without you as you turn up on the quayside, it will sit there at anchor for several more hours. Or days, maybe. The *Spes* had a second mate whose duties included passenger management. That meant he ordered them to arrive early and stowed them at his leisure while nothing else was going on; at sea, his role was to hear their complaints and keep them calm in a storm. He inspected their baggage keenly when they first came aboard because in a *bad* storm, while the mariners struggled to control the ship's wild movements, it would be his task to decide what to chuck overboard to lighten it. There are rules, hated but fair, about how to divide any losses between owners if actual cargo is thrown off in an emergency—but casual passengers have few rights. I could see Aulus was extremely popular with the second mate. Aulus was a lad; his "essential" luggage was extremely heavy. If a tempest should blow up, he was on the list to surrender all his treasures first.

We put Aulus on the ship. Then we had to wait so long that he became restless and came off again. He and I sauntered around the port. He wanted to make his parents worry that he would miss the boat, while I had the excuse of trying to find drinks for the children.

Yes, we had brought the children. Julia and Favonia both loved a chance to run very fast toward the edge of a wharf above a crowded harbor full of deep water.

Nux had actually been *in* the harbor. Water called to Nux like Circe at her most sirenous. Before I could stop her, Nux had leapt off the wall and paddled around crazily until she realized there was no way out. At that point, I thought I might have to jump in myself to save her; the children were shrieking at the thought of losing their doggie and even Helena was agitated by the imminent drowning. Since I could not swim, it was a relief when a sailor fished Nux into his bumboat and returned the bedraggled lump to us—in return for the customary bribe, or price of a drink as it is ridiculously called. No drink ever cost that much.

"Now I'm all wet from the damned dog. That bumboat swine lured her in on purpose . . . We may have to abandon you, Aulus."

"I never asked anyone to come," grumbled Aulus. That was true, but of course he was touchy at the thought that we might dump him. Now he felt lonely—and he had not even left the country.

"Oh, Julia Justa will make us stay. Your mother still loves you."

"Well, thanks, Falco."

I was surprised to find that the customs desk on the arrivals wharf was manned by Gaius Baebius.

"What happened to permanent sick leave after your beating?"

The clerks he supervised all stared curiously. Gaius looked shifty. "I'm still in agony, Marcus. Some days I can hardly move for the pain . . ."

"Skip it, Gaius."

"You have no idea what my suffering is like——" I could imagine the diatribe if he got started.

I said if Gaius really wanted to make a complaint, he could find Cratidas at the Aquarius—though I warned him not to go alone. Hearing my short sharp tale of knives and uplifted benches, Gaius thought he might instead hire a lawyer and sue for damages. A good move, I thought. It would be very neat if a vicious ransom gang was broken up because their leading man had to flee legal action from a malingering civil servant.

"And how is darling Junia?"

"Back home in Rome. I was not aware you were so fond of her, Marcus."

Nor was I. I had slipped up by even mentioning her.

On the quay nothing much was happening.

The first officer sauntered aboard. We took that for a good sign.

The first mate arrived, bringing some sailors. They were typical mariners. I saw Julia Justa stiffen as she noted their farmyard accents, their missing eyes and their limps, their rough tunics and bare feet. She wanted her boy to be safe in the hands of elegant master mariners with boots, cloaks, and Phrygian caps. Nothing less than Jason and all his Argonauts would be good enough to row Aelianus. We soothed her. Julia Justa knew we were being insincere.

The captain, Antemon, arrived. He turned up at the quay with the ship's guard, carefully escorting his owners, Banno and Aline. The ransomed wife scuttled aboard, still ashen-faced. The husband remained at the end of the gangplank and stared back at the port for a moment, looking resentful.

I went up to him. "I'm sorry your trip ended so badly. Now you are safely leaving, is there anything you will tell me about what happened to your wife?" Above us on deck, Antemon was watching warily.

More furious than frightened now, this time Banno told the story. Most matched what other witnesses had said. Aline had been seized here at Portus, almost as soon as they landed. Banno was soon handed a letter which arranged a meeting in a bar. He had to go alone, and ask for the Illyrian.

"Can you describe him?" Banno looked vague. "Anything you remember about his height, his build, his coloring? Did he have hair or was he bald? Teeth? Ears? Scars? Clothing? What did he wear?"

I got nothing. Either the witness was shortsighted, or too cowed. He did tell me one thing: the location of the bar. It was on the river frontage at Ostia, quite near to the Aquarius. He had had to take the ransom money to the bar right next door.

"Does Aline remember anything?" She had been sure she was drugged, and was kept lying on a bed in a small room where she thought there was a woman, with children. "Or might it have been a single boy, Banno?"

Banno could not answer that. He was unwilling to ask the still-traumatized Aline, and there was no time anyway. He left me abruptly, almost in midsentence. The *Spes* was finally sailing.

We all stood on the quayside with that mournful feeling that afflicts people as they watch somebody else leave the country. We saw the gangplank pulled in and the mooring ropes cast off. Nux barked loudly. The ship was maneuvered by tugboats and its own oars, gradually prized out from its tight-packed berth, then towed slowly into the center of the great harbor. Sailors worked frantically to adjust the square sail. The vessel turned laboriously to face in the right direction. At the rail, Aelianus, who was wearing a dark red tunic, soon became a blurred dot; we had all long stopped waving to him.

We stayed until the *Spes* started to move independently. The tugs with their heavy towing masts fell back from her. She slipped free and made her way toward the harbor exit, sailing smoothly out through the passage on the south side of the lighthouse.

"He's gone!"

Aulus had his good points. Even I would miss him.

XXXV

The senator had told his carriage driver to wait at our apartment. If the Camilli drove back to Rome straightaway, they would hit the wheeled vehicle ban and be stopped at the city gate, so we delayed their journey by having a very late lunch. Helena went to fetch Albia, who had chosen not to come with us to Portus. She was not a slave; she had the right to free time, and apparently Aulus was no great draw for her. Helena herself enjoyed time alone, so had always allowed the young girl moments with her own thoughts.

I settled everyone else in one of the courtyards at the Aquarius. Nowhere else was so convenient, and I would not be deterred by an antisocial Cilician. The place was big enough to cope with a large influx, and had a pleasant, respectable atmosphere. If you overlooked the fact that armed pirates accumulated there sometimes, it made an ideal family restaurant.

Anyway, there was no sign of Cratidas.

We had a good, if slightly subdued meal, which with rather slow service took most of the afternoon. However much we reassured ourselves that Aulus was doing the right thing, and that his ship was sound and well managed, a sea voyage is always dangerous. It would be several weeks before he landed and could send a letter to confirm his safe arrival, then weeks more before the letter found its way to Rome. If Aulus remembered to write. His mother said he had a bad record in that sphere.

When we finished, the senator and I wrangled over the bill, but in the end he paid it. I had things to do, but it was only polite to return to the apartment for farewells.

"Don't worry, Mama darling—" Helena was feeling mischievous. "The *Daily Gazette* says that rumors of pirates operating again are untrue . . ." As Julia Justa stared in horror, I quickly signaled the driver to start off.

After we had watched the carriage disappear, a sense of anticlimax downed us. While the children scampered off, looking for toys they had abandoned the night before, Helena, Albia, and I all walked back slowly into the courtyard. It seemed forlorn after our great family banquet.

Helena wiped away a tear. I hugged her. "Aulus will be all right."

"Of course." She became more brisk. "Now we are alone, Albia and I have something to show you. While she was here this morning, we had a visitor."

"Entertaining a follower?" I teased Albia. She looked hot.

"Don't," warned Helena. "It was just as well that I came home to fetch her; Albia found him a handful."

Now I was a furious head of household. "I'll sort him! Who was the bastard?"

"A slave called Titus."

Titus? That chirpy extrovert who worked for the landlady at the Marine Gate rental—the slave who cleaned Diocles' room. I could imagine how the pushy tyke would be too flirtatious with Albia if he found her alone. He would take her for a slave or freedwoman, for one thing.

I looked across at Albia, who was kicking her heels. Helena had interrupted the unwanted advances; there was no harm done. "He brought you some things, Marcus Didius." Albia had already learned that I needed efficient reports: "First, his excuse was that there were two good tunics Diocles had left at the laundry. These have 'come to light unexpectedly,' so Titus says."

"Wrong size for him!" I grinned.

"I said this was not enough to earn him a tip."

"Excellent. The last girl I kept in the office to take messages was a soft touch."

"Lies," murmured Helena, to whom I had been referring. "Tell him the rest, Albia."

"Notebooks."

"Notebooks! I thought we had those—mostly empty."

"These new ones are written in. There are quite a lot. I believe Titus had kept them, hoping they might be valuable. Now he is frightened he will get into trouble!" Albia spat. It was a habit we had yet to cure. "So he will. Sooner or later, and I think sooner . . ." Prophesying doom for men gave Albia much satisfaction. "Titus said—or he pretended—he had been asked to look after these tablets by your scribe. To put them in a safe place, and not tell anybody. That is why he kept them secret from you. But some men came to the house asking about them yesterday, and Titus is now very scared."

"Who scared him?"

"He knew no names."

"I had a quick look at the tablets," said Helena. I imagined her speed-reading before she rushed back to the Aquarius for lunch. "Two different authors, I would say. Some look like old diaries—don't get excited; it's not love affairs of the famous. They are ships' logs, or similar."

"Boring! I can do without a load of notes saying '*wind nor' by nor-nor' west, sea choppy; had beans for supper, farted hilariously.*'"

Helena had been teaching Albia to read on quiet evenings. Albia must have scanned the tablets too and now piped up, "Marcus Didius, it is more like '*Termessos: sold five from the Constantia; good price for the wine . . . Off Samos, met the Iris. Brisk but a result.*'"

"Who wrote these logs?"

"It does not say. There are a lot of 'meetings.'" Albia was a bright girl. She knew we had been talking about pirates. "Most are 'brisk' and end with a list of good prices."

"Sold five what?" I met Helena's eyes. Like me, she suspected the worst.

"The lists of sales are endless," Albia told me unhappily. "Are they *people,* these numbers? These fives and tens and threes and even twenties? Are they people, being sold into slavery?"

"The tablets are old and battered," Helena tried to reassure her. "I think we'll find these events happened many years ago."

Realistically, Albia knew that not all stricken people could be saved from their misfortunes as she had been. Eventually she said in a low voice, "Wrapped in one of the clean tunics was a sword, Marcus Didius."

"Did Titus say anything about it?"

Albia saw Titus as one of life's lowest characters. "No, he shrugged it off as unimportant—but he is keen to get rid of it to you now."

I told her she had better show me, so we went indoors.

The sword was a plain, short-bladed model in an ill-fitting, twisted leather scabbard. No soldier or ex-soldier would have given it a second glance, but an imperial palace freedman, brought up among bureaucrats, would not have known it had poor balance and blunt edges. There was rust on the blade, which had never been oiled and looked after, and a great deal more rust where the handle was attached with a crude weld. One sharp blow and I reckoned the ensemble would fall to pieces. I doubted if Diocles had ever used this weapon; he must have had it for re-assurance only.

So when he went out the last time, Diocles had left the weapon in his room, because he thought he was going somewhere safe, either alone or among people who meant no harm to him. More importantly, he had believed that he would be coming back.

XXXVI

I left Helena with the new note-tablets. The children were contented, so she was ready to read and interpret this written work. There were enough tablets to cover a side table. Most looked ancient, their wooden boards bleached and dried up; these were filled with uneven scribbles of the kind Albia had described earlier. A few newer tablets matched those we had found before in Diocles' room. Perhaps they would give a lead as to what had happened to him.

Helena assured me this task needed one person to review everything—that was, her. I went out instead to investigate the two bars where Banno had told me he went to negotiate his kidnapped wife's release.

I found the bars fairly easily. One charmless nook was called the Clam, its neighbor was the Venus. Blurred pictograms advertised them. They were one-room holes of the type that occur in rows fringing every seafront or riverfront: smoky innards where food and drink were prepared, with crude tables outside squashing up against the next establishment in an unending line. The waiters—when customers could find one to take an interest—seemed interchangeable. These places prided themselves in serving excellent fish meals—which meant they overcharged mightily for a weak bowl of soup with shell in it, a very small piece of yesterday's bread, plus red wine so acidic that if it was painted on your corns your whole toes would drop off.

I approached the bower of the love goddess first, on principle. Given its name I was not surprised to find a pale waitress with a weary expression, whose duties must include going up the back stairs with customers who wanted extra services.

"Something to eat, sir?"

No thanks. I was grown up now. I knew what would happen if I ate in a dump like this. I could not spare the time to be that ill. "I'm looking for the Illyrian."

"Not here. Get lost."

"Has he ever been here?"

"If you say so. Everyone seems to think he has."

"Who's everyone?"

"A stupid stiff from the vigiles." Brunnus. "Did you hear me?—Push off!"

Brunnus had messed up the scene just as well as he could for me. Then when I emerged from the Venus, cursing, what should I hear but his voice?

I ducked and hid. I realized what was going on: it must be the Ides of August today. The Fourth Cohort had just arrived to take post in Ostia, and their vexillation was being shown around by the departing Sixth, led by Brunnus, on the traditional familiarization walk. That is, identifying the enormous corn warehouses they were supposed to guard—as a prelude to trying out the local bars.

The Fourth had been in Ostia before. They must remember the place from two or three years ago, though to be fair, since the vigiles had a six-year turnover among their ranks, a proportion of the present detachment might be new. The warehouses had not moved position. But some of the bars might have changed hands or altered their wine suppliers, so old haunts might no longer feel the same. Men of action would need to reconnoiter urgently.

Before they could spot me, I dived into the Clam. Few customers ever bothered to venture indoors from the tables outside. There might be a latrine out at the back, but most men walked over and peed in the river; I could see one customer doing exactly that.

First, the chef and waiters thought I must be in here to complain. Once I reassured them, I was treated as a novelty. Forewarned at the Venus, here next door I straightaway moaned about Brunnus. It worked. Soon I was told that the Illyrian sometimes dropped in for business purposes. Of course they claimed to have no idea what business he was furthering. Many trades need to operate through their proprietors meeting people in bars—or so many proprietors would have you believe. Publishing. Racehorse owning. Pimping. Fencing stolen goods . . .

The Illyrian knew the ropes. He gave the waiters a tip in advance, so they would point him out to anyone who asked for him. He left another tip on the bill when he left. While that meant he could be sure of a welcome if he came here again, the lavish behavior also meant the staff very clearly remembered him.

"It sounds as if he knows how to behave . . . But I am told he's rather sinister?"

My informant, a spotty young male in a filthy tunic, laughed. "He never scares me!"

"You mean he's not as fierce as he makes out?"

"No, I mean he wears eye paint and silly slippers." In a lifetime of unexpected answers, that came as a genuine surprise. "The Illyrian?" The waiter thought my remark hilarious. "He's as fierce as a wet sponge. He's just a scrawny old queen."

A couple of vigiles looked in at the door. I took that as my cue to leave.

I had no wish to hang around while members of the Fourth Cohort jumped all over the place like fleas on a scruffy dog. But the night was young, and I needed to think. I started to walk.

A short stroll took me away from the river and into the Forum on its western side. As an attempt to avoid the vigiles, that was a disaster: more of the Fourth were lined up in rows at the foot of the Capitol. I could see Rubella with them, so although they looked sick that they were missing the wine-shop inspection, they were on their best behavior. In general, most never saw the cohort tribune. They stared at him curiously.

Petronius was seconding Rubella, chewing his thumb and looking bored. I also recognized Fusculus, Petro's deputy in Rome. Fusculus, an increasingly rotund, happy fellow, appeared to be the duty officer in charge tonight. He had formed up a small group in a halfhearted honor guard. The vigiles do not wear uniforms or carry armor, so they cannot parade with their gear highly polished, and insofar as they drill, it consists of lifesaving tips and equipment practice. They are reluctant to march. A vigiles salute is likely to be derisive. Neat lines don't put out fires. If someone in the crowd here had screamed for help, the Fourth would have shown themselves to be good men. But ceremonial was not their strength.

So a shambolic group, of all heights and body weights, were shifting about in their motley homespun tunics, while Fusculus gave benign instructions when he felt like it. Relaxed by nature, Fusculus enjoyed catching villains; that was so he could pick their brains for a treatise on the underworld. He was an expert on criminal cant; this hobby had taken him far beyond the norms of laundry-snitching and the confidence trickster's happy finesse of a plump mark, into farricking, boogle-squiddling, and the long toddle (which he told me once was a shorter version of marathon-running, which in Aventine street slang means fleeing justice). However, Fusculus defiantly had no interest in tonight's long-winded civic bollocking, where his men had to stand arse-aching beside a diplomatic podium. Diplomacy? The Rome vigiles do not bother with such etiquette.

A cluster of locals was clearly unimpressed with our lot. Penned behind a temporary barrier, these folk were cheering a homegrown team: a large, brutally well-organized contingent from the builders' guild wheeled in and began putting on a welcome for the new vigiles.

These men were good. They knew it too. Their crack troops were out today, demonstration-marching as if the Emperor was reviewing them. The display was skilled and meticulous. They could march and salute— and salute while marching. They stayed the correct distance from one another as if measured with a swagger stick. Their lines were straight.

Their double and triple rows were square. Their right-angled turns were crunched to perfection. They swung and they spun and they halted on the spot as if parade drill was wondrous fun. (To anyone with a real military background, that was blasphemy.)

The toy soldiers all wore fake army uniforms in gaudy colors, with shorter tunics than normal. Startling epaulettes plumped up the already wide shoulders of their so-called officers. Each man carried a very clean rope and a shiny grappler. I found their gear a hoot, but the stamp of massed workboots made the ground tremble. It was sinister, and I reckoned it was meant to be.

I soon learned from bystanders that members of other guilds were always known as the plebs, but the builders called themselves the "booted ranks." They had sixteen troops. Each troop consisted of twenty-two heavy men, headed up by a decurion. The decurions were all hoping to become a president. The guild always had not one, but three quinquennial presidents. They also owned a tame town councillor. Ostensibly appointed by the civic government "because of the builders' extreme importance in Ostia," he was a conduit for obtaining contracts. In any other town this would be called graft. Ostia, I was proudly informed, was different. I did not ask how.

No town can support a paramilitary group of over three hundred and fifty hard bastards without their influence in civic life becoming dangerous. Gaius Baebius and I had seen the boot-boys being obnoxious on fire duty and this closer look did not fill me with joy. They went in for sleeveless tunics that would show off bulging biceps. They had big, boozers' bodies. I knew what they would be like off duty too—big mouths and bloody politics.

The Ostians seemed happy, but this carnival had given me a chill.

I stood in the press outside the Curia. The quickest way home was to cross in front of the Capitol, where Rubella and Petro still stood glumly, beneath a canvas awning supported on posts; reluctant to be seen, I waited. Normally I would have hailed Petro. I was not in a mood to fraternize.

As the display reached its noisy climax and ended, top men in the guild approached Rubella. He and Petronius obligingly shook hands; their polite response seemed genuine, though I guessed otherwise. To the fore was Privatus, with his dark strands of stuck-down hair shining on top of his bald head. He had grown the back hair too long, so he looked like a vagrant from behind, despite wearing his holiday tunic and toga, all of brilliant white. With him was a man someone told me was the tame councillor; apparently the guild were about to erect a statue in his honor and there was no secret that it was a thank-you for favors. One of Privatus' fellow presidents of the guild was an imperial freedman. Ostia seemed to attract ex–Palace functionaries. They could never take a formal position in civic life, but through the guild, where they could rise to the highest title, they might become big names lo-cally. The biggest guest tonight was the Pontifex of Vulcan—the top priest, who came attended by his own little set of functionaries and public slaves.

I despised them all. That was not because of their origins. I hated them sliming a way into business deals through their trade camaraderie. The councillor who was now being gracious to Rubella would be praised on his statue plinth for his good works; the good works were nothing less than benefactions to the building contractors, in the form of fiddled con-tracts. I wondered if Diocles had discovered this.

The entertainment was breaking up. Whoever planned it must have intended that members of the Fourth Cohort would at this point mingle with the boot-boys. They reckoned without the Fourth Cohort, who were melting away. The boot-boys took no notice; they had their own associates. The troops who had given the display were being greeted and flattered by others in their guild. As they swanked about, I recognized one of the marchers: he had heavy sideburns and matted curls, plus an unforgettable swagger and sneer. It was the leading deadbeat from the fake vigiles guardhouse, in the street where the scribe's aunt had died. Once I spotted him, I soon picked out the others.

It would have been fatal to make myself known. There were too many guild members present, and this was their turf. As the Forum piazza began to empty, I made my way discreetly across to the Decumanus. Spotting a large foodshop, I stopped to order wine. At the sound of my voice, a man standing at the counter next to me turned around, ex-claiming to the waiter, "He'll buy me another too!"

The shameless scrounger was my father, Didius Geminus. He was with a friend, a friend who had no objection to me buying *him* a drink as well.

XXXVII

My boy," said Pa, acknowledging our relationship. He managed not to sound disparaging. I made no comment.

His companion tilted his winecup to me. No introduction was offered, though he looked vaguely familiar and viewed me with a whimsical air as if he were about to slap my back and remember some incident I would rather forget. I must have seen him around the Emporium. I assumed he was one of the group who had come from Rome today: as Justinus had warned me, Posidonius had recruited a few colleagues who had known him for years to help him find his daughter. My father had descended on Ostia among an informal posse of do-gooders. If these righteous old swine were all like Pa, for them it was just a good excuse for a seaside tavern crawl.

"If you all plan to thrash Theopompus into offal, Pa, don't tell me."

Pa looked cheerful. "I am sure the young man will respect our point of view, son."

"Oh yes. Six or eight of you back him into a dark alley, and give your opinions in the customary manner—he'll hand her back as quick as spit. The problem will be making the lovelorn girlie see her predicament."

"Fathers know how to explain things." From mine, that was rich.

"Posidonius is a kindly fellow. He won't push her too hard, he brought her up very nicely, and she will see his reasoning—"

I laughed bitterly. "Plainly you know nothing about daughters!"

"Don't be like that, son." As usual, my father was shocked to find anyone criticizing his past behavior. He really had convinced himself that abandoning a wife and infant children was fine. Now he was hurt and I was angry. Some things don't change.

I noticed his silent companion watching us with a kind of reserve. He was older than Pa by as much as a decade—if the entire crowd supporting Posidonius were of this type, the vigilantes were hardly in their prime. This man was overweight too, flabby and hook-shouldered. I wondered if he was another auctioneer, like Pa; I could imagine him fingering fine art objects with those chubby, rather white fingers. He wore what must be a valuable cameo ring, vivid white glass over deep lapis blue, which appeared to show a miniaturized pornographic scene. It was the kind of thing that appeals to men who call themselves connoisseurs, men with cold eyes, who subject their wives to buggery and then talk openly of their perverted streak, as if vicious taste makes them better than the majority.

Pa was completely different; he had simply fathered too many children then could not endure the domestic results. In despair at him, I tried to drink up quickly. The wine had been flavored with spices and honey; it was too sickly to knock back in a hurry. As a distraction, I mentioned the builders' guild. This pair must have noticed the noisy display. "Petronius has a house on loan from their president—one of their *three* presidents. I gather they do nothing as a singleton that can be a triplet."

"They act as if they own the streets," said Pa.

"Maybe they really do—public works are the main activity at Ostia. I reckon they are trying to take over." I licked my lips, agitated by the honey's stickiness. "This is a sick town."

"What do you think?" Pa asked the man with him.

"Marcus is right."

Cheek. Calling me Marcus was too damned informal. But with my father always ready to see me as prudish, I bit back my irritation. Sons are treated as children by their fathers' friends. Arguing about it gets you nowhere.

Never one to be outnumbered in a vote, Pa changed the subject. "Marcus is chasing Cilician pirates."

"I am looking for a missing scribe," I corrected patiently for the other man. "Pirates, I am reliably informed, do not exist—and absolutely not in Cilicia nowadays."

"So who's doing the kidnaps?" scoffed Pa, while the other man looked on in silence.

This time I grinned. "*Ex*-pirates."

Pa's companion finally allowed himself to be drawn. "Only to be expected." He spoke in a dry, depressed tone, which chimed in with my own attitude more than I had expected. Having made the statement, he stopped. He seemed to enjoy leaving his listeners hanging.

"How's that?" I prompted. I was still being polite, but something about him was getting on my nerves. He gave the impression he enjoyed being controversial.

"They had a way of life," he said. "Some called it piracy; to them it was their natural mode of business. If it was all taken away from them, they were bound to find a new occupation. People have to live."

"You sound sorry for them."

"I understand their position." He seemed detached, yet added, "We had the same thing here, with the dispossessed farmers. It caused absolute misery."

I could remember my grandfather, the one on the Campagna, sounding off about old land "reforms," which drove countrymen out of tenancies where they had farmed for decades. Gramps kept his farm—but we all thought he had done it by tricking someone else. All his neighbors thought so too. "So you view the Cilician pirates as unfortunate displaced persons?"

"Naturals for a life of crime," Pa sneered. He hated most other nations. He would say that was because he had done business with them and learned what they were like.

"Naturals to be *blamed* for everything, anyway," his friend said. "So what do Cilician pirates have to do with your missing scribe, young Marcus?"

Once again I tried to ignore his overfamiliarity. "Diocles may have been writing memoirs for one of them—but my hunch is that he was really interested in this kidnap racket. Theopompus and Posidonius' silly daughter may yet gain a mention in the *Daily Gazette*."

"We won't be the only ones chasing Theopompus!" growled Pa. "His comrades won't thank him for publicity."

"You have tied the kidnaps to the Cilicians?" asked the other man of me.

"They h̶ ̶e inadvertently let me identify a couple of their group."

"Co̶ ̶ be dangerous for you."

"If ̶ y scribe turned up, I'd be out of here. The kidnappers have both t̶ ̶avy and the vigiles on their tail now. It can't be long to a show-̶wn."

"So then good-bye, Cilicians! If the navy and the vigiles are closing in, they may find your scribe for you. You might lose your fee." *Well, thanks for that!* "Favonius, I have to go . . ."

The man had slipped away almost before we registered his polite self-extraction. He left behind a whiff of shaving unguent and, for me, a slightly cheated feeling.

Nobody at the Emporium called my father Favonius. He was Geminus, his long-adopted cognomen. Geminus to everyone. Well, to everyone except Ma, in one of her vengeful moods. She insisted on using the name he had had before he ran away from us.

"You do know who that was?" Pa was signaling the waiter to refill our cups. He had already laid money on the marble to cover it so I was trapped.

I shook my head. "Should I?"

"Too right, my boy! That weird streak was your Uncle Fulvius."

I gazed at Pa. He nodded. Suddenly, I grinned back. Now I could see it—though Fulvius had gained age, weight, and a much more truculent attitude. "As dreary as I remember! It's hard to see what all the fuss was," I commented—though my uncle's deliberate way of annoying people explained a lot about his reputation.

Pa and I both saw ourselves as members of the solid Didius clan; we were two bumptious boys from Rome, the only place worth living. So now we two kings of society lifted our winecups, saluted each other with a clink, and were for once at peace together. Now we were doing what town boys really enjoy: laughing at an eccentric country relative.

XXXVIII

Helena was intrigued when she heard of my meeting. "So why didn't you recognize your uncle?"

"It's been years since I met him. I never saw much of Fulvius anyway. I can't have been more than five or six the last time—it was before Pa left us. My long holidays on the farm were later; Ma used to take us all to run around and tire ourselves out—when she could get somebody to give us all a lift into the Campagna. By that time Fulvius had gone."

"Gone to do what?" asked Helena. "What is the real story?"

"He didn't fit in."

"He was driven out by the others?"

"No. Fulvius voluntarily took himself off."

"Unhappy?"

"Just bloody awkward, I'd say."

"Oh, nothing his nephew inherited then!"

I got out of that by asking how Helena was progressing with the Diocles tablets.

She had read them all already. I was not surprised. On a waxed tablet of her own, she had quoted bits she wanted me to see. A large proportion of what she had collated involved the meetings Albia had described, which were clearly confrontations between ships, where the named vessels came off worst. People were sold into slavery. Goods were seized and marketed for profit. Then occasionally deaths were noted.

"Deaths? Unnatural ones?"

Helena gave out a restless sigh. "No doubt of it. 'We took three losses.' Another time, 'Too many to handle; five overboard.' I think that may mean *thrown* overboard. Later, 'They lost ten, the master caught it; would not give up—Lygon finished him.' Yes, Lygon is named. Do you think that's the same one you are interested in?"

I shrugged. We had no way of knowing—though it seemed a big coincidence. "Any other familiar people?"

I was hoping for Damagoras or Cratidas, but was disappointed. Helena looked up her own notes to be sure. "No, but Lygon is mentioned twice. The second time is horrible—'Woman screaming; Lygon took her head off for us; silence!' "

"Hey! I'm sorry I let you read this stuff."

As I shuddered, Helena embraced me. I hoped that would distract her from the horror. We then sat huddled together, looking through the tablets. Try as we might, we could find no internal evidence as to who wrote them. Unfortunately, only schoolboys sign their personal note-tablets *Marcus owns this. Hands off, or the kindly Furies will strike you . . .*

The logs must be from a captain. He never said what his own ship was called. It had traveled widely around the eastern Mediterranean, operating for years, from the Greek islands across to the Phoenician seaboard. His trade was bloody, and there was no doubt it was criminal. Nobody could call it anything other than piracy. This vessel preyed on other shipping. Plunder was its sole reason for putting to sea. It never took a cargo out, though almost always came back to land with one or more commodity for sale.

To us it was theft. To the ship's captain, it was fair trade.

Although we could not identify him, clues made us sure that he was a Cilician. First there was the name of his crony Lygon, who—if he was the one I knew of—came from Soli/Pompeiopolis. Apprentice sailors were mentioned, sometimes with their place of origin, also in Cilicia; many were farmhands and despite claims that the people of the mountains had no part in piracy, it became clear that there was a regular progression of young men being sent from the land to find experience, reputation, and riches at sea.

From time to time the logs recorded alliances with other groups and nationalities. "Agreed a treaty with the Pamphyllians—Korakesians (Melanthos). Side men in, but they won't hold . . . Off Akroterion met the *Fideliter* and the *Psyche*. Cattle and slaves; Melanthos took the cattle; he won't stay true . . . Meras of Antiphellos and his Lycians joined us. Meras left us again after could not agree over the hides . . . Sailing off Xanthos. Good pickings if the season holds, but the Lycians don't like us being here. Met a large trader out of Sidon but Marion came up during our action and we had to fight him off. Later followed the *Europa*, out of Thera, but no luck; Melanthos got that . . . Offer to partner the Illyrians but they are faithless and too violent . . ."

"Too violent"? That was hilarious. Once he had stripped his victims of valuables, the writer never hesitated to hurl people overboard to drown. He only took prisoners if they were suitable as slaves. Otherwise, he eliminated witnesses. He and his seamen lived by the sword. If stabbing failed, they used strangulation. Helena had found repeated notes of wounding during robberies, limbs lost on both sides, frequent records of mutilation and reckless killing. Sometimes they would go ashore in search of booty; once they sacked a shrine.

"I looked for mention of Illyrians," Helena said. "This sole mention of Illyrians being faithless and violent is all. But assuming the writer is Cilician, he does make partnerships from time to time, often swearing oaths of alliance with those he has quite recently quarreled with or accused of breaking faith."

"Could 'the Illyrian' we know of just be a nickname?"

"I suppose so, Marcus. But it must have some link to where the negotiator comes from."

"Now," said Helena, gathering up a small pile of tablets she had placed separately, "the interesting part. I shall tell you what I believe Diocles was doing."

"These other tablets are his own notes?"

"Yes. The handwriting and layout match the notes we found in his room. In these," she went on, speaking calmly and without drama, "the scribe is making a summary of the old logs. You could call it an outline of a proposed new work—"

"Do you mean that Damagoras told me the truth—Diocles really was going to help him put together his memoirs?"

"No doubt of it." Helena pursed her lips. "But it makes Damagoras a liar. First, he assured you, Marcus, that he just had a couple of brief discussions with Diocles, after which the scribe decided not to proceed. But for Diocles to make all these notes, the two of them must have gone into great detail together."

"I was puzzled that he had given Rusticus, the vigiles recruiting officer, an address in the country, not the rental house at the Marine Gate . . ."

"Yes." Helena was with me. "Diocles probably went to live for a while at the villa. He worked up these notes while staying there. So Damagoras lied about how close their relationship was. But the main area where he lied—and he's lying through his teeth, Marcus—is this. If these ship's logs are what Diocles had to use as the raw material for the memoirs, then there is no doubt, no doubt at all, about what Damagoras used to do for a living. The captain who composed these old records was a pirate."

I nodded. "And I'll tell you something else, my love—I don't believe the virtuous claim that he has long ago retired. He was a pirate—and I reckon he still is."

Next morning I began to read the note-tablets myself. I took them down to the courtyard and sat on a bench in dappled sunlight, with Nux fast asleep up against me and the children nearby. From time to time I had to break off, because Julia Junilla was playing at shops and wanted me to buy some pebble that was supposed to be a cake. This happened so often that I asked for a trade discount—only to be given the same surly reaction I would get at the counter of a real shop.

Helena had just come down to mediate in our commercial wrangling. As she agreed with Julia that I was being mean, someone came in through the entrance looking for me. It was Virtus, the slave from the vigiles patrol house. I was surprised to see him, and even more startled that Petronius Longus had sent him with a message.

"Fusculus and Petro have been called out to an incident. Apparently you will be interested, Falco. Some madman drove a chariot off the road in the middle of last night. Seems the 'accident' wasn't an accident, though—the horses both had their throats cut. They found a body. I can't stop; apparently the chariot is a known vehicle and I've got to go and see that man Posidonius—"

Tablets scattered as I stood up abruptly. "Sounds as if the worst has happened. They must have killed the girl—" I had been too abrupt; Helena gasped. "Sorry, love. Give me directions, Virtus."

Helena was now calling for Albia to bring her a cloak and look after the children. I normally kept her as far from death as possible. But in Rome she had talked to the foolish girl, persuading her to confide her hopes and dreams. I knew that Helena would be determined now to pay her last respects to Rhodope.

XXXIX

We had to go out to the old salt workings. Salt was the staple that brought about the founding of Rome. A large marsh lies out on the Via Salaria—the Salt Road—just before Ostia as you travel in from Rome. Virtus said the wrecked vehicle was there. The chariot had been spotted by passing drivers that morning, off road and upended.

Helena and I set off down the Decumanus on foot, intending to hire donkeys if we saw a stable. Luck was with us; an open cart rattled past, bearing a group of vigiles fresh from their patrol house. They were going out to the scene of the crime, and they let us hop on board with them. It would be a short journey. We could have walked, but it would have taken time and effort.

"What do you know about it, lads?"

"Debris was noticed at dawn. Salt workers were alerted and went over to see if there was anything to salvage. When they saw the situation with the dead horses, they got scared and sent a runner into town. Rubella dispatched Petronius; he passed back a message that we are to meet him on site, bringing transport and gear. Chariot fits a description of one we were looking for."

"What's Petronius want the gear for?"

"Lugging back the chariot."

"Get away! It's not his style," I joked glumly. "This is a rich boy's passion-wagon. Lucius Petronius is a stately oxcart man."

The vigiles grinned nervously. They were restrained, because I had Helena sitting silent beside me. I was feeling anxious myself about bringing her. The body we were going to see was probably mutilated; if my suspicions were right, we had a witness being silenced—silenced by men who controlled their victims through fear. Next time they took a female captive, they would make free with ghastly details about what had happened to today's corpse.

I had seen violated bodies. I did not want Helena to experience that. Clinging to the sides of the cart on that short bumpy trip, I never managed to think up a solution to spare her.

When the cart stopped, I jumped out feeling queasy.

This was a lonely place for anybody to be brought to die.

There was high ground up ahead toward Rome, but these wetlands formed a great marshy hollow, probably lower than sea level. Parts had been filled in by dumping the rubble from buildings destroyed by Nero's Great Fire in Rome, but the dumps only made the place seem even more unwelcoming. Most salt was now produced north of the river, but there were still a few workings here, as there had been since the dawn of Roman history. The main road ran on a raised causeway. The Tiber must be some distance away to our left. A brisk breeze was whipping across the low ground when we arrived, though when it occasionally faltered, the sun was burning. Wind and heat are the tools of salt manufacture.

In the marshes on our right stood the hunched wattle huts of the salt-pan workers, among the shine of low rectangular drying pools. By one of the huts dilapidated carts were waiting to ply their ancient trade up the Salt Road to Rome. Hillocks of sparkling salt grains were mounded beside a turning area where they loaded up.

Nobody was about. Everyone had gone to stare.

The wreck was on the other side of the main road. "Better wait here," one of the vigiles suggested to Helena, but she stuck tight next to me. We walked down a slip road onto the marsh. Under our feet, the rutted path had a white gleam; we trod with care in case it was slippery. The worst risk was turning an ankle in a boggy hole.

Old crystallization pools were everywhere, though on this side of the road they looked unused. There was no reason for anyone to stop on this road, unless they had business at the saltpans. A lover might possibly bring his girl out here for a giggle somewhere private, but he would have to have heard there was a very good moon that night to romance her by.

It was a stupid place to try driving a chariot off road deliberately. Everything was far too spongy underfoot.

Birds flew above us as we walked over to the scene of action. We could just make out two wheel scars where the vehicle had careered in a long curve across the saline floodplain, sinking deep into the wet ground and crushing the coarse vegetation. It was amazing that the chariot had made it so far without bogging down completely. Maybe it had had a lot of help.

The sad corpses of the two once-handsome black horses were lying together beside the vehicle. A knot of people were gathered around. One chariot wheel was off, the other leaning at an angle. From the road, you would think it had simply careered from the highway and crashed. Close to, I thought someone had used a mallet on the coachwork.

Petronius Longus was talking to some locals. He saw us approaching; he gestured for me to keep Helena back.

"Stay here."

"No, I'm coming."

"Your choice, then."

The vigiles who had brought us immediately did what they were trained to do: they moved back the gawpers. The salt workers were gnarled little men with particular features and little to say. Their ancestors had stared at Aeneas in the same way these were staring at us now; their ancestors' ancestors knew old Father Tiber when he was an adolescent lad. Others in the audience were contract drivers who had noticed the crowd and left their carts up on the road. The men stood about with their thumbs in their belts, giving out opinions. Carters always know what's what—and they are usually wrong.

I walked up to Petronius. We clasped hands briefly.

Helena had gone straight to the chariot, but it was empty. "We had to hunt for the body." Petro muttered, but ever alert, she heard him. "Come and see."

He walked with us across the marsh, away from the cluster of people. When we had gone beyond earshot and our feet were soaking wet, we saw something lying up ahead. Helena ran forward, but stopped in shocked surprise: "It is not the girl!"

A sudden rush of tears caught her. I stood at her side, bemused. There was some relief not to be looking at Rhodope, but at the body of a man instead. Petronius watched us both.

"This is Theopompus."

"Thought so." Petro and I were now back on old terms.

Helena had crouched to look at his face. It was not pretty. Theopompus was lying on his side, curled slightly. He must have been dead here half the night; what remained of his clothing was sodden. He had been beaten and then robbed of his finery. Troubling discolorations covered what we could see of him, though at least there was little blood. It looked as if he had been finished off with strangulation.

"Not easy to see what the girl saw in him!" Petro commented.

Theopompus must have been twice Rhodope's age. He was short-limbed and sturdy, deeply tanned even where his braided crimson tunic was drawn high up one thigh; the fine material was now filthy and stained. If it had stayed clean, we would probably have found him naked; his belt, his boots, and all his jewelry had been taken. Some of the gold at least had been worn a long time so it had left white skin on removal: a tight arm bracelet, finger rings, even earrings probably, because a trickle of blood had dried on his neck.

I was not convinced the killers stripped the corpse. Those salt workers would have had a good look this morning; that could even explain how Theopompus came to be so far from his vehicle. The salt workers might have dragged the corpse away before they lost their nerve and sent for the vigiles. But he may have been alive when the chariot crashed, then ran for his life until he was brought down and finished off.

Though none too handsome by classical standards, he had had more or less even features, before someone broke his nose for him last night.

His dark, triangular face was slightly hook-nosed. I supposed he was attractive—to a young woman who was ready for adventure.

"I don't imagine the girl did this." Petronius was in the dry, brutal mood that often afflicted him when faced with a vicious death. "Well, not unless she was built like a barracks, and she had just found out he was a love rat . . ."

"Her name is Rhodope," said Helena, in a tight voice. "She is timid and slight, aged seventeen. I hope she never saw him like this." She gazed around anxiously. "I hope she is not out here!"

Petronius shrugged. For him, the girl had tangled with the wrong people and her fate was her own fault. If anything, he blamed her for making him and his men have to come out here and deal with this.

"So where in Hades is she?" I mused.

"We don't know if she was with him. If she was, and could walk after the crash, she may have wandered off," said Petronius. "Fusculus has gone to the river to look." We could see remote figures, moving slowly along a line of vegetation that marked what must be the course of the Tiber. It took a long loop away from the road and right around the marsh.

"Was Theopompus brought here dead or killed here?"

"Can't tell. I suppose it's just as bad being beaten to pulp in a tavern—but there's something about this place . . ." Petro tailed off. He was a townsman. He hated the thought of murder taking place in isolated country spots.

"Did the salt workers see or hear anything last night, Petro?"

"What do you think? Not a thing."

"They huddle in their huts and if late-night marauders come out from Ostia in crazy vehicles, they bolt the doors?"

"They don't want trouble." Petro sounded restless and irritable. He might pretend a scene like this left him untouched, but he was wrong. "Drunks come out here for crazy fun. They see the people on the salt marshes as weird sprites, just waiting to be knocked on the head by town sophisticates. And revelers looking for trouble suppose they will get away with it."

"The killers of Theopompus probably will."

We started to walk back toward the crashed chariot. "We have nothing to pin this on anyone," Petronius grumbled. "I wouldn't want to go to court with it. A defender could argue that those bruises were acquired when the chariot went off the road . . ."

"Hard work explaining the slit throats on the horses," I reminded him.

"True. But unless we come across someone who actually saw Theopompus with his killers, they may be in the clear."

"Rhodope may have seen something," Helena interrupted.

Neither Petro nor I pointed out that Rhodope was perhaps also dead. Even if not, if she saw the killers, that put her straight back in the kind of danger that had made me earlier suppose it was her body we would find lying here.

Petronius looked at me. "I've been told the girl's father is in Ostia trying to find her. Rumor has it, he brought muscle. Know anything about that, Falco?"

I toyed with denial. Petro continued to stare, so I said, "As far as I know, the muscle consists of just a few old-timers, looking for a good day out."

"I shall ask where her papa and his day-trippers were last night," said my old friend, with a distrustful grunt. It sounded as if he were passing them a message through me. "I bet they will all give each other nice little watertight alibis."

"I'm sure they will." I did not want to be involved. "Can you blame them, once they find they are being scrutinized by you?—You know the other kidnappers silenced Theopompus," I growled. "Somebody said only yesterday that if he drew attention to their racket, his cronies would not thank him."

"Who said that? Are they connected to the gang?"

"No, just an uncle of mine who I happened to run into. We were chatting generally."

"I didn't know you had an uncle here."

"Neither did I."

Helena walked away from us and went back to the road. She stood on the causeway, where a brisk wind blew her mantle against her body. The fine blue cloth flapped like tent canvas, fighting its embroidered border, which moved to and fro more heavily. Helena hugged her arms close around herself, staring across the opposite marshes.

"What's your plan for the chariot?" I asked Petro, as I prepared to go to Helena.

"Drag it to the Forum. Stick up a board saying, 'Anyone see this fandangle yesterday?' Then put a man alongside to take notes. One good thing—it was a *very* noticeable craft."

I nodded, and went to my girl. I tried to hold her, though she turned away from me. Her dark hair had been tugged free by the wind; she was still clinging on to her mantle with one hand while struggling to collect loose hairpins. I stroked her hair, gathering the long loose strands in my own hand, then held her hard against my chest.

Both of us must have been thinking about that momentary sighting we had had of Rhodope and Theopompus when they drove into Ostia— he, showing off madly and barely able to control his high-strung black horses, she screaming with excitement at the sheer thrill of being with him.

Calmer now, Helena became less unresponsive in my arms. So for a short time there were, after all, two lovers clinging together for comfort, in that wild place.

XL

We watched the recovery of the chariot, which was manhandled up to the road and then fixed to the vigiles' cart. Its Hellenic ornament looked tawdry and cheap, now the paintwork was battered. Harness bells jingled forlornly. While its rescue was accomplished, the body of Theopompus was taken up too. Fusculus appeared, having found no sign of any other passengers.

So we all trekked back to Ostia. I checked for news at the station house with Petro and Fusculus. In view of the kidnap connection, Rubella had assumed command. Petro looked annoyed, and became even more friendly to me behind Rubella's back.

"The girl is alive. The father came in," announced Rubella. "She was returned to him late last night. He answered the door and she was pushed indoors, screaming, wrapped up tight in a cloak. Posidonius just grabbed her; he claims he never saw who brought her. She's not telling him anything."

We listened. We were all tired, windblown, and depressed. Rubella had merely sat at the patrol house letting the evidence come to him. Now we were ready to let him take the initiative. "Somebody has to interview the daughter. Petronius Longus, can you get your wife here? The girl may be overawed; I think we should start with the kindly approach and a chaperone."

"Helena Justina knows Rhodope," I suggested. "Helena is already here; she is waiting for me." Petro shrugged; he was easy. Rubella went along with it.

Fusculus sat outside the interview room with Posidonius. If there was anything more to extract from the father, Fusculus with his easygoing manner was likely to obtain it.

Inside the room, we seated Rhodope on a chair. She looked boot-faced and uncooperative. Helena tried to reassure her, but the girl remained sullen. Either she had been frightened into silence or she now just hated everyone; she definitely did not intend to help us. Petronius, calm and understated, introduced himself and said he had to tell her we had found her lover dead. He first implied he thought it was a road accident, gently leading in to saying that Theopompus had been murdered. No reaction. Rubella pulled rank and tried the heavy stuff, but had no luck either. They told the girl she might be in danger herself; clearly she did not care.

"I don't know anything about it." That was Rhodope's constant refrain.

Now Rubella decided to use the *really* heavy stuff. Gripping her by the arm, he marched the girl to a room where the troops had flung the bruised body of her lover. Curtly, he ordered her to look. To her credit, she managed not to scream or collapse, though she can never have seen a murdered corpse before. Tears she could not stifle ran down her cheeks, yet she braced herself as if defying us. She had lost everything. Nothing more could affect her. She stood stiffly, staring down at Theopompus, with her grand hopes all ruined. This was a very young girl, who had gone out of her depth through no real fault of her own; harassing her made the rest of us feel grimy.

Her father appeared in the doorway. Shocked, Posidonius recoiled from the corpse and took his daughter in his arms. He sheltered her and perhaps she wept then; we could no longer see her face.

Helena was furious with Rubella, and she told him what she thought. In the end the vigiles had to say that Rhodope could go.

★　　★　　★

First, there was a brief coda. Helena looked after Rhodope while the father was reinterviewed by Rubella, asking questions about the vigilante group. Posidonius said his friends, including Geminus, were staying together down by the port. Rubella sent men to bring them in. I stuck around, in case I had to bail my father. It was more than he deserved from me; my mood darkened.

Posidonius and his bereft child had gone. Helena came to see Rubella.

"Tribune, I managed to make Rhodope say something, while you were speaking to her father." If Rubella was riled, he forced himself to hide it. He needed the details. Helena reported coldly: "The couple were staying in a room near the Temple of Isis. Men came suddenly last night and told them they would have to part. Theopompus was hit, to keep him quiet, then he was dragged out of the house—he must have known what lay in store for him. Rhodope was simply bundled up and returned, unharmed, to her father."

"Well, that's what we thought," said Rubella, seeking to escape.

Helena insisted on making him hear everything. "This is what you don't know: Rhodope was insistent that Theopompus knew the men who took him."

"So they were *not* her father's friends from Rome?"

"You must decide that," Helena replied quietly.

Even though Rhodope's statement put them in the clear, Rubella kept the Emporium cronies at the patrol house for a long time. They were brought in, grumbling and truculent. He himself grilled them individually. You could call it being thorough and unrushed—or wasting time.

I was not allowed to attend any interviews, but I eavesdropped from outside. They all said the same. Men of my father's age and temperament know how to fix an alibi.

According to Pa, who was the last to be interrogated, it was all innocent: "We never tracked the bastard down, and that's a fact."

"What would you have done to him, had you caught him?" Rubella asked sarcastically.

"Explained that he should look elsewhere for love," smirked Pa. "Posidonius was planning to give him a big payoff—though we all thought that was a big mistake."

"You should have known better. You could all have ended up battered to death at the saltpans!" Rubella stormed, at his most pompous.

"Is that what happened to the lad?" Pa asked meekly. "Not nice!" Then I heard my father harden his tone. "*We* didn't do it—and this is what proves it: *we* wouldn't have left the body where a bunch of nosy passersby would find him straightaway!"

That made some sense.

Rubella kicked him out. As we trundled out of the patrol house, I heard Rubella commanding tetchily: "Round up the usual suspects!"

"Sir, we only just got here on the Ides," Fusculus protested. It was dusk now, and nobody who went to the saltpans had had lunch. "We're new boys and don't know who is who in Ostia—"

"The Cilicians," Rubella enlightened him. "You'll find them all named on the 'Cilician pirates' watch list."

So there was a list. And Rubella had just confirmed that the vigiles saw Cilicians as still involved in piracy.

XLI

I would have liked to see the roundup, but I had the next best thing: Petronius would tell me later about it. I went to dinner at his house.

By the time I arrived, having gathered up my family, Pa was there as well. He had decided to move in and lumber Maia and Petro with his presence. The other friends of Posidonius were going back to Rome, their task done—or at least, rendered unnecessary by Theopompus' attackers.

Maia looked momentarily flustered by the sudden influx. She was embarrassed because Privatus, who owned the house, was making one of his visits. She could hardly object if he wanted to inspect his new statue installation—the weeing Dionysus, now positioned on a new plinth in a garden pond—but although Privatus always assured them that they were welcome to treat the place as their own, and urged them to entertain as much as they liked, Maia shared my reluctance to be under too much obligation.

"We could all go out to eat—"

"No, we won't," decided Pa. "Let the builder give us a treat!" He had still not recovered from having a new bathhouse built. I was only surprised he did not immediately invite all of Posidonius' other friends to call in for refreshments before they hit the road. He would have done it, if he had thought of it.

Winking at Maia, I went to talk to the contractor myself, as a polite gesture. All I could think of was to mention that I had been impressed by the display put on by the booted ranks in the Forum yesterday.

"Why thanks, Falco! Our lads always give a good show." The man with the strands of hair raked over his bald patch positively preened. I had found him adjusting the pressure in his wine god's outlet pipe. He was wearing a particularly obnoxious tunic with a bad shine on the nap, and was obviously sneering at the less impressive display by the Rome vigiles; I was sorry I had volunteered to make friendly overtures. "How's your search?" he inquired of me. "You were telling me last time about your missing scribe?"

"Still missing."

"How does this look?" He was still fiddling with the fountain water-works.

"His kidneys are in fine fettle—but I'm inclined to say, the effect is a bit diuretic."

"Has something terrible happened to him?"

"Your Dionysus?—Oh, my scribe. It seems likely."

"But you're no closer to solving it?" Privatus seemed very keen to point that out.

Gritting my teeth, I found myself retaliating. "By the way, is it some of your boot ranks who set up that phony vigiles patrol house by the Temple of Hercules?" Privatus looked startled. "Better tell them the game's up," I said gently. "Brunnus may have been relaxed about it, but Marcus Rubella is very hot on scams. It's not just time for your boys to move on, Privatus—it's time to close their bribery shop down."

"I don't think I like what you're saying, Falco."

"I don't like it either," I commiserated. "One thing I have found out about Diocles is that his aunt died in a house fire, needlessly. Apparently Diocles had gone for help to your fake group. All the local people know better of course, but he was from Rome. He must have really believed that if an alarm was raised, they would come running."

Privatus was listening now. He was like a wound-up automaton, moving slightly from one foot to the other, full of pent energy, ready to dart into action. But there was nothing he could do.

I carried on with the torment. "Of course now I've recognized them as your boot-boys, it could raise the whole issue of the builders' role in firefighting . . ." Privatus assumed the utterly reasonable gaze which contractors use to delude complaining clients. I expected him to talk about suppliers having let him down despite incredible efforts on his part. Or to blame the weather.

"What evidence do you have that we let this man down, Falco?"

"Enough," I assured him. "It's been a year now, hasn't it? And as you see, the affair of the scribe's aunt simply will not go away." I slapped him on the shoulder. "Of course your guild is extremely powerful; I'm sure you can survive a negligence claim, should it happen. Though with Diocles missing, who is there to claim? But the Emperor may hear about what happened. He will be sent reports on how your guild operates . . . Did you know that the scribe's aunt was an imperial freedwoman?" Vestina's time at the Palace would have predated the current Flavian dynasty, but I failed to mention that. Privatus knew he must keep smiling. I had him on the run; I left him to squirm.

"By the way, Privatus, I don't like the look of that outflow. I think your wine god needs a good doctor to squeeze his prostate."

Privatus did not join us for dinner.

Petronius came in after we had finished. While Maia produced a food-bowl she had kept for him, he told me that every Cilician with a name known to the vigiles was now residing in custody. It was quite a large number. Rubella was in his element processing them; Fusculus, still on duty, was deeply unhappy; soon, they would have to call in caterers to supply gruel for the prisoners, but there was little hope of Fusculus himself getting a meal tonight. Petro's chubby deputy already had a rumbling stomach.

"I can see the logistics are not easy." I smiled. "I bet Rubella himself has a three-course snack with a red wine chaser hidden in his office . . . Did the Cilicians come quietly?"

With a wry smile back, Petro nodded. "They are all farmers nowadays, Marcus, my boy. Farmers are model citizens. You should know that. You're half rural."

"Nothing odd about me. All good Romans have country cousins—you included."

"None of us can match you for the weirdness of the cousins, though."

Petronius looked tired. He had had a long day, starting when he was called out to the saltpans. His skin looked stretched, his hair stuck up in untidy spikes, his eyes had a faraway stare. This did not seem the moment to confess that I had been taunting his landlord. He reached for wine, drinking fast, for numbness.

"So who did you get?" I asked him. "Who are the stars on your Cilician watch list?"

"Cratidas, Lygon, Damagoras—"

"I thought the old fellow had no record?"

"He does now. I put him on the list, after you discussed him."

"Oh it's my fault! What about the negotiator, the so-called 'Illyrian'?"

"We still don't know who he is. Rubella has to persuade a prisoner to tell him."

"No chance. It would amount to a confession."

"Quite."

Petronius was so weary, he just stared into space. Maia reached over and took his winecup from him gently, knowing that any moment he would nod off and drop it. He was almost asleep, or he would have stopped her taking the cup. Maia drained what was left. He shook his fist vaguely; my sister captured his hand and held it. The fond couple. So long as one or other of them was too exhausted to fight, they would survive together.

I sat for a moment, thinking about the Illyrian. I did not rate that tale he told the kidnap victims, that he was an outsider, a neutral intermediary. He always handled the ransom money; he must have an umbilical cord straight to the gang. Maybe he was the ringleader.

He would have heard by now that all of the others had been rounded up. I wondered how he would react. There was nothing he could do, except lie low in whatever lair he frequented. But he must be questioning whether the vigiles had serious evidence or had just made a hopeful pass. He would realize that he himself had never been identified or he would be in a cell now. In this situation, some villains would flee. I reckoned the Illyrian's nerve would hold.

"I keep wondering if it's a pseudonym for Florius," said Petro abruptly. He was so keen to capture this gangster of his, he saw Florius everywhere.

"No, I reckon it's my long-lost tricky brother Festus, returned from the dead."

"Festus!" Petro sat up in pretended horror. "Now you're talking serious shit!"

He slumped back, and we let him start nodding off again.

Helena and I took our leave quietly. Helena, who was fond of Petronius, leaned over him and kissed his cheek; he smiled sleepily, acknowledging that he was too far gone to move.

In the hallway, Maia was waiting with a bundle. "You left this!" she accused me, drawing in her crimson skirts in distaste. It was Diocles' baggage. I had dumped the dirty laundry days beforehand, hoping that would be the last I saw of it. The house slaves had cleaned up the tunics, on the assumption that the garments belonged to their master; I peered at the results, but there was nothing I would be seen around town in. These looked like the clothes Diocles wore when he was disguising himself as some kind of laborer. There was a particularly vile slug-colored number. I told Maia she could give the lot to the slaves.

Pa appeared. It was just like him to delay us at the wrong moment. "What did you think of old Fulvius?" he asked me.

I yawned rudely. "I thought we went through that."

"What is he doing in Ostia?" Helena asked of Pa, as he held her cloak for her while she carried our sleeping daughter Favonia.

"He came home. It's allowed, even if you're Fulvius."

"And was that story true about him going to Pessinus but catching the wrong boat?"

"The way he tells it now, he was just shipwrecked on the way."

"So why ever was he going to Pessinus in the first place, Geminus? I looked it up—it's right in the middle of Phrygia!"

"Attis syndrome," Pa replied, trying to be mysterious.

Helena was unfazed. "You mean Fulvius was a follower of the cult of Cybele?"

"Well, Fulvius had a bit of a mixed-up personality . . ." In front of Helena, my father was now curiously shy. She glared until he told her what had always been rumored about my uncle. "Helena, this may shock you—we got used to it—but for a while, poor old Fulvius reckoned he wanted to be a woman."

"Being one of my uncles," I said gently, "he had to go the whole crazy way."

Pa completed the story: "He left home to go and see the experts at the shrine of Cybele about removal of a certain body part . . ."

"Castration?" demanded Helena clinically.

Pa blinked. "I think he joined the navy instead."

"That's hardly a solution to his problem!"

"You don't know sailors, sweetheart."

"No? What happened to the legend that sailors have wives in every port?"

"They miss their wives when they are at sea."

Helena shook her head at Pa reprovingly. "So is Fulvius happy now?"

"Happy?" Pa and I looked at each other. "Fulvius will never be happy," I told Helena. "If he had succeeded in getting to Pessinus and cutting off his implement, for him it would only have been another problem."

"He would have spent the rest of his life regretting that he snipped his stick," Pa agreed with me.

Helena calmly wrapped the end of her cloak around the child in her arms and let the conversation drop.

Helena and I set off back to our apartment. The outer wall of Privatus' house still had my ropes and cleaning material beside it from when I was on watch. That would never have happened in Rome. I retrieved my bucket.

At the old town gate, there were no lights in the upper room. I had forgotten to ask Petronius whether the woman who guarded the kidnap victims during their ordeal, Pullia, had been pulled in along with her lover Lygon. And if so, what had happened to the seven-year-old we met that day, the lad Zeno?

We had arrived at the right moment to find out: Fusculus and a couple of his men clattered down to street level. They had taken in Pullia earlier, and had just finished searching the gatehouse.

"We found a load of drugs," said Fusculus, gesturing to a basketful of glass phials now being removed. "Opium poppy, I reckon."

"So tomorrow we can expect to see the vigiles staggering about the streets, blissfully comatose?"

Fusculus grinned in his happy way. "You want to volunteer to test the extracts?"

"No, he doesn't," said Helena. "But if none of the kidnap victims will testify, don't forget Marcus and Lucius Petronius once saw Pullia herself insensible after she had sampled the sleeping draft."

"Looks as if the woman is the only one we can snare with evidence," Fusculus told us. "Rubella thinks he may have to release the males—"

Helena was angry. "A whole gang of men are terrorizing victims, raping teenagers, extorting, and killing—but you will hold only their female assistant!"

As she stormed off growling, one of the vigiles let out a shout from the interior of the gatehouse. A small figure scuttled out, ducked around Fusculus, and hared off up the road. It was Zeno. No one made much attempt to catch him, and he legged it out of sight.

XLII

There are various problems in letting the generals run a battlefield: mainly, they pay too much attention to their budgets.

Marcus Rubella, the tribune of the Fourth Cohort of Vigiles, was keyed up to solve the Ostian kidnappings ahead of rival troops. However, he had already been forced to authorize a light supper and night-soil removal for thirty unexpected prisoners. When he realized that as a result he now had to choose between giving them breakfast or providing the customary Saturnalia drinks to his own men next December, it was no contest. The thought that by evening the pirates would be eating supper at the expense of a new candelabrum in his Rome office clinched it. He had set his heart on improved lighting and had spotted a faux bronze upright four-branch model with an Ionian top which he thought would do just nicely. So Rubella scrutinized his meager interrogation notes; he saw there was bugger-all chance of making charges stick; and he let the Cilicians go.

That said, Rubella was not stupid. Nor, possibly, was he corrupt.

His brain, according to Petronius Longus, worked on different principles from those of normal human beings, but brain there was beneath that short-haired, low-profile cranium. In fact Petro regularly tried to persuade Scythax, the vigiles' doctor, that Marcus Rubella's brain needed maintenance, in the form of having a hole drilled through his skull for inspection purposes.

Trepanation would have been a good idea for the normally prescribed purposes: relieving pressure. Rubella liked to think. This was well-known. He spent long hours in his office on the Aventine apparently doing nothing at all, but in rare moments when he confided in people, he claimed that his method as a cohort commander was to do the thinking other people chose to omit. According to him (and Petronius had been given the benefit of this theory at some length, at one of the cohort's legendary Saturnalia drinks parties) this method of leadership enabled Rubella to foresee problems, to anticipate criminal tendencies, and to plan cunning ambushes that other cohort commanders, with their less intellectual methods, would never achieve.

Thus, on the next sunny morning when many of the vigiles were despairing of their leader's stupid action, we were informed that when he let the Cilicians walk, Marcus Rubella had had a clever plan. This plan had been formulated as a result of research he had conducted in the few days between me paying him that visit in Rome and him bringing his men to Ostia. In order to be at the top of his profession in the matter of outwitting pirates, or pirates' descendants, or ex-pirates, the thinking man had been to a library and borrowed some scrolls. The cohort tribune was now an expert on Cilician habits and Cilician ways of thought.

"Stuff their habits!" muttered Lucius Petronius, who was no fan of literary research when it came to men who strangled their associates out on lonely salt marshes. "I want to see the bastards strung up on crosses where they can't do any more harm."

"So do I," said Rubella (who as well as a working brain beneath the crewcut had two big ears, one each side of his head in the customary manner, and both as sharp as a bat's). "Stop mouthing off to Falco like a schoolboy in the back row. And in any case what's bloody Falco doing here at my morning briefing?"

Everyone looked at me. The vigiles were feeling extremely depressed, so picking on me came as light relief. They were usually friendly, but just at this moment each one of them would happily have seen me lightly roasted in a bread roll with a piquant dressing of fish pickle.

I explained, with my informer's mild manners, that I had dropped into the patrol house to inquire what progress—if any—had been made in solving either the kidnappings or the killing of Theopompus. Rubella said to get lost. This was what I expected; he had a limited repertoire. I started to move away slowly, but when he began talking again I stayed put. Informers also have their traditions. Hanging around at briefings where we are not wanted is one of ours.

"You may all think that I have gone crazy—" Rubella's men dutifully looked as if they were thinking, *Oh no, sir.* I was thinking how glad I was not to be one of his men. "Trust me. I've done the right homework. What you have to understand about Cilicians is that they pay great respect to their elders. They have key leaders who are called Tyrannicoi—that's a Greek concept, just equates to a local king; we Romans view tyrants in a rather different light, of course—" By now we all reckoned Rubella had finally gone crazy. "Now, whether they are on board ship, where they elect their captain, or on land, where their leaders are more territorial, the oldest tyrants are the ones they honor most. We happen to be holding one who is about as old as you can get. So although it seems as if I have made a mistake in letting the rest go free, have faith. I kept back the fellow who matters. We are still detaining Damagoras."

Somebody cheered. Rubella could recognize a jibe; he glared. He glared at me, on principle, although I was not the culprit.

Petronius was blunt: "Damagoras claims he has retired."

"And the rest all claim they are innocent!" Rubella retorted. "I don't believe them either, Lucius Petronius."

Petro sniffed, but had to allow the point.

"I like the neatness of this," Rubella congratulated himself. "The people who take hostages are faced with a hostage themselves. Damagoras is being held against their good behavior. One slip, and their esteemed chief is for it." Rubella favored us with a benign smile. "And to make sure we can find them again, I instructed them all not to leave town."

Well, that was reassuring.

Of course if the Cilicians did leave town, Rubella would in one sense be vindicated. The kidnappings would stop. Then the tribune would be able to claim he had eliminated an extortion racket using minimal manpower and with little impact on the budget. Either way, Damagoras would cost nothing to keep; now that he had people on the outside, they sent in provisions daily. The pirate chief would be living a life of luxury, his only complaint being that he had to stick in his cell. Still, it was already a beautifully furnished cell.

Unfortunately for Rubella, almost at once proof arrived that the extortion would continue. While we were still at the briefing Helena Justina hurried to find me with some startling news. Holconius and Mutatus, the two scribes who commissioned me, had just arrived in Ostia from Rome, wanting my advice. The *Daily Gazette* had received a letter which said kidnappers had captured Diocles and removed him to Sardinia. His captors had now brought him back to Ostia and a large ransom was demanded. They ordered the scribes not to tell anybody of the ransom demand, and not to involve the vigiles.

"Still, you appear to have done that," sneered Rubella.

"It seemed vital you should know," Helena said, just managing to keep her temper. "This is a chance to lie in wait and catch the ringleaders while the ransom is being paid."

An ambush! Marcus Rubella, the thinking commander, was now a happy tribune.

XLIII

Rubella might have been cheerful. I was annoyed.

"Helena Justina, would you care to explain to me exactly why you just did that?"

Helena squared her shoulders. We were walking home. There was always a danger when we quarreled in the street that one of us would walk away forever. (Or at least until we thought the other party believed it might be forever just enough to enable a reconciliation scene.) We were both headstrong. Having two children, an adopted orphan, and a dog at home complicated matters slightly. Before striding off with too much hauteur, someone had to look over their shoulder and make sure the other one was going to look after the family.

Today I was being far too grown-up for that. I wanted to stick around and make my presence felt.

"You know why I did it, Falco." If I was Falco, that meant she was determined not to be impressed by the head-of-household bombast. Marcus was allowed more slack.

"Pardon me; I left my personal priest at home today. Read me the auguries!"

"Stop shouting."

"When I shout, believe me, lady, you will know all about it."

People had turned to look at us. I certainly was not raising my voice any more than the occasion demanded. Helena kept walking. An interfering idiot stopped to ask the respectable stole-wrapped matron if that unpleasant man was bothering her. Helena said yes. "Don't worry; he is my husband."

"Oh, sorry! Have you considered divorce?"

"Frequently," said Helena.

We walked on. I was biting my thumb. Too soon, we arrived at the entrance to the courtyard of our apartment. We stopped.

"Explain now. We don't argue in front of the children."

"Wrong, Falco. Anyway," said Helena in a tight voice, "I think it's best if *I* decide what should happen with the children. I am the one they have to rely on to be here looking after them . . . I'll tell you why I went to the vigiles. Two reasons, really. One is that I genuinely feel Mutatus and Holconius are wrong not to involve the authorities. And then, what would have happened if I had just let you go and see them privately, Marcus? You know as well as I do—you would have taken on the issue, and you would have done it all alone. Aulus has sailed off, Quintus is crooning over his baby, you wouldn't have wanted to tell Petronius what you were up to—and so *you* would have dealt with the ransom demands. Am I right?"

I said nothing. I tried to think up alternative courses of action I could pretend would have been my choice. None came to mind.

"So once again, Falco, I would have had to live with the terror of you going off into danger, on your own, ignoring sense—"

"I never ignore sense."

"You are ignoring it now."

"No, I'm adapting. I've just had a shock today. I thought you and I were partners. We consulted on important issues—"

"You were not here. Just for once I did what *I* wanted. And I chose to save you."

"I really did not think I had to say this, Helena: don't interfere with my work!" That hurt her. I hated the sound of it myself. Now we really were quarreling. I tried to soften it. "Be reasonable. I've been going off alone on cases all the years that you have known me—"

"Seven," she said bleakly.

"What?"

"Seven years. That is how long I have known you. You could be dead in seven minutes if you make the wrong choice, in the wrong place, with nobody to back you up—"

"Don't make me feel too old to cope."

"You are not too old. But you are no longer a lone informer, giving your soul to a mission. You are a family man with a full life, and you need to readjust."

We glared at each other. There was no easy way out of this. "Are those your grounds for divorce, Helena?"

"No. I'm still thinking up the grounds. They will be much more colorful; I want a big splash in the *Gazette*."

"Don't even try. I'm the man of the house. The divorce is mine; I deal with legal niceties."

"Do what you like with the niceties," scoffed Helena offhandedly. "Don't forget *I* deal with the accounts."

"Oh, you may do—but don't expect an expensive settlement!"

We were still glaring. I convinced myself there was a difference in the glare.

"So. Are you going to buy my forgiveness now by telling me where they are staying?" When she failed to react, I nudged: "Holconius and Mutatus."

"How do you know that I know where they are?"

"Helena Justina, you're the best partner I could have. You are efficient, farsighted, and although you would deny it, bossy. You didn't mention this to Rubella—but I know, Helena, you will have asked for their address."

She knew the address, and she told me. Then she denied she was bossy.

I thanked her gravely. "Be reassured, sweetheart. This is the first stage only; I am just exploring the situation. It will be perfectly safe. I'll go now. Do I get a kiss?" Helena shook her head, so I kissed her, very firmly. We looked at each other, then I left.

* * *

I walked back to Helena. She was still standing where I had left her, in the shadow of the courtyard arch. She looked shaken. I sympathized; it was how I felt.

"Come with me."

"You don't need me for this."

"No. But come anyway."

"It's big of you to allow it."

"That's right," I said. I tucked her hand in my arm and kept it there. "I'm getting old and easy to outwit; even so, I should still be able to manage talking to a pair of *Gazette* scribes. But this way, if I find myself in any danger, I can use you as a shield."

XLIV

Holconius and Mutatus were sitting glumly in their hired room. Between them, spread on a carefully laid-out cloak, lay an unpacked packed lunch, looking like food they had brought from Rome with them. They had divided it neatly into two portions, but seemed too disheartened to start.

I introduced Helena, as if I forgot she had met them that morning. We both assessed them thoughtfully: two lean, middle-aged freedmen with excellent Latin accents and grammar, who must be equally smart at Greek. Two sophisticated, literate men, who seemed ill at ease outside their natural environment.

"Marcus had heard you were both on leave," Helena said, settling herself. As she spread her skirts and readjusted her bangles, Mutatus shook his head. It was a rapid, nervous gesture.

"With our responsibilities, we are always available in emergencies."

I wondered if Diocles had been growing into a similar bald, bewildered-looking misfit. Somehow I thought not. The missing man had regularly covered worldly stories; he traveled; he could offer himself for work in diverse trades. Diocles was feckless and he drank. He owned a sword. The man could have been an informer—had he been able to choose a decent weapon.

Holconius and Mutatus did not look like men who had brought swords. I doubted that either owned one. Nor could I easily imagine either with family connections. Both had the narrow, obsessed air of experts. Bachelors, or men with dim wives who were expected to admire their husbands' culture and intelligence from the background. Holconius, the elder, was in a white tunic with cream undertones; Mutatus was in white that had a grayish tinge. Otherwise they matched as well as a pair of table ends.

"Do you want to see the ransom note, Falco?" Holconius demanded.

"All in good time. It is true that there has been a kidnap racket operating in Ostia—and that Diocles may have stumbled across it. But my first consideration, when a ransom demand is delivered like this, has to be whether it is genuine."

"Genuine?" They looked startled. Holconius scoffed, "Why should you doubt it?"

"It's too long since your man vanished."

Even Helena was watching me curiously. This was our first chance to evaluate what was going on.

I had been thinking about it as Helena and I walked here. "This does not fit the pattern, Holconius. In the abduction cases we know about, there are strict rules: they carry off women, not men; they make their demands for money normally on the same day; they close the deal fast; they choose foreigners who will leave the country if threatened. Basically, they avoid coming to the attention of the authorities."

Holconius nodded. His role at the *Gazette* was to take the notes in the Senate. It must have been a pleasant change to hear a worthwhile argument, with points listed cogently.

"What choice do we have?" demanded Mutatus. "None. The race is fixed. Somebody's got Diocles; the outcome is a dead cert." Mutatus covered the games. As a sports commentator he made swift assessments, then perhaps thought about it afterward while other people were howling that he was a complete idiot.

"Kidnappers work by trading on their victims' inexperience," I told him. "They want you to be so scared for Diocles, you follow their instructions exactly. You two have never been in this situation before, and it fills you with consternation. But I am thinking it through. For one thing, they claim they have had Diocles ever since he disappeared, having transported him to Sardinia. Is this credible?"

"It sounds like a cover-up." Helena reinforced my argument. "Some opportunist has seized on the fact that people are looking for Diocles, and is hoping to cash in."

I agreed. "Someone has just heard that Sardinia is full of bandits, and they decided that would sound good. When people go missing, especially when there is high-profile anxiety about their fate, such nonsense happens."

"Cranks, maniacs, and confidence tricksters are drawn to a tragedy," Helena told the scribes. "Families who lose loved ones in unexplained circumstances can be horribly exploited."

"That is why I have to advise you whether to take this demand seriously," I said. "Frankly, I am doubtful."

"You don't want us to pay the money?" asked Mutatus.

"I don't."

"But we brought the money with us!" This kind of illogical reasoning would be joy to a ransom gang or to any kind of exploiter.

I realized that the cash must be sitting in the large chest beneath the cloak upon which the two scribes had laid out their lunch. Perhaps they thought robbers would fail to look under their tablecloth. Most likely, the daft pair had given absolutely no thought to security.

I told them to take their loot for safekeeping in the vaults of one of the Forum temples. "To be sure, tell them you are depositing imperial funds." I paused. "Does the Emperor know about all this?"

They looked shifty. Eventually Holconius admitted with a lofty wave of the hand, "In view of the circumstances, and the need for secrecy, we were granted funds by the cashier in the Chief Spy's office."

I drew breath sharply. "I take it Anacrites is still at his holiday villa?" They both looked surprised at the familiarity with which I spoke of him. "He will be livid when he knows that you two have siphoned off his petty cash."

"It's more than petty cash . . ." Holconius blushed. "We told them you had authorized it."

"You told them a lie then," I replied quietly, keeping my temper. Helena covered her eyes with her hand, despairing. Anacrites had always posed a threat against me that frightened her. This was asking for more trouble. "You owe the Chief Spy a confession, and me an apology. Your action will gravely damage my relationship with Anacrites—" Nothing could damage it. We had no relationship. He and I were permanently out to get each other. These two ninnies had just given him the upper hand.

"Show me the ransom note now, please."

"We left it in Rome." Upset by my attitude, Mutatus tried bluffing.

"Holconius offered it to me. Let's be sensible, shall we?"

They produced the document. I read it and gave it back to them. They seemed surprised I did so. That was the difference between scribes and informers. Scribes wanted to keep everything for their archives. I was used to learning the crucial parts of correspondence, then ditching the evidence. (Or replacing it exactly as I had found it in the owner's ivory scroll box, so he or she never knew that I had read it . . .)

This was a waxed tablet, written in Latin, legible but not produced by a secretary. It said the usual: we've got him, you want him back; give us the money, or Diocles dies. The arrangements were in the letter. There was no mention of any Illyrian. The scribes were to leave the cash at a drop site. It was in Portus Augusti, an establishment named the Damson Flower. I was able to inform them that their venue was close to a bar called the Dolphin, and that I thought it was probably a brothel.

Helena looked impressed by my local knowledge. The scribes simply looked shocked.

"This is a confidence trick," I assured them. "If you give them the money, you will lose it and never see Diocles."

"They will kill him even if we pay?"

"They won't kill him—because they don't have him." We had covered this already, but Holconius and Mutatus simply had not heard me. "Look, I wish I could say my investigation will lead to me finding him drinking with a maudlin face in some portside bar. All I have learned so far leads me to dread his fate—though in my opinion, he has not been kidnapped."

"You think he is dead already?" Holconius was blunt.

"It seems a possibility. Maybe he has ended his own life, suicide for personal reasons after suffering depression. But there are other alternatives, some of which involve people and stories he may have wanted to write in the *Gazette*. I asked this before, but I will ask you again, was there any particular scandal that Diocles told you he intended to cover?"

The scribes shook their heads.

I warned them again not to pay the ransom. They thanked me for coming to give them this sound advice. They had not the slightest intention of following it.

They forgot, I had had many clients before. I knew the signs.

XLV

As Helena and I were going out, we met Rubella and Petronius coming in. We all stopped to confer on the doorstep of the lodging house.

"It's a swindle," I announced to the two vigiles. "Nothing about this matches the methodology of the Cilician gang. I advised Holconius and Mutatus not to deliver the money. They promised—but of course they will ignore me. I'm going to lie in wait at the drop site."

"We'll see you there!" breezed Rubella, in a jovial mood.

"Do you know where it is?"

"Falco, if you can get it out of a couple of scribes, we damn well can too." Rubella paused, and became less jocular. "So what about the missing man? *Could* he have been kidnapped?"

"It's possible."

"Who would take a prisoner and hold him for two or three months, without contact?" Petro asked. "The story is illogical. What do you think?" he then asked me.

"One: Diocles could have topped himself while in some mental crisis over a dead aunt, his only relative. Two: he upset Damagoras, a likely suspect. Or three: something bad happened because Diocles held a grudge against some members of the builders' guild—more suspicious bastards."

Petro and Rubella cheered up at three, delighted to have their fire-fighting rivals implicated.

"What's the betting?" Rubella demanded.

"Honestly, I don't know."

"Typical informer!"

Helena looked defensive, then asked Rubella, "How did you know the scribes lived here?"

"Oh, we have ears everywhere, young lady!"

Petronius was more open: "They arrived in Ostia in a big carriage, clearly carrying a chest of gold—and at the Rome Gate they stopped to ask directions to a good lodging house."

I groaned. "So the whole of Ostia knows they have something to steal? The money box is in their room; help yourselves before somebody else does . . . I advised them to stash the cash at the Temple of the Capitoline Triad."

"We'll recommend the Temple of Rome and Augustus," scoffed Rubella. "That should confuse the stylus-pushers nicely."

The two vigiles officers were going upstairs, no doubt to repeat the conversation Helena and I had just held there. We parted in lighthearted mood. We were all fired up because at last we could make progress. Whether we caught the real kidnap gang or some other chancers, at least now there was an opening for action.

"Oh, by the way," Rubella called back to me. "That silly girl, Posidonius' daughter, came to plead for the body to bury. I allowed her to have it." I was amazed he had been so gracious to Rhodope, but I knew why: it saved the vigiles having to dispose of Theopompus themselves. "I said she had to hold a decent Roman funeral at a quiet local necropolis, not some damned great pirate feast on the beach, and she is to let me know in advance where and when the ceremony is."

I gave him a light salute. "See you there as well then!"

Rubella had paused again. Two steps above him on a flight of stairs, Petronius watched us. Petro knew what was coming. "Another thing, Falco—she let slip a curious fact. Theopompus was not one of the Cilicians. He was an Illyrian."

I raised my eyebrows. "Not the one who acts as an intermediary; his description is quite different . . . So, Rubella, what does this mean?"

"I have absolutely no idea," admitted the tribune. "But if Illyrians and Cilicians have been working in partnership, maybe we can somehow put a rift between them."

"Play politics!" exclaimed Helena admiringly. Rubella looked suspicious, but was unable to tell whether she was mocking him.

When we reached our apartment, Julia and Favonia were engaged in a screaming quarrel. Albia let out a final exasperated yell at them, failed to make any impact, then ran out to sit by herself in the courtyard. Helena and I seated ourselves on either side of her, each holding one of her hands in consolation as we listened to the high-pitched volcanics up above.

"Just to let you know," I told Helena over Albia's head, "when we get divorced, I shall provide decent necessities without protest, and I am surrendering all my paternal rights to the children."

"Oh, they must live with you, Falco. I am a traditionalist," Helena lied.

"No, I absolutely insist on this. Little children should be with their loving mothers. I am a generous man. I shall compel myself to make this sacrifice."

Helena gazed back at me. "We could both run away," she suggested, rather wistfully. "They have two grandmothers who will fight for adoption rights."

"Done!" I cried. "Let's run away together; that sounds like fun."

Other tenants were starting to look out to see what the noise was. Some wag asked us whether we wanted him to call in the army to quell the tribal rebellion. Leaving Albia to sit in peace, Helena and I went up dutifully to wrench apart our offspring. So long as we only had two, we could grapple with one each. Normally the bruises went down after about five days.

If the two scribes followed their instructions, they had to take their money to the drop the next morning. Rising when it was still dark, I prepared for action. I hammered loose studs back into my best boots. Nux was lying on my feet. Albia had come from the other room and was observing the ritual.

"I don't have a boot-mender in Ostia."

"You won't use a boot-mender in Rome, Marcus Didius." We both spoke in hushed voices.

"True." By the light of an oil lamp, I checked bootstraps methodically. "Menders are useless." I wiped the oil from my sword, having first produced the weapon from my hiding place, to Albia's astonishment. Turning it to the light, I checked the blade and sharpened it with my sharkskin buffer. Then I filed my dagger with pumice, just to keep occupied. "Tell me, solemn girlie from the wild north, why are you so intent on what I am doing?"

"Aulus Camillus said, if there was to be any action, I should watch you getting ready."

"Aulus, eh?" I winked at her. People tended to assume Albia was a pallid soul, but she could take teasing. "Watch for what, exactly?"

"He said it always impressed him to see you change from a clown to a soldier."

"Aulus thought well of me, eh?" That came as a surprise.

"He said: 'When the eyes stop smiling, you can feel safe.' Of course," Albia assured me quickly, smiling herself, "I feel safe all the time now myself. He meant, that was how he felt, if he was in an action with you."

I stood up. The dog jumped back, and whined softly. She knew something was up, and that she would not be taken out with me when I left. I made sure I had on a tunic which allowed free movement of the arms, tightened my belt a notch, buckled on my sword.

"I did not know you had a sword with you," Albia observed gravely. "You never wear a sword in Rome."

"In Rome, it is against the law."

"So it is safer for you here, where you can wear one?"

"No. It is more dangerous, because here there may be idiots wearing weapons who don't know how to use them properly."

"But you do?"

"I do."

"Have you ever—"

"Albia, don't ask." I had to say good-bye to Helena now; she was in the other room with the children, pretending not to know what I was doing.

"Do me a favor, Albia. When I have gone, tell Helena Justina what her brother said."

Albia nodded slowly. "That will comfort her."

"Perhaps. If not, just remind her that on this operation I am not alone; I am going out to play with the big boys from the vigiles."

Instinct had brought Helena to the doorway. Nux ran to her, seeking help to deter me from going; Helena bent to stop the dog pawing the flimsy undertunic she wore in bed at night. Seeing me ready and with my sword on, Helena closed the door gently between me and the children. Julia, who was always too alert for convenience, was already just the other side of the door, silently staring. Behind her, I glimpsed Favonia sleepily standing up in the crib. "Given what I know of the vigiles, should their presence reassure me, Marcus?" Helena kept her voice low.

"Trust in what you know of me." I took off my gold equestrian ring, then gave it to her for safekeeping; sometimes it was best not to reveal my status. I kissed her quietly. Only Helena could tell whether my eyes were still smiling.

"Don't fall into any water," she answered. An old joke between us. An old, and very loving joke.

She was still anxious, but I had all her affection. It shows what great forbearance Helena allowed me—given that she knew I was going out now to a brothel in the port.

XLVI

The lighthouse had gone dark. Its great bonfire had been allowed to die down as dawn wanly lit the wharves. The working day in Portus had begun long before I arrived, even though I had crossed the river on one of the first ferries. There could have been only a few hours between the last sailors rolling back to their ships after their night's carousal and the arrival of the most hard-worked laborers. The brothel appeared to be closed.

I made my way slowly up the mole, gazing at the moored ships. Everywhere was quiet, but activity had begun on some of the vessels. A sleepy sailor spat into the harbor; I pretended to assume it was nothing personal. At the customs post, a clerk was sluggishly setting up the table. Ships with taxable goods could arrive in port even this early; in fact, a vessel was out by the lighthouse, maneuvering so badly it was impossible to tell whether it was going out or coming in. The clerk and I exchanged faint nods; maybe he had seen me recently, talking to Gaius Baebius. Neither he nor anybody else seemed surprised to see a stranger at the port this early. On the docks, people take most things for granted—apparently. More likely, eyes were watching my every move.

The three naval triremes were still moored together, still apparently deserted. Matched pennants wilted on their sterns, from which lines ran

down to bollards on the quay. The usual sordid harbor litter bobbed in
the dark water between them.

The air was chilly. I had come with a cloak. It would be a nuisance
later when the sun started to burn, but this way I could keep my sword
out of sight.

Reaching the far end of the mole, in the shadow of the lighthouse I
turned and walked back the way I had come, tripping over half the ropes
I had managed to avoid the first time. I could have wandered all around
the other mole, but it was too far from the venue. Instead, I joined the
men who stood at the bar of the Dolphin, warming themselves with hot
drinks and breakfast snacks. Most had the glum fatalism of those starting
their day's labor. One stood out: my brother-in-law. My heart sank.

"Hello, Gaius. This is a surprise."

"Marcus! I've taken a real liking to this place," Gaius Baebius informed
me. His pomposity was already irritating. "It has become my local, since
that day you and I discovered it."

As he took my order, the noncommittal eyes of the proprietor told me
the delight was one-way.

"Ha! 'Discovered' makes us sound like territorial pioneers. All we did
was walk along here with Ajax. How are your aches and pains?"

"Still agony—"

Cursing myself for asking, I cut in brutally: "Anyway, what are you
doing here so early?"

"I always come down to the port at this time. I like to get settled.
Sometimes the view of the sunrise is very affecting." I was not capable of
replying to poetic ideas, not at this hour—and certainly not from Gaius.
"And you are working too, I suppose?" he asked me loudly.

"I enjoy a good sunrise myself." There was no point kicking his shin
as a hint to shut up; he would want to know, equally loudly, why I had
kicked him.

"Yes, I thought you must be here on surveillance; there are some of
your friends from the vigiles." I groaned.

As the somber working men at the Dolphin all turned from their
breakfast in one synchronized motion to stare, Petro, Fusculus, and a se-

lection of their troops sauntered from the ferry direction in twos and threes, unobtrusively—or so they had thought. The stevedores and bumboat rowers might have noticed the newcomers anyway; port workers could smell law-and-order men a mile away. But the vigiles' arrival was enough to disperse the breakfasters, leaving only a couple of stubborn loaders who watched what happened next with sour expressions, chewing their handfuls of bread and refusing to be bumped out of their routine.

The vigiles replaced the departing breakfasters at the counter, where they ordered snacks of their own.

"Got an operation on today?" Gaius asked, with his usual lack of tact. Fortunately, Lucius Petronius was chewing at that moment so could not bite off my brother-in-law's nose.

"The sunrise will be lovely," I informed Petro as his brown eyes spoke movingly of overwrought feelings.

"Nice!"

Standing at the bar of the food stall, we turned our backs to the counter, elbows on the marble. That way, we could gaze across to the Damson Flower unobtrusively. I saw a couple of the men go over to the building, then start surreptitiously checking for the back door. There was bound to be one. No self-respecting bar or brothel lacks a rear exit for a quick getaway—or to serve as a secret entrance for those who burst in for armed debt collection or a surprise mass raid on the purses of the customers.

"That place over the road does a roaring trade," observed Gaius. For a sleepy bug, his feelers were acute. He had homed in dangerously on our object of observation. "The Damson Flower."

"Yes, the first rays of sunlight are just starting to glint charmingly on the wonky roof finials," seethed Petro. "Oh look, now the worn-out pornographic board is shining in the newborn light . . . Gaius Baebius, shouldn't you be at your tax table?"

Gaius Baebius turned his large watery eyes to Petro, and made a huge show of catching on. "Yes, Lucius Petronius, I must supervise those slackers who work for me."

"Good man."

Gaius left. The atmosphere improved immediately.

★   ★   ★

The door of the Damson Flower opened a crack. A young man in a rust-colored tunic and with rather short hair slipped outside and came over to the bar. He ordered bread and a drink, as if he had just come from a bout with a good-time girl. Maybe he had. But he was undoubtedly a vigilis. He gave a slight shake of the head to Petronius, drank up, and then left. Another man, in a streaky green tunic, arrived on foot from the direction of the Island, and went straight to the brothel, where he was soon admitted. He definitely belonged to the Fourth Cohort; I recognized him.

I remarked to Petronius, "Some people will volunteer for anything!"

"Sad, isn't it?" He grinned.

The rest of his men gradually dispersed around the locality. Most had first obtained a bite to eat; the vigiles regard this as a sacred rite, which they must follow impeccably in order to placate the gods and guarantee the survival of Rome, Senate, and People. Once satisfied, they merged into nooks around the port. Fusculus was slumped on his back against the base of a crane, looking like a bundle of rags or a partner in one of the criminal scams that fascinated him. I half expected a sidekick to be hiding nearby, ready to jump out and rob anyone who bent down to see if the apparent heart attack victim needed help.

Petro and I remained at the Dolphin, with its excellent view of both the Damson Flower itself and the approach road from the ferries. We were talking about family issues. We took as our starting point Gaius Baebius, which led to how I had always loathed my brothers-in-law, and the curious fact that my best friend was now one of them. "You may have to ditch Maia."

"How about I adopt her? Then she stops being your sister, so I can't be your brother-in-law—"

"But Maia becomes your daughter so you are not allowed to sleep with her."

"Bad plan!"

Still filling in time, we discussed which of my brothers-in-law I hated most. This provided inexhaustible repartee. I could not decide between Verontius the road contractor, who was an obvious scab on society's nether regions, and Mico the plasterer, who looked fairly harmless, but who had a lot of faults—especially his terrible plastering. But Petronius had a particular down on Verontius, whom he once tried to arrest for bribery on official contracts; Verontius had gotten off without a stain on his character (he bribed his way out of the charge). We avoided all mention of Famia, who had been married to Maia until he died a couple of years back; I could not remember whether Petronius had ever been told of Famia's greatest moment. It was being kept a secret to save the children from the shame: Famia had been sent to the arena in Leptis Magna and eaten by a lion.

Famia was a drunkard with an uncontrolled tongue, which was how he incurred his fate. But he had not achieved the depths of dirt, deceit, smelliness, and absenteeism which were mingled into a flavorsome brew by the toothless water-boatman father of my favorite nephews, Larius and Gaius. As soon as we mentioned Lollius, Lollius won outright.

Time went by.

Around us, the port had come to life. The few early loaders who had seemed to be working on their own initiative had now been joined by organized teams. Singing and joshing, they set about complicated maneuvers, which often involved long periods of inactivity where men stood on the quayside and talked through how to approach their task. At other times they seemed to have no problem, but swung into action with practiced assurance. Then sacks and barrels kept coming ashore or going on board in great quantity. At intervals along the mole, cranes had creaked into action, raising stuff from deep holds; usually the crane had a lonely operator, working with unseen companions who never seemed to communicate from the ship. If a load slipped, the operator had to leave the crane and remedy the disaster on his own. If he was lucky, a seagull came to watch.

Handlers shifting produce manually crossed from one tightly packed ship to another, sometimes several, using gangplanks as bridges as they hauled amphorae of wine and olives or threw sacks and bales from hand to hand. Awkward items provided us with plenty of amusement. A whole string of Spanish horses had to be coaxed down a gangplank, teetering riskily even when someone suggested they be blindfolded. Divers arrived to work in one area of the dock, where a valuable commodity had been dropped in the water the previous day.

We were there half the morning but the divers still had not found what they were searching for. We never discovered what it was. Petro wandered over to make friends with their supervisor since a contact among the divers might be useful to the vigiles.

A new ranker arrived from the Island, looking nervous. He began to approach Fusculus, then noticed Petronius, who had spotted him and was hurrying back to the bar.

"Sorry, chief—bad news. The scribes won't be coming after all."

Petronius adjusted the position of his wine beaker on the counter; the gentle movement was deceptive and the scared messenger knew it. "Tell me."

"It's all a fix." Nervous of Petro, the ex-slave was rushing the story. "They started out, sure enough, got as far as the ferry, then had the money snatched off them while they were on the boat."

Petronius now showed he was livid. "I cannot believe what I'm hearing! How was this cocked up?"

"The ferry was attacked by another boat."

"What?"

"Sure thing, chief. A gang had hijacked a tugboat. Four or five of them. The two scribes were coming over on one of the big Lucullan ferries—" Four different ferry services plied across the Tiber daily. The Lucullan line had multiple oars and took both passengers and heavy goods. They were big, unwieldy vessels.

"And where were all of you?" asked Petro coldly. "I told you to keep a close tail on the scribes."

"We were in one of the vigiles skiffs, most of us. Parvus was supposed to stick with them on the ferry. Rubella said only one man was to be that close, in case they got suspicious."

"*Rubella!*" Petronius came even nearer to the boil.

"If a tribune wants to come on a mission, chief—"

"If he does, you lose him! Tell me the rest of this disaster."

"Parvus couldn't get on the right ferry, because of the crowds, so he was squashed on the Rusticelian one—" Just a rowing boat for passengers. "But it was crossing at the same time, more or less parallel. He could see what was happening. The gang rammed the Lucullus ferry, jumped aboard, and ransacked the purses of everyone—all the passengers. Rubella reckons robbing the others was to make it look good—"

"He thinks the Damson Flower instruction was just to get the scribes on the river?" snarled Petro. "This was how the money was always going to be collected? So the scribes had their chest taken in the scrum?"

"Whipped off them and passed to the tugboat before you could blink."

"So where was Rubella while this pastoral scene unfolded?"

"In our skiff. Jumping up and down and spitting fire. He kept yelling to be rowed nearer, but to be honest, none of the lads is very good at steering." Every time a vigiles detachment was assigned to Ostia, the troops had to learn to manage their boat. In Rome they did not need one; there were bridges.

"And where is Rubella now?"

"Ostia. Comforting the scribes and explaining to them they are just victims of a trick."

Petronius ran his hands through his hair, taking this in. Always concerned for the men's safety, he asked in a more temperate voice, "Anyone attempt to fight back? Any casualties?"

"Parvus. He jumped into the water and swam over from the ferry he was on. He managed to get aboard the Lucullan. He's a mad devil—he whacked one of the gang with an oar, nearly split his head open—" As firefighters, the vigiles are an unarmed force. They can do a lot with fists and feet, or they improvise. "But then someone poked Parvus in the guts and he fell off the ferry."

"Is he all right?"

"He went under. Rubella and some of the lads jumped in after him. We fished him out, but that held us up. By then, the gang were back on the tugboat, laughing at us all as they rowed off at a lick downstream. We tried to follow but the ferries got in our way—"

"On purpose?"

"Well, there was chaos. The current was swirling boats everywhere.

The thieves seemed to know what they were doing on the water, but there were some collisions. I thought we were going to sink. We found the tug soon afterward. They beached it by the Isis sanctuary; there's no sign of them now, and of course nobody saw anything suspicious when they landed there—or so they all say."

The man fell silent, looking guilty. After a moment, Petro clapped the vigilis on the shoulders, to show there were no hard feelings. Then he signaled to Fusculus (who had been listening in, though at a careful distance). They summoned the troops and set about a full internal search of the Damson Flower.

"Take this joint apart!" ordered Petronius. Sometimes he showed greater respect for people and property. But he had to relieve his feelings somehow.

XLVII

It was not the first time Petro and I had been in a brothel—always for professional purposes, of course. We had once risked our lives and our reputations in the biggest love nest Rome could offer, vainly searching for the gangster father-in-law of Petro's bugbear Florius. By comparison, the Damson Flower was tiny and its services basic, though like all port establishments it had its own salty color. Small cells on two floors offered little more than hard, narrow beds. The deluxe ones each had a clothes hook outside in the corridor. The imperial suite boasted a cupboard containing a piss pot.

Despite looking deserted from the quay, when we burst through the main door with belligerent vigiles greetings, the interior coughed up a slew of disreputable occupants. Sheepish sailors emerged from all quarters, many carrying kitbags and looking as if they were using the place simply as a cheap hotel. The girls came in many flavors, from sloe-eyed Easterners, through dusky dames from inner Africa with amazing busts and backsides, to a skinny Gaul with no bust at all who kicked Fusculus in the groin unexpectedly. They all had garlic breath and foul language. Several tried the old trick of shedding their clothes to disconcert us—where they were wearing clothes to start with. The madam called herself a Spanish dancer, but could never have been farther than the Rome Gate at Ostia in her life. In doing this job for decades, she had probably acquired more technical knowledge of binnacles and foremasts than most ships' carpenters.

The bouncer, at whom Ajax had barked so furiously the other day, was wearing a tunic that had played host to most of the moth population in Portus. It had more holes than cloth in between them; when he moved I expected clouds of little winged creatures to stream out as if we had disturbed a bats' cave.

"Have you even been in a bats' cave, Falco?" demanded Petro scathingly. I was a spare-time poet; he had always disapproved of my fanciful tendencies.

"Imagination is a rare talent."

"How about you apply it to helping us process these desperadoes?"

The madam had refused to speak to us, it being a tenet of her trade that since she was a legal outcast because she was a prostitute, law officers from Rome had no jurisdiction over her. That was how she put it, anyway. Fusculus argued against this circular philosophy with the vigiles' trenchant wit and good manners: he socked her on the jaw. It may seem harsh, but at the time he had been trying to drag her out of doors and she was standing on his foot; she weighed a lot and must have known her so-called Spanish dancing shoes had formidable high heels.

Because of her noncooperation, Petronius was squeezing the bouncer's balls. We wanted him to tell us whether any of the customers hailed from Cilicia. "Or Illyria," I added. Petro reinforced the question manually.

"Is that near Agrigentum?" The bouncer had been well trained in playing dumb, even when at risk of becoming a eunuch. We gave up on him. As a symbol of us giving up, Petronius clouted his ear. Petronius then explained to the watching customers that he was eager to try out his squeezing and clouting techniques on other parts of the anatomy, so anyone who wanted to give him any trouble could be a volunteer.

This was too sophisticated, and anyway most of them were foreign. Or so they claimed. It was true that they all had great difficulty even understanding a request for their names and livelihoods.

Petronius Longus put the men in a line, guarded by his troops, and said he would now go through the process of checking whether the cus-

tomers were free Roman citizens or runaway slaves; he explained that although he hated xenophobia, he would be obliged to pay particularly
close attention to those who were foreign. Anyone who did seem to be
a runaway would be put in a heavy neck-collar and imprisoned until a
countrywide search for his master had been carried out; due to pressure
of work there was no guarantee at the moment how long these searches
might take . . . But not to fear: all anyone had to do to be in the clear was
to produce his valid certificate of Roman citizenship.

Nobody carries their certificate around with them.

Many citizens in Rome do have a birth certificate (or did when they
were born and registered), freed slaves are given a tablet, and all ex-army
personnel acquire their diploma of release (which we tend to keep carefully, in case we have to disprove accusations of desertion). In the
provinces, where most of these men originated, citizenship is a loose
concept. The gaggle of seafarers, loaders, negotiators, and short-order
chefs all looked abashed, grew scared, and then played our game. A list of
names, hometowns, and trades was created rapidly.

Nobody owned up to being Cilician or Illyrian. Or Pamphylian,
Lycian, Rhodian, or Delian. There was a Cretan, but he was on his own,
only four feet high, had bandy legs, and threw up from terror when we
questioned him. We decided he could not possibly be part of the scam on
the two *Gazette* scribes—so we made him promise not to do it again
(which he did even though he was innocent, swearing some peculiar
Cretan oath). We let him go. As he scampered off down the quay, he
cursed us. Fusculus looked nervous.

"He has done *something*," Petro decided darkly, with the voice of experience. But it was too late now. For a man whose legs were so bandy
you could drive three goats between them, the Cretan could move like
an Olympic sprinter who had the promise of a hot date if he came home
from the stadium with a wreath. That was another reason for suspicion;
most of the rest had sauntered off, deliberately looking unconcerned.

"Lemnus," said Fusculus, double-checking the list. "Lemnus from
Paphos. Works as a building site concrete mixer, freelance. Out of a job
currently."

"So what's he doing on the docks?" I asked.

"Looking for work, he says."

"On a cheap whore's mattress?" We all laughed. The madam of the Damson Flower then shrieked at us that her women were all highly trained and did *not* come cheap.

Life had made this hag an excellent businesswoman. When the vigiles packed up to leave, she promised them a trade discount if they visited on a quiet night.

Petronius Longus was taking his men back to Ostia. Rubella would not welcome my presence at the debriefing for that morning's episode on the river. I told Petro that if he saw Helena he should reassure her that our mission had aborted on us. But while I was over here at Portus, I thought I would stick around and sniff about.

The vigiles left. I went back to the Dolphin. Everything seemed to be over—but now I was alone without backup. For me, that was where the day's adventures began.

XLVIII

I bought lunch. In open defiance of the imperial food-stall rules, dish of the day at the Dolphin was a hot fish stew. It should have been pulses but the waiter had a line over the harbor wall; fish were free. Portus was awash with officials, from the corn-supply aediles to the tax beetles to the harbormaster, the lighthouse staff, and the watchmen; this should have been a completely regulated area. No chance. In ports disobedience is as common as silt.

I was mopping my bowl with a lump of rustic bread when who should I see come trotting back to the Damson Flower but Lemnus. His bandy Cretan legs were still kicking up dust like a house-slave in a flaming temper. With a furtive glance over his shoulder, he scampered inside the brothel. A minute later so did I.

The male bouncer had gone off to lunch. A short, round, gloomy girl was now guarding the door. "You again!" she greeted me.

"I love to be so memorable—where's Lemnus?"

"Mind it."

"Listen, fatty-chops—take me to the Cretan, fast!"

"Or what?" She was expecting a threat so I showed her a half-denarius.

"Or I won't give you this." I was not intending to give her that much money whatever she did, but she was less than bright and she fell for it.

With what she thought was an alluring smile, she led me along the corridor. She was about as alluring as a pregnant duck, and she only looked about fourteen. Bad enough to be overweight and miserable at that age if you have a decent life; working in a brothel as well must have been deadly.

Lemnus was sitting in a cell by himself.

"Now then, little man from Paphos, what are you doing back here?"

"Hadn't finished." Petro's men had already established that under questioning Lemnus whimpered. He only showed his real style when he was out of reach. Then the curses flew as fast as his bent little legs.

"Since you are in here on your own, the jokes are obvious and crude, Lemnus. Has he paid?" I demanded of the girl from the door, who was still hanging around in the hope of the coin.

"He has a slate." She tossed her hair derisively, which caused a mist of dandruff and cheap scent. I let her see me put away the coin I had offered, so she went back to her duties. "Time-waster!" she muttered, scowling.

"I assume that's you," I told Lemnus cheerily—just as he stopped being a timid weasel, flicked open a folding knife, and lashed out at me.

I had expected trouble. I elbowed his arm up and just escaped slashing. Lemnus barged out of the cell past me, but I had my boot out at ankle level. He crashed to the floor. I would have disarmed and overpowered him, but the doorkeeper had turned back and jumped on me. She was still after that half-denarius—and prepared to fight dirty for it.

I freed myself from being choked and gave her a kneejerk that doubled her up, squealing. The Cretan had legged it again at top speed. As I followed, women appeared from all directions. The madam had been right: they were all highly trained—trained to get in my way. I shouldered aside a desert princess, squashed her pale friend against a doorpost, deflected one fury with my hip and another with my forearm. Lemnus had bolted out of doors and when I burst back onto the quay he had vanished from view. However, men were staring toward a public latrine as if a fugitive might have rushed in there, so I raced inside too.

There were five men taking philosophy breaks, all strangers, all immersed in their tasks. No sign of Lemnus. No other exit. It would have been rude to run in, then run straight out again. I took a seat.

Enthroned on a spare spot, I recovered my breath, growling quietly. Nobody took any notice. There is always one loser who talks to himself.

At least there was a benefit in chasing a suspect in a high-grade imperial area: since Claudius and his successors might be caught short while inspecting harbor facilities, the twenty-seater latrine was fit for an emperor. The five-to-a-side seating benches were marble-clad, with the smoothest possible edges on their beautifully designed holes. The room was an airy rectangle, with windows on two sides so passersby could look in and spot their friends; if Lemnus did come in here, maybe he had vaulted out of a window. The cleansing water ran in channels that never flooded. The sponges on sticks were plentiful. A slave mopped up drips and splashes. What's more, he wore a neat tunic and was discreet about expecting tips.

The conversation among the porters and negotiators was banal, but after a long morning out I had better things to do than chat. Informers normally have to manage without relief. In an empire that prides itself on high-class hygiene, bodily retention forms the main challenge for men in my profession. Slugging it out in fights or making your tax declaration creative is a cinch by comparison.

I sat lost in thought about the bad aspects of my work—the traditional musings of a man who has entered a lavatory alone. A couple of people left. Two new ones entered. Suddenly I heard my name: "Why hello, Falco!" This was the other traditional drawback: the idiot who insists he must talk to you. I looked up to see a white-haired, elderly fusspot, being very particular about checking that his seat was clean and dry: Caninus.

It was natural to run into the sea biscuit at Portus, though of course I felt annoyed. When navy men have the opportunity to enjoy decent facilities on firm ground, instead of being hung out over the stern of a prancing ship in a fierce wind, they tend to take their time. Caninus now looked set in here for days, and I was stuck with him.

In latrine etiquette, the others present were now able to relapse into private contemplation, while they pitied me for being spotted. I was forced to be pleasant. "Caninus! Hail."

"Not your usual drop-in, Falco?"

I shook my head. "Just passing through." This is an old army joke, but the navy seemed to know it too.

"So!" breezed the nautical menace with a meaningful glare. "Were you involved in that activity at the Damson Flower this morning, Falco?"

"Confidential," I warned, to no avail.

"Yes, I thought you must have been. A ransom that went wrong, I hear?"

"You must have your narks in all the right places."

"Was it connected with that case you mentioned? The missing scribe?"

"Diocles is supposedly up for ransom." I saw no harm in the admission, even though the four other men present were now listening intently while pretending not to. "I think it was a try-on; nobody has kidnapped him. I just wonder how the speculators knew he had disappeared—and that people were sufficiently anxious about him to respond to a demand for money."

"You were asking me about Cilicians," said Caninus. "Traditional behavior. They sit in taverns and brothels, on the lookout. Exactly how pirates used to work: picking up news of ships with decent cargoes that they would subsequently follow out of harbor and assail."

"Now the bastards stand at bar counters, listening out for recently landed rich men, who have wives or daughters with them," I agreed. As a professional courtesy I lowered my voice: "You didn't tell me, last time we met, that you were in port to follow up this racket."

"Oh—didn't I?" Caninus was offhand. "You never said it impinged on your missing scribe."

"I didn't know."

We fell silent. The change of pace in our conversation allowed two of the other men to finish off and leave. The remaining two, who presumably knew each other, began a conversation about racehorses.

Caninus was being very friendly. "By the way, Falco—somebody pointed out a fellow recently who is supposed to be an uncle of yours."

I was surprised to find myself known as a character around Portus— or to hear that my family tree provided wharfside gossip. "Are you sure you don't mean my father, Didius Geminus? Everyone knows him for a rogue."

"The auctioneer?" I was right. Everyone knew Pa, including naval investigators. It was no surprise. Geminus had shaken hands on plenty of dodgy deals. In fact, one of the men talking about horses cast a very quick glance at me then made his escape; maybe he had been involved in one of Pa's murky art purchases. The endless supply of Greek athlete statues that Pa sold off in Pompey's Portico were knocked out for him by a repro marble specialist down in Campania, but he had told me some rhytons and alabastrons which he supplied as cheap "old" vases to interior designers came in by sea. According to Pa they were genuinely Greek and almost certainly old—it was the source he preferred not to discuss. "No, I'm sure it was your uncle," Caninus persisted.

"Fulvius," I conceded. "Until last week I hadn't seen him since I was a child . . . Why the interest?"

"I thought you might be working with him."

"With *Fulvius?*"

"You were seen drinking with him and your father. Geminus came down here to look for Theopompus, didn't he?"

"For heavens' sake!" I was amazed and indignant. "I had a quiet drink with some relatives at a Forum bar; we only met by chance. Yet it got re- ported to you—and you decide we are an organized team? One that might tread on your toes, presumably?"

"Oh . . ." Caninus could see it was ridiculous now, and backed off quickly. "I was just in discussion with a fellow who thought he might have known your uncle abroad."

"I don't even know where he has been," I said bluntly. "He is most fa- mous for setting off to Pessinus and getting on the wrong boat. That was years ago. As far as I know, it wasn't a boat to Cilicia." If it sounded as though I was telling Caninus it was none of his damn business, then fine.

"Pessinus?" Caninus looked puzzled.

"Ancient shrine of the Great Mother," I confirmed. I kept my tone solemn. "He wanted to modify himself. Uncle Fulvius takes religion all the way."

"I thought it was illegal for a citizen to mutilate his—"

"Yes, it is."

"Or to dress up and dance about in women's robes?"

"Yes. Fortunately, Fulvius hates dancing. But as you may know, citizens are allowed to give money to the cult. Uncle Fulvius is so charitable, he could not bear to wait for the annual festival in Rome. He just wanted to contribute to the upkeep of the eunuch priests as quickly as possible—"

I was inventing freely, unable to take it seriously, but Caninus lapped it up. "He sounds intriguing."

"With his lack of geography when booking a sea passage? No, I could not have had a more interesting uncle." Ma would have been proud of me.

"And has he really cut off his whatsit with a piece of flint?"

"Not as far as I know." Even if I thought Fulvius had done it, self-castration was an offense and he was still my relative. I was not going to give the navy an excuse to lift his tunic and inspect him. They could get their thrills elsewhere.

I stared at the attaché, wondering just why my long-lost uncle so fascinated him.

The fourth stranger, an unobtrusive man in his forties, was busying himself with a sponge. Caninus glanced at him then decided it was safe to continue. Without changing his tone or his expression, he told me the point: "The word on the docks is that your Uncle Fulvius came back here after living in Illyria."

"That's news to me," I retorted in annoyance. "Last I heard, Uncle Fulvius was shark-fishing."

I saw no reason to make polite excuses. I stood up and left.

XLIX

Coming out onto the quay again, I felt sick. I had no idea where Fulvius had spent the past quarter of a century. Even if he had been in Illyria that was no proof that he was involved with pirates and kidnappers. But the sea biscuit's sly insinuation had a sure ring. I was related to several entrepreneurs whose business deals were best left veiled. Fabius and Junius were just embarrassing, but their elder brother had a streak of dark intelligence, plus loathing of the social rules; he took a joy in doing people down. I saw it clearly: as the kidnappers' intermediary, Fulvius would fit.

The allegation that "the Illyrian" was a "scrawny old queen" also rang true. Fulvius had tried to run away to a cult whose goddess, according to myth, was born double-gendered; Cybele's male partner was then created from her excised masculine genitals, only to castrate himself ecstatically . . . That was a family I did not envy. When they sat around the fire at Saturnalia swapping medical histories, it must be grim. But no hapless nephew had ever had to explain to Cybele, the Great Idaean Mother in her turreted crown, that Attis was not just a eunuch in a starry cap, but lead player in a nasty ransom scam.

I was tough. But not so tough that I wanted to be stuck with this. The specters of *my* mother and of Great-Auntie Phoebe on the family farm rose up alarmingly. We informers may not be known as scared of our mothers, but we are accustomed to assessing dangers correctly—so of course we are.

I walked back inside the lavatory. The other customer came out past me, giving me a funny look. Caninus was now in close conversation with the young attendant; tipping him, presumably. The youth turned away quickly. The navy man looked up, surprised and wary.

"I think you are wrong," I said. "If you *are* wrong, you just libeled a senior member of my family. If not, Caninus, don't waste my time with insinuations. You raised the issue—you must turn Fulvius in."

I left again. This time I would not be going back.

I was striding along toward the exit that would take me to the Island and the return route to Ostia when I saw them. It was just a glimpse. The sun was high, the day was hot. A haze had arisen over the open sea. All around close at hand the stone wharf was shimmering. I had a long morning, lunch, and a brisk chase behind me. I was tired and angry. I was angry with the navy man and more angry, *much* more angry, with my uncle for exposing me to the navy man's allegations. I wanted to go home. It would have been easy to dismiss what happened next and to leave Portus.

But I had just seen two men in colorful costumes, who were carrying a wooden chest.

I first noticed them as they passed between a crane and a pile of grain sacks. In a second they were hidden by the clutter on the dock. Then, as I waited, they emerged farther on. They went trotting along at a comfortable speed, one at each end of the chest, which must have convenient handles. It looked a good weight, but not impossible to maneuver. Yesterday when the two scribes were having their lunch off their booty box, I had not been able to look at it properly, but this container was about the same size. The two carriers appeared to be seafarers.

I glanced around. Sometimes the docks are crammed with officials. This was too close to lunchtime. No assistance was available. I set off after the men alone.

It was tempting to shout. I was too far away from them. If they ran with the chest I could catch them, but they wouldn't do that; they would drop it and scatter. I was gaining, but they were still too far ahead to confront. I dodged around a mound of marble blocks, leapt over a whole bundle of mooring ropes, snaked among untidy handcarts—and found that the two men had vanished. I ran on, and reached a clear part of the quay. I had been here this morning. Everywhere seemed deserted. The berthed vessels rode quietly, crammed into moorings, all looking empty of people. Then a wizened deckhand popped up his head on a merchantman. I asked if he saw the chest-carriers go by; he reckoned they had taken the treasure trove aboard a trireme. I asked if he would come and help. Suddenly unable to understand Latin, he dived out of sight again.

His explanation seemed correct. The first trireme was the next ship along from me, tied up with its stern to the quay; the second and third lay beyond it. Had the two men continued far along the dock past the triremes, they would still be in sight. They could only have turned off and boarded.

The trireme rode high, its deck eight or nine feet above the water. I could not really see up to the deck. In the tightly packed harbor, these enormously long vessels must have been backed into their moorings, either punted in or perhaps hauled by the crew with towing ropes. Now steep gangplanks came down on either side of the curved stern ends; they had light halyards across them to deter boarders. I scissored over the nearest. Then I walked carefully up the incline and stepped out through the knee-high side rails onto the quarterdeck.

I had been on military ships before. As a young recruit I had sailed on army transports, perhaps the bleakest experience of my army life; I could still taste the fear as we were carried across to Britain, all wanting to go home to our mothers and throwing up throughout the whole freezing journey. Later, I had had a brief experience in calmer waters in the Bay of Neapolis, feeling the huge surge of speed as a trireme chased conspirators, the unbelievable smoothness as its rowers turned expertly almost on the spot, the almost undetectable crunch as the ram struck home and wrecked our suspects' boat. Triremes were supposed to be unsinkable. Such a comfort.

This long ship slept in silence, oars shipped and sails furled, eerily deserted. A narrow gangway stretched away up the center. At the far end
the beaked goose figurehead nodded gently. On the bow at water level, I
knew a great armored ram bared its fangs to the waves—six or seven feet
of reinforced wooden jaw, sheathed in bronze, with teeth for forcing apart
the planks of ships being attacked. These warships were Rome's weapon
of control for the pirate menace.

I walked the full length of the ship. At the fo'c'sle end was a tiny cabin
beneath the deck, for the captain and the centurion. The complement of
two hundred or so crew, including a handful of peacetime soldiers, were
provided with little shelter, though a light canopy protected them from
missiles and some of the weather. The cabin was locked, but I looked
through its tiny window: no wooden chest.

As I walked back, I wondered where they all were. Six hundred men,
from the three boats, had melted away. I had seen no obvious ratings'
presence at Portus or Ostia, no boastful trierarchs getting drunk in their
loud, legendary way. Caninus was supposed to have put spies in the bars,
but six hundred was a lot of spies to secrete. Maybe some had gone up to
Rome. The two Mediterranean fleets had permanent offices there. The
Misenum Fleet's central staff were quartered in the Praetorian Camp,
though rumor had it they were to be moved nearer to the Flavian
Amphitheater soon, because sailors were to operate the proposed great
awnings that would shade the crowds. The Ravenna Fleet headquarters
was over in the Transtiberina District.

None were here. The entire ship was empty. There was not even a
watchman.

Nothing for it. I walked across the warm quarterdeck to the far side
and cautiously crossed to the next trireme. I could have gone down one
gangplank and up another, but I had wasted enough time. Each trireme
had an outrigger running its length, to support the upper bank of oars; I
climbed out and jumped across from one oarbox to the next. I did it with
trepidation, nervous that I would slip and fall into the dock.

The second trireme was empty too. I searched it quickly then made
my way with increasing discomfort across its deck, then jumped over to
the third vessel. Being alone on these enormous empty ships was start-

ing to unnerve me. Each time I crossed to a new one, explaining my presence became a more difficult option. Boarding one warship without permission was probably treason. Boarding three would be three times as bad.

From habit now, I walked right across the last trireme and looked over the far side. There I saw another ship, lower in the water and so previously invisible. It was a monoreme liburnian, a classic light galley. For some reason a gangplank ran down from this trireme's quarterdeck to the liburnian. Had triremes carried a cargo, I might have thought the liburnian was raiding it. When moored parallel to the quay, with the smaller vessel farther out in the harbor, it would be customary to allow access to land with a link—though any commercial ship's captain would think twice about using a navy warship as a bridge. But this had no obvious explanation. Still, the lower ship also looked deserted. I took the handy gangplank and went down.

Almost at once I heard somebody coming. There was no way back to the dock without meeting the arrivals face-to-face. I braced myself to tell a good story.

They shot into view on the quay, coming fast aboard. In battered seaboots and colorful trousers, these bare-armed, wild-haired sailors smacked of the Eastern seas. There were just two of them, but one was being hauled along, stumbling and helpless. A great, very recent bruise disfigured his swarthy face, and an ear was swollen to twice its normal size. He was being helped aboard by a determined seaman with great gold brooches on his shoulders, who must be as strong as a small ox, judging by the easy way he half carried his concussed crony. He saw me on their ship.

"What happened to your friend?" I played it cool.

"He walked into an oar." I felt a chill. One of the Fourth Cohort, Parvus, had struck a thief with an oar, during the fracas at the river.

We glared at each other. The man in charge was dark, domineering, and displeased. His fierce gaze suggested he was ready for a fight.

"What are you doing here?"

"Making some routine inquiries. The name's Falco."

"Cotys."

"And—?"

"Arion." The wounded man had stiffened up; now the pair moved apart, covering my escape route.

"Where are you from, Cotys?"

"Dyrrhachium." Where in Hades was that?

"Not on my personal trade route—" I guessed wildly: "Would that be Illyria?"

Then as Cotys nodded, I rushed his wounded crewman.

I had reckoned Arion was the easy target because of his wounds. Wrong. Arion laid into me in an offhand way. Disposing of trouble was routine; he wanted it over quickly, and if I died on him he didn't care.

I broke free, barging Arion into Cotys to delay them, and legged it for the shoreward gangplank. Someone whistled, summoning reinforcements. I didn't stop to worry about the crew coming up on deck; others had arrived on the quay, blocking my escape. Then a huge blow between my shoulders felled me. I crashed to the deck and felt my back wrench painfully.

I was dragged upright. Many hands threw me between them. After some playful Falco-tossing they hurled me half senseless back on the deck.

Around me began more action than I liked. This vessel's crew were masters of the rapid getaway. The ship had close to fifty oars, single-banked each side; from nowhere rowers had appeared to man them. Smaller and chunkier in build than the elegant warships, it could have been moored there beside the triremes for days, weeks even—but it was leaving now. Energetic activity had the liburnian edging out into the harbor without benefit of a tugboat.

All was not lost—or so I thought briefly. As we pulled out beyond the trireme, I suddenly saw above me the white-haired head of Caninus. He looked down over the trireme rail curiously. I struggled upright and yelled for help. Caninus merely raised a languid arm. Maybe he was waving farewell to me—but it seemed a signal to Cotys. Any hopes of rescue by the navy faded abruptly.

I had one chance to help myself, while the sailors still busied themselves with leaving. They had not even searched me. As the ship approached the harbor exit and the lighthouse, I whipped out my sword and held it to a seaman's throat. But nobody noticed me. My frantic cries to the officials at the lighthouse were lost. At that time of day, the port officials high above had too many vessels in sight.

Sailors threw themselves upon me, ignoring the danger to their colleague. Their reaction was automatic. These men were used to acting fast. They didn't bother to disarm me; I was dragged to the rail and thrown straight over it.

Like the warships, this liburnian had outriggers. These structures extending out from the hull are standard on warships with banked oars, but normally unnecessary on monoremes. But if they expect combat, as—say—a pirate ship might, outriggers protect their oars from being raked and smashed by an enemy. At least it saved me from the drink. I fell into the outrigger but as I grabbed its upper rail, I lost my grip on my sword. It slipped through the gap next to the hull, and fell into the sea.

As I myself risked slipping between the brackets that supported the oarbox rails, the Illyrians decided to pull me back aboard before I could do damage. Knives were drawn; clinging to the fragile woodwork, I didn't fancy being sliced. As hands reached out, I let myself be pulled back in. I scrambled from the outrigger to the deckrail, then dropped back on board.

They would not kill me in full view of land. This time they roped me to the mast to keep me out of trouble. I calmed down. As my heartbeat steadied, I assessed the situation. It seemed clear from the way this ship was loaded and crewed that Cotys was planning a lengthy cruise.

"Where are you sailing to?" I croaked at a passing sailor.

His face split into a vicious grin. "We're going home, Falco!"

Hades. These bastards were carrying me off to Illyria.

L

Nobody on shore could have spotted my plight. Hopes of pursuit and rescue soon faded.

The liburnian galley was another craft I knew from a past adventure. Camillus Justinus and I had once commanded such a ship down a river in Germania Libera. A lad with well-placed friends, Justinus. One of his friends was a beautiful priestess in a German forest, the lost love he never talked about to his wife, Claudia. The priestess happened to have possession of a liburnian galley (which made her more useful than any lost loves of mine!) and she had let us borrow it . . .

This liburnian from Dyrrhachium had the classic lightness of her class, and she produced a good turn of speed. She was half decked, and with my limited experience I could tell she was sailing low in the water as if fully laden; who knew what illicit cargo lurked beneath the deck, though I made some guesses. They are nippy vessels, large enough to feel secure, but excellent for reconnaissance, river navigation—or piracy. On the high seas a liburnian can spurt out of nowhere, overhaul a heavily laden merchantman, and grapple to it before defensive action can be taken.

Soon we had sailed out of the harbor, passed the Tiber mouth, and turned south along the coast. It was a wonderful time for sailing, as afternoon sunlight sparkled on the blue waves below a cloudless summer sky. The gracious villas of the rich looked like toy houses all along the shore.

Once we were under way, I was released from the mast and brought forward to be sport for Cotys. He swaggered up, eyes bright with anticipation. His men stripped me of my cloak, sneering; it was a simple, functional garment which I wore for camouflage, not fashion. Judging by their exotic gear, they would all have preferred to capture playboys in fancy silks.

Cotys was ready to conduct the ritual humiliation. "So—what have we here? Your name again?"

"Falco."

"Slave or citizen?"

"Freeborn." There was a chorus of jeers. I was hardly free now.

"Oho—are you a man of three names?" Increasingly, I wanted to extract this joker's insides with the bilge pump.

"I am Marcus Didius Falco."

"Marcus Didius Falco—son of?" Cotys was ragging as enthusiastically as if he had done it many times before.

"Son of Marcus," I answered patiently.

"So, Marcus Didius Falco, son of Marcus—" The ritual phrases had a threatening ring. This was the rubric someone would carve upon my tombstone one day—if anybody ever found my corpse. "What's your tribe?"

I had had enough. "I really can't remember." I did know that pirates made a habit of hurling anti-Roman insults at their captives. Pirate insults feigned admiration of our social system—then led spitefully to drownings.

"Well, Marcus, son of Marcus, of the tribe you can't remember, tell me: why were you spying on my ship?"

"I came aboard following two sailors with a chest I thought I recognized."

"My cabin monkeys, bringing my sea-chest aboard." The response was instant. Cotys was lying. His voice dropped; it acquired more menace. The surrounding crew were enjoying themselves hugely. "What did you want with my sea-chest, Marcus?"

"I thought it contained the ransom for a man I am trying to trace. I wanted to discuss the situation with the people who say they are holding him."

"What man is this?" Cotys scoffed, as if it were news to him.

Informers hope to take the lead in questioning, but when your job entails invading places where you are unwelcome, you soon learn to let interrogations proceed the other way around. "His name is Diocles."

"Is he a spy too?"

"He is just a scribe. Do you have him?" I asked quietly. I had absolutely no hope that Diocles was aboard this ship—though he might have been here once.

"We do not." The declaration gave Cotys great satisfaction.

"Do you know who does?"

"Does *anyone* have him?"

"If you are asking that question, do you know that he is dead?"

"I know nothing about him, Falco."

"You knew enough to send his friends a ransom note."

"Not me." Cotys grinned. The way he spoke made me believe him this time.

"Ah! So you knew somebody else had sent the note? You then ambushed the money, stole it from under their noses—"

"Would I do that?"

"I think you're clever enough." He was certainly clever enough to know I was issuing compliments to soften him up. As he chortled at the flattery, I asked quickly, "So who sent the ransom note, Cotys?"

He shrugged. "I have no idea." He knew, all right. This man would steal from anyone—but he would want to be certain whose loot he was hijacking.

"Oh come! If you are going home to Illyria, what do you have to lose in telling me?" If he was going home, his partnership with the Cilicians must have broken up. So they could have issued the ransom note and Cotys treacherously took advantage. "I'm not official; my mission is a private one," I cajoled. "All I want is to find Diocles and rescue the poor sap. So, do the Cilicians have him?"

"You must ask them."

"I hope I have the chance!" I grinned, acknowledging that this depended on what Cotys did to me. He grinned back. I was not reassured. Hairs rose on the back of my neck. "Why have you brought me on your ship?"

"Someone is worried!" Cotys informed his leering crew. "Relax, Falco!" he then sneered. "We are just dipping the oars in the ocean on this fine afternoon, while we test out some mended leaks. It's a long journey back to our home country—but we have a funeral to attend before we sail. So we'll take you safely back to Portus, never fear. There was no need for your swordplay and screaming for help." I was careful not to ask whose funeral it was. Their countryman, Theopompus.

I had no faith in this promise of a safe return to land. If the crew once decided I had been watching them too closely, I was definitely done for.

I lost priority. Cotys turned away, to discuss some ship's business with a big, competent-looking man who seemed to be his sailing master. They checked over the side at intervals. A sailor asked Cotys something and glanced at me wickedly; further mischief was being planned. The sailor, a runt with a broken nose who looked as if he spent both voyages and shore leave fighting with all comers, disappeared down a half-ladder that led to the storage hold.

A few minutes later, the same sailor ran up on deck, carrying a swath of white material. Inwardly, I groaned. Cotys snapped back into taunting mode. "Look—a toga! Marcus, son of Marcus must wear his proper toga, lads!"

They hauled me to the middle of the deck. Forcing me to hold my arms out, they wrapped me tightly in the white cloth. It may have been a bedsheet; it felt like a shroud. They spun me around and around, as if hoping I would grow dizzy. "That's better. Now he looks the part." Cotys had grown hoarse with yelling derision. He came closer, his stubbly chin barely an inch from mine. "You're nervous again, Falco." It was a low growl. "I wonder—do you know this game my lads want to play?"

"Oh, I think I do, Cotys."

"I bet that's right. You look like a man who knows a lot—" This was a warning that Cotys was aware how clued up I was on his criminal role.

A bumboat boy ran up and placed a wreath on my head, amid delighted whoops from the others. The chaplet was several days old, a relic of some party, its fragile leaves now desiccated and scratchy. "A crown for a hero—hail, Falco! Acknowledge our homage, acknowledge—"

I forced myself to salute them.

"You are fortunate." Cotys aimed his final dart. "You have fallen among men of honor. We know of your privileges as a Roman citizen. Appeal to the Emperor. Is that right, Marcus, son of Marcus?"

I nodded wearily.

There was mock applause as I was pushed and pulled toward the liburnian's guardrail. Knowing what was coming, I tried to resist. It was useless.

"Don't think badly of us, Falco," Cotys instructed. This man just loved play-acting for his disreputable crew. "Far be it from us to hold a Roman prisoner." He gestured to the head of a rope ladder which one of his men had just hung overboard at the rear of the ship. I had heard of this trick. I knew the rest. "You are free to go, Falco. There is your road home—take it."

I looked overboard. The ladder ended two feet from the water. It was swinging about madly. Slowly, I climbed up onto the guardrail and pre-pared to descend. A burst of laughter greeted my reluctant move. Clinging to a rope, I remained upright on the rail. The wooden top was wet and slippery. The fine goatshair rope I had gripped cut into my hand. As the ship surged forward, every wave threatened to upend me.

Once I started down the ladder, my fate was certain. I would be flung off it, either by accident or with assistance from the crew. Far out in the open ocean, where the famous Tyrrhenian currents raced, even a good swimmer would stand little chance. And I could not swim at all.

LI

Seamen began to flick at me with ropes. At least the mock toga in which they had wrapped me protected me from the lashing. I climbed onto the ladder.

"That's right—down you go!" Cotys grinned.

Feeling for the sagging rungs, I lowered myself glumly. I could see a couple of fishing smacks, a long way from us. The shore looked far off too. We were in one of the Mediterranean's busiest shipping lanes—on the only afternoon that the route into Portus appeared to be empty.

Above, I heard the rowers return to their stations; they were given a new order. The ship took up its course again. I was so close to the oars that as they dipped and rose they splashed me. Something was done to the mainsail. I clung on desperately as we turned out to sea on a long tack against the current, leaving the coast even farther behind us, then I swung madly as we maneuvered again. The rowers were working hard. Every time the steering rudder swung around to change direction, the ladder bucked outward or bounced me against the hull; each time it was harder to avoid being thrown off.

I managed to shed the mock toga. I pulled off the battered wreath and dropped it. A seaman, watching me from the rail above, cackled with laughter. I might still be a fool in the eyes of the crew, but I felt better.

I was alive. So long as I clung on, there was still a chance for me. Still, I was helpless on a rope ladder, inches from the rising oars, on a ship sailed by professional kidnappers who knew I had uncovered their trade. Returning me to land was a lost promise. I knew too much about their activities and I had nothing to bargain with. They might be ignoring me at present, but I was nowhere near safe.

I was still reviewing and discarding action plans when a new disaster struck. Above me on deck the crew were busy. The sailing master was still passing to and fro inspecting the hull; occasionally I saw his head as he looked over. Cotys had disappeared.

Cotys must have gone to investigate the stolen money chest. I heard a roar—a yell of utter fury. Commotion broke out on deck. The rowers ceased their efforts and must have left their seats; the oars hung idle. The ship staggered and lost her momentum. *"This is a box of rocks!"*

Now Cotys leaned over the rail above me, shouting. In one hand I glimpsed big gold coins. In the other were pebbles, which he hurled at me. I ducked. One or two stung me. Seamen were crowding the rail; there must have been over forty in the crew that afternoon and most of them had left their posts to harangue me.

"You did this! You cheated me—"

"I had nothing to do with it—"

No use. Cotys wanted a culprit. "Anacrites!" I bawled at Cotys. This was typical of the Chief Spy and his staff: even when he was away, Anacrites' cashiers had automatically worked a fiddle. Knowingly or not, Holconius and Mutatus had become party to a classic scam. The ransom chest must have had coins in the top layer to look good—but it was mainly loaded with stones. This scam usually failed; criminals know to check a payoff thoroughly. But if one group of pirates is stealing from another in a hurry, they might omit this precaution.

"Cotys, the money was issued by the Chief Spy's office. He always plays dirty—"

Cotys knew nothing of Anacrites. "You did it!" he shouted. "This is the end of you, Falco!"

The crew were all yelling abuse. Someone began shaking a boathook, though I was too low down for them to reach. Cotys disappeared again for a moment—then he was back with an ax. He was so angry he was willing to sacrifice a decent ladder just to dispatch me. He slashed at the ladder. Like all sailors, he knew how to cleave a rope in a crisis. One side gave way. As I swung and crashed against the hull, I cried out for him to stop. He sawed through the other rope. I fell.

I had just time to hope that some passing dolphin who liked to play with Roman boys would swim up and save my life.

Then I took a last breath, flailed madly amid the tangled ladder rungs, and sank beneath the deep, cold waves.

LII

*D**on't fall in any water . . .*

Helena had known almost since I met her that I could not swim. She had once saved me from tumbling into the River Rhodanus, after which it had been her personal mission to prevent me from drowning. She had tried to teach me how to stay afloat. *Hold your breath and just lie back; you will float on the water. Have faith, Marcus—*

I went down. I came up. I held my breath and looked up at the sky. Water rushed over my face and I sank straight back down under.

I was trapped in ladder rungs. I was being dragged beneath the water by their weight. Stupidly, I was still holding on. I let go my grip and fought to free myself. Terror almost overwhelmed me.

I broke loose. Suddenly lighter, I knew I was free. *Don't panic; just keep still . . .*

I came up and hit the surface. Warm sun lit my face. Coughing, I nearly sank again. *On your back, Marcus; you're quite safe . . .* I kept still. I took a breath and did not sink.

Fine. Thank you, lady.

The Illyrian ship was sailing fast away from me on the northbound coastal current. The shoreline was so far away it was virtually out of sight. I had been battered and tormented, then thrown into the ocean. I was floating, but when I tried to move, I floundered. I had swallowed seawater. I knew I would be cold and exhausted all too soon. I felt sick. Cramp was moments away. There were no friendly dolphins wanting to rescue me, though I knew there would be sharks. Neptune and Amphitrite might have invited me to dinner, but they must have gamboled off with their hippocamps to elsewhere in their salty domain.

Nobody knew I had even left Portus. Now here I was, all alone in the middle of the Tyrrhenian Sea.

In despair, I struggled to point myself shorewards. Then I saw a fishing smack.

The small boat was motionless with its spritsail furled, not too far from me. Nobody was visible. I tried calling for help, with no result. Slowly, I tried paddling and at last, after ages of effort, I struggled right alongside the bobbing boat. It was too soon to start feeling proud of myself. It was too soon for relief. As I called out and made my presence felt, someone at last reacted. He was very displeased to see me. In fact, as I tried to grab a rope and appeal for help to come aboard the craft, he abruptly stood up above me. In horror I saw him raise an oar, about to crash it on my head with sure intent to kill me.

I kicked off from his damned boat. I would have cursed him but there was no time and I went under the water again. The man I had seen was wide, sturdy, in his sixties, and with wild gray curly hair. Although I only glimpsed a blurred outline through the water in my eyes, I knew him. I tried to shout his name but swallowed a pint of sea instead.

It was too late. I was drowning now.

Then I blundered into something which nearly took my ear off, and heard a cry of "Grab the bloody oar!" After which that familiar voice said with casual irritation, "I've given birth to an idiot—"

So I grabbed the oar and gasped with my usual filial respect, "Shut up and pull me out, before I die here, Pa!"

LIII

Nice of you to drop in, Marcus. What are you doing, fannying about here all on your own, half dead?"

Half dead was right. I was lying barefoot in the bottom of his boat, completely collapsed. I could not even thank Geminus for the welcome. Someone thumped me between the shoulder blades. I threw up a lot of seawater.

"Gods, nothing changes with this boy—he was just the same at three months old—oops, there he goes again! Let's try and aim him over the side next time . . ."

Someone else was in the boat.

With a lot of concentration, as other people hauled me upright, I managed to squirm around enough to be seasick over the rail as requested. Applause greeted this feat of willpower. I lay with my face on the rail, shivering uncontrollably. "Take me home, Pa."

"We will, son."

Nothing happened. The fishing boat continued to bob gently where it was. I was aware that Geminus was taking his ease, completely unconcerned. Eventually, I managed to squint around enough to see his companion: Gornia, Pa's warehouse assistant. Beside him, my belt had been looped around a spar and my boots upended on the rowlocks to drain. Both Pa and Gornia were wearing hats. They had draped a tiny piece of sacking to provide shade for me. The August sun sparkled off the ocean, its light implacable and dazzling.

I could not face the major issue of why my father just happened to be drifting about the Tyrrhenian Sea. So I lost myself in wondering why Gornia, who ought to be supervising the warehouse back at the Saepta Julia in Rome, was instead sitting with my father in the same ridiculous boat. The answer was beyond me. Gornia, a little old chap who had spent many years with my father, just sat there and grinned at me with almost toothless gums. I did not waste effort on an appeal to him. He always let Pa take the lead in conversation, and Pa was a master of holding back essential facts. Gornia could have worked at some respectable establishment, where the pay would have been as scanty and the hours as long, but he gave the strange impression he enjoyed the thrills at the Geminus cavern of mysteries.

"Take me home, *please,* Pa!"

"All in good time, boy."

Nothing had changed. I could have been five years old again, overtired and overfed with honeyed dates, at some long-winded auctioneers' party to which Pa had been told to take me to get me out from under Mother's feet for a few hours.

With two young children of my own, I knew all too well how to respond: "I want to go home *now!*"

"Not yet, son."

I gave up. Maybe I had really drowned and this was a nightmare in Hades. "Pa, is it too much to ask—exactly what are you doing here?"

"Just a quiet fishing trip, Marcus."

"Sharks?" I snarled, thinking of Uncle Fulvius. I could see a couple of lines dangling overboard, though neither Pa nor Gornia was paying them any attention. I could not remember my father going fishing before, ever. He was a grilled-pork man. Or as we used to joke, roast peacock, if ever he could impose himself on a dinner party where the host served such a luxury to spongers. Since nothing would ever happen until my annoying parent decided he was ready, I roused myself a little and struggled out of my wet tunic. Gornia kindly spread it out to dry.

Pa gave me a flask of water. After tentatively sipping, I recovered enough to ask if he knew where exactly Fulvius had spent his exile after he missed that ship to Pessinus.

Pa looked surprised, but answered, "Some dump called Salonae."

"Where's that?" Pa shrugged. I prodded, "Is it in Illyria?"

"Well . . ." He had known all along. "I think it's more north."

I did not believe him. "Not Dyrrhachium?"

"I told you, Salonae."

"What was Fulvius doing there?"

"Bit of this, bit of that."

"Don't wriggle. This could be serious." I had some more water. "Bit of what, Pa?"

"Serious, how?"

"Uncle Fulvius could soon be arrested—"

"For what?" Pa seemed alarmed.

"Piracy."

"You are joking, son!"

"No. What has he been doing in Illyria, do you know?"

"Just buying and selling." That would give Fulvius an appeal to Pa; anyone in commerce overseas was a potential contact. Before I could ask, selling what, my father volunteered, "He was a supplier to the Ravenna Fleet. A negotiator."

"Negotiator covers a whole range of business—legitimate or otherwise."

"You look as if you're going to be sick again, lad," said Pa earnestly.

"Don't distract me. I'll be fine if you ever row me back to land. I'm wet and I'm cold, and I've had a bad experience. If you hadn't turned up, I would have drowned. I am grateful, believe me, I am very grateful— but why can't we go? For heavens' sake, I'll buy you some damned fish. I'll get you a whole bloody swordfish and let you say you caught it yourself, Pa—"

Pa let me rant. When I stopped, he just said peacefully, "We can't go yet."

I looked at Gornia. The emaciated porter just grinned. Both he and my father seemed strangely at home out here.

"Whose boat is this?" I demanded suspiciously.

"Mine," said Pa. That was news. It was an old boat. How long had my father had a boat?

"Where do you keep it—and what is it for?" Pa just smiled at me. I tried again: "Do you often row out as far as this, and just sit whistling under the sky?"

"Very health-giving."

"Very dubious, Pa." Gornia thought this was so witty he chuckled. Well, that was a first. He too seemed quite content to stay here forever, doing nothing. I stood up, managed not to faint, and grasped a long rowing oar. In theory I could handle small boats, though I was not as adept as Petronius. "If you don't tell me what we're waiting for, I'm going to scull us ashore myself, Pa."

My father didn't bother to get up and grab the oar; he knew three strokes would finish me. "We are waiting for a catch, Marcus. All that's bitten so far is yourself—a delightful surprise, don't get me wrong—but Helena won't thank me if I grill you for supper . . . Sit down and stop playing up. If you're hungry you can have my lunch."

"He looks as if he'll chuck up again." For once, Gornia was moved to comment. He was worried that if I took after Pa, I would eat his share. Still, it looked a large hamper.

I worked things out. They had done this before. More times than I would like to know. Of course they were not fishing; they had an assignation. I could guess what for. Pa was expecting some international trader to drop goods overboard to him. He would take the booty ashore in secret, without paying import duty. I could hardly complain, since he had rescued me, but I now understood why he had been prepared to bash anyone who tried to climb aboard.

I was furious. My father was smuggling works of art—and if the vigiles or customs apprehended him today, I would be arrested too. I explained how inconvenient this would be to a man of my superior equestrian status—and Pa told me where to stuff my gold ring. "You'll get caught, Pa."

"I don't see why," my father assured me in a bland tone. "I never have before."

"Just how long have you been doing this?"

"About thirty years."

"It can't be worth it—"

"It bloody is!"

"What's import duty—two, two and a half percent? All right, so you have to add one percent auction tax but you make your clients pay that—"

"Duty on some luxuries is twenty-five percent," intoned Pa, and let me absorb why such a swingeing tax made sitting in this boat worthwhile.

"It gives me a good feeling," my father chortled eventually, "every time your sister Junia inflicts that fart-arse husband of hers on me!"

"Oh, if we're cheating Gaius Baebius, well done!" I slumped down in the boat and prepared for more punishment.

For the next few hours I shivered and was seasick and acquired vicious sunburn, until I wished I had waited much more patiently for a chance to hitch a lift ashore with a dolphin.

Finally the expected ship approached, a flag was dipped, Pa and Gornia leapt to their feet, waved cheerfully, and when the vessel hove to, they sprang into action as various oddly shaped, heavy packages were lowered in rope cradles. I stayed where I was, pretending to be comatose. My two companions caught the bundles expertly and stowed them, working at speed, filling this fishing smack and the little jollyboat which it towed behind. Gornia, who had once seemed a complete townie, clambered between the boats with unexpected agility. Even Pa, as he began trimming up the sail, looked like some old whelk who had lived in a fishing village all his life. Gornia manned an oar with all the aptitude of a ferryman.

The merchant ship had moved off again, and at last we were heading shorewards. I dragged my salt-stiffened tunic back on over my head.

"Where will you land, Pa? I can't face a long trip back to Ostia."

"No need, son. Soon be all over—you'll be tucked up in a cozy bed with some hot spiced wine to lull you off . . . We'll look after you." I gazed at him. A new secret was about to break. Some hideous revelation that I would feel obliged to keep at all costs from my mother. "I have my own villa," Pa meekly informed me.

Well, of course; he would. Stuffed with art galleries full of Greek stat-ues. Paid for by contraband. "You should let him show you his collection, Marcus," Gornia confirmed enthusiastically. Pa looked shifty.

A thought struck as I glared at him. "Fulvius acquires stuff for you—has he been a long-term supplier?"

"Don't tell your mother." Ma would strangle Fulvius.

"How astute! You two have been contacts for years?"

Pa nodded. That meant, if Uncle Fulvius was in league with modern pirates, so was Pa. I closed my eyes in despair.

"Nearly there," my father soothed me. "This has been a wonderful treat for me. Sea and sun. A happy day out in a fishing boat, with my boy . . ."

It was dusk when we arrived at his villa. It was as luxurious as I expected. I tried not to look.

There was no shortage of slaves. A messenger was sent to Helena.

"You might have consulted me. What did you say, Pa?"

"Nothing to worry about, darling—gone fishing with Geminus." Oh great. I tried to think of other things. "Isn't this villa close to Damagoras?"

"He's just up the coast. Is it true he's banged up?" Pa wheedled.

"Jailed in a vigiles cell."

"Is that a nice way to treat an elderly man?"

"No, but the vigiles are heartless—so watch out! What do you know about Damagoras?"

"We don't mingle," uttered Pa. "I hold my soirées at my place in Rome; I keep myself to myself here. Lot of interlopers—you never know what class of person you might find you're dealing with."

I said I could well see that a smuggler would not want to mix in with a pirate chief—and that was when I went to bed.

The bed was as comfortable as promised, and I slept as soundly as any man who had been tormented and thrown into the sea to drown, before he endured ghastly family revelations and drank a lot of wine to blot out a horrendous day.

☆　　☆　　☆

A night's recovery time was all I needed. I was anxious to be on my way. I slept in longer than I meant, but still found the breakfast buffet (served by yet more slaves) before Pa put in an appearance. Gornia, an anxious type, was already up and packing a discreetly covered wagon. He took me up to Ostia. He dropped me close to my apartment, then drove on toward Rome. I walked swiftly home, only to find a note written on the back of the one Pa had sent Helena yesterday. *Dear skiver, If you turn up, have gone to funeral. Necropolis at Rome Gate. I trust you caught a big one. HJ*

I washed in cold water, changed into new clothing and my second-best boots, tried and failed to put a comb through my salted curls, then stood for a second beside Favonia's crib. My family were absent, but it helped me reconnect with them.

I detoured via Privatus' house. My children were there, being looked after; I did not disturb them. Young Marius and Cloelia were in the peri-style garden; they had discovered how to fiddle with the Dionysus statue's waterworks. The wine god now performed a huge, arching pee at which they fell about in fits of giggles. Then they looked up, saw me, and threw themselves upon me with delight. Nux and Marius' young dog Argos, who were sleeping in a patch of shade, looked up, wagged lazy tails, and went back to sleeping.

"Uncle Marcus! Everyone has been searching for you."

"I'm in trouble, then."

"Well, if they kill you at the funeral," Cloelia consoled me, "that will be convenient. Would you like red roses or white ones on your bier?"

"You choose for me."

"The double ones are my favorites."

"I lost my sword," I told Marius. "Does Petronius have a spare here?" My nephew was not supposed to know, but he did and he fetched it for me straightaway. It was a basic weapon in a plain scabbard, but sat in the hand well and was perfectly sharpened. Buckling it on, in the familiar high military position under my right armpit, I felt better at once. "Thanks, Marius. Kiss the girls for me."

"We'll be their guardians," Cloelia assured me in her solemn way, "if Mother and Aunt Helena make you fall on the sword." While Marius was fetching the sword she too had scampered off, to return with Petro's second-best toga so that at the funeral I could be properly clad, with my head veiled in its capacious folds.

Nice children. I decided not to mention that their great-uncle was a pirate's associate and that their grandfather smuggled art.

LIV

Marcus Rubella may have tried to prevent the funeral of Theopompus from becoming a wild party on a beach; what he had achieved was a wild party at a necropolis. Since Rhodope had chosen to give her lover his send-off at the Rome Gate, this was about as public as it could be. When I arrived, the event had been in full flow since sunrise, and its fervor showed no sign of abating. Everyone who passed by on the main road to and from Ostia must have been aware of it. Rubella looked glum as he supervised a group of vigiles, who were attempting to divert the crowds.

"No entry!"

"You tell them, son."

With a cheery wave to the tribune, I eased in past his traffic controls. Aiming for the noise, I made my way between the rows of columbaria. The necropolis was laid out like a small town of miniature houses for the dead. They were solidly brick-built, many with pitched roofs. Some had their doors standing open; most had a main room, with niches all around the walls at two levels, for receiving urns. One wide, travertine paved street ran parallel to the main road from Rome; it was full of people, all heading for the Theopompus send-off.

"Stop right there!" A fist hit my chest. "Is that *my* toga?"

"Oh, damn. I thought I hid that blob of sauce you copped last time you wore it."

Petronius Longus was a sharp-eyed bastard—and he was growling. "That toga was clean when you filched it, Falco. I can see it's mine, not the hairy affair you normally trip over." My own toga, which I had left in Rome, had been inherited from my brother Festus, who had favored a luxurious nap and an exceedingly long hem. I had never yet had it altered because I hated wearing it.

This one was too long for me as well; Petronius Longus is half a head taller. I draped a fold of the borrowed garment over my lugged curls. This created a sad parody of a devout man going to a sacrifice, but I pulled a long face and used mincing steps for extra effect. Petro whistled flirtatiously. "Stop sounding like a brickie on a scaffold, Petro—I need to be disguised."

"Hiding from Helena? So where in Hades have you been? I had to give the whole port a going-over for you yesterday—then some mad message came."

"Pa on good form—" I did not give him away. "How is Helena?"

"Apart from furious?"

"I'm innocent. If the harbormaster had done his job, he would have seen me being stolen away by a cutthroat gang of Illyrians."

"The ones who are here today?" Petronius perked up and attached himself to me. "Oh fun! Will they be angry you've escaped? I'll come and watch."

He poked my toga, felt the sword, then showed me the pommel of the one he carried beneath his cloak. I admitted that I had borrowed his own spare. "Mine is at the bottom of the sea. I wish I hadn't wasted effort polishing it first."

"Lucky it wasn't you who fell in."

I grinned weakly.

The funeral was taking place in the middle of the wide road, which at that point was packed with people. The ceremony was getting under way, but it looked as if nothing much had been happening for several hours. Mourners who knew one another were sitting around in groups trying to remember the name of that fat man who got very drunk the last time they went to a funeral. People who knew nobody were stretching their stiff limbs and looking bored.

There was no sign of the grief-stricken girl's father, but his money was well in evidence. That poor hound Posidonius must have paid for everything, starting with an enormous pyre, tended by half the funeral directors in Ostia, with a full Roman entourage—an orchestra, massed ranks of hired mourners, and religious celebrants. The very best in white mourning wear had been lavished on Rhodope, plus a mighty great feast for all comers. Hangers-on who had never met Theopompus were greedily tucking in.

The procession had ground to a halt; Posidonius presumably did not own a tomb at Ostia so the cremation was taking place in the middle of the roadway. A cinerary urn, in the kind of Greek black-figure my father imported, was ready on a stand. Pa knew Posidonius; I wondered if the ancient art had come off a ship near the Laurentine coast just yesterday. The corpse was still lying on its flowery bier. This looked a bit lopsided; one leg of the bier was being discreetly leveled up by attendants poking stones underneath it. Florists and garland-twisters had had a happy time, but the perfumiers would walk away with the crowns for best effort. We could smell the exotic oils from thirty strides away.

Theopompus, last seen half naked and barefoot, had now been dressed up like a barbarian king. He would have loved the finery. Skillful work had been done on his bruises too. I thought the face paint effect was a little too much, and Petronius criticized his barber. Petro was a stickler for classical straight bangs. The undertakers had puffed up Theopompus' luxurious haircut and given him a radiant crown of locks. "Very Greek!" said Petronius. By which he meant . . . what Romans mean by very Greek.

We were still admiring the embalmer's art when our womenfolk found us. Helena was flanked by Maia and Albia; they approached me like a trio of Furies who had premenstrual headaches and some unpaid bills to query.

"Anything to say?" demanded Maia, keen to see me squirm. Helena Justina, tightly wrapped in a heavy stole, said nothing. Albia looked scared to death.

"It was not my fault."

"It never is, brother!"

I strode past my sister and clutched Helena in my arms. She could see my wrecked hair under its formal veiling and she felt me flinch as the sunburn hurt. She knew something bad had happened. I just held her. She buried her face in the shoulder folds of Petro's toga, shaking. I could have buckled and wept myself, but people might have thought I was upset over Theopompus.

Maia had been watching us; with her head on one side. She put her arms around both of us briefly, pulled back my veiling, and kissed my cheek. She had had troubles in her life; seeing other people with stretched emotions made her gruff. She took Albia to see the torches being lit to burn the bier.

Petronius stayed with us, his eyes raking the funeral guests for known faces. To bolster myself, I began telling him quickly all that had happened yesterday after he left me at Portus. With her head on my shoulder, Helena listened. I got as far as being hijacked on the ship, trying to minimize talk of drowning. "Then it turned out that Cotys had the chest with the scribes' ransom money; it must be the Illyrians who carried out the raid at the ferry—"

"I'd like to arrest this Cotys, if he shows," grumbled Petro. "Bloody Rubella has ordered that unless it becomes unavoidable, we are to avoid confrontations."

"Can't we *make* it unavoidable? Is Rubella obeying religious scruple or political diplomacy?"

"There's just too damned many of them, Falco. We've got Illyrians here—plus the Cilicians too." I raised an eyebrow. He explained tersely, "We reckon they have been working the kidnaps together—an alliance."

"Blood brothers? So who," I asked, lowering my voice slightly, "is current favorite for killing Theopompus?"

"Fifty-fifty bets."

"And what about the ransom attempt? There must have been plenty of witnesses when the ferry was raided."

Petronius scowled. "Yes—and all anyone will say is that the raiders were exotically dressed."

"Cotys and the Illyrians."

"Yes, but did they send the ransom demand? Or," said Petro, "do they just know who the real kidnappers are?"

"Assuming Diocles actually was kidnapped."

I mopped Helena's wet face on a corner of my toga. With Petro's stern eye on me, I checked nervously in case coloring came off on his precious garment, but she was bare of makeup. As the stole fell back I saw too that her hair was loose; she had put on no earrings or necklaces either. It was appropriate to disregard your appearance at a funeral. Even so, I felt that lump in the throat again.

"I'd better confess, love—I've been in the sea."

"Marcus, I told you not to fall in water."

"I didn't fall; I was slung off the Illyrians' ship. But I followed your instructions about lying with my toes turned up and looking at the sky." I held her tighter. "Thank you, sweetheart."

"You must be a better pupil than I thought—" I was a better pupil than *I* had thought. "How," asked Helena pointedly, "did your father come into this?"

Petronius was also looking at me skeptically. Anything that involved Geminus must involve a scam; still, investigating my dear father would be more trouble than it was worth.

"Pa was fishing."

"Catch anything?" asked Petro in a dour tone.

"Just me."

"I'm surprised the old scamp didn't throw you back."

I suppressed a sudden vision of Geminus with that oar raised up to crack down on my head.

Maia came back with Albia. My sister said she had had enough and was going home. She hated funerals. It might have something to do with losing her husband when he was abroad, and her guilt at not being able to attend his send-off. I never liked to stress how little of Famia had remained to be given a send-off; the lion who dispatched him had not been a picky eater.

★   ★   ★

Helena had been sent a personal invitation by Rhodope, though so far she had been unable to speak to the girl. We went and found her, in a glittering white mourning gown and veil (and several gold necklaces), installed on a thronelike chair on a low plinth, among a large group of dark, thin women who were presumably Illyrian. They had created a bower with a corona of modest curtains, then they stuck the girl in it by herself. This gave the impression that Rhodope was a valued member of their clan—yet they were all talking to one another, while she sat alone in misery. She made a pitiful widow, suspiciously like a prisoner.

Helena firmly trod a path between the women, who were mostly sitting cross-legged on the ground. They looked hostile, but whenever she stepped on a hand or crushed a skirt, she bestowed a sweet patrician smile on the victim. Every inch a senator's daughter, Helena Justina was bringing condolences and patronage without questioning whether she was welcome. Trampling on provincials seemed to be her heritage.

I knew she was angry on behalf of the bereaved young girl. Whatever support the teenager lacked, Helena intended to offer it now. "Rhodope! This will be a hard day for you—but what a wonderful turnout. He must have been extremely popular. I hope it's some consolation for you."

The pale girl looked suspicious. Only Rhodope had her large sad eyes fixed on the bier. Everyone else here was using the funeral as an excuse for a party. With free food and music, none of them spared a thought for Posidonius, being fleeced yet again, and few seemed to care much for seeing off Theopompus to the afterlife either.

It was a segregated event. Women stayed together; so did men. Different groups of men clustered separately from each other. The formal Roman undertakers were going about their business, more or less unnoticed, while among the knots of seafarers foreign musicians played exotic instruments, oblivious to the mournful Roman flutes that were supposed to signal high spots in the ceremony. From private cooking fires, scents of roast meat and fish mingled with the incense. The overall effect was completely disorganized. It also had the feel of a party that would last for the next three days.

A veiled man barged past me, his hairy arms holding a portable altar high on his shoulder. Acolytes scurried after him, towing a sheep and bringing implements for sacrifice. There were whoops from the rough element, who were eyeing up the sheep as potential spit-fodder.

Since nobody else wanted Rhodope's attention, Helena was able to stay there and talk. While she introduced Albia, I stopped with them. After Maia left, Petronius had mooched off to inspect the mourners. As the only male in this group, I was out of place—but it was nowhere near so dangerous for me as joining angry men with sea-knives in their cummerbunds.

The pyre was struggling to light. I could see the priest's lips moving as he cursed under his breath.

"What will you do next?" Helena asked Rhodope quietly.

"I am going to Illyria with his people."

"Is that a good idea? Joining them along with Theopompus would have been different. Without him, will you be welcomed?"

"Oh yes. They are my friends for his sake." A couple of gap-toothed old women looked up and smiled vaguely. They might not be talking to Rhodope, but they were definitely listening.

Helena let the subject drop. It was Albia, herself the child of loneliness and suffering, who burst out irritably, "You are being foolish. Life will be hard and you will be a stranger. They will make you marry some man who will be cruel to you. You will be a drudge."

Rhodope shot her a displeased look. In different circumstances the two young girls could have made friends. "You know nothing about it!"

"I know more than you think!" retorted Albia. I met Helena's eyes as the two teenagers argued; she looked proud of Albia, who now said flatly, "I have lived without a family, among very poor people."

"They are not poor!" flashed Rhodope. "Look at these women—see how they are dressed." It was true that they were richly adorned: among their crimson, blue, and purple robes, chain necklaces were draped in clusters, rows of bangles lined their thin arms, anklets and earrings twinkled with gold disks and spindles.

Sure of her victory, Albia proclaimed, "There burns your man. Your hopes are flying up to the heavens in the smoke. Sit and weep for him. Helena Justina will comfort you." Albia gathered her skirts in one hand and began to pick her way disdainfully between the seated Illyrian women. As if emphasizing their lack of interest in Rhodope, she offered, "I will go and fetch food and wine for you."

"They are hung with gold!" insisted Rhodope, almost beseechingly.

Albia turned back. She was a few years younger than Rhodope, yet visibly more sensible. Perhaps she realized that Rhodope's father must have allowed her uncontrolled shopping throughout her short life. "Gold," Albia commented drily, "which they are not allowed to spend, I think."

LV

When the trouble began, it happened unexpectedly.

The sheep had had its throat cut, which caused unusually loud applause. The priest barely had time to drop the entrails in a dish before unexpected assistants snatched the carcass and had it slow-roasting. The pyre had now been lit, though it was not drawing well. As the smoky flames began to flicker around the corpse, close male relations of Theopompus should have been giving his eulogy, but none of the Illyrians stepped forward for that role. Still, we all knew he had been a flashy dresser who drove too fast. Rhodope would probably give him a huge memorial stone later, extolling virtues his colleagues had never noticed. Despite her conviction that she was among friends, I thought few would linger until she inaugurated the stone.

The flames began to crackle around the flower-decked bier at last. I saw Albia boldly seeking refreshments for Rhodope as she had promised. She had pushed her way past nearby groups who were cooking up their own cauldrons and approached a grand feast set out on a temporary table, the official catering provided by Posidonius. She helped herself to a bowl and a goblet, waiting for a turn with the food and drink. Picnics with the dead at the necropolis were standard. This was just being done on a huge scale. There was a disorganized buffet queue.

The caterer had sent slaves to empty the hampers and lay out the delicacies neatly, but the nervous waiters looked overwhelmed as Illyrians and Cilicians started taking over. Women grabbed serving dishes; men leaned to snatch the best morsels, while holding out cups to be filled by overworked waiters. Albia refused to be ignored or barged aside.

Helena had her eye on our girl, and so did I. Albia was young and on her own there. It was no surprise that one of the men in seaboots was eyeing her up. As she turned back to us, he followed, not realizing Albia had a wild past. He made his move. Barely stopping in her tracks, she elbowed him away and flung the contents of the goblet she was carrying right in his face. Then, unperturbed, she brought the food bowl to Rhodope.

"Someone jogged me. I shall fetch you more wine—"

"I'll come with you!" Rhodope had seen what happened. She stood up in sudden solidarity. The little queen of the party now flushed with embarrassment and turned into a good hostess.

I was already removing the man, with stern advice he didn't want: "Let's not spoil the party. Suppose you get lost—"

"Wait, Falco!" Rhodope's voice rang out above the hired mourners' moans. Something had disturbed her. She seized one of the pyre-lighting torches and brandished it overhead. It was broad daylight, a blissful August day; she did not need to light the scene.

Albia, looking impressed by the theatrical stand, squared up beside her. Rhodope flung out her white-clad arm dramatically. *"Ask that man where he obtained his boots!"*

He tried to squirm out of sight. I grabbed his arm. He was a sallow, unshaven wretch with eyes that wandered off on their own somewhere when anyone looked at him. He wore a loose gray tunic and a rather good black belt, probably stolen. The boots to which Rhodope was pointing were soft tan-colored calfskin with red straps crisscrossed up the shins. They had bronze hooks and tiny bronze finials on the ends of the straps. I would not have been seen dead in them—but clearly this fabulous footwear was special to the stricken teenage girl.

The trouble had started.

Rhodope was too distressed to sustain her initial rage, but she could still manage drama. "I know those boots," she whispered in horror. "I bought those boots for Theopompus. He was wearing them when he was dragged away, the night he was taken from me. Whoever killed him must have stolen them . . ." She decided to faint. Albia was having none of it and hauled her back upright.

"He's a murderer!" squealed Albia. "Don't let him escape."

I was conscious that we were surrounded by a huge crowd, many of whom were this man's relatives. Slowly, people stood up, amid a wave of muttering.

Petronius Longus appeared at my side. Now they had two of us to attack. So far, they were holding back. Petro was larger than anyone else present. He was *much* larger than the man in the disputed boots, whom he now gripped with an arm up his back, lifting him by the neck of his tunic so his toes dangled. "Let's have the boots off him, Falco."

I removed the boots. It entailed dodging wild kicks until Petro made sure, very efficiently, that his captive stopped struggling. This was entertainment for the crowd, who saw we could be violent and began to revel in the scene. The man who had been wearing the fine bronze-toggled boots ended up white-faced and trembling; Petronius dandled him playfully.

Helena stepped forward, took the boots, and carried them to Rhodope. "Are you quite certain these are the boots you bought for Theopompus?"

As the center of attention, Rhodope revived. "Yes!" She tried fainting again, but again Albia dragged her upright, shaking her fiercely, like Nux with one of the children's rag puppets. Albia had a no-nonsense attitude to first aid. No slumping or whimpering would be allowed.

Petronius told the captive not to give him any trouble, or he would end up as ashes on the pyre. By now members of the vigiles had become aware of the problem and were filtering toward us through the mourners. Petronius turned to the assembled groups of sailors. Thrusting the captive in one direction then another, he cried harshly, "Which of you brought this boot-thief to Italy? Whose is he?"

Laughter came from Cratidas, surrounded by grinning Cilicians. Petro aimed the captive at him. He answered with his usual sneer: "Not ours."

Lygon, who was alongside in his flamboyant coat, also shook his head quickly. Then they jeered at another group, who must be Illyrians.

I pretended to watch the action, but I was searching the crowd. Eventually I found the man I was looking for: Cotys. I wanted to tackle him myself but there was too much opposition here.

Edging up to Rubella, I muttered, "Group over there by the food table: villain in the plum-juice cloak—can your boys take him?" The tribune appeared not to hear me. I had faith. Rubella himself strolled over to the buffet as if he wanted a fistful of skewered meat, nodding to one or two vigiles troopers as he made his way. He was fit and fearless; one thing you always had to say for Rubella was that when it came to action, he was utterly sound. A drunken innkeeper hit him once and said it was like punching masonry.

Cotys sensed trouble. But he was still drawing his knife when Rubella—one-handed—knocked him flat. Then the tribune stood on Cotys' knife arm, and calmly ate his skewered tidbits while he waited for the noise to settle down.

There was a hush. When a heavy ex-centurion stood on someone's wrist with his whole weight, everyone could sympathize—but certainly not try to help the man on the ground.

"This the one you want, Falco?" Rubella called conversationally, as if he had just picked out a flatfish at a fishmonger's. He cleaned his teeth with his little-finger nail. "Who is he, and what has the bastard done?"

I retrieved the boots from Helena. "He's Cotys, an arrogant Illyrian. He took me on a forced ride on his leaky liburnian, tried to drown me, and he stole my sword—for starters. These boots come into the story. Yesterday, I saw the man Petronius has arrested clomping around in them. He and another filthy character carried a chest aboard the ship. Cotys claimed it was his sea-chest but—you'll be interested in this, Tribune—it's the same one the two scribes brought to Ostia with their ransom for Diocles."

"Thanks. I like a clear indictment!" Rubella bared his teeth in what passed for a grin. Then he lifted his foot and pulled Cotys upright by the arm with one strong movement, a movement Rubella must have known was liable to dislocate the man's shoulder. Cotys yelled with pain. "Seems a bit soft," commented Rubella. The vigiles have simple rules. One is: always undermine gangster chiefs with insults when their men are watching. After my ordeal aboard the ship, that suited me.

"So—you raided the ferry yesterday and stole the chest, did you?" Rubella demanded.

"Nothing to do with me," whined Cotys.

"You sent the ransom note?"

"No! I told Falco—" This time he was truly indignant.

"How did you know about the money then?"

"A rumor at a brothel—a load of cash was to be exchanged at the Damson Flower."

"So you decided to lift it before it got there? Who were you double-crossing, Cotys? Your friends the Cilicians?" The Cilicians began muttering.

"We would never cheat an ally!" Cotys was not convincing them. The Cilicians howled and grew ready to turn nasty.

"Have *they* got Diocles?" I saw Rubella's eyes sum up the situation with the crowd. Mutual suspicion between the two national groups was simmering dangerously. The tribune sniffed. "Cotys, I'm arresting you for stealing Falco's sword. Let's have a discussion about the rest at my station house—Clear the way, people. Bring the barefoot wonder, Petro."

There was a flurry of white. "No—wait!" Once again, young Rhodope tried to intervene. She was still grasping the torch, its flames threatening to set fire to her flimsy dress. Helena and Albia rushed to dissuade her. "It cannot be right. This is Cotys—"

"Noted," snapped Rubella. He needed to get out of there. Looking as calm as possible, he began walking his prisoner through the crowds. Some of his men tried to link arms and make a clear corridor.

"No, no—Cotys was Theopompus' chief. Cotys," the girl wailed, "would *never* have had Theopompus killed!"

Rubella stopped. Cotys was still held in his brutal military grip. Whatever kind of centurion Rubella had been in the legions, it never entailed tucking up recruits in their campbeds with a gentle good-night lullaby. "Listen to that!" marveled Rubella to Cotys, inches from the pirate's face. "The little princess says you couldn't have done it—because you were the dead man's chief. Sweet, isn't it?" Then he about-faced the prisoner and set off, pushing Cotys ahead of him, fast. Over one shoulder, the tribune shouted, "Set her straight, Falco! Take her somewhere for a chat—look after her." He meant, get the girl away from the rest of the Illyrians urgently.

My task was tricky. Men I remembered from the liburnian were now surrounding Rhodope with clear intent. Petronius, alert, passed his own prisoner to a pair of vigiles and moved toward us. Even women were pushing forward, glaring openly at Rhodope. Quick-witted as ever, Helena and Albia tried to gather up the girl to rush her away.

She was in peril, though completely unaware of it. The Illyrians knew she could give evidence on being taken for ransom, perhaps naming names. She could identify the snatch-squad who took Theopompus the night he was killed. Theopompus might have told her all sorts of secrets. Even the Cilicians were beginning to realize the danger. The Illyrians, now leaderless, milled about uselessly, but Cratidas and Lygon exchanged a glance and headed straight for Rhodope. With drawn swords, Petro and I were already stepping in. *"Go, Helena!"*

Vigiles were at our sides—officially unarmed, yet suddenly equipped with staves and poles. We could have held up the Cilicians and the day could yet have been salvaged. But Rhodope, a bereaved teenager with huge emotions, had remembered that she was presiding over her lover's funeral.

Breaking free from Helena and Albia, she burst through our safety cordon. She shifted Lygon from her path by swiping him full in the eyes with her flaming torch. She dodged around Cratidas on nimble feet. Groups of women fell back, screaming. Men pulled up, bemused.

"I loved him!" shrieked Rhodope, as she scrambled to the pyre.

She knocked over the portable altar. She cursed the sacrificing priest as he cried out at the ruined augury. She barged through the scattering acolytes and slipped past the musicians (they had seen trouble at funerals many times and were nipping aside). The hired mourners were slowly circling around the pyre, which at last was burning up well, as they intoned and tore their hair. Rhodope pushed through them; she clearly intended to throw herself upon the burning bier.

An alert young flautist grabbed her by the waist. As the distraught girl tried to immolate herself, he seized her like a rather ham-fisted god grappling a reluctant nymph just before she turned into a tree. Rhodope's torch and his flute tumbled to the ground. She flailed in his arms; the youth, who was fat and clearly good-natured, dug his heels in and stuck with the tackle. Her hands grabbed for the flowered borders of the pyre. The flute-player kept pulling her. Rhodope struggled forward, desperately yanking at the expensive garlands. The lad hauled on her stalwartly, suddenly taking them both backwards at a run. Long snakes of plaited lilies and roses tore away from the bier and came with them. Then the bier tilted. Two legs on the pyre gave way; it upended. Garlands snapped. The bier fell back in place.

But first it had catapulted Theopompus upright—where he stayed on his feet, stiffly at attention. His dead body was outlined in the prettiest licking flames. His head, with its elaborate long hairstyle, was encircled in an enormous green halo of fire.

LVI

People scattered in hysteria. Petronius and I were running forward.

"Whatever pomade that corpse had—I want some!"

We collected up the sobbing girl, bringing the flautist for his own protection. With Helena and Albia at our heels, we raced from the funeral area. We passed a side turning, out of which stepped some vigiles. Petro shouted an order. They tackled our pursuers; though they were heavily outnumbered, it gave us space. We almost reached the end of the necropolis before heavy footsteps came pounding after us. "Quick, in here—" Petro pushed us all inside an open tomb and with his shoulder shoved the door closed. Five of us gasped a bit, then sat down on the floor in darkness.

I did a quick recount from memory. *Six* of us.

As we struggled for breath, I gasped quietly, "Lucius, my boy; that may be the most stupid thing you have ever done."

He was fired up to silliness: "Wonder who lives here?"

Helena Justina found my hand and held it. "And I thought *you* were irresponsible."

"What's your name, son?" murmured Petro to the flautist.

"Chaeron."

"Well, Chaeron lad, I'd just like to say, before we get hauled out, finely chopped, and turned into soup by a nasty gang of pirates—well done."

The flautist giggled.

Nobody tried the door. We could hear nothing from outside. Petro decided that meant they could not hear us either.

"Now, young Rhodope," he chivvied, firmly addressing the invisible cause of our discomfort, "we may be here some time. While we are stuck, I shall ask you some questions."

"I want to ask one." Rhodope had spirit. Abandoning the hysterics, she reverted to her stubborn streak. "Was my Theopompus really killed by his own people?"

"Yes."

"Why?"

"Because—" Petronius could be very softhearted, with girls. "He fell in love with you. Cotys will have been annoyed that Theopompus had endangered the group."

"How? I loved him. I would never have given away any secrets."

Petronius did not know how to tell her that she had already done so. She was vulnerable and young; her father had been so desperate that he ignored instructions to keep quiet about the kidnap and went to the vigiles. Posidonius' name in the file at the station house led me to him, then to her. Rhodope led us to Theopompus. Theopompus led us to the Illyrians, who had not even been suspects until then. After months, if not years, the vigiles had a line on the kidnappers, Cotys was in custody, and more arrests would follow. It could have happened some other way, but Rhodope was still the only victim who had ever told us anything worthwhile.

From the kidnappers' point of view, the real blame lay with Theopompus for seducing the girl. From that moment, the clever ransom scheme, which depended on terror and silence, had begun to unravel. He told Rhodope his name. Then, for whatever reason, he eloped with her. His colleagues knew who deserved retribution.

I wondered why Rhodope had been left alive. They could have killed her at the same time as her lover. They were too scared of the outcry, perhaps.

I no longer thought the Illyrians had ordered Theopompus to fetch the girl from Rome. Had they wanted to stop her talking, she would be dead on the salt marsh too. He must have gone after her on his own account. The pleasant deduction was that he genuinely loved her and could not bear to part from her. The cynical, most likely, reason was that he could not bear to part from her father and his money. Theopompus saw that if he held on to Rhodope he could extract ever more from Posidonius. If he was taking the proceeds not for the group but for himself, *that* could well have made his cronies turn on him. By acting alone, he made himself an outcast. Theopompus had signed his own death warrant.

I had feared that Rhodope came to be seen as dangerous when I mentioned her to Damagoras. But at that time I thought Theopompus was a Cilician, working with Lygon and killed by the group led by Cratidas. Probably my talk with Damagoras had had nothing to do with the elopement or with Theopompus being killed. The Illyrians may never have heard about my visit to Damagoras. They took their own revenge.

Or maybe there had already been trouble brewing between the Cilicians and the Illyrians. I provided ammunition to the Cilicians. They complained about Theopompus to his own people; the Illyrians were forced to act, perhaps?

Either way, resentment then festered, and the Illyrians later stole the scribes' money chest—though it seemed likely to be the Cilicians who had sent the Diocles ransom demand. Maybe Cotys was annoyed at not being informed of the plan. Each side now saw the other as faithless—all because of my missing scribe.

I wondered how he would feel about all this. I had always thought Diocles enjoyed seeing trouble in action and would not be averse to causing some.

None of it brought me any closer to finding him.

The unlit chamber was growing hotter. Already the air within was stale. These tombs were built solidly, as I had earlier noticed. It was never intended that anyone living should be inside with the door closed. Breathing had not been allowed for.

I had ended up with my back against the door. Now I tried to move it. It was solidly jammed. I commented to Petro that the doors of tombs are not meant to be opened from inside.

"I'm frightened." That was Rhodope.

"I'm sure we are all a little nervous." Helena was aware of the danger of letting the girls become hysterical. I was tense myself. "At least we are all together. Lucius, is anybody likely to come and let us out?"

"Don't worry."

"No, of course; you will get us all to safety." Only someone who knew Helena well would detect her faint note of sarcasm. Not one to dwell on a situation she could not control, she then said, "Now Rhodope; you have seen the truth, I hope. Theopompus was madly in love with you, but his people take a different view. You cannot go and live with them—"

"But I said that I would!"

"Forget it," I told her gently. I could hear Albia grinding her teeth at the other girl's lack of logic.

"Promises made under duress have no validity," Petronius assured Rhodope solemnly.

"It was my own choice . . ."

"You were shackled—by love." He had a ten-year-old daughter. He was a good father; he knew how to lie sincerely when it was for some young girl's own good.

"Isn't it time you told us, Rhodope, what happened when you were first kidnapped?" Helena then asked.

It took some coaxing. But with Helena's quiet pressure and shielded by the darkness, eventually Rhodope yielded. She told us how she had been snatched from the dockside at Portus, whisked away among a group of both men and women, then taken to Ostia; they had crossed the river— not on a ferry, but in some small boat of their own. A cloak was put around her so her face was hidden from others and she could not see where she was taken. They took her a long way away from the river, as far as she could tell.

"Do you think you were drugged while they had you?"

"No."

"Are you certain, Rhodope?"

"Yes. The Illyrians don't drug people." The girl sounded shy now; she knew she was giving away secrets. She was also sure of her facts: "Theopompus explained that the Cilicians work in a way his friends think is dangerous. They have a woman called Pullia, who knows about herbs."

"Yes, Pullia. She tests the herbs on herself . . . So you are sure that the Cilicians and Illyrians have both been involved in these kidnaps."

"Yes," agreed Rhodope in a small voice.

"They used to work together?"

"Yes."

"Do they—or did they—exchange information and share the profits?"

"I think so."

Helena worded it carefully: "So . . . if they don't use drugs, tell me sweetheart, how do the Illyrians keep their prisoners subdued? What happened to you, Rhodope?"

Now we could hear real panic as Rhodope muttered, "I—don't want to remember."

"Did something really bad happen?"

"No!" That came out very definite. Helena waited. "No," said Rhodope again. Then she sighed quietly. "That was the point. I was too frightened to do it. Theopompus intervened and said I didn't have to go there."

"Go where, Rhodope?"

"Into the pit."

"What pit?" demanded Petronius, shocked. Like me, he had been expecting her to say she had been subjected to some physical abuse. Unpleasant—but straightforward in its way.

"I don't know. It was somewhere . . . I could smell incense. I remembered that today, at the funeral . . ." We heard her voice catch. Her concentration shifted. "What is happening to my Theopompus?"

"The priest will reconstruct the bier," I assured her quickly. "Theopompus will go to the gods properly. The undertakers will bring you his ashes later." I made a mental note to ensure that they took her *some* ashes. Preferably in the urn she herself had chosen.

Posidonius had paid for a high-class funeral company. Once they stopped scampering away in fright, I hoped the undertakers would creep back to continue with the cremation . . . I could not say to the girl: for heavens' sake, he was just a lecherous, stupid pirate! She still held information. And she still had the rest of her life to lead; duty dictated that we shepherd her into the future kindly.

"Tell us about this pit," Petronius Longus reminded her.

"It was underground. I was terrified to go in there—that was when Theopompus first became my friend. He was wonderful . . ." We could almost hear Rhodope trying to think. "It was in a place that was religious. I don't remember how we got there, I don't remember anything about that. I was too scared then."

"Tell us what you can," Helena coaxed.

"A narrow room . . . lamps . . . There was an arched entrance and steps leading down; people go belowground as a test of their devotion. The other men were trying to push me down there to keep me hidden. I started screaming—I was so scared that day—I didn't understand why I had been captured. I thought that I would die there underground. They hurried me; they pushed me; they were trying to force me to go down into the dark—"

Terror took over again. This pitch-dark tomb was the wrong place to remind Rhodope of that ordeal. She broke down. Helena soothed and comforted the girl, while next to me I could hear our own tough Albia muttering disparagement.

"But Theopompus was kind to you," Helena murmured. Rhodope agreed, then gave way to her grief for him.

When the distressed girl finally settled down again, Helena tried a new tack. "You must help us, so that nobody else has to undergo such a frightening experience. This is important, Rhodope. Did you at any time meet the man who is the negotiator for ransom money?"

"Once."

"How did that happen?"

"He came to see us when Theopompus brought me back from Rome."

"Was he angry?"

"He was furious. Theopompus laughed about it afterwards—though I didn't like the man. He was very scary."

"What did he look like?"

"Old."

"What else?" Rhodope hesitated. Helena suggested calmly, "We have heard that he dresses oddly."

"Yes."

"Eye paint and slippers, somebody told Marcus."

"Yes."

"Well, that sounds extraordinary. So he looked like a woman?"

"No, he looked like a man, but he had masses of eye paint—more than you should wear—and very elegant slippers."

"Were his manners effeminate?"

"No."

"And does he have a name?"

"He is called the Illyrian." Once again Rhodope paused. "It's a joke."

"How's that?"

"Well, Cotys and his men were the Illyrians—but *he* is not."

"That's very helpful!" said Petronius in a hollow voice. Beside me, Albia shook with a brief burst of wicked laughter.

"So what nationality is this man?" Helena asked, ignoring them.

"Roman," said Rhodope.

People were silent. We were all having problems finding air.

After a while Petronius told me, "I know what that pit must be. It's the ordeal trench for initiates—she was in a Mithraeum."

I thought about that. My brain had slowed down, starved of air.

"It makes sense, Falco. Rhodope, listen. There is a religious cult that many soldiers join, and I believe it is common among pirates. Their god is called Mithras. This cult is secretive, but the initiates have to rise through seven ranks. One of their tests is to lie alone in a covered trench all night. I think that was where you were to have been put."

"I don't know."

"Did they take you to a sanctuary indoors somewhere, maybe in a private house? You would have gone through a changing room, where the

men put on various colored robes. The shrine would be downstairs, perhaps with a statue of a god riding on a bull. Try to remember. Was there
a room underground where they held daily services, and this pit underneath the nave?"

"I don't think it was like that." Drowsy with grief and lack of air,
Rhodope had lost interest and become unhelpful. "It's no good going on
at me, I don't know!"

Helena shushed her.

I said to Petro, "It's not Mithras. I searched for temples all over town.
I know every damned place of worship in the whole of Ostia—I never
found one Mithraeum."

"Mithras is a secret religion. They don't have temples. Did you know
what to look for?"

"I know as much as you!" I felt bound to ask him, "Are you in the
cult?"

"No." Petronius was also wondering. "Are you?"

"No."

We were both glad to have cleared that up.

I was fairly sure that before he died, my brother Festus had tried the
whole Mithraic ritual of lying in a trench in the dark and having the blood
of a sacrificed bull rain down on him. I doubt if he ever progressed beyond
the first level; after initial curiosity, having to be serious about the cult would
have put him off. The bull's blood would be enough to deter me.

"Of course," jibed Helena, "as it's a secret male cult, if either of you
were in it, neither would own up." Neither of us answered her.

"Petronius is right," I said at last. "If this pit is in a Mithraeum, it will
be hidden away at the back of a private house or place of work—and we
will never find it." Wickedly, I added, "Unless, Petro, you have a file at
the vigiles station house, with a list of them?"

"We have the file," he answered, a little reluctantly. "It's the empty one."

The young flautist started coughing. He sounded asthmatic. That
could be a contradiction, but the breath control when he was playing the
flute helped him. That was what he told Helena, as she took up the new
task of calming him.

"This is a wonderful young man, Rhodope. It was quite superb how he rescued you. He is brave, athletic, polite, sensible—and he has a steady job. When you recover from your grief you should think about settling down with somebody like this." I expected an outcry from the girl, but she was always up for new adventures. "Are you married, Chaeron?" Helena asked.

"No!" answered Chaeron, eagerly.

Who knows where the matchmaking might have led. But Helena fell silent apprehensively, as our hot, cramped tomb suddenly echoed to a hearty knocking sound.

LVII

I felt Petronius shift his bulk alongside me. He reached behind us so he could return the same knock with a dagger pommel. Someone then shoved the heavy door inward against our backs, so we tumbled in a heap. Familiar voices came in with the cool air. Hands reached to pull us out onto the roadway. Fusculus and some of the vigiles were our rescuers.

Wiping the sweat from my brow as I cooled down, I caught Petro's eye. "Prearranged bolthole!" I applauded his forethought.

Angry noise was still coming back up the track from the funeral site. With nervous glances, Fusculus quickly arranged for the women to be taken under escort to Petronius' house; the escort would stay there on guard. Rhodope was a valuable witness. On the excuse that her father had reported her missing, she would be kept secure—whether she wanted it or not.

I kissed Helena and promised to be a good boy. "Don't make promises you can't keep, Marcus!"

Petro and I, with Fusculus and the remaining men, walked back to the party scene.

As I had hoped, the undertakers were true professionals. They had rebuilt the pyre, lashed down the corpse as if he had never jumped up for a look around, and rekindled the flames amid a fresh douche of scented oil. The priest was busy at his altar while the rest ensured that Theopompus would go down to the underworld with *somebody* paying him attention.

But all around this somber, stoical group, chaos raged. The Illyrians and the Cilicians had each decided their blood brothers were bastards. Fusculus wondered what took them so long to fall out; Petro pretended to be a romantic who thought it was just a lovers' tiff; I had never believed they were sincere in the first place. Now they had torn up their pact and were pounding each other like true marriage partners on the brink of divorce. The fight was as good as any last-night brawl after a tense series of games at a provincial amphitheater, a melee when one set of locals thinks the other bragging bullies have been cheating all summer with the magistrate's connivance, while the others have just found out that the first side's chief gladiator accepted their bribe but then failed to throw his fight. *And* his oversexed brother never turned up for training because he was too busy getting their trainer's wife in pod . . .

Petronius, Fusculus, and I found ourselves a mixed platter of finger food from the remains of the buffet, and watched in admiration as we chewed. These men-who-must-not-be-called-pirates really knew how to create fighting theater. Fists flew. That was only the start of it. Weapons were used, including knives; free-flowing blood soon told its story there. In addition, fingers, feet, elbows, knees, and heads were all part of the action. Several times, Lygon produced his speciality: he launched himself high in the air, then floored some unfortunate opponent with a two-footed kick. Cratidas was head-butting all comers, going at it like a demented woodpecker. Some of the women must have fled. The remaining few egged on their favorites.

We were just in time obtaining our eats; the table went over. Three men, locked in a passionate knot, demolished the shaky construction. Now food was squashed and slimed underfoot on the gray thoroughfare slabs, adding to the risk of skidding and falling. Petronius advised the caterers' slaves to go home. Like any sensible skivvies, they took the wine with them. We let it go. We already knew the flavor was merely adequate. I, for one, was to be grateful for my abstemiousness later.

Members of the vigiles tiptoed around unobtrusively, retrieving those who could be tidied out of the way. After bodies had been sorted by nationality they were laid in neat lines on either side of the road, Illyrians to the left, Cilicians to the right A particularly pedantic trooper then sorted them into further categories: dead, dying, and comatose. In his free time he checked that he had placed all in each category satisfactorily in height order. This must have been to assist identification afterward. An Illyrian (or Cilician) flew out of the fighting center and staggered backwards into our group. Petronius quickly wiped his mouth on a napkin, then propelled this seaman back into the fracas by applying a boot to his backside.

The fight was thinning out. Among those still on their feet, Cratidas and Lygon were the most prominent. Even they reeled uncertainly. They could still summon up physical resources, but like all the rest, they were starting to fade. Petro decided the fighters had tired themselves out enough. He gave a whistle. What followed was brief and methodical. His men entered the action and set to, me among them, finishing off whoever was left standing. Before long, they had all either run away or lain down in surrender. Petronius and Fusculus had Cratidas and Lygon under arrest.

Orders were given for dealing with the dead and immovable. We set off along the roadway, taking the prisoners who could still walk. Behind us, I heard the mournful *swoosh* as the priest doused the pyre with water from a ritual vessel. Theopompus had now traveled with full Roman pomp to whatever barbaric gods he honored. Only his ashes remained. Sealed in their black-figure urn, they would remind his young lover of their fleeting time together and the innocence she had so eagerly given away.

At least, as the past gradually came to be an embarrassment, Rhodope would always know that her dream lover had had a spectacular send-off. If it turned out that he had left her pregnant, she would think of Theopompus in his halo of green fire every time she was combing her child's hair.

LVIII

Once out of the necropolis, we hit the main road and approached the Rome Gate. It was formed of an entrance and exit, between square towers set in the city walls—the very walls which were built by Cicero as Consul, after the devastating sack of Ostia by pirates. The protective walls were now half buried in habitation. Within a few years of their construction, Pompey had cleared the seas. Freed from fear of attack, people had built houses and workshops behind, abutting, and sometimes right on top of the defenses. A marble plaque told a poignant story. First it commemorated Cicero's creation of the city walls; five years afterward Clodius, Cicero's archenemy who was a kind of urban pirate himself, had erased the Consul's name and covered it with his own, in blood-red lettering. Cicero, approaching political decline, had bitterly complained.

The old orator would have had caustic things to say about the modern interlopers we held in custody. The vigiles caused quite a stir as they hit the main road and held up the traffic in both directions so their parade of downcast prisoners could be marched in through the gate. As our battered human trophies emerged on the Ostia side, a familiar white-haired figure hove into view. He was the navy man, Caninus. The vigiles neither looked at him nor paused. But I did both. I glared him in the eye and planted myself right in front of him.

"If you're going to the funeral, it's over."

"I was unaware of it until too late. I should have been there on surveillance."

"Well, the vigiles have wrapped up the kidnapping problem—and solved the Theopompus murder." He gave me a bland smile. I remained unmoved. "You were a damned failure yesterday, Caninus!"

"Clearly no harm came to you, Falco—"

"No thanks to you! I didn't expect you to row a trireme by yourself, but a word to the harbormaster, and a search party, would have helped. I'm amazed that when a citizen is being carried off by force, the navy just give him a cheery farewell."

"Sorry. I thought you were just waving a greeting—"

"Caninus, you let the Illyrians take me. You never expected to see me alive today."

"Oh, be reasonable, man. A trireme in harbor cannot be moved without retensioning the main cables, the *hypozomata*—" I raised an eyebrow and let him burble nervously. "Run fore and aft; hold the timbers in a lock along the length. We slacken off the hawsers, to rest the frame, when we dock for any period—standard practice. It's impossible to sail like that; the ship could break her back." The attaché, who had always talked too much, finally stopped.

"Caninus, I never expected pursuit by trireme. Tell me—how come a bunch of Illyrians who are working new versions of the old trade, ever felt comfortable with their liburnian moored tight against three naval warships? Do the Cilicians cozy up to you in the same way? Caninus, what exactly is your game?"

"Excuse me—" He was turning away. "I will be needed to brief Marcus Rubella."

I had already briefed Lucius Petronius with my own thoughts on Caninus.

We walked in silence until we came to the side street that led to the vigiles station house. The prisoners and their escort must all be inside already.

"Aren't you coming, Falco?" Caninus asked in some surprise when I made it plain I was heading off down the Decumanus.

"I'm still looking for my scribe. Besides, I have a sense of family. I have no wish to be present if you are intending to proscribe my Uncle Fulvius."

A small tight smile disfigured the navy man's well-barbered face. He turned down the side street. I continued along the main highway toward our apartment, hoping to find Helena Justina there.

I never made it. I ran into Passus. He was on Petro's team, a comparative new boy though he must have been with the Fourth for a couple of years. Headhunted by Petronius, Passus was short in stature, with clipped hair, and big hands and feet like a puppy. That belied his casual competence. I gave him a quick roundup of the day's events. He told me he had been trusted by Rubella as the sole invigilator on Holconius and Mutatus, and was watching their apartment in the hope of developments.

"So what's the word, Passus?"

We had worked together previously on the murder of an art patron; Passus knew me well enough to open up. "I think I bungled it," he said.

"You were on your own," I sympathized.

"All the lads were on the necropolis exercise so I had to manage . . . A child brought a note. I had nobody to send for backup. Either the scribes had spotted me, or someone warned them. So they both came out, but they split up. I tailed the one with the boy—Holconius. But he and the boy just walked around in a bloody big circle, then he went back inside the apartment. The boy ran off. I am depressed, Falco."

"You think the scribes have a new ransom demand? Mutatus gave you the slip, and went alone to a meet?"

Passus nodded and swore bleakly. Then he took himself off to report to Rubella. I gave up my plan to find Helena, and went to see Holconius.

Of course at first he denied everything. But sitting alone in the apartment had sapped his courage. He admitted the new ransom demand. Rubella had firmly warned the scribes to do nothing—but again they ignored advice in case it rebounded on the so-called captive Diocles.

They still had money. Mutatus had gone to fetch the cash. The new ransom note said only one man was to handle this exchange. Mutatus would be contacted.

"So you see, Falco," Holconius declared self-righteously, "I cannot tell you anything about how the money will be handed over—because *I* don't know!"

I ordered him to go to the vigiles station house and confess to Rubella. I made Holconius tell me which temple was their bank. Then I set off there.

LIX

I stood on the steps of the Temple of Rome and Augustus, thinking.

This temple must have been one of the earliest symbols of imperial power. Built by Tiberius in honor of his stepfather and of our lucky city, it was entirely composed of marble. Six fluted columns adorned the front area, which had a platform whence political speakers could bore the luckless crowds on festive days. A couple of extra columns turned around each side to entrances where stone stairs led to the interior. To call the edifice triumphalist would be an understatement. Not only did Victory fly her stuff on tiptoe from forty feet up on the top pinnacle of the fancy frieze, but indoors the cult statue was Roma Victrix—a large lass dressed up in an Amazon costume. She had a figure like Helena—though Helena would kick me for saying so. Let's say, Roma Victrix was in good shape, but as the incarnation of the Golden City she headed up a great new trading empire which imported tidbits from every part of the world—and quite clearly she enjoyed her food.

Roma was shown as an Amazon, with one extremely round, awkwardly prominent breast, revealed naked among her curiously full draperies. Amazons are usually famous for wearing nothing but a short skirt and a snarl. Roma mainly dressed sensibly. Her other breast was properly covered up, and seemed less well developed. It may have been amputated, as is supposed to happen in the best Amazonian circles, for purposes of avoiding her bowstring. She had one sturdy foot steadying a little globe and looked as if she were about to kick off at the start of a ball game.

I had had plenty of time for these musings. I had been inside, but now I was outside again. Indoors, I had glimpsed a priest of the cult, a snooty flamen who thought I was about to steal the ritual vessels and donated treasure. Once I was spotted by this haughty factotum, the temple-keeper—an ex–town slave who did all the work around there—was sent to ask if he could assist me. That meant assisting me back outside onto the front podium.

Now I stood there, pretending I was a little boy who wanted to be an orator. I surveyed the Forum. It was a long rectangular area, with the tall Capitolium at the far end, the statutory Temple of the Capitoline Triad. That was where Rubella and Petro had been trapped the other day, when they watched the builders' guild stamp around in their marching display. I could see a shrine, which I knew was dedicated to the city Lares. Midway across the Forum ran the Decumanus Maximus. To my left, I had the Basilica and Curia. To my right and behind me were baths, public latrines, and shops. Ahead, on the far right-hand corner though more or less out of my vision, stood the house of Privatus where Petronius lodged.

Things here were not progressing. If Mutatus was on the premises, he must be downstairs in the strongrooms beneath the temple podium. The keeper had refused to let me down there. Saying I wanted to talk to a visitor who was making a withdrawal had failed to impress him. The keeper was doing his job, protecting money on deposit. He might already know that Mutatus and Holconius had had some of their cash stolen—for all he knew, by thieves who had followed them after they came here and made a withdrawal.

The temple-keeper had courteously promised he would let me know when Mutatus came up from the strongrooms. To his credit, he did give me the nod—though he waited until the scribe had left.

I knew Mutatus had not passed through the Forum. I would have seen him. The piazza was packed with people, the late afternoon surge of pedestrians going to the baths and workmen walking home, but I was on a vantage point and I had the whole Forum area in plain sight. Mutatus must have gone out at the back, and on the Basilica side; from my position, which was on a corner, I had been watching the other exit.

I walked down the steps and went to the rear of the temple. At a street-corner caupona no one could tell me anything. I crossed the back of the temple. Here began the main road to the Porta Laurentina. This was a seriously important part of town, and although light industry—cornmills and laundries—lurked among the private houses, the neighborhood lacked the proliferating bars and brothels that clustered around the Marine Gate and the riverfront. It was not the kind of area "the Illyrian" had favored for meetings. This convinced me that someone else had muscled in. The ransom demand for my scribe was a new scam.

My scribe. He was mine by now. I was determined not to give up on him until I knew his fate.

"Spare a copper for a bath!"

In the littered shade at the back of the most prestigious buildings, there are beggars. This wit knew how to suggest his request should be granted urgently; he was filthy. In fact he was so filthy he looked as if he had covered himself with grime on purpose. Anyone charitable would shoo him to hot water and a strigil. (Anyone who then thought twice would remember that most towns offer free public baths. This beggar was dirty from choice.)

I held up a coin. Then I gave it to him. There was no point holding back; he would just say what I wanted to hear in order to obtain the money. "Seen anyone leave the temple just before I came around the corner? Which way did he go?"

A grimy arm, swathed in dreadful rags, waved vaguely down the Cardo Maximus, toward the far Laurentine Gate. The man was probably drunk. He looked too verminous to question at close quarters. I had to decide whether I believed him. With nothing else on offer, I set off up the road.

"I'm Cassius!" he croaked after me.

"I'll remember!" I lied, fleeing. The last thing I wanted was to be stuck with a madman with dangerous politics. Having a bust of Cassius in your house still counts as treason. On the birthdays of Brutus and Cassius, all sensible men are very careful not to hold dinner parties that could look like memorials.

Compared with the Decumanus, the Cardo was a narrow little street, gently sloping downhill and deeply shadowed by the buildings alongside it. I had been here before, though I was riding not walking, as I went to see Damagoras. One of the houses near the Temple of Rome and Augustus had been a smoking ruin, the morning Gaius Baebius and I first encountered the firefighting bullies of the builders' guild. I had also come here during my temple hunt. The road to the Laurentine Gate had become a motif of this mission.

Cassius did not let me down: I was halfway to the Gate when the traffic coming toward me thinned and ahead of me I saw a boy. I recognized the slight figure: Zeno. Zeno, from the gatehouse, that thin little street rascal whose mother was Pullia, the Cilician kidnappers' drugs queen. Walking alongside Zeno and talking to him earnestly was a well-built elderly man. I knew him too. It was my Uncle Fulvius.

Fulvius had one hand on Zeno's shoulder. The boy looked up at him with a trusting expression. Pullia had been in custody now for several days. Lygon was only captured today, but he had never himself lived at the gatehouse, and he had appeared indifferent to Pullia's child. Without his mother, Zeno would have had to fend for himself. Fulvius must have befriended him.

Maybe they knew each other even before Pullia's arrest. If Caninus was correct in identifying my uncle as the negotiator, "the Illyrian" used a young boy as his runner. All along, little Zeno could have been that boy. Now, if the Diocles ransom demand did, after all, come from the Cilician gang, the pair could be going to meet Mutatus.

Even if not, there were good reasons to investigate what a young child was doing in my uncle's company.

I followed them hotfoot. I wondered if they were heading outside the Gate, so my day would be ending as it began, at a necropolis.

Sitting in a tomb in the pitch dark had been bad enough. Now, had I but known it, I was heading somewhere worse.

LX

When they turned off the Cardo it was just before the town Gate, but even though they were not going to the necropolis I had a gloomy premonition.

I knew this place. I had been here one quiet morning, during my extended search for temples. It was no use to me then, and I would rather not have had it become significant now. Fulvius and Zeno had entered the sanctuary of the Great Mother: Cybele. That was bad enough. Even before I got there, I could hear that this was not a quiet occasion.

The old city walls provided one boundary for a large triangular area; it was bigger than any other temple campus I had seen at Ostia, bigger than any religious sanctuary in Rome's crowded public areas, apart from the sacred heights of the Capitol and Arx. We entered this haunt from the Cardo, halfway along, through a row of little shops. Directly opposite, stood the main Temple of Cybele. A corner to my left had a cluster of other buildings, one of which I knew was the shrine for Attis. Cybele kept her castrated consort at a distance, although a colonnaded portico beside the old city wall did provide a sheltered route for their eunuch priests to meet. A jumble of buildings on my right were, I thought, for adherents of the cult. Maybe the priests' living quarters if, as at Rome, this exotic cult's celebrants were kept away from daily life lest Eastern mysticism contaminate our sturdy Western values.

My task now was hopeless. The sanctuary was far too busy. People were everywhere; as a meeting place where kidnappers and victims could be unobserved, this site had been chosen cunningly. I could not now see Fulvius and the boy. Nor could I spot Mutatus, nor anyone who might be meeting him. I had had some ideas of whom to expect. The presence of my uncle—wherever he had disappeared to—had implied that I was dealing with the old gang still. Caninus must be correct: Uncle Fulvius was "the Illyrian" and this would be, after all, yet another exchange manipulated by the same people as all the rest.

A cult initiation was apparently due tomorrow. Priests in their long effeminate robes were milling about, some escorting a large black bull to the pen where he would spend the night before sacrifice. He was led in a short procession, with Eastern music and dancing—and he sensed that all this fuss foretold something dangerous. Maybe he could smell the blood of his predecessors. At any rate, the colorful costumes and unusual surroundings were badly upsetting him. He started bellowing and tried to break free. He was a big lad. Luckily they had him secured with more than flower garlands; stout work with ropes contained him until he was half dragged, half shouldered into the pen. Lustral water was splashed about; he did not care for that too much either.

All this took place in the complex of small temples to my left. There was further activity in the long colonnade. I would never identify anyone I wanted here.

I pulled the toga I was wearing up and over my head like a man attending a sacrifice; it offered some anonymity. Nobody who knew me as an informer would be expecting to see me in formal dress—well, not unless he already knew I had been to a funeral today. I set off straight across the open grass, heading for the main temple in the far corner of the site.

It was late afternoon. The sun was above the temple, making it a dark outline only. Anyone there was lost from sight, invisible against the building. However, if they looked this way they would see me, a well-lit togate figure, striding toward them in the open, quite alone. If I was approaching villains, they might not suspect I still had Petro's spare sword hidden in my clothing. On the other hand, if they knew why I was tracking them, they might guess I would come armed. They would be armed themselves. Since they were in a religious complex, their weapons would be hidden too. Any number of them could be lurking here. They were likely to know me; I might not recognize them.

I reached the Temple of Cybele. Discreetly, I searched it. The toga helped make me acceptable. The Great Mother had a rectangular temple of modest proportions, within which she reclined in her turreted crown; she turned a calm gaze upon me as I invaded her silent sanctum. In the presence of powerful women, informers are respectful men; I apologized for disturbing her.

Empty-handed, I strode back outside. Impatiently I shook the toga from my head, to feel less muffled; I ran a hand through my curls, still caked with salt from my enforced dip yesterday. From these gray temple steps, I now had the light in my favor. It should have been a magical time: early evening, with the August sun still hot and some hours from setting, the sky deep blue above, the strength of the sunlight not yet lessening, though the day was now passing toward a late dusk. The stones of the temple beamed warmth. Absorbing the atmosphere as my nightmare feeling grew, I was aware of the sea, close by behind me, and the town running away to the left.

Many of the people who were in the sanctuary moments ago had already vanished. Those who remained walked about quietly. The music had stilled. Within the campus all was now peaceful. Sounds from the town and the port and the nearby gate to the open country seemed to come from another world. I could smell wild oregano. Seagulls gently soared overhead.

I stood still, watched and listened. My right hand found its way through the heavy folds of the toga to the sword hilt.

Then, as I continually scanned the enclosure, searching for someone I recognized, at last I thought I glimpsed Uncle Fulvius. He was right at the opposite end of the campus, moving around the huddled sanctuary of Attis. I jumped down the steps of the Great Mother's temple, and on light feet began running through the long colonnade.

*   *   *

Fulvius had been making his way around the shrine. I thought he had gone into the building—but when I arrived, panting, I had no luck there. I started to searched the area. This corner of the sanctuary was full of nooks, well-heads, altars, and mysterious entrances. Devotees did not need to have tile labels on the doorposts as if the buildings housed physicians or accountants. But I could not tell what anything really was.

There was one dreadful possibility: I knew I had to find it. The rites of Cybele are as dreadful as the rites of Mithras, and one is very similar. Somewhere nearby must be a tauroboleum pit: a man-high hole underground into which initiates must descend. There they would stand alone in darkness for a ghastly test of their devotion.

It would be some kind of cellar, with a grid above the underground pit; upon that grid tomorrow, priests would slaughter the great bull who was still bellowing mournfully in his pen nearby. His spilled blood would rain down onto the novice, who stood alone in pitch darkness, being showered from head to foot with stinking gore. The rite of removing initiates from the pit in their foul robing of bull's blood was notoriously repulsive.

I found the tauroboleum. At the back of the Temple of Attis was a tower built into the corner of the city wall. Part now formed a narrow shrine. Pine trees cast a perfumed shadow. Inside, niches held statues of Cybele's consort, signified by his starry Phrygian cap and his pine cones. The nave was already lit with lamps, adorned with flowers, and scented with incense.

As soon as I entered I knew this was the place to which the Illyrians had once brought the terrified Rhodope. Ahead of me were steps, as she had said: a short flight down which they must have struggled with the girl as they tried to force her to enter the dark, arched mouth of the tauroboleum pit. Initiations must be rare. On days when this shrine was out of use, its remote tauroboleum—a kind of ghastly drain or culvert—would have made a perfect hideaway. Any cries from victims would go unheard. And afterward, the women who had been imprisoned here would be utterly traumatized, their future silence assured.

I was standing inside the dimly lit shrine when I thought I heard someone outside. I was torn, but the tauroboleum pit was nearer than the exit, so I moved that way. Descending the steps, I had to crouch low to peer inside; it was too dark down there to see anything, though a faint glow from the lamps behind would have outlined me. Outside the shrine a voice called "Who's there?" I nipped down the steps. Too late, I heard movement, then hands reached up to grab my garments, pulling me down and underground. Someone dug me painfully in the ribs and shushed me. We were squashed too tight for me to draw my sword. Not that I wanted to. My companion was not threatening me. Well, not in the usual way.

Somehow I knew who was in here with me: It was Fulvius. I was coping well with this development, until someone up above us in the shrine suddenly slammed shut a metal door on the pit and locked us in.

"Marcus, you damn fool!" muttered Fulvius. "That was bloody careless—we're really stuck now."

I refused to see this as my fault, but what he said was true. Our prison was damp, musty, and not built for two. We could stand up, but this pit was constructed for one man alone. I could not help remembering that when I was small, people had told me to avoid Uncle Fulvius because he disliked children. Many years later I had realized that that was the family way of saying he liked little boys too much. Now I was trapped in a pit in the dark with him.

O Mother!

LXI

We can't see much, but light is getting in through the grid and so is air—" To my surprise, my uncle seemed to be taking charge. Now he began calculating odds. I was the ex-soldier; that was my job. "There's one of him, and two of us—"

"I have a sword, though no room to use it." We were packed in very tight. Fulvius could not avoid knowing that I had come armed.

"We are safe enough down here." My uncle was a complaisant swine.

"That's nice," I said sarcastically. "Some maniac has locked us in and we're stuck until they come with the quaking initiate tomorrow morning."

"Scared, Marcus?"

"Only of what I am about to find out—I really want to know," I said, as patiently as possible, "what *your* position is in this. I was told by Caninus that you are the Illyrian."

"You were told wrong."

"So put me right."

"Did you believe him?"

"How should I know, Uncle?"

"There is an alternative—"

I got it in first: "The Illyrian could be Caninus himself?"

"Oh, smart boy!"

"So the navy is *not* investigating the ransom scam—"

"Maybe they are," said Fulvius. "What do you think *I* am doing here?"

My uncle was an *agent?* "Can you prove this statement?"

"I don't have to prove it." When I said nothing, Uncle Fulvius insisted, "You have never seen me damned well dressed like a woman."

"Face paint and slippers are just not your style? Such a relief for the family! All I know is, you were going to Pessinus but you got on the wrong boat—"

Fulvius chuckled. "I got the boat I wanted. Did you meet Cassius?"

"No—" I remembered the beggar behind the Temple of Rome and Augustus. "*Cassius?* . . . Of course—I thought the grime looked self-applied."

"He likes to throw himself into things," Fulvius boasted. An innuendo I preferred to ignore hovered crudely. "Cassius and I have been together for a quarter of a century." Well, that answered one question. They were a stable couple.

"Mother will be so pleased you have settled down! Cassius was on the boat, I take it. The boat you decided was the right one?"

"He was on the boat."

"I am happy for you, Uncle. But we're wasting time. We need to get out of this."

"We have to stay put."

"Sorry, Uncle, I'd prefer not to make Cassius jealous by lingering—" I tried shoving the door. Uncle Fulvius allowed me to exhaust myself, grunting in protest as I crushed him.

"Shut up and sit tight. The shrine above is the meeting place. Zeno told me. When the money is handed over, we can listen and collect the evidence."

"Zeno was the boy runner?" I was getting my breath back. "You be-friended him? So where is Zeno now?"

"A priest of Attis is feeding him hot milk and sesame cakes." That did not reassure me. Still, the child could be extracted later. Extricating us might be more difficult.

★   ★   ★

"Will your Cassius bring help?"

"Of course." That was reassuring, but I still did not like being trapped underground in the dark. Waves of panic swept over me. There must be drainage, but caverns that have been drenched in gore acquire a horrendous smell. I fought claustrophobia. If initiates could stand this in isolation, I could live through the fear . . . Possibly.

"Whatever did you have for lunch?" demanded my uncle pompously. I was breathing in his face; there was no alternative.

"Funeral fare."

"Onions." Oh, Fulvius was fastidious. Now I wanted to laugh.

While we waited for something to happen, I nagged my uncle to tell me about his role in this fiasco. He said he worked for the navy, as a corn factor; Pa had told me that. And I knew that the army—so presumably the navy too—often made use of their corn factors to gather intelligence. Fulvius had been involved with supplying troops for years. From Salonae, where he lived, his contacts were with the Ravenna Fleet. "He was at Ravenna—"

"Caninus?"

"Got it!"

"I am an informer, Uncle. Whatever you've heard from the family, I happen to be good at it . . . I find this unlikely"—I found it appalling—"but are you saying you do similar work to me?"

"Maybe."

"No need to be secretive. I was an army scout. Now I take on imperial missions."

"Good for you, boy!" Fulvius changed the subject, without admitting anything. "Our paths never directly crossed until now."

"Well, I'm glad that this business has not ripped up old friendships . . . So he tells me you are the Illyrian—and you say it's him."

"You just listen to me," ordered Fulvius.

"Perhaps I will—" Or perhaps not. "How did Caninus go bad?"

"He made the wrong friends when he was supposed to be monitoring the Illyrian seaboard."

"Wrong friends? When we talked at that bar with Geminus, you were defending the coastal folk yourself."

"I was explaining what has happened to the dispossessed," argued Fulvius. "The men you call pirates come from poverty-stricken communities, where the options are few. Young lads off the land are sent to sea because it is the only option."

"Cotys and the others—the Cilician community—seem happy with their lot."

"Don't despise them as riffraff," said Fulvius. "There was a long tradition of coastal groups giving shelter to men fleeing poverty—often seamen of talent who simply found they could not get a ship. What you call pirate ships were high-class vessels, manned by the best-quality mariners."

I had picked up a nuance. "One of those communities gave refuge to you and Cassius?"

"Oh, Salonae is perfectly civilized!" Fulvius cried angrily. "But I know people in Illyria. I know the good and the bad. I had been to Dyrrhachium. So I was asked to keep an eye on Cotys unofficially, when he seemed to have been lured into new, unacceptable ventures. I soon spotted that he was being protected by a bad apple in the Ravenna Fleet. When Caninus got himself transferred here, ostensibly to shadow Cotys, then I was asked to shadow *him*."

"Was it the first time you had been used in intelligence gathering?"

"No."

A horrid thought struck. "Who asked you to do it? You don't work for Anacrites?"

Uncle Fulvius uttered something quiet and crude. "I do not." Interesting. He obviously knew who Anacrites was, though.

"Who commissions you then?"

"Who wants the seas kept sweet and clean?"

"The Emperor?"

"I suppose so, though we try to ignore that dreary aspect."

"'We' is you and Cassius? And who pays you two?"

"You don't need to know, Marcus." If I was ever to trust him, I did need to know.

"Don't treat me like a lad. I've done enough stinking official missions of my own."

"We are not offering you a partnership."

"I would not take it!"

We both seethed quietly. It was like a low moment at a family birth-
day party. After a while I asked the inevitable professional question: "So
what is the going rate for intelligence, with the Ravenna Fleet?"

"More than you get, probably."

His arrogance was hard to take. Now I knew why, in the family,
Fulvius had always been unpopular. "Don't be too sure of that!"

The discomfort was getting to me. "What's happened?" I wondered rest-
lessly. "Mutatus set off hours ago from the temple with the money. If this
is the rendezvous, where has he gotten to?"

"Fake trail," Fulvius said curtly. "According to Zeno, Mutatus has been
sent to a series of false drop sites. He'll get about three messages until he
is passed here. It's to unnerve him, and perhaps shake off any follow-
ers . . . By the way," said my uncle offhandedly. "I may have let you reach
the wrong conclusion earlier. It wasn't Caninus who locked us in; that
was Cassius."

"What?"

"If Caninus sees the door locked, he will never suspect that anyone is
down here listening. I need to overhear what happens. He is an official;
we have to trap him with hard evidence."

Oh great. So Fulvius and his life's partner were not just government
agents, they were a pair of idiots. I should have foreseen this. I was not
sharing a well-planned exercise with a master spy; I was stuck in a hole
with my mother's elder brother. Fulvius was a sibling of Fabius and
Junius. It followed that he was a lunatic.

"Clever?" asked Fulvius, condescendingly.

"Not clever! At least Cassius is still at liberty, on the outside."

"We can't rely on the navy. He's gone to fetch the vigiles."

"And I suppose," I said viciously, "you and Cassius think that they live
in an old shop by the Temple of Hercules Invictus?"

That caused a silence. I just had to hope Uncle Fulvius was deliberately riling me.

⋆   ⋆   ⋆

Fulvius complained of swollen ankles. I too had aching legs and feet, plus a pain in my back as I tried to avoid collapsing on my uncle.

Suddenly we heard noises above us. Footsteps. We strained our ears to work out who was now in the shrine. It could be a priest, unconnected with our mission. I was hot and increasingly uneasy. None of my own associates knew where I was. Our only backup was Cassius. Thrills.

Faintly audible, someone paced about. I was all set to risk calling up to ask if it was Mutatus, when a new person joined him.

"Where is the money?" Caninus—muffled, but recognizable. Not close; probably near the shrine door. Fulvius nudged me excitedly.

Mutatus, closer and louder, answered. "The money is safe." He must be right beside the floor grille, immediately above our heads.

"Where?"

"I can get it. Falco was right. We don't believe you have Diocles, but if you really *can* produce him—"

"Falco—hah!" There came an abrupt movement. Things went wrong. We heard an angry shout. Caninus—closer—exclaimed, "You fool!" Something clanged and skidded, like a weapon falling on the grid. Down in our vault, Fulvius shouted out, but went unheard.

Feet went pounding away from the shrine. Two sets? I thought so. "All you had to do was hand over the money!" Caninus, voice retreating, somewhere outside. A short scream, then more sounds of pain and fear.

In the distance the sacrificial bull started bellowing, agitated by the commotion.

Someone returned to the shrine, moving slowly. Filled with dread, Fulvius and I kept quiet. There were three awkward footsteps, a thump directly above us, then footsteps running out. The trace of light that had once penetrated the tauroboleum pit through its upper grille had vanished.

"I have a bad feeling," I said softly.

Fulvius listened. "Something is dripping down on us . . ." Then he added in horror, "It feels like blood!"

It was not the bull. We could still hear him bellowing . . .

Fulvius and I realized the terrible truth: just above our heads lay Mutatus—either finished already, or now bleeding to death.

LXII

My uncle groaned once and called out to the scribe. There was no answer. We could do nothing to help Mutatus—and I knew it was probably all over. For the scribe's sake, I hoped so. Like Diocles, he must have owned a sword and brought it here, in a crazy act of defiance and bravery.

Unbelievable.

We seemed to be there for hours. Eventually we heard Cassius arrive. He cursed, then hastened to release us. We fell out through the opened door, gasping, and he dragged us up the steps. Light and air dazzled us.

Wiping sweat from my brow, along with who knows what, I stumbled to the body. It was Mutatus of course—and, of course, dead. I pulled him off the grid; he was not some damned cult sacrifice. I straightened him up on the floor of the shrine. His fingers had been shredded where he had tried to fend off blows from his own sword. Caninus had carved him as crudely as a raw recruit. Trust the damned navy not to know how to handle weapons. I knelt down in the pool of blood and closed the old scribe's eyes. Then I shut mine, genuinely grieving.

When I stood up, the other two were watching me. Cassius, looking familiar now, must be fifteen years my uncle's junior. He had shed the beggar's rags and wiped off some of the grime, though he still had dirt camouflage stripes blackening his face. What a poser. I had not filthied up my face for an action since I stopped creeping around northern forests as an army scout. With only a bunch of toadstools to hide behind, at least there was some point.

Gray-sideburned as he was now, in the straight nose and brown eyes I could still trace the handsome younger man for whom Fulvius had fallen. Biceps strained against the tight sleeves of his tunic, his big calves were muscular, and there was no fat on him. I had seen him before: he was the fourth man from the public latrine where only yesterday Caninus had taunted me about Fulvius.

Together, they were as noncommittal as a married couple; they would share a commentary later, in bed, possibly. I preferred not to think about that.

"He managed to avoid me," Cassius complained. The action man in the partnership—not doing much to help us. "I found a blood trail leaving the sanctuary, but he slipped past me somehow—"

"Damned amateurs!" I was angry. At my feet lay a scribe who had exceeded his remit in the bravest way. Mutatus should have been pensioned off with honor, not crudely slain—with four or five ragged strokes—because this pair of incompetents could not round up one aging corrupt attaché who had already been wounded.

Fulvius and Cassius exchanged glances.

"I'll go after him," offered Cassius.

I pushed him aside. "No, *I'll* go!"

But it was no longer necessary. Passus and a group of vigiles rushed into the shrine. They had men out already searching for Caninus, closer on his tracks than we would ever be now. Passus bent and inspected the departing trail of blood spots. "I'll get a scent dog in."

"You know it's Caninus we're after?"

"Brunnus had told us. He's been checking up in Rome. The Ravenna boys are trying to keep it all quiet, but the big epaulettes in the Misenum Fleet overruled them. A full-scale hunt is on—but you know Rubella; he intends the Fourth to get all the glory."

At the uproar of the vigiles' arrival, the bull had begun to vocalize again; I found the noise unbearable. "The Fourth will have to catch Caninus then—"

"You know us, Falco!"

I could relax. The experts were taking over. Shaken in body and sick at heart, I staggered outside. The evening was beautiful. The selfish gods must be unmoved by our tragedy. I threw up on the steps of the Temple of Attis, to the horror of a priest.

Uncle Fulvius calmed down the bull in due course. Well, he was born on a farm.

Once it was clear I was no longer needed, I left them all without a word and went home to my wife and family.

LXIII

Next morning, Helena kept the children quiet so I slept in long after everybody else had breakfasted. When she woke me, I was not pretty. A rough attempt last night to wash off the salt, blood, sweat, and dirt had failed to produce much improvement. I was rested, but felt shaken and deeply depressed.

Helena knew all that had happened. I had unburdened myself to her before I fell asleep. Now she fed me, then told me a messenger had called that morning. Damagoras, still imprisoned by Rubella, was asking to see me. Helena reckoned she knew what he wanted.

"While you go out to play at dares with the boys, Marcus, I just sit alone at home, surrounded by old note-tablets . . . I had been thinking about the tablets, actually. I suspect Damagoras wants his ancient diaries back. Remember you told me that Cratidas and Lygon made some joke about discussing literature?" If she said so, she must be right. Too much had happened recently for me to remember. "Maybe Damagoras had asked Cratidas and Lygon to retrieve his notes; when that dreadful slave, Titus, came here and saw Albia, *he* said that somebody had been asking about the tablets."

"Albia said Titus was frightened."

"Yes, Marcus; he would be scared stiff, if he had been threatened by Cratidas or Lygon."

It all seemed long ago. But I still wanted to find Diocles; in fact, with Mutatus' death so much on my mind, I wanted it more than ever. Mutatus had paid a terrible penalty for his lost colleague. I owed it to both not to give up now.

"Go and see Damagoras."

"I could take the shipping logs back to him—"

"No!" Helena instructed in her crisp way. "You just find out if Damagoras is willing to exchange information for them." She looked at me, with her head on one side. "You're very quiet. Don't give in to him."

"No chance," I assured her gently. "Believe me, fruit—anyone who gets in my way today will find me very tough."

Helena produced clean clothes and my oil flask, accepting my filthy condition with no other comment. My daughters, playing down in the courtyard, were less diplomatic; they ran up to greet me, took in my disgusting state—then ran away squealing. Albia turned up her nose too. Nux came with me happily. Nux liked having a master who growled around the house and stank.

I went out to the set of baths by the vigiles station house. That was deliberate.

The baths were handsome and comfortable, built by the old Emperor Claudius when he first brought the vigiles to guard his new corn warehouses. After I cleaned up and slid into a new tunic, I left the dog sleeping blissfully on the filthy old one. She was loyal, but I saw no reason to subject her to the kind of scenes I knew I would find at the station house. While his men continued to search through Ostia and Portus for Caninus, Marcus Rubella would be interviewing prisoners. I knew his methods. Since he got results, nobody ever argued. But for him, "interviews" were never an intellectual exercise.

On leaving the baths, I crossed the street and entered the dark gatehouse. To me in my current dismal mood, these crumbling barracks reeked of misery. I could hear no Cilicians or Illyrians screaming, but the subdued manner of the vigiles in the exercise yard told its own story.

Marcus Rubella was a master of pain management: the excruciating mixture of torture and delay.

I met Fusculus. He told me the prisoners were still reluctant to speak, but Rubella was slowly putting together a case. The vigiles had tracked down Arion, the man who was wounded with the oar during the ferry heist; with my evidence that I saw Cotys take him aboard the liburnian, this was enough to tie Cotys and the Illyrians to stealing the ransom chest. Rhodope's testimony damned them for abducting her. Against Cratidas, Lygon, and the Cilicians, evidence was more circumstantial.

"Oh gods, Fusculus—don't say the Cilicians will get away with their part!"

"No, Petronius is on that aspect. He's out trying to find that boy, Zeno."

I pulled up. "Last seen at the Temple of Attis. My uncle had some priest looking after him—"

"No sign of your uncle," said Fusculus, looking at me carefully.

I scowled. "Uncle Fulvius is famous for one thing—running away."

"Well, you know Brunnus came yesterday with information from the fleet headquarters. According to him, they don't want their agent exposed."

I told Fusculus that in my experience Uncle Fulvius was a grumpy, unhelpful bastard anyway, then I went to see that other reprobate, the Cilician chief.

"You are my only hope, Falco! That tribune says I have to give up all my little luxuries."

I leaned on the doorframe at Damagoras' cell. So far he had managed to hang on to cushions, rugs, bronze side tables, a portable shrine, and a well-padded mattress. "There are worse jails, Damagoras. If you want to see a hellhole, try the underground tomb at the Mamertine in Rome."

The old pirate shuddered. "Nobody gets out of there."

My voice was cold. "I did!"

He gazed at me. "You're full of surprises, Falco."

"Sometimes I surprise myself. At this moment, knowing that you run organized kidnap rackets, I am surprised to find myself talking to you . . .

You had nothing to say when I approached you for aid before. Why do you want to see me, old man?"

I noticed now that Damagoras was thinner and older-looking than when he dealt with me so arrogantly at his villa. Time was running out for him. This cell in the decrepit barracks was no place for his ancient bones, already aching after a long, active life at sea. "You still want to find Diocles, Falco?" he asked.

"In return, I am to offer you . . . ?"

"My old ship's logs. You have them, don't you?"

"Evidence." That was stretching it. Only Damagoras himself was implicated in those old sea fights—and only if he admitted that the logs were his. Reference to the Cilicians' violent past was mere color. But the way Rubella worked, a sympathetic magistrate would be asked to review evidence like this—circumstantial but yet shocking—then his condemnation would send the kidnappers straight to crucifixion or to the arena beasts. Nobody would see a trial. The sailors were men of humble background, unlikely to possess proof of citizenship, and what's more, they were foreigners. Enough said.

I came farther into the cell. "All right—what have you got for me?"

"You'll give me the logs?" Damagoras demanded eagerly.

"If I find the scribe, I will give you the logs." He was eighty-six. His own activities must be limited and any of his cronies who remained free after Rubella's purge would be kicked out of Italy, so he would lack subordinates. Things were different now, in any case. Damagoras was on a watch list.

He leaned forward from a battered chair. "The scribe and I were closer than I may have said." I nodded. "Diocles knew a lot about me."

"He stayed at your house."

"You knew? He was with me for a couple of weeks. When he disappeared, I had my boys find out what had happened."

"He is dead, isn't he?"

"I reckon so, Falco. That was why I stopped looking."

I crouched down in front of Damagoras, elbows on my knees. "So what did you find out?"

"He really was going to write my memoirs, you know." Damagoras spoke now as if he was describing a good friendship. "We went into everything in detail—"

"I know that. Diocles made copious notes."

"You've got his notes?" demanded Damagoras. I gave him a tantalizing smile. "We got on well. I trusted him, Falco. I told him all about my past—and when he had had a drop to drink, he told me what was on his own mind. He had troubles."

"His aunt had been killed. He blamed the firefighters—not the vigiles, the builders' guild."

"You're right. He had come to Ostia to do something about it."

"Is this how he came to grief?"

"All I know," said Damagoras, "is that he started working for one of the builders. He got himself a job as a carrier for a concrete maker, Lemnus—"

"Lemnus from Paphos!" I shouted, leaping up. Lemnus—the bow-legged Cretan who attacked me at the Damson Flower, then scarpered . . . Petronius had reckoned he had a conscience about *something* . . . Well, Petro could pull him in now, if he could still find him.

Lemnus was freelance, though. "Whose contract were they working on?"

"I don't know, Falco." Lies. The old pirate was far too busy making sure he did not look too shifty.

"Not good enough, Damagoras! Tell me the contractor."

"You can't touch the man; he is too big in this town—"

"Nobody is too big for me." I grabbed Damagoras by the front of his white tunic and hauled him from his chair. He was taller than me, but he quailed. "It was the man Diocles blamed for his aunt's death, wasn't it?" I shook him.

Damagoras dropped his voice. "Shh! He's always hanging around here—he wants the contract to rebuild this station house—" He drew a finger across the top of his head, to signify stranded hair. "Privatus."

I let the old man stagger back and find his seat. I believed the story. The scribe's working tunics had been covered with mortar splats. Privatus ran the guild. He made a lot of noise about that. If the builders' guild boot-boys had been fatally incompetent, Privatus would seem responsible.

Diocles may simply have wanted to expose the guild—but if he talked about his plans, word would have gotten back. If he complained to Lemnus, Lemnus may have snitched. For Privatus, Diocles spelled awkward trouble. In his personal anguish, Diocles may not have realized how much Privatus had to lose. Threatened with the loss of his social standing in Ostia, the builder might have reacted more viciously than some senator Diocles accused of sleeping around. The scribe had misjudged the danger.

But Privatus had contracts all over the place—both at Ostia and Portus. Unless I could identify where Diocles had been employed when he disappeared, there was little hope of discovering his fate.

I strode out into the yard. Members of the Fourth were making efforts to clear away abandoned equipment. I left a message for Petronius about Lemnus.

Collecting Nux from her long snooze at the bathhouse, I went home. Life there was normal—the aftermath of tantrums. Little Julia was now sitting very quiet and sucking her thumb with a tear-stained face. Albia looked flushed. Helena looked harassed. As far as I knew, neither woman ever used the threat of waiting until Father came home to dole out punishment . . . Well, not yet.

I asked what Julia had done. She had found the empty note-tablets left by Diocles, and covered the boards with wild scribbles. Because of the risk that they would ruin important case-notes, we had a family rule that the children should only play with writing equipment when they were supervised. There had been incidents with inkwells, for one thing.

You could not expect a three-year-old to remember and obey a family rule. Mind you, I would probably be saying the same thing when Julia and Favonia were twenty-five and married.

Helena had rescued the tablets. Julia had only defaced the empty ones; the ship's logs and the scribe's notes were safely put away in a chest with the scribe's sword. The only tablet where my daughter spoiled something significant was the one on which Diocles had sketched what we had thought was a board game.

"Of course!" Suddenly, when I needed the answer, I saw it. The diagram was not solo chess. This was a map, a rough plan knocked out as a memo, with a couple of landmarks initialed. It was the kind of sketch a man would draw to remind him how to find a site where he must work tomorrow.

I recognized the location now. Having come straight from the station house, I could see exactly where the sketch depicted: there was a V for the vigiles, a B for the Claudian baths in which I cleaned up this morning, a squiggle for the wine shop in the street—and an important C. That was circled.

Petronius Longus had once told me that underneath the station house lay a moldy old water cistern.

LXIV

I do not like water cisterns. They are always dark and sinister. You can never tell how deep they are—or what may be moving beneath those vague ripples on the surface. This one did not disappoint me. We had scared off the rats when we all tramped in on the walkways, but we could sense trouble.

The place was separate from the station house, across a small lane that ran parallel with the Decumanus. Unused for years, nobody seemed to know why it was here—though all agreed that the obvious answer, to provide water for firefighting, did not apply. Fusculus was taking charge of the search; he thought the cistern had been built to supply ships with drinking water, in days when they used to moor right up along the river before Portus was built.

We set up lights. Their eerie flickering showed a cavernous interior, divided into five or six echoing bays. Virtus, the clerk, had looked up site management records. They confirmed that Privatus and his firm had been engaged for structural repairs here at about the time that Diocles disappeared.

We spent some time listening to drips and scurrying rats, while we were waiting for the diver. The diver, who knew there would be no salvage fees in this search, took his time coming out from Portus. Still, there was no hurry.

The diver arrived. Full of technical bravado, he assured us that weight was no problem; he was used to retrieving amphorae, so if he found a body he would need no help to bring it to the surface. He boasted that he had no fear of the job. We did not disabuse him. When, after swimming around for a couple of hours and searching several of the bays, the diver burst out of the water with a terrified screech, the vigiles—who had known what to expect—were tolerant. Someone took him off at once for a large drink.

With the right location identified, the vigiles did the rest. Concrete is a fabulous material; it sets under water. Despite a large lump weighing down the body, they freed it and brought out the remains late that afternoon.

They laid what was left of Diocles on an old esparto mat in the street. He must have been in the water since the day he disappeared. He was bloated beyond recognition; I would never know now what he had looked like when he was alive. But we were sure it was him.

The scribe still had his own dagger, in its sheath. Holconius would be asked to identify that later. We could not tell how Diocles had been killed, but Fusculus was sure that Lemnus from Paphos could be persuaded by the vigiles that he wanted to reveal details. Whether any retribution would strike the contractor, Privatus, I doubted. He would have been stupid to kill Diocles with his own hands; guild presidents use other people to do their dirty work—and to take the rap. Even so, Rubella could make life difficult for him in the short term, and the records would stay on file—one of the files that cohorts passed on each time a new detachment arrived to take over.

There was the usual fuss, the usual standing around endlessly while men disputed theories of what might have happened. At last the corpse was carted into the station house, the vigiles went off to wash, the diver left. I sat alone outside the adjacent wine shop, raising a sad beaker to the scribe's memory.

Petronius Longus came down the side road when I was getting into my second drink. He held little Zeno by one hand. Petronius nodded, but they passed me without speaking. At the entrance to the station house, Petronius paused; I heard him say words of reassurance. Then he led the boy inside. Zeno went with him sullenly, but with an air of resignation. He was used to being told what to do; someone here would entice him to cooperate. Treated right, Zeno would give the vigiles names and events. Perhaps later, if he was sufficiently helpful, someone would have the kindness to release his mother.

I was expecting Petronius when he returned to the street soon afterward. I knew he would not process Zeno himself. He had no taste for interrogating children.

He sat down beside me. I had already obtained a second cup and poured wine for him from my jug. We talked about the situation briefly. He asked me about Fulvius. I said honestly that the story of Fulvius working as an agent for the navy seemed convincing—but that I would not be surprised if his connections with the Illyrians from Dyrrhachium were murky. Given his history, I reckoned he had fled abroad again. This visit to Ostia would be one more confused sighting over which my family would mutter and argue all through Saturnalia.

Petronius then told me that the vigiles had been given a lead on Caninus' whereabouts. Gaius Baebius, of all people, had reported seeing him. When Gaius was taking his breakfast at the Dolphin in Portus that morning, Caninus had slunk into the brothel opposite, the Damson Flower. Rubella and Brunnus had taken a posse and would arrest the attaché if he was still on the premises.

"Brunnus is still lusting for glory for the Sixth."

"While Rubella is of course above such ambitions! Do we want to go and join the fun?"

"Let them jostle. We two have more sense."

We did not have to wait long. While we sat there, Rubella, Brunnus, and an armed group brought the captured attaché for his reckoning. We remained at our post, merely pulling in our feet to avoid the dust they kicked up. The prisoner was almost invisible, at the center of the escort. But I noticed that, perhaps to disguise himself at the brothel, Caninus was heavily painted. Of his fabled beaded slippers there was no sign: his feet were bare. His long tunic hung off him in rags. He slumped limply, as the vigiles held him by the arms. They must have started working him over at the brothel.

Petronius and I watched grimly as they dragged the prisoner backwards down the side street to the station-house gate. He was a corrupt official; the ex-slaves in the vigiles would be merciless. Vespasian had already had enough bad legions to clean up; he would not want a naval scandal too. The Caninus affair would be buried. No trial or conviction would feature in the *Daily Gazette* court reports. Caninus was due for silent elimination. We saw him being hauled inside the station house. No one would know when, or if ever, he came out.

The prisoner and escort vanished into the shadowed interior. Then for once someone hauled the mighty doors across behind them. The vigiles were seeking their own dreadful privacy for what would happen next. The thud of the heavy bar which clenched the tall doors shut echoed up the empty street.

Petronius and I then sat on in the afternoon sunlight, two old friends with very long memories, sharing a quiet drink.